TRIPLE TROUBLE

A MIA MURPHY MYSTERY

STEPHANIE ROWE

COPYRIGHT

coincidental and not intended by the author or the artist. There are excerpts from other books by the author in the back of the book.

WHAT READERS ARE SAYING ABOUT MIA MURPHY

"A hilarious and twisty ride! ...I definitely need more Mia Murphy in my life." Five-Star Goodreads Review (Tammy M.)

"I was catapulted into the story and remained captivated until the end... Down right laugh out loud!" Five-Star Goodreads Review (Elizabeth)

"Stephanie Rowe has such a way with words! Her offbeat humour and madcap adventures are absolutely mesmerizing!" Five-Star Goodreads Review (Laura C.)

"A hoot! " Five-star Goodreads Review (Margie)

"I am so in love with Mia and her friends...this series just has me literally laughing out loud...Non-stop high jinks, great characters, and above all, wonderful and engaging writing." Five-star Goodreads Review (Penny)

"[Mia] had me laughing out loud constantly. Also, I think King Tut might be my favorite water-loving bodyguard/ kitty cat companion that I've ever read! I absolutely cannot wait until we get the third book!" Five-star Goodreads Review (Danielle B.)

"I love this book, this series and this author!" Five-star Goodreads Review (Riding Reviewer)

CHAPTER 1

X.

I stared at my phone, stunned at the text that had just come in from an unfamiliar number. My brain immediately shouted at me that the X meant bad things, bad, bad things.

Then I remembered that I wasn't ten years old in the middle of a con with my mom. She wasn't standing on the other side of a luxurious room crowded with celebrities, holding up two crossed fingers, giving me the X sign that meant "abandon the con right now because it's going south."

I was, in fact, a grown woman who had walked away from that life and my mom ten years ago. I was currently standing on my dock in the gorgeous morning sunlight on a beautiful Maine lake, going over my list of all the must-do items still undone prior to the grand reopening of my new marina.

Not a celebrity or con in sight. And definitely no mom.

I took a breath. Wow. My head had gone to old places in an alarming hurry.

I grinned at my massive rescue cat, who was perched on the end of the dock, his tail twitching in anticipation of the next unsuspecting fish to swim past. "It's all good, King Tut."

He ignored me, but I knew that the love was still there.

My life was great. I had friends, a home, and a marina that I was determined to turn into a success. I looked down at my phone again, studying my list. The landscapers were due to finish today, and—

A second X popped up.

My heart sped up, and I sucked in my breath. *What the fudge?*

Tentatively, almost terrified of getting a response, I texted back. *Mom?*

I got an immediate, automated reply stating that the phone number was not in service.

I felt both relieved and weirdly sad. Of course it wouldn't be my mom. I hadn't had any contact with her since I'd left her when I was seventeen. Granted, I'd always felt that she knew exactly where I was and what I was doing, but even if that were true, why would she be texting me XX after all these years?

One X had meant abandon the con. XX had meant that it was getting dangerous and to get out as soon as possible. Get out? From my own home? That made no sense. But I couldn't help but take a more careful look around me.

The lake was relatively quiet, but there were a few boats around. Across the cove was Jake's Yacht Club, with its upscale blue and white awnings. Staff in their navy shirts and khaki shorts were strolling around helping customers. Everyone was calm. No danger that I could see.

I studied each driver of the boats that were near me, but I recognized everyone. No one new.

I turned around to examine my marina. The painters were working, the landscapers were making things beautiful. The front window that had been shot out my first week, almost killing one of my new besties, had been replaced, so the big plywood board was gone.

Everything was coming along well.

But despite all the warm fuzzies surrounding me, I could feel panic starting to build in my chest. I'd been relaxed for days, so the sudden descent into panic was throwing me. I was out of practice being on guard for my life.

I looked at King Tut again. He was my gold-star surveillance system. He'd sacrificed morals, pride, and common decency to save me more than once. "King Tut!"

He didn't take his gaze off the lake.

I took a breath, trying to get my head back into focus. The fact King Tut wasn't concerned meant there wasn't a threat. Granted, it could also mean that he was so deeply immersed in predator mode that he had no mental space for anything else...

My phone dinged again. My heart jumped, and I looked down.

X.

Three Xs.

Three Xs meant *get out fast, no matter what it takes.*

I looked around again, the hair on the back of my neck prickling even as I tried to talk myself out of freaking out. It was a few Xs. There was nothing special about an X. Anyone could type an X. Glitches could produce Xs with zero effort.

I was at home at my marina. What could possibly be so dangerous that I needed to get out as fast as I could? My mom's messes hadn't been mine for a very long time.

Then my gaze settled on Vinnie, the sometime-gang-leader-ish guy who was currently acting as my unofficial bodyguard, due to the fact that my real one had been murdered (by a person unrelated to me and my life). The feds still couldn't figure out who had put surveillance cameras in my marina, so Vinnie had taken over keep-Mia-alive duty.

It had never once occurred to me that the spying had anything to do with my mother. I'd assumed it was connected to my ex-husband, who was currently in federal prison for being a drug kingpin. I'd put him there, and his mom had tried to kill me for it.

Vinnie was standing in the parking lot, his arms folded as he scanned the area. He looked dangerous and armed, despite the fact he had already admitted he would never shoot anyone for me, due to his aversion to a life of guilt and trauma, and things like that.

But at six-foot four, muscular, and wearing just the right amount of bling for a gang leader, he looked like a deadly force, so I doubted anyone would try while he was around. Plus, honestly, after spending so long looking over my shoulder, I'd gotten used to the possibility of being a target.

I was chill now.

Except, apparently, when being triggered by my past.

I looked down at my phone again, trying to think of a reply that might help me figure out if the sender was my mom.

My mom had been a code person, because living a life of crime had taught her that paper trails were never good for the criminal.

I tried to remember something from the code we'd used, but all I could think of were the made-up symbols that we'd created, none of which were on the keyboard of my phone (go figure, right?). I couldn't quite recall how any of them went together anyway.

I did remember the symbol for my name, though.

I quickly knelt on the dock, dipped my finger in the water, and then drew the symbol on the wood. I took a picture of it then texted it to the number.

Again, an immediate reply that the number was not in service.

Then, right after that, another text came through. *XXX.*

Alarm shot through me, the kind that she'd triggered in me so many times as a kid. *Run, Mia, run!*

"King Tut," I shouted. "Let's go. Now." I didn't know where to go, but I had to get out, and get out fast. I had no idea what was happening, but I liked my life too much to be willing to die. "Vinnie," I shouted. "We gotta go!"

Vinnie started running toward me, but King Tut ignored me. I ran to the edge of the dock to get him. Leaving my cat behind didn't qualify as "no matter what." He was my family, and there was no way I was leaving him. "King Tut! We gotta go—"

He shot off the dock and dove into the water, disappearing under the surface. "Hey!"

I immediately jumped in after him, knowing that sometimes King Tut vanished for hours once he got under the water. I didn't know where he went, but wherever he came up for air was out of my sight. It used to freak me out, but I'd gotten used to it.

But now was not the time to lose my cat for hours. The late June water was warming, but still a shock to my system as I hit the lake. I immediately ducked under, searching the crystalline water for my black cat.

I didn't see him.

I stood up, water dripping off me. Vinnie was already at the end of the dock. "What's happening?" He looked alarmed.

"Where's King Tut? Can you see him? We need to get out of here, but I need to get him first!"

"King Tut?" Vinnie pulled off his sunglasses and scanned the water.

At that moment, I heard the roar of the lake patrol boat. I whirled around and waved my hands at Devlin Hunt, the too-handsome-for-anyone's-good cop who was driving it. "Stop!" I shouted. "King Tut's under the water! Turn off your propeller!"

Because we'd done this drill many times since I'd bought the marina a few months ago and discovered that my cat was an avid underwater hunter, Devlin immediately shut his boat off and leaned over the edge to search the water.

For a long moment, there was silence as the three of us scanned the water for my baby.

"There!" Devlin pointed close to the beach, and I sloshed through the water toward where he was pointing, my heart pounding.

"Something's wrong!" I shouted as I hurried after King Tut. "I'm in danger!"

"What?" Devlin stood up and put his hand on his gun. "What's going on?"

"I don't know!" I saw a black shadow under the water, and I lunged for him. My hands wrapped around King Tut's waist, and I dragged the yowling beast out of the water. "I need to go!" I started running toward the shore. I had no idea what the danger was or where it was coming from, which made me even more alarmed.

Just as I reached the shore, fighting to hold into a sodden ball of long-haired anger, an extended-cab pickup truck shot into the parking lot. I knew that black truck. It belonged to one of my two best friends, Hattie Lawless, a seventy-something chef who ran a café in my marina and raced cars on the side. "Hattie!"

She hit the brakes and the truck skidded to a stop. She jumped out, grabbing my shoulders as I ran up. "What's going on? Why do you look like you're freaking out?"

"A triple X! I think my mom sent me a triple X!"

"Is that porn?" Hattie looked intrigued. "I had no idea your mom was into porn. I mean, not surprising because she's a wild card, but porn? Can I see it? I assume it's girl power porn, right? She seems empowered."

"Porn?" I stared at her. "No. It's our signal that the con has gone south, and we need to run."

"A con?" Her eyebrows shot up. "You're running a con with your mom? What con?"

"I'm not. I mean, that I know of. But I got this text from this random number, and it could have been her, and—"

"Wait a minute." Hattie put her hands on her hips. "Mia Murphy. Pull yourself together. You're not running a con. You own a marina in the charming town of Bass Derby. You don't engage in illegal activities, except to help others. And you haven't heard from your mom in over a decade. Whatever you think is going on, isn't."

I grabbed my phone and handed it to her as Vinnie ran up. "See?"

Hattie took the phone, and the two of them peered at it. "This?" Hattie frowned at me. "Some random text from a number that doesn't even work? You're freaking out about *this*? How do you know it's her?"

"I don't *know* it's her, but what if it is? What if there's something going on and she's trying to warn me and—"

"Hey!" Hattie cut me off. "Take a breath, girlfriend." She held up her hands palm up and inhaled. "Deep breath. Channel your inner river."

I blinked. "My river?"

"Yes. A calm, scenic river. Tranquility. Peace. Serenity. Imagine chiseled, charming men lined up on the banks, singing about how wonderful you are."

I stared at her. "Seriously?"

"Yes. Imagine their deep voices, singing 'Mia is a badass. She rules the world!' Maybe they're even dancing for you, some manly, synchronized beauty. How can that not feel good? Breathe in. Breathe out."

Devlin finally caught up to us. "What's going on?"

"Keep channeling your river, Mia. I got this." Hattie held up my phone. "Mia thinks this text is from her mom, signaling that the end of the world is upon us, and she must run away. To where? She doesn't know. From what? Also unknown."

Devlin took the phone and frowned at it. As he studied it, I found my pulse slowing and my panic easing. Devlin was a local cop in the small town of Bass Derby, but I was pretty certain he had a black ops background.

His buddy, Agent Hawk Straus, who I called Griselda to reclaim my personal power, was the FBI agent who had coerced me into a two-year-undercover sting against my ex. When I'd moved to Bass Derby, Griselda had asked Devlin to make sure no one from my ex's life assassinated me. He trusted Devlin with my life, which means I did, too. With Devlin standing by my side, no one would be able to get to me.

Plus, the river visualization had been surprisingly helpful.

I took the deep breath Hattie had wanted for me, and she nodded her approval as she studied me. "It's not like you to freak out like that," she observed. "You're very unflappable when it comes to danger like assassins, guns, and other imminent threats to your life. Why are you having a fit over this?"

Devlin looked over at me. "Hattie's right. This could easily just be some random text."

They were right. I usually was pretty calm. A childhood of crime had inured me to the small dangers in life. In fact, it had instilled in me an affinity for a high-risk life, which I tried to suppress as much as possible. "I know. It's just...well...it's my *mom*."

"It's probably *not* your mom," Hattie said.

"I know. I just meant that she triggers me." I let out my breath again. "The purpose of the triple X code was to get my attention when I wasn't taking things seriously. She would use it to freak me out and get me to do what she needed me to."

Hattie cocked her brow. "That sounds a little manipulative."

"When you're a criminal, sometimes you can't mess around." I looked over at Devlin, who was frowning at me. "What?"

He held up my phone. "I'm going to have Griselda, I mean Hawk, track this number and see what he can figure out."

I nodded. "Okay, great. Thanks."

"But in the meantime, I agree with Hattie," he said. "Keep an eye out, but we're already on alert, so I don't think we raise the alarm any higher. Unless you know something else?"

I looked at the three of them, and buried my chin in King Tut's soggy head. "You know, I think you guys are right. It makes no sense that my mom would be telling me to run from here." My tension eased even more. "It was an old trigger, I guess."

"We all have those," Devlin said softly.

I knew he understood. He'd been in a gang when he was a kid, so I imagined he had his own share of childhood land mines that came up from time to time. "Thanks."

He nodded. "It's all good, Mia." But he continued to study me. "You do look like hell, though."

"Thanks." Not too long ago, Devlin had declared his interest in dating me. On the same day, Griselda had made the same announcement. They were besties. Griselda had warned me off Devlin. Devlin had warned me off Griselda. I didn't want to ever date anyone again.

It was awkward.

And yet somehow, I'd agreed to have dinner with Devlin tomorrow night. Umm…

Hattie peered at me. "You know, you do look haggard. It can't all be from that text."

"Mia was up all night working on the marina," Vinnie offered. "She's freaking out about having it ready in time for her grand reopening."

Empathy flashed across Hattie's face. "Sweetie, it looks amazing. It's going great."

"I know, but it's just that I have to overcome the marina's reputation and mine. Do you know that the sheriff came over here with some woman a couple days ago? She'd lost her diamond ring and accused me of taking it, due to my criminal history and all."

Devlin narrowed his eyes. "I didn't know about that." No one in the entire town was impressed with our sheriff, not even the mayor, who had hired him. She also happened to be his mom.

"Well, the lady found it under her own bed," I said.

"Which you could have put there," Hattie said. "It doesn't exonerate you."

I looked at her. "How is that helpful?"

"Just wanted to remind you of your awesomeness. Just because someone doesn't appreciate your specialness or sees it as a threat doesn't make you any less awesome." She put her arm around my shoulders. "You need a vacation."

I sighed. She'd offered this trip about forty times in the last two weeks. "I can't take a vacation. I'm opening my marina in ten days."

"And yet, you were ready to abandon it all forever, because of a random text," she said.

I grimaced. "So I freaked out a little."

"A lot," Vinnie said. "You dove in after your cat like he was about to be murdered."

I tightened my arms around my soggy cat, who was now purring and happy to be snuggled. "I thought he was in danger."

Hattie put her hands on her hips. "As I have told you repeatedly, I'm going to visit my cousin Thelma for a couple days to celebrate her birthday. Come with me. It's a five-star island resort on the coast of Maine. You'll come back rested, refreshed, and ready to receive all texts with a clear mind."

I wanted to go so badly, because having friends was a precious new treasure, and I loved every second of it. But setting down roots in my new town was critical for me, and getting accepted by the town was more difficult than I'd expected. I had a lot riding on this grand opening, and I needed to be here working, not on vacation. "I already told you I can't. I have the grand opening—"

"If the triple X *was* from your mom, then leaving for a couple days seems like a great idea as well," Hattie interrupted.

Huh. "You're not wrong about that," I admitted slowly.

"And Lucy's coming on the trip," Hattie said. "Girl bonding. You know you love it."

Aw...Lucy was going, too? Now I really wanted to go. The three of us had become such a tight trio since I'd moved to Bass Derby.

"I think it's a good idea to go," Devlin said. "Get off the grid for a few days while we figure this out."

I looked at him, both disappointed and relieved at the idea of missing our date. "Our dinner?"

He grinned, looking pleased that I'd even remembered we had plans. "I don't know about you, but I'll still live in this town when you get back. We'll figure it out."

I bit my lip. The idea of stepping away from the marina for a couple days did sound good. I was drained, I loved Hattie and

Lucy, and a little part of me was worried that the text really had been from mom. "Is the resort cat-friendly?"

"I don't think so, but hang on." She pulled out her phone and made a call. "Beau. It's Hattie."

Beau Hammersley was a reclusive, wealthy mystery writer who claimed to hate the world, except for me, my mom, and Hattie. I suspected he liked people a lot more than he claimed, but I adored him either way.

"Mia needs to leave town for a couple days because her mom might have just sent her a cryptic text about danger. Can you come over and grab King Tut and watch him?"

I grinned. Beau was obsessed with my mom. He'd run across a documentary on the infamous Tatum Murphy when he'd been researching one of his books, and the obsession had been born.

Hattie hung up the phone. "He'll be here in a few seconds. He's around the corner. He's out boating."

My arms tightened around King Tut. "I don't want to leave King Tut behind—"

"Yo! I'm here!" Beau came flying around the corner in his boat, shouting and waving his arms. He sped up to the beach and ran his boat right onto the sand. He leapt out and came racing up. He was wearing his bejeweled sandals, denim shorts, and his tee shirt with the bloody dagger on it. His hair was ratty from the wind, and the only sign of wealth on him was the brand of his sunglasses. "Your mom's in danger?"

I almost started laughing at his delight about my mom being involved. "I don't know. Maybe."

Hattie pointed to King Tut. "Mia needs King Tut safe."

Beau eyed the cat. "Tatum might come to check on him?"

"She might," I agreed. Who knew what my mom might do? No one. Checking on my cat was as possible as anything else.

"Then he's safe with me." Beau held out his arms. "Come on, King Tut. Let's go." The reclusive mystery writer liked to put on a tough persona, but in his heart, he was a good man. If he said he'd keep King Tut safe, he would. He'd do whatever it took. After decades as a mystery writer, the man had ideas about danger, death, and murder that no one wanted to know.

King Tut gazed at Beau and didn't budge from my arms.

Beau met his steely gaze. "I have caviar."

King Tut immediately leapt out of my arms, raced down the sand, then jumped into Beau's boat. He sat down on the bow, flicked his tail, and gave us all a sullen, serious glare with his unblinking yellow eyes. Even with his black fur still dripping with water, he looked huge, menacing, and dangerous.

"Damn, girl." Hattie grinned. "If you decide not to go and deprive that cat of Beau's caviar, you will never be safe from that feline again."

"I need to channel King Tut's attitude for my next villain," Beau said. "Look at that threat. It's brilliant. Subtle. Unyielding. And yet disarming in that kitty-cat ball of soggy fluff. It's almost diabolical. I love it! He's my new muse. Get me his life jacket, and we're off."

I bit my lip. "I've never been without King Tut since I rescued him."

Hattie put her arm around my shoulder. "King Tut will be safe away from the marina, and you'll be safe too. Plus, both of you will have fun."

"I think it's the best call," Devlin said. "Give me a couple days to figure out what's going on." He looked over at me. "I'll keep an eye on the marina."

"I will, too. I know what the contractors are supposed to be doing, and I'll manage it," Vinnie said. "I'll sleep in the spare storefront. It'll cost you, but I'm worth it."

I looked at the three of them, and my heart got all mushy. These were my friends, people who cared if I died, cared if my cat was safe, and cared about my marina. I might not have had my breakthrough with the rest of the town yet, but I'd found a little niche of home, and I appreciated it with all my heart.

The truth was, I did want to go with Hattie and Lucy. I wanted to go with every fiber in my being. "How long's the trip?"

"Three days and two nights," Hattie said. "The ferry leaves in four hours, though. We need to hurry. How fast can you pack?"

I looked over at her, and suddenly, I knew she was right. They were all right. Those texts might not be from my mom, but they were the impetus I needed. I was supposed to go on this trip, and I wasn't going to miss it. "Fast."

CHAPTER 2

FOUR HOURS LATER, I was sure we were going to die.

Not by an assassin.

By Hattie.

"Slow down! We're not going to make the ferry, no matter how fast you drive!" I gripped the handle on the car door and braced myself as Hattie careened through the crowded parking lot for the Harmony Island ferry. "Hattie!"

"We have to make it! It's the last ferry of the day! You're a slow packer so you don't get to complain!" Hattie whipped the steering wheel to the right, and her massive pickup truck screeched into a parking spot.

Lucy yelped and covered her eyes, and I closed mine.

But the truck stopped and there was no sound of crushing metal.

I opened my eyes and looked back at Lucy. She rolled her eyes and gave me a thumbs up, and I grinned. We survived. Rock on.

"Let's go!" Hattie tried to open her door, but there wasn't enough space. "Son of a biscuit!"

I peered out my window and saw that I was only a few inches from the car next to us. "How did you even fit in here?"

"And at that speed?" Lucy added.

"Magic. I'm a magician behind the wheel. You both know that." She rolled down her window. "No time to move it. Let's go." She braced herself on the doorframe and pulled her feet out from under the steering wheel.

I watched her with increasing alarm. "We're not climbing out."

"Of course we are. God, Mia, you'd never guess you grew up in a life of crime! You're so unimaginative now!" She moved into a crouching position and then leaned out the window.

Oh, no. That wasn't good. "No, Hattie, seriously. We're going to be on the island for two nights. You can't leave the windows down that whole time!"

"We're not missing that ferry! It's Thelma's birthday!" Hattie hauled herself out the window. "I'll hold the ferry for you. Get my bags!" She took off running across the parking lot toward the ferry boat that was tooting its last farewell.

Lucy leaned over from the back seat and hit my shoulder. "Mia. She'll jump onto the ferry. You know she will. She'll die, and we'll never recover emotionally!"

"I'll stop her." I yanked off my seatbelt and climbed across the seat to the driver's side. I hoisted myself out the window and then dropped to the pavement. "Hattie! Wait!"

She didn't even turn around. She just ran even harder as the ferry boat tooted again.

Crap. I sprinted after her. "Hattie! Stop!"

Up ahead, the attendant put the chain up across the ramp to the ferry.

"Let me through," Hattie shouted. "I'm coming!"

He looked up sharply, and alarm flickered across his face, as would be the normal reaction upon finding a fuchsia-haired sassy senior running at you and screaming. He waved his arms, trying to flag her down. "Stop! The ferry is leaving."

"It's right there! I don't even have to jump!" She ducked under the chain. "Out of my way!" Hattie raced down the ramp, but the attendant had closed the gate on the ferry, and the boat was already moving away from the dock.

If she tried to jump, she would be in trouble.

"Hattie Lawless, don't you dare jump!" I shouted. "We'll find another boat!"

"Yes, we'll hire someone to take us!" Lucy yelled from behind me. "Stop, Hattie! Just stop!"

Hattie started to slow to prepare to jump. Dammit. The woman believed she was unstoppable, but there were limits to even Hattie's greatness. "Hattie!" I screamed, fear clamping in my throat. "Don't!" I ran harder—.

"Hattie Lawless!" Someone else yelled. It was a voice I didn't recognize. "Stop that right now!"

Hattie looked over her shoulder, then grinned. "Vera!" She stopped and waved, inadvertently stepping right in my path.

Oh, crap! "Hattie!" I lunged to the left to avoid crashing into her and knocking her into the ocean. I tried to stop, but my feet hit a wet spot and I lost my balance.

I landed on my hip. My momentum carried me down the angled ramp at an alarming pace.

"Mia!" Hattie reached for me as I slid past her, but I ducked her outstretched hand, not wanting to pull her off balance.

I lunged for the railing, but my hand slipped off the metal. *Oh, no.*

I shot off the ramp with a yelp, staring down in horror at the dark, cold ocean. "Oh, God."

It was a long drop.

"Mia!" Lucy and Hattie shouted in horror, but it was too late.

I barely had time to plug my nose and suck in a breath before I plunged into the bottomless depths. Water rushed past me, and I could hear the whoosh of bazillions of tiny bubbles.

The water felt heavy and thick, and I could taste the salty brine in my mouth. My eyes stung, and the shock of the cold water reverberated through my body.

Panic seized me. *I don't want to die this way. Or now. Nothing about this is how I want to die.*

I started thrashing my arms and legs frantically, fighting with everything I had to stop the fast descent and get back to the surface.

I was so deep that I couldn't hear my friends shouting.

But what I could hear was the churning rhythm of the propellers, thudding through the water like some ominous music in a horror movie.

Come on, Mia! Gravity finally lost its battle with my frantic kicking, and my trajectory shifted. I started making progress toward the surface. I swam up fast, and I nearly cried with relief when my face broke the surface...and then realized that I was right next to the ferry, near the back end.

The business end.

The massive boat stretched up right in front of my face. I felt like I was at the base of a skyscraper, its smooth, black battered sides stretching so hopelessly high. People were leaning over the railing, staring down at me, and pointing, like I was a freak show at the circus.

An alarm sounded, a wild shrilling blast that was nearly deafening.

The piercing sound broke me out of my stupor. I jerked into action, swung my feet around, planted them on the side of the ferry boat, and then pushed off as hard as I could.

I swam backwards frantically, using every muscle that the heavens had given me, including all the ones I'd never had a reason to use before.

I couldn't take my horrified gaze off the massive black ferry. I wasn't far enough away yet, and the propellers were getting closer. The water was swirling, spinning me in directions I didn't want to go.

Something hit me in the face, and I screamed, sucking in mouthfuls of water.

"Grab it," Lucy yelled. "Grab on!"

The water was churning up so much I lost my bearings. My head went under, and suddenly, death felt real, more real than it ever had before. I flung up my arm and my hand brushed against whatever Lucy had told me to grab. I flailed at it, trying to find something to grip. Finally, my arm locked around it, and I hooked my elbow through it.

"Hold tight!" Lucy yelled.

I hugged it to my chest. It took off through the water, dragging me through the frothing swells. I fought to keep my head above the water, coughing and spitting to try to keep the ocean out of my lungs.

My grip started to slip, and I fought to hold on.

Then, suddenly, just as quickly, the churning stopped, and the water settled enough that I was able to get my bearings. I realized I was holding onto a round life preserver, which was attached to a rope that led up to the dock I'd catapulted off. The ferry propellers had shut off, and the ocean was no longer pulsing with the throbbing of those blades coming to get me.

Hattie and Lucy were leaning over the edge of the dock, yelling at me, along with a lot of other people, many of whom had their phones out, videoing my almost-death.

I hauled myself up on the cushion, resting my upper body on the white foam ring. The rope was taut, keeping me from drifting back toward the ferry, which was still only yards away, but thankfully only floating silently instead of preparing to chop me up.

I leaned my cheek against the foam and coughed. My lungs ached. My chest hurt. My throat burned. I'd come deathly close to drowning, and I didn't like it one bit.

I was resilient when it came to danger, but that was because I was smart, capable, and under the illusion of having some control.

The ocean had just taught me that it had all the control, and I didn't like that one bit.

I was out.

I was going home, back to my marina, and focusing on what mattered: my future in Bass Derby.

Girls weekend?

Over before it began.

CHAPTER 3

"MIA. You're being dramatic. You didn't drown, so you're fine." Thirty minutes post-near-death-by-drowning, Hattie put her hands on her hips, regarding me impatiently as I walked out of the bathroom stall at Vera's Lobster Shack, freshly changed into dry clothes.

"Dramatic? Really?" I dumped my soggy clothes in the sink. "Have you ever fallen off a high dock and almost been run over by an ocean ferry?"

"Well, no, but—"

"It's not as fun as it sounds."

Lucy was leaning against the sink, her arms folded over her chest. Her dark hair was braided in an intricate pattern that she said had taken almost twelve hours for her stylist, LaShonda, to do. Even under the fluorescent lights, her brown skin was radiant. She looked put together, tough, and gorgeous, which basically summed up who she was. "Honestly, it doesn't sound that fun."

"Right? And it's less fun than that." I eyed myself in the bathroom mirror. My hair was tangled from the ocean water, I had a scratch on my cheek, and I still looked a little haunted. That was good. I could get sympathy if I looked traumatized.

"You're being a wimp," Hattie said, blatantly disregarding the fact I deserved sympathy. Her fuchsia tipped hair was still perfectly coiffed, and her matching Hattie's Café tee shirt was not only spotless, but it was also dry. Because she hadn't fallen in the water. "You love adventure, Mia. Your eyes light up whenever I mention the possibility of picking a lock, sneaking in somewhere, or blatantly ignoring the orders of assorted law enforcement officials."

"Actually," Lucy said, "Mia usually reminds us that she's no longer a criminal and that she's only helping this *one* time. *Then,* her eyes light up."

Hattie grinned. "Exactly. So stop being a wuss, Mia. You're not going home. We have a big trip planned. It will be a blast."

I squeezed my salty hair out over the sink. "I love the adventure of a well-planned con. Or outsmarting a jerk with bad morals. I'm good at that, and I feel confident. Falling in the ocean? A whole different ballgame." Honestly, I did still want to go on the trip, but our destination was about seven miles offshore, and the thought of getting on a boat for a seven-mile ride felt like a little much for me. "Why don't we just stay in a hotel here? We already missed the ferry."

"Can't," Hattie said. "Thelma's counting on us. I'm not going to bail on my cousin. It's her birthday, and I never leave her alone on her birthday. Now that she's a widow, she requires extra care."

I looked over at her. "She's a widow?" How could I abandon a widow on her birthday? If Hattie was telling the truth, then we had to go. Or maybe just Hattie had to go. I mean, I'd never met Thelma, right?

"Yep, her husband died a few years ago," Hattie said. "He was found in the Whispering Caves. Heart attack. Now he whispers with the others."

Lucy and I looked at each other, and the sudden concern on Lucy's face bonded us instantly.

"What are you talking about?" I asked Hattie.

"Whispering Caves are about a mile from Harmony Island. The caves are haunted. At high tide, you can hear the whispers of anyone who has died there, including Roger. Can you imagine poor Thelma? Her husband's spirit whispers during every high tide at a haunted island that's only a mile away from her beautiful, ocean-front house. You think we can possibly leave her to celebrate her birthday by herself?" Hattie put her hands on her hips. "You two are heartless wenches."

I turned to face her. "Are you making that up?"

Hattie grinned. "You'll just have to go to Harmony Island and find out."

"How? How would we even get there? We missed the ferry." Three cheers for that little fact. I was all-in for never venturing out on the ocean for the rest of my life. I mean, I *would* if I could, to support Thelma, but since we'd missed the ferry...

Hattie grinned. "We did indeed miss the ferry," she agreed, much too cheerfully.

Lucy narrowed her eyes. "Hattie," she said warily. "What did you do?"

"Nothing yet, but Vera said she'll ask around. She'll be along in a moment."

Vera was the owner of the Vera's Lobster Shack that we were currently in. I hadn't met her because I'd been in the ambulance being brought back from the dead when she had trotted out to see what all the fuss was about, but Lucy had told me that Vera was a short, sassy, take-charge-boss woman, exactly the kind of woman Hattie would be friends with.

"Ask around for what, exactly?" I'd packed only enough clothes for two nights and three days, so I was already down an outfit. "Look—"

At that moment, the bathroom door flew open with so much force that Lucy and I both jumped back.

Hattie, however, just grinned as a sixty-something hot-ticket strode into the room. "Vera! I'd like you to meet Mia and Lucy. Ladies, this is Vera Jimenez, one of Thelma's best friends, and a fine chef."

Vera was about five-feet tall, olive skin, hair as black as King

Tut, and a smile that literally lit up the room. "Mia! So glad you're all right!" She practically bounded across the room and wrapped me up in a big hug that felt fully genuine. "Any friend of Hattie's is a delight to meet. I'm thrilled you're not dead!"

"Um, thanks. Me, too." I wasn't used to hugging strangers unless I was trying to pickpocket them, but she was such a great hugger that I embraced her right back and left her wallet where it was, although I couldn't help but notice which pocket it was in, where her phone was, and how easy it would be to get her keys.

I *was* reformed, but old habits never died. In fact, they were always thriving, vibrant, and ready to be released back into the world.

Hattie hadn't been lying when she said I had a certain love for the thrill, unfortunately.

Vera hugged Lucy, then beamed at me. "Every summer, some careless tourist dies in the ocean, and I'm delighted it wasn't one of Hattie's friends. Luck is on your side, my friend. I hope it stays with you."

"Mia's difficult to kill," Lucy said cheerfully. "The universe has tried a bunch of times."

"And yet she's still here," Hattie added. "She's like a cat."

"Hopefully not a cat," Lucy said, "or she's almost out of lives."

I raised my hand and waved it. "Hello? I'm right here. I can hear you giving away my chances for survival."

"It keeps you on your toes," Hattie said. "Complacency serves no one." She put her arm through Vera's. "You guys are meeting royalty. Vera owns the two best lobster spots in the entire state. One here, and one on Harmony Island. She built her entire business from nothing while taking care of her baby girl. She's an idol of single moms everywhere."

To my surprise, Vera's smile faltered slightly. It was barely noticeable, but my childhood had made me addicted to observing people, and I knew that something Hattie had just said hadn't set right with Vera. Her daughter? Her business? Lobsters? Something in Vera's little world wasn't quite right.

"Hattie's the superstar," Vera said, quickly deflecting the topic away from herself. Had anyone else noticed she'd done that?

"Oh, they already know I'm a superstar, but it's always a good reminder to the world," Hattie said cheerfully. "You're coming to Thelma's party tomorrow night, right?"

Vera nodded. "You bet. Wouldn't miss it."

"Don't wait too late. There's a big storm forecast," Hattie said.

"I know. I'll be over in plenty of time." Vera grinned, her smile lighting up the room again, almost making me wonder if I'd imagined her hesitation. But I hadn't. I was better than that. "I found you guys a ride over, but he's leaving soon. Blanche also missed the ferry, so she'll split the bill with you."

"Blanche?" I hadn't heard that name before. "Who is Blanche?"

"Blanche Bickstrom is the President of the Knitting Queens," Hattie said, with a shade less enthusiasm than she'd introduced Vera with. Before I could ask what the Knitting Queens were, Hattie moved on. "Why is she over here on the mainland? I thought she was in charge of the party."

Vera leaned in and got a delighted, gossipy expression on her face. "There's a rumor Blanche has a boyfriend over on the mainland, but she won't spill. She came over on the ferry last night and then missed this one." She wiggled her brows. "You'll have to find out what's going on with her on the ride over."

"On it," Hattie said. "I love gossip, especially when it involves illicit activities with men." She picked up her bag. "We're ready. Where's the boat?"

"Captain Jim's boat is called Lady Cassandra. It's a blue and white boat in the last slip on dock number three. Do you know where that is?"

"I can find it." Hattie paused. "Captain Jim," she said thoughtfully. "Why does that name sound familiar?"

Vera grinned. "I dated him about ten years ago. He's a good guy, but he wanted to settle down, so we weren't a fit."

"Right? Who wants to settle down with a man?" Hattie rolled

her eyes. "Freedom is so fantastic." She looked over at us. "Ready ladies?"

"Isn't Harmony Island seven miles out into the ocean?" I put my bagged wet clothes into my roller suitcase.

"About that, yes," Vera said. "Why?"

"How big is Captain Jim's boat? I mean, there's a storm coming in, right?"

Vera raised her brows. "Are you scared? Hattie said you take down assassins."

"I don't want to be in a little boat on the ocean," I admitted. "It does scare me."

"It's a lobster boat," Vera said. "Captain Jim has been a lot further out than that in plenty of storms. You couldn't be in better hands. And the storm isn't coming until later. You're good. Enjoy the day, Mia. It's a grand one."

"Aren't they all?" Hattie grabbed her bags, which she'd set on the child changing table so she didn't have to put them on the floor. Not that the bathroom was dirty. It was actually kind of cute, in a lobster shack kind of way, with a smiling cartoon lobster painted on the wall, and blinged scallop shells super glued to the mirror. "How about a coffee for the road? And how's your baby girl?"

The two sassy seniors headed toward the door. "Simone's not a baby anymore, Hattie. She's in her thirties!"

"That's impossible," Hattie said. "You're much too young for that."

Vera laughed. "Of course I am."

I picked up my bags and started across the restroom, Lucy walking beside me. My sneakers squelched with each step, a gruesome and visceral reminder on how short life could be when a woman's best friend was Hattie Lawless. I felt the ocean in my sneakers, my lungs, and my hair, and I stopped. "I can't do it, Lucy. There's literally no way I can get on a little boat and head out into the ocean."

I was tough, but my two years undercover against Stanley had shaken me, and I was still trying to recover. I'd had a few panic attacks since I'd come to Bass Derby, and Lucy had seen one of them. She knew what secrets I tried to hide when it came to my resilience.

I wasn't as tough as I pretended I was. I wasn't as tough as I wanted to be. Trauma will do that.

Lucy's face softened. "You're more capable than you give yourself credit for, Mia. Plus, you know how to swim."

I let out my breath. "I know, but—"

Hattie stopped and spun around. "Mia, I'm deeply appreciative that you sacrificed yourself to save me, but my gratitude doesn't extend to the point of letting you become some spineless wimp willing to give up on living dangerously just because of a little near-death incident."

"I'm sorry. I can't hear you. There's water in my ear." There *was* water in my left ear, but unfortunately, I could still hear her. "I'm going to call an Uber. It'll be fine."

"It won't be fine," Lucy said. "We'll miss you."

"And no Uber driver will drive you back to Bass Derby from here. It's too far," Hattie added. "We're not in Boston anymore, Toto."

I looked back at her. "Really? Am I Dorothy? And my drug-lord-wife life is Boston?"

"Yes. You're a wimpy little girl too afraid of life to embrace the magical adventure you've been given."

"It's true," Lucy said. "Hattie's treating us to a five-star resort on a glorious island. You can't seriously walk away from that just because you're scared of the ocean."

I grimaced. "I do want to go," I admitted.

"Then do it," Hattie said. "It's okay to be afraid. But it's not okay to miss out on life because of fear."

That was something my mom would have said.

My mom.

The triple X was still on my phone, which I'd declined to leave with Devlin, in case she tried to reach me again.

25

My mom had spent a lot of time teaching me how to manage fear, and knowing when to listen to it, and when to ignore it. It was funny how I could be so confident dealing with assassins, but be terrified of going out into the ocean in a small boat. Fear was weird like that, wasn't it? It didn't always make sense, but it was real.

"Mia," Lucy said gently. "You'll be fine."

I looked over at Vera. "You're sure Captain Jim is capable?"

"Absolutely. And very dashing."

"I love dashing men." Hattie grinned. "I bet he even has life jackets Mia could wear."

I fisted my hand around the handle of my bag. Missing the chance for a girls trip with Hattie and Lucy was pretty much tragic for me in my infancy of the world of girl bonding. Was I really going to let fear deprive me of that?

I couldn't. Fear could never win. It just couldn't.

Lucy grinned. "Mia's in. I can see it in her eyes."

"Captain Jim's boat better be in good shape," I warned. "Or I'm not getting on."

"Oh, it is," Vera said. "I promise."

"All right then." I grinned. "Let's do this."

CHAPTER 4

WHEN WE ARRIVED at dock number three, there were three boats moored.

Two beautiful, white boats that looked like they were treated with love and serviced regularly.

The last boat looked like it was at least fifty years old, and still had remnants of the blue paint job that it had been given when it was made. Oh, boy. "Tell me that's not Lady Cassandra."

"Um…" Lucy hesitated. "It matches Vera's description, but she did say it was a good boat."

At that moment, a gray-haired, tough-looking man with dark brown skin, a faded gray shirt, baggy jeans, and high red rubber boots, and what looked like a gray Irish cap walked out on the deck of the sad-looking boat. He saw us coming and waved. "Hellooo," he bellowed, his voice echoing like it was in a cave, even though he was in open air. "Made it just in time!"

"Oh, well, isn't he rugged?" Hattie said cheerily. "Happy day to us!" She left us behind and went trotting down the dock, waving at Captain Jim.

My feet felt glued to the dock. "Lady Cassandra looks like she'll sink the minute we untie her."

"Captain Jim is a lobsterman." Lucy pushed my back to get me moving. "He can't have a sinking boat, or he'd be broke."

"Maybe he's a really good swimmer and sinks boats on a regular basis." My heart started to race as we neared the boat. It had a high bow that sloped down to a stern that sat much too low in the water. There was a small white cabin with a blue roof in the middle of the boat, and all the paint was peeling off that as well. "I don't want to get on that."

Lucy put her arm over my shoulder as Hattie hurled her bag onto the boat and hopped up with evident glee. "You're a freaking badass, Mia. Nothing stops you from what matters to you."

I watched Hattie's animated face as she chatted with Captain Jim. I didn't want to miss this weekend, not for anything. "Maybe he has life jackets."

"I'm sure he does." Lucy squeezed my shoulder. "Don't worry. I'm a great swimmer and I'm fearless around water. I'll save you if you fall in."

I looked over at her. "I don't want to actually fall in and need to be rescued."

"It'll be good for you to fall in. It will get you over your new fear of the ocean before it has time to settle in permanently and trap you forever."

Fear. I hated being afraid, but the ferry moment was trying to dig its ruthless talons of fear and disempowerment into my psyche. Which meant I had to face it and tear it down. I raised my chin and pulled my shoulders back. "I refuse to live in fear. It'll be good for me to get out there again."

"Exactly. Nothing conquers fear like action." Lucy waved at Captain Jim as we approached the boat. "Hi! I'm Lucy Grande. This is Mia Murphy."

I waved at him. "I almost died falling in the ocean earlier today, so I need to know you can keep us alive." Yes, I was trying to ditch the fear, but a little warm reminder of his job as our captain was never a bad thing.

He stared at me, then burst out laughing. "Can't promise nothing like that. Life ain't like that, especially not on the ocean."

Great. Captain Jim and I were clearly going to be great friends.

"Oh, come on, Mia," Hattie said. "We're going to have an adventure. Captain Jim said he'd take us past the haunted caves on the way."

"Haunted caves?" How had Hattie already had time to get a personalized tour arranged? She'd been chatting with him for less than thirty seconds.

"Yep." Captain Jim held out his hand to help me on board, his grip reassuringly strong and steady despite the visible number of decades on his face. "It's where bodies are found."

"Bodies?" I grabbed a life jacket from a crevice in the side of the boat and yanked it over my head. "What kind of bodies?"

"He said all kinds!" Hattie said cheerfully as Lucy hopped on board. "Back in the pirate days, they found some old pirate booty and skeletons. And now, people go check it out, and get stranded at high tide, and oopsie!"

"Oopsie? Isn't that a little cavalier for people who drown in caves?" I had a new, very strong empathy for people murdered by the ocean.

"Oh, it doesn't happen much," Captain Jim said as he started the engine. "Folks don't die, unless a storm causes an extremely high tide, like we had a couple days ago. Then the caves fill with water, but no one goes out in that kind of storm. Normally, people simply get trapped out there for a few hours, and that's when the ghosts come out."

"Ghosts!" Hattie looked thrilled. "I knew about the whispers, but actual *ghosts*? Isn't that spectacular?"

I rolled my eyes, recalling the ghost whisperer that we'd recently had to deal with. "Ghosts are overrated." Did they even exist? I wasn't about to claim I had the answer, but I was definitely skeptical.

"You're too young to be so boring, Mia," Hattie said. "With all the corpses we've run into lately, you'd think you'd have a little more imagination."

"Corpses?" Captain Jim put the boat into reverse and began to back out of the slip. "You guys run into a lot of bodies?"

Before we could answer with our long list, we were interrupted by a loud holler.

"Hey! Hey! Wait for me! Captain Jim! Hattie! Yoohoo!"

Captain Jim glanced down the dock, then put the boat in neutral. "Whoops."

A woman about Hattie's age was running down the dock...if you could call it running. It was more of a shuffle with about every fourth step being a run. She was pushing a cart that was loaded with shopping bags. Balloons were flapping around, bouncing off her face. She kept whacking the balloons away, trying to see past the myriad of colors. Her hair was gray, reaching almost the middle of her back. It looked like it had been a few days since she'd brushed it, but it could have just been the wind. Was this Blanche? I'd totally forgotten about her.

Hattie grinned. "Dang it. I thought we'd gotten away in time." She stood up. "Hurry up, you lazy dog!"

"Coming, you old rat!" she shouted back.

Lucy leaned over and caught a piling as Blanche hurried up. "Captain Jim," Blanche hollered, "you let that ancient bat distract you. Never trust that woman."

He grinned. "I never trust any women. No news there."

"You can trust me," Hattie said. "I'm a goddess in every way." She walked over to the edge of the boat and eyed Blanche's cart. "Is this for the party? It's tomorrow. Cutting it a little close?"

"Have you ever tried to buy balloons on the island? Or sexy party supplies? Well, let me tell you, they don't have any fun stuff on the island. You need to go to Portland for that." Blanche held up a bag. "Come on, let's load up."

"Sexy party supplies?" I glanced at Lucy, who wiggled her eyebrows at me.

"Of course sexy party supplies." Blanche thrust a bag at me.

"It's important to always remember that you're a vibrant, passionate woman no matter what age you are, or how you feel. Gotta keep that spirit burning bright! Come on, people! Let's take action!"

I liked Blanche. She was ornery, bossy, and called Hattie names. She was going to be fun, I could tell. With her ordering everyone around, it took only a few minutes to unload her cart. I saw a few items poking out of bags that made Captain Jim look twice and then hide a grin.

Within moments, we were all settled. Lucy and I were on a bench in the middle. The cart was upside down over the balloons so they wouldn't get whipped around by the wind. Lucy had her foot on the cart to keep it from sliding. Hattie was next to Captain Jim asking him questions about the engine and gears, and Blanche was sitting on a bench opposite us, rifling through her bags.

"Let's go, ladies!" Captain Jim put *Lady Cassandra* into reverse for a second time, and the boat eased away from the dock. "I gotta know about the corpses," he said. "You guys really find a lot of them?"

Blanche looked up sharply. "A corpse? You found a *corpse*? Where? Who? When?"

"Lots of them," Hattie said. "Mia's the Corpse Whisperer. They follow her wherever we go."

I wished the boat came with seatbelts. "I'm not the Corpse Whisperer."

"You are." Lucy climbed up on the bench and leaned over the side, hanging out over the water. "But it's good. It makes life fun. We love you anyway."

"We love you because of it," Hattie said. "That would be awesome if you'd attract another corpse adventure for the weekend. Can you do that?"

I folded my arms across my chest. "I'm not attracting another corpse."

"*Another* corpse?" Blanche stared at us, alarm on her face. "You find bodies? Like murdered people?"

"We do," Hattie said. "If there's a body around, we'll find it."

"And solve the murder," Lucy chimed in cheerfully. "We're better than the cops! It's fun!"

Blanche sat up, looking at us. "You guys solve *murders?*"

"Not officially," I said. "It just happens that sometimes we get a little tangled up in them."

"But it is fun," Hattie said.

"I bet it's fun," Captain Jim said. "Murder is sexy. I'm looking to boost my fishing with some local boat tours. I could sell myself as the guy who found a corpse. If you guys find one, can you bring me in on it?"

"Murder isn't sexy—" My protest was drowned out as Hattie agreed enthusiastically to keep Captain Jim in the murder loop.

"Fantastic." Looking absolutely delighted with how the day was unfolding, Captain Jim opened up the throttle, and the boat shot forward.

The old boat went startlingly fast, and it lurched over the waves, bouncing me nearly off the seat.

I grabbed the edges of the seat, while Lucy let out a whoop of delight.

"Murder's a tourist money-maker," Captain Jim shouted over the wind, the crashing waves, and the roar of the engine. "Every time there's a new body in those caves, it amps up tourism."

"Every time?" I shouted. "How many have there been?"

"Roger Gold about three years ago. There were three about ten years ago, and then, before that, it had been maybe thirty or forty years."

"Three?" I shouted. "All at once?"

"Nah. It was over a couple months. That's when the cave really got its reputation."

"Cool," Lucy yelled. "Who was it?"

"The then-manager of the Pirate Pines resort, and a couple of its staff," Captain Jim said.

"Wow," Hattie shouted. "That's crazy, since Thelma's husband was the manager!"

"What?" I stood up. "Seriously? Is the resort cursed?" Cursed and ocean-locked? This was looking like a worse idea for a weekend by the minute.

Blanche was listening to the conversation with a very alarmed expression on her face.

Lucy kicked me with her foot. "You don't believe in curses, do you? You seem way too practical for that."

"No, but isn't that weird? Four people who worked at the resort wound up dead in the same cave?"

"I'm telling ya," Captain Jim shouted over the roar of the engine and the wind. "People like to go into those caves. They get trapped, and stuff happens."

"Were they murdered?" I had to ask. Not that murderers scared me anymore, at least not as much as they should, but there were too many pieces involved here to be a coincidence.

"They all were unsolved. Murder or accident? No one knows," Captain Jim replied. "But their ghosts still hang around, so maybe they've got a reason to be sticking around."

"Have you seen the ghosts?" Hattie asked.

"I haven't," Captain Jim said.

Hattie looked over at Blanche. "What about you? Have you seen the ghosts or heard the whispers?"

"I don't go to the caves," she said. "I've never been."

"What? How could you not go?" Hattie looked surprised.

"It's not my thing." Blanche looked away as she said it, avoiding eye contact. "Can I drive, Captain Jim?" She stood up and walked over to him and Hattie, changing the topic.

Lucy looked at me and raised her brows. I agreed. Blanche had a little secret about those caves. All these women with their secrets! Who needed murderers? We had Blanche, Vera, and haunted caves.

Lucy patted my legs as she plopped herself down next to me. "Aren't you glad you came?"

Hattie's roar of laughter drifted over the engines and the wind, and I looked over at her. She was standing beside Captain Jim again, and he'd let her take the wheel, while Blanche poked fun at her. Hattie gave me a thumbs up, a huge grin on her face. The wind was whipping through her fuchsia hair, whipping her curls into oblivion, and she didn't care at all. She was pure joy, and I felt it begin to infect me.

"I am glad I came," I admitted. "We do have fun."

"Right? And we never die, either!"

"Yet. We never die, *yet*."

Lucy grinned. "'Yet' is all we need. And honestly, we're not going to the Harmony Island for bodies. We're going for a VIP treatment at a gorgeous resort. How can that not be fun?" She grabbed my arm and tugged. "Come on! To your feet, you land lubber!"

I laughed and let her pull me to my feet. The ocean stretched ahead of us, dark gray, rough, and bottomless. For a moment, I felt a little vulnerable in this old boat in the middle of the ocean, and then I looked over at Captain Jim, Hattie, and Blanche. They were having a blast, cracking each other up, and completely comfortable.

They knew they were safe, and I decided to trust them, and go with it.

I put my arms up in the air, mimicking Lucy's pose, and was just about to let out a howl of delight when the boat slammed into something. The impact threw me and Lucy forward, and we crashed into the bow. I almost shot over the front of the boat, but Lucy grabbed my life jacket and hauled me back as the boat thudded again, this time the thud coming from under the middle of the boat, as if we'd hit something and then run over it.

Captain Jim stopped the boat. "What in the hollering lobsters was that? Nothing should be in the water here," he said. "Gotta check that out."

It was going to be a body. I knew it.

Only minutes into our girls weekend, and we were already going to find a body.

CHAPTER 5

WE ALL JUMPED up and searched the choppy waters. I was looking for a long, dark shape that would be the right size for a body, but all I saw were whitecaps and the ominous gray swells of the water.

"I got nothing over here," Hattie yelled.

"Me either," Lucy said.

"I don't—" I cut myself off when I noticed a glint of something in the water. "Wait! What's that?" I pointed, and everyone came over to my side to look. Captain Jim drove us closer, until I could see that it was a flat, shiny-ish object, floating on the surface of the water. It was pale gray, just light enough to be a contrast to the water.

"That's definitely not a body," I said happily.

"Don't be so pessimistic," Hattie said. "It could be a torso."

Blanche hit Hattie in the shoulder. "You're a monster, you wrinkled, old menace."

"I'm a vibrant, enthusiastic participant in the joys of life," Hattie retorted. "I see joy everywhere!"

"Even in someone's tragic death?"

"If that's what the universe challenges me with, then I'm in for the win," Hattie said.

Hattie had never talked about Blanche before, but I was deeply enjoying their banter. They felt like sisters or besties who had known each other since they were stealing each other's toys in the sandbox. "If I start calling you a wrinkled, old menace, will that bond us even more?" I asked.

Hattie shot me a deathly look. "Don't you dare, you smartass little thief."

I grinned. She'd called me a name. I was in the club.

Captain Jim turned the boat around. "Someone grab it off the stern as we go by."

I gripped my life jacket. "I'm good." There was no way I was leaning out over the ocean to drag that thing in.

"I got it," Lucy said, moving past our bags to the back.

"Put on a life jacket," I yelled.

She ignored me and sat down on the bench across the very back of the boat. The rail was only a few inches high, easily low enough for her to tumble off, right into the propeller.

"Do you have a hook or something I could use, Captain Jim?"

"Yeah, here." He handed a metal pole with a curved hook to Hattie, who passed it on to Lucy.

Maybe for pulling in lobster traps? That was so handy.

We all leaned over to watch as Lucy fished for the item.

"I think it's a suitcase," Blanche said.

"A suitcase? No chance that was a suitcase," Captain Jim said. "The impact was too hard."

I inched over to the stern to look more closely. It was a rectangle object, shiny metal. "It looks like a metal storage trunk." I had some of those in the maintenance shop at the marina.

"Definitely a trunk," Hattie agreed.

I grinned. "Well that's good. I thought it might be a body."

"Me, too," Hattie said. "Honestly, I'm bitterly disappointed right now."

"I'm not going to lie. I'm disappointed as well," Captain Jim said.

"Could still be a torso," Blanche said dryly. "Just stuff that sucker right in there. Maybe the head is in another trunk we'll run into."

"Oh, right! Great attitude!" Hattie said much more cheerfully. "Whoever said you can't teach an old dog new tricks hasn't met you yet."

"I'm younger than you are," Blanche snapped.

"In your mind!" Hattie winked at me as she said it, and I grinned.

Lucy hooked a handle onto the end of her rod, and began to carefully pull the trunk in. "Got it."

Captain Jim cut the engine and came back to supervise as Lucy dragged it closer to the boat. I was impressed with her precision. Despite the waves and the bouncing boat, she never lost her grip on the trunk, and within a few moments, it was right up behind our boat.

She stepped out onto the platform on the back of the boat, and Captain Jim did the same.

Hattie immediately climbed out there with him, despite the fact that the platform was only about twelve inches wide. "Come on, Mia."

Ohh… "I'll stay here and supervise."

"Me, too," Blanche said. "Someone needs to be smart enough not to fall into the ocean and clearly that's going to be me, today."

"Mia needs to fall in again," Hattie said. "Mia, get your butt out of the boat. All the good stuff in life lies on the other side of fear."

"By 'good stuff,' you mean pulling a trunk out of the ocean?" I didn't care that she was calling me scared. I knew that I was tough, but I also had my limits. Falling into the ocean had scared the bejeebers out of me, and I was owning it. "Is that the kind of 'good stuff' worth risking my life for?"

"Oh, for the sake of all that's sweet and sour in the world, you're not risking your life by being out there." She bounced up and down on the transom. "See? It's all good!"

"Am I in your will?" Blanche asked. "Because if I am, you keep right on bouncing."

"I'm leaving everything to Mia's cat. That's a soul worth supporting."

My heart got all warm and fuzzy. King Tut was a special treasure for sure.

"Then die, old lady, die, for all I care."

"Oh, for heaven's sake, stop that!" Lucy went down on her knees. "No one's going to die, and you two need to start hugging instead of pretending you hate each other."

"Hate?" Hattie looked surprised as she and Captain Jim bent down to grab the trunk. "I don't hate Blanche."

"Who could hate Hattie?" Blanche said. "She's just so much fun to torment. No one can keep up with me except Hattie."

"Exactly. It's my job to keep her on her toes," Hattie said. "That's what friends are for."

"Well, then friend this trunk onto the boat," Lucy said. "Let's go."

I considered trying to force myself to climb over the transom, but I was inspired by Blanche, who was owning her right not to climb over and risk her life for a trunk.

I folded my arms over my chest and stayed where I was. The ocean was just so bottomless, and I still had the salt in my soul from my last plunge. "In case you guys fall in, Blanche and I will rescue you." That was actually true. See? Sometimes fear was wise and helpful.

Lucy rolled her eyes at me, but I felt empowered by setting boundaries. Yay me.

"Toss me a rope, then," Lucy said.

I looked around and found a rope tucked in beside the other life jackets. I grabbed it and handed it to Lucy. While Hattie and Captain Jim held the trunk next to our boat, Lucy quickly tied a rope around her handle, then handed me the rope. "Don't let go," she instructed me.

"Got it." Delighted to be feeling useful even though I wasn't out on the boat's precipice of death, I wrapped the rope around my hand a few times to get a good grip while my pals all grabbed the handles.

Blanche leaned against the edge of the boat. "You all sure you want to bring that thing on board? Could be anything. Maybe not something you want."

"Or maybe it is," Hattie said. "Where's your sense of adventure, you old stick-in-the-mud?"

"I have plenty of adventure, you old bat. I just don't waste time with stuff that doesn't matter."

"On three," Captain Jim ordered. "Mia, you pull as well."

"On it."

We all braced ourselves, which wasn't that easy with the boat bobbing in the water.

"One. Two. Three!"

I leaned back, using all my body weight to pull on the rope while my friends hauled on the handles. The trunk came out a few inches. "Come on!" Captain Jim yelled. "Don't be a girl!"

With a loud grunt, Lucy hauled her end up onto the boat, then dragged it back toward her, basically hauling Hattie and Captain Jim's end out of the water as well. She dropped her end on the transom with a thunk and glared at Captain Jim. "You just used 'girl' as an insult? A *girl* just pulled that whole thing out while you were trying not to fall in." She flipped her braids at him, then hopped back into the boat.

I grinned, and I high-fived her as she landed in the boat. "Well-played, my friend."

She winked at me. "One of my greatest joys in life is when men underestimate my strength."

Hattie let out a whoop. "That's my girl," she told Captain Jim. "Don't mess with my girls!"

Captain Jim saluted Lucy. "I surrender," he said. "You kicked ass on that one. Let's get this on board."

It took five minutes, a lot of sweat and curses, but we finally got the trunk over the transom and into the boat. As it thudded to the floor of the boat, we stood around it and inspected it. The trunk was about eighteen inches high and wide, and about thirty inches long. It was a shiny, smooth metal, with reinforced rivets on every corner.

It was locked. Not a padlock, but an actual lock. More of a challenge, which was always fun.

"Can you open it?" Hattie asked.

"Maybe." I knocked on it. "It sounds like solid metal."

Lucy frowned. "In the movies, it's the kind of case that would contain a nuclear warhead. Or some kind of virus that will kill ten million people in three seconds. It has that look."

I stared down at it, frowning. "You're not wrong."

"It does have a bit of an end-of-the-world apocalyptic feel to it," Hattie agreed as she stood beside me. None of us made a move toward it.

"Never seen anything like that," Captain Jim said. "Maybe it's alien."

"Alien?" We all looked at him.

"Yeah." He didn't take his eyes off it. "Or military."

"Military?" I frowned at that thought. "It does look pretty official."

"I agree," said Lucy.

"Me, too," said Hattie. "All the more reason to open it."

"Unless it contains the virus." I paused. "Give me a sec." I quickly pulled out my phone and Facetimed Griselda, the FBI agent who had handled my two-year undercover stint against my drug lord ex-husband. He'd stopped answering every call at every moment after the sting was over, but since he'd recently declared his interest in dating yours truly, I hoped it meant he'd be a little more on it with my calls.

It was tricky. Especially since I didn't want to date anyone ever again...and yet found both Griselda and Devlin irritatingly tempting.

But would I use them to make sure I wasn't going to have my face melt if I picked the lock? Yes. Yes, I would.

Joyfully for me, Griselda (aka Agent Straus) answered on

probably the last ring before I would have hung up. He was wearing a tee shirt and sunglasses, and he looked like he was on a river. I expected him to glare at me and bark out some question like, "Where are you?" like he always did.

But instead, he flashed a dimpled grin at me and said, "Hey, Mia." His tone was friendly, warm, and almost sounded happy. What. The. Devil.

I stared at him. "What did you do with Griselda?"

His brows went up. "What are you talking about?"

"You're being nice. You greeted me like a normal person. That's almost creepy coming from you."

He smiled then said, "The playing field has changed. I'm trying to appear dateable now. Answering your call politely felt like a good start."

"I don't want the playing field to change." I was so used to Griselda being a pain in the butt, annoying, and aggravating. I hadn't expected his declaration that he wanted to date me to result in him answering the phone like a civilized human being. "I like being annoyed by you."

He didn't look remotely apologetic for being nice. "I'll still annoy you. But I figured I needed to up my game. Were you calling to invite me on a date? Had a little time to think about my offer, and you're ready to give it a try?"

"No. God, no. Never." The minute I said "never," a little voice inside me said I was lying. I wanted it to be never. But I couldn't promise. He was making things complicated, and I didn't want complicated. Ack. I felt like I was choking. I had not been ready for grumpy pants to turn on the "I want to date you" switch right now. "Stop it."

His smile widened, and amusement flickered in his eyes. "You're flustered. I've never seen you flustered."

"You're an idiot." I waved the phone in the air. "Someone else talk to him."

Lucy grabbed the phone and waved. "Hi, Griselda."

He gave a grumpy sigh that felt reassuringly familiar. "My name's Hawk. And hi, Lucy."

"Hi, there!" Hattie leaned in and blew him a kiss. "I'd call you Hawk, but girl solidarity prevails, so you're Griselda in my book."

"Hi, Hattie." He sounded resigned now. His tone was a little cooler, now that he realized I probably wasn't calling him for dating talk, which made me so much happier. "Devlin said that it's trouble when the three of you are together."

"And me!" Blanche leaned in and waved. "Blanche Bickstrom. President of the Knitting Queens."

I could almost feel Griselda's pain in his grunt of acknowledgment. He was a high-level FBI agent, and I was sure there were many things he'd rather be doing than Facetiming my friends.

And yet, he was doing it anyway. Point for him.

"Plus me." Captain Jim leaned over Hattie's shoulder. "Who are you?"

Griselda narrowed his eyes. "Who are *you*?"

I took the phone back and quickly did a brief intro. "Captain Jim, this is Agent Straus from the FBI. Griselda, Captain Jim is transporting us to Harmony Island for a girls trip, but on our way, he ran into a floating, locked trunk. We fished it out of the ocean, but before we opened it, I thought we better check to see if you recognized it."

He frowned. "Me? Why would I recognize a trunk you found in the ocean?"

"Because it looks kind of official." I flipped the camera around and aimed it at the trunk. "What do you think? Because we don't want to open it if it's going to melt our faces off or something like that."

"You think it's a torso?" Hattie asked hopefully.

"Walk around it," Griselda said. "Let me see it from all sides."

I glanced at my friends when he spoke. The fact he'd immediately gone into business mode told us that we hadn't been wrong that there was something to this trunk. We all waited silently while I walked around the trunk, giving Griselda a three-sixty-view of our finding.

When I'd walked around twice, Griselda swore under his breath. "I'm not sure what it is, but I agree that you shouldn't open it. I'll call a local contact and have him meet you on shore. What dock are you near?"

We looked at each other, including Captain Jim.

"Mute him," Hattie whispered.

I hit the mute button and turned the volume off as Griselda's mouth continued to move. "What?"

"We need to open that trunk," Hattie said. "What if it's something cool?"

"I agree," said Lucy.

"Me, too. It's my boat. It's our find. This could be great for business," Captain Jim said.

"You guys are trouble," Blanche said, "But I'm in. Finders keepers if it's good. We throw it back in the ocean if it's bad."

"We're not polluting the ocean," Lucy said.

"What if it's asps?" Hattie said. "What if a thousand poisonous snakes are there? Do you want to stay on the boat with them?"

She raised her brows. "Asps."

"You never know."

"Fine. If it's asps, we'll let them drown."

"Smart girl." Hattie turned back to me. "Open it."

"But keep Griselda on Facetime," Lucy said, "just in case it's something that could get us in trouble, like a body. Then he can be our witness that we didn't kill the guy."

"Good call." Hattie snatched my phone out of my hand. "I'll keep the camera on you while you open it."

I hesitated for a moment. "When I found cocaine in my china cabinet, it changed my life forever. You can't ever go back and wish you hadn't found it. What if it's something like that?"

Hattie put her hands on her hips. "Finding that cocaine landed you in Bass Derby with two besties, plus freedom from a drug-dealing husband, who would have had to kill you at some point if you'd stuck around. Best thing you ever did, finding that cocaine."

She had a point. "All right." I went down on my knees and pulled out my lock picks. "You can unmute him."

"What are you doing?" Griselda nearly shouted as I leaned down to inspect the lock more closely.

"Don't yell, or we'll turn off your volume again," I said. I checked my lock picks and selected the one I thought would work.

"Mia, I swear to God—"

"Don't swear to God," Hattie said. "That's very rude. And we're keeping you with us so you can witness whatever we find, in case it gets ugly fast."

Griselda swore, but he knew me well enough to know that nothing he could do would stop me. Now that the sting operation was over, he didn't control me or my life, and I would never let anyone control me again the way he had.

The boat, including Griselda, fell silent as I worked. It took a few tries, and more creativity than I'd had to draw on in a while, but it wasn't long until I heard the audible click of the lock giving way.

I looked at my friends. "You ready?"

They all nodded, but took a couple steps back.

Right. Okay. I flipped the latches holding the case shut, then I raised the lid.

It wasn't a body.

It wasn't a torso.

It wasn't even drugs.

But it *was* money.

A. Lot. Of. Money.

"Holy mother of magic," Hattie whispered.

Griselda swore. "Close that case and get back to the dock. Now."

"It's mine," Captain Jim said. "Finders keepers."

I grabbed the bundle nearest to me and lifted it up. I flipped through and saw that the entire stack of bills were twenty-dollar denominations, nicely wrapped and stacked. My gut congealed with fear, because I knew what kind of person had money like that. I held it up to the phone and showed Griselda. "Drug dealer? Arms dealer?"

"I don't know," Griselda said, "but whoever lost that will do whatever it takes to get it back from the four of you. Close the trunk, lock it, cover it, and haul ass back to the dock. What dock, Captain Jim? And how far out are you?"

While Captain Jim conversed with Griselda about location, I slammed the trunk shut and locked it, well aware that Captain Jim might try to help himself to a few bills when no one was looking. I looked at Hattie and Lucy. "The people who this belongs to probably have lots of guns and like using them," I whispered.

Hattie looked slightly alarmed. "That's a lot of money," she whispered. "I'd kill over it too if it was mine."

At that moment, I heard the rhythmic thud of a helicopter. I looked up, and I saw one flying low over the water toward us. "Holy crap!"

"Boobs out," Hattie shouted. "No man notices anything when boobs are out!" She ripped off her top, revealing thankfully that she was wearing her bathing suit under her clothes.

Captain Jim hurled a tarp at us, and Lucy and I yanked it over the trunk. Captain Jim hit the gas, while I threw a couple beach towels on top of the tarped-up trunk. Hattie sat down on the trunk and leaned her head back, thrusting her breasts into the sky.

Blanche jumped next to her and tore off her shirt as well. The two sassy seniors struck poses worthy of Marilyn Monroe, the two of them covering the whole trunk with bare legs and boobs.

Lucy and I looked at each other, and with a sigh, we both pulled off our shirts. I didn't have my suit on, but I had a sports bra, so off my shirt went, along with the lifejacket I'd been clinging to so dearly. Lucy leaned back against the transom and pulled her foot up by her ear, which almost tore my own hamstring simply by watching her.

I grabbed my phone from the dash, where Captain Jim had left it, then I leaned against the side of the boat and took my hair out of the ponytail, trying to look like part of Captain Jim's harem as our boat picked up speed.

The helicopter flew toward us, and my heart started racing. It was definitely coming to check us out.

"Head toward the island," Hattie shouted at Captain Jim. "That's closer than going back to the mainland."

"You got it!"

We were hurtling across the waves now, but this time, I wasn't feeling so worried about flying out of the boat, because you know, priorities and all that. "Don't look at the helicopter," I shouted. "Let's just have fun."

"I am having fun," Hattie yelled. "I love adventures!"

The helicopter was so close to us. I looked up at it, because it would have looked suspicious to pretend I didn't notice the helicopter flying over our heads. I turned my phone so Griselda could see the helicopter.

The wind kicked up into a frenzy as the helicopter passed over, flying so low I felt like I could reach up and grab it. We all looked up, and I saw a man leaning out of the helicopter, looking down at us with binoculars.

Holy crap. They weren't messing around. Which was better, being chopped up by a ferry boat or gunned down by a drug dealer? Neither. Definitely neither.

I needed to get them away from us, and fast. If this money was illegal, they would want to stay off the radar. "Video them," I shouted. "Pull your phones and record them!"

I held my phone up, making it obvious I was recording them, except I was actually Facetiming Griselda. I looked at the others and held up my phone, gesturing for them to do the same.

They immediately grabbed their phones and did the same, so all four of us were filming them.

The helicopter peeled off almost immediately, speeding away as it quickly gained altitude and got out of range of our phones.

"Holy mammoth lobster," Hattie said. "What the heck was that?"

"I don't know," I said, "but I want to get off this boat. Captain Jim, get us to the island." The fact that the helicopter had taken off when we'd started to record them was a possible indication that all was not on the up and up with them. *Crap.* Griselda was yelling at me about something, so I hung up on him.

No one got to yell at me, even if I was in the middle of an arms deal.

"Heck, yeah!" Captain Jim opened up the throttle even more, and the boat took off across the water, bouncing and leaping across the waves. I grabbed my lifejacket and strapped it back on, then made my way across the boat to my friends.

Lucy and I sat on the back side of the trunk, our backs against Blanche and Hattie's.

It was too loud to talk, but we sat together, squished on that trunk full of money.

Wondering how long it would take until Binocular Guy in that helicopter realized what Hattie and Blanche had actually been sitting on. Could we make it to shore before they turned around and came back for us?

CHAPTER 6

THIRTY MINUTES LATER, we were docked at the Harmony Island pier and out of *Lady Cassandra.* We'd helped Blanche unload her party supplies, and we had all our luggage on the dock. Still alive. Yay for us.

"Heck, yeah," Hattie said as we gathered on the dock. "See why we missed the ferry? Because we were meant to have that adventure!"

Blanche grabbed the handle of her cart. "Eh. You want adventure, come to Thelma's party."

"You want help setting up?" I asked.

Blanche snorted. "Heck no. I have most of it set up at Thelma's already. It's a surprise for all."

"Her house?" That surprised me. "Why not have it at the resort?"

Blanche winked. "Because there are rules at the resort. We don't like rules, do we?"

"Heck no," Hattie answered. "No rules! Can't wait! Thelma's meeting us on the beach. We'll keep her occupied until you're ready."

Blanche grinned. "You keep being so helpful and I won't need to drive you out of town at dawn."

"You wish I'd stay forever," Hattie retorted.

"I'm not going to lie, I do. You liven up the place, and we need it here. Thanks for the ride, Captain Jim."

"You bet. Can I come to the party?"

"Girls only!" Blanche shouted as she trotted off down the dock, towing her overloaded cart behind her. "We'll use you as a party favor if you show up!"

Captain Jim looked speculative as he watched her go. "Might be worth it," he said under his breath.

"To be a party favor?" Lucy asked. "I'd think that would scare you."

He laughed softly. "Everything about those women scare me, but they're good people. Especially Thelma. Don't see her much these days, but she's one heck of a woman."

The three of us looked at each other. Did Captain Jim have an affinity for Thelma? "Are you married Captain Jim?" Lucy asked.

"Me? Nah. Been waiting for the right time and the right woman."

"All this time?"

He shrugged. "When you know what you want, you'll wait." He took his gaze off Blanche's retreating figure. "You all still want to go to the haunted caves tomorrow? Maybe Thelma would like to come?"

I grinned. Oh, yes. Captain Jim was holding a torch for Thelma. I wondered if she knew that.

"Don't know about Thelma, but we're a yes for a trip," Hattie said. "I'll text you."

"Great! I'll look forward to it." He looked at Lucy. "Help me drag this trunk out of the boat. I don't want that thing on my boat any longer."

"Out of the boat?" I unfastened my life jacket and handed it back to him. "Aren't you taking it back to the mainland for the FBI?"

Captain Jim snorted. "No way. No money is worth that. I'm dumping it on the dock here, and then I'm jetting."

"What?" Alarm shot through me. "No. You can't leave the trunk here! Those people will come to the island to get it!" The island was our oasis for the next two days, so it couldn't also contain a magnet to attract gun-toting bad guys. "I'm not giving them a reason to come after my boat. I'm not dying just so the FBI can check them out."

As much as I didn't want that trunk sticking around the island, I didn't blame Captain Jim. "Hang on." I stepped away and called Griselda again.

He answered on the first ring. "Where are you? I have people waiting at the main dock."

Ah...that was the old Griselda. Right to business. I was so much more comfortable with this Griselda. "After that helicopter incident, we wanted to get off the water, and Harmony Island was closer. So that's where we are."

There was silence.

I grinned. Griselda was so adorable when he was outraged by my lack of malleability. "Captain Jim wants it off his boat," I continued. "He's not going back in the ocean with it. Can you have someone collect it here?"

Griselda unleashed a litany of curses mixed in with my name.

I put it on speaker phone and let everyone enjoy his creativity. Captain Jim grinned. "I feel like I need to take notes. This is some good stuff right here."

After a while, Griselda calmed down enough to speak. "Tell Captain Jim to stay where he is. I'll have someone there within an hour—"

Captain Jim barked laughter. "Screw that. I'm not going to stand around here and guard it. Anyone who wants that thing can take it. I'm going to go get a beer and fried clams at Vera's. If it's still in my boat when I get back, I'm tossing it overboard and taking off. I gotta leave in thirty minutes so that's how long you have. My boat's name is *Lady Cassandra*, and she's at the last slip." He punched the disconnect button on my phone and walked away, leaving me holding my phone.

Wow. Captain Jim had hung up on an FBI agent he didn't even know. I loved that.

Captain Jim suddenly paused and turned around. "You ladies need me? You guys okay?"

Aww…that was sweet. "We're good," I said. "But thanks."

He nodded. "Hattie, you have my number. Call if you need anything." He winked. "I like you ladies. The world needs to keep you in it." Then he turned and strode away, leaving us staring after him, surprised by the warmth from the grizzled lobsterman.

My phone rang, interrupting our moment of man-appreciation. I looked down at the screen. "It's Griselda."

Hattie waggled her finger at me. "Silence that phone, babycakes. We're on vacation now."

Captain Jim was already halfway down the dock, whistling as if he didn't have a care in the world.

Maybe he didn't. Maybe he was resilient and carefree.

I admired that so much. Captain Jim might be my new idol. I took a breath, and decided to let the whole trunk scenario go. We'd made it to the island, the helicopter wasn't in sight, and it was girl time. "I'm in. Let's do this!" I silenced my phone, shoved it in my pocket and picked up my backpack. "Girl time!"

Lucy grinned and put her arm over my shoulder. "This is going to be a great weekend," she announced. "I'm ready to be pampered!"

"Me, too." Hattie extended the handle on her pink and blue flowered bag and started wheeling it down the dock. "Margaritas, beach time, and birthday fiesta, here we come!"

I noticed she didn't say corpses, which was fantastic.

She'd gotten her excitement for the weekend, and now it was just going to be peace and quiet.

Hattie beamed at us. "Wait until you meet Thelma. She makes me look boring!"

Lucy and I exchanged glances, and then we both grinned.

So maybe not peace and quiet, but the kind of fun that

included crazy sassy seniors and girl bonding, not corpses and machine guns.

The kind of weekend I'd been dreaming of my whole life. I couldn't wait.

———

THIRTY MINUTES LATER, we were in heaven.

"This is the best," Lucy announced. "I should have become friends with you years ago, Hattie."

"Agreed," I said.

"You weren't ready," Hattie said. "I'm a lot. Not everyone can handle me."

I laughed. "You're perfect."

She grinned. "I didn't say I wasn't. This is the life, though, ladies, isn't it?"

"Yes," Lucy and I both agreed.

We were, at that moment, lined up on lounge chairs on the most gorgeous Maine beach I'd ever seen, not that I'd seen a lot of them, but it was still beautiful. We each had a royal blue umbrella positioned perfectly above us, and our personal tent was behind us, just big enough for a little party if we decided to go inside.

We even had a cabana boy named Nate, who was like an over-hyped puppy committed to living his best life every single moment. The sun was warm, the sand was pristine, and the waves were crashing in perfect Maine attitude. "Maybe I should have bought a place on this island instead of Bass Derby," I said. "This beach is amazing."

"You'd never survive here," Hattie said. "Not enough excitement." She was wearing a massive, pink straw sun hat, a pink bathing suit with a skirt, and sunglasses so large that they covered most of her face.

"But the perfect amount for a girls vacation weekend." Lucy had already stripped down to her bikini. Her brown skin looked fantastic against the yellow and gold glittery fabric, and her muscles from years of baton twirling and sledgehammering dock posts into the lake gave her arms and abs that I was definitely jealous of.

"I'd be thrilled if absolutely nothing happened the entire rest of the trip," I said. "Peace and quiet is glorious."

Hattie snorted. "There's no chance of peace and quiet once Thelma shows up. Enjoy it while you can."

"Where is Thelma?" Lucy said, looking around. "You said she was meeting us here."

"She'll be here when she's ready," Hattie said, wiggling to get more comfortable in her lounge chair. "She likes to plan an entrance. Relax, ladies, because once Thelma shows up, there will be no more relaxing."

"I'm in." Lucy flopped down and put her tee shirt over her face. "It's such perfect weather today."

"It is," I agreed. It was a gorgeous afternoon. The ocean stretched out before us, and I didn't see a single helicopter buzzing across it, so I was happy.

It was a pristine beach, sparsely populated with guests. A few families building sandcastles, some sassy seniors knitting in the shade of their umbrellas and screeching with laughter, and a beach volleyball game. It was pure vacation, and I felt something inside me begin to unfurl, relaxing for the first time in a very long time.

I smiled contentedly and looked down the beach. The resort's roped off section ended beside us, and there were a row of privately owned cottages dotting the bluffs.

Not more than twenty yards away was a cute, gray house. It had a deck, steps down to the beach, and big glass windows. There were also blue flashing lights reflecting off those windows. "Um, Lucy?" I poked her with my toe.

She lifted the tee shirt to peer at me. "What?"

I nodded toward the house. "Do you see that?"

She turned to look, then grimaced. "Already? We've been here for less than an hour."

"See what?" Hattie sat up and turned around. "Are those police lights?"

"No." Lucy lay back down and put her tee shirt over her face. "There's nothing untoward happening anywhere near us."

"Definitely not," I agreed quickly.

Hattie was on her feet now. "Those are definitely lights from a police car."

Lucy started to snore.

I picked up my phone and began to read the new book I'd downloaded for the trip.

Hattie shaded her eyes to look more closely. "Why are the cops at Thelma's house?"

"Thelma's house?" Lucy made a sound like she was gagging, and I groaned.

Of course it was Thelma's house. The one house that we couldn't ignore.

"Yes. I wonder if Blanche hired a cop stripper to kick off the fun. Let's go check it out." Hattie shoved her feet into her flipflops, grabbed her flowered purse, and then started trotting across the sand toward the weathered staircase.

Lucy stopped snoring, but she didn't take the tee shirt off her face. "I refuse to be entertained by a cop stripper."

"Me either." I started to laugh. "Imagine if we told Devlin we saw a cop stripper? He'd be so offended. Or Griselda?" My FBI handler didn't have the kind of sense of humor that would put up with that.

"Oh!" Lucy clapped her hands. "You could make Griselda and Devlin do a strip-off to see who wins you. The local cop versus the FBI agent. I love that. I'll judge, since you won't be impartial."

Oh…"I've seen both of them without shirts," I admitted. "It would be a tough choice."

"Right? Six-packs on both of them." Lucy grinned. "I'll take whoever you don't pick. I don't care which it is. Griselda's moodiness is utterly charming, and Devlin's competence is very attractive."

"I know," I sighed. "Griselda is a control freak, but he also respects my instincts, which I love. And when Devlin gets worried about assassins coming after me, it's really sweet."

"Plus, they're both strong enough that they keep you challenged." Lucy grinned. "I think you should try for a throuple. All that testosterone would be awesome."

I started laughing. "A throuple?"

"I'm sure Hattie would support the throuple concept," Lucy said. "The more the merrier when it comes to men."

"Unless they're the wrong guy, then zero is merriest." That was how I'd wound up at my zero goal, after the fiasco with my ex. Unfortunately for me, both Griselda and Devlin had elements of appeal, so it hadn't been that easy to completely ignore their declarations of interest.

So a vacation was a great break for me. With no men around, I couldn't get sucked into their charm and accidentally green light one, or both, of them.

But that law enforcement vibe was following me around, if the flashing blue lights were any indication. I sat up and turned around so I could watch Hattie heading to Thelma's house. "What if it's not a cop stripper at Thelma's house?"

Lucy made a noise of someone being strangled. "Thelma is Hattie's cousin. If it's not a stripper, then what are the odds that it's nothing to be worried about?"

"Zero," I said. "The odds are zero."

"Yes, that's what I was thinking." Lucy yanked the tee shirt off her face. "Listen, I really want this girls weekend. We all need it, including Thelma, from what Hattie said. Let's take control and save this birthday retreat, Murph. I didn't bring a gun. Maybe I can borrow one—"

Guns? Oh, heaven help us. "No. Do not get a gun. The cops are up there. We don't need guns."

"But do we *want* guns? Need and want are very different." Lucy was already pulling on her yellow mesh beach robe.

"We neither want nor need them, but we do need to go see

what's happening." I put on my sneakers, wishing that I'd brought my cat, King Tut, along with us. I always felt a little safer with him around.

Lucy grabbed her backpack. "It's a cop stripper," she said firmly. "Probably in his eighties. There are plenty of eighty-year-old hotties, right? It will be fun. Show us that sex is still in our future even if it takes us another fifty years to meet our one and only."

"Hopefully." I had a bad feeling, though.

I yanked on a pair of shorts, keeping an eye on Thelma's house. Hattie reached the top step, then I saw her speed up when she reached the deck, a new urgency to her step. *Crap.* "Something's wrong up there. We gotta go."

"Of course there's something wrong. There always is when it comes to us."

We both ran across the sand. As we reached the steps and started jogging up them, I could hear Hattie arguing with someone.

Lucy and I looked at each other, and then we bolted up the stairs. We ran around the side of the house, and then stopped in stunned surprise.

"Oh, Lordy," Lucy whispered. "The Corpse Whisperer strikes again."

CHAPTER 7

"THIS IS NOT MY FAULT." My stomach dropped as I took in the scene in front of us, which included Hattie and a woman who I was guessing was Thelma in animated discussion.

Two cops were leaning over a hot tub.

There was an attractive silver fox in that hot tub.

In a tuxedo.

With his feet up on the edge, still wearing his polished dancing shoes.

And a pair of knitting needles in his chest.

Dammit. "I'm not the Corpse Whisperer."

Lucy looked over at me. "At what point do you stop denying it? Is it ten corpses? Twenty? Fifty? Or is it a timing thing? Like if the gap is more than five days between corpses, it doesn't count?"

"Maybe he's not really dead."

"There are knitting needles in his *chest*."

"There *appear* to be knitting needles in his chest. This is a birthday party. Who knows what Blanche organized? Maybe it's a zombie stripper. He looks pretty fit. I'd like to see him dance. Wouldn't you like to see him dance?" Speaking of Blanche... I looked around. "Is Blanche even here?"

"Maybe that's the rules she was talking about breaking. Murdering people. Maybe we've walked into a horror movie. We're on this isolated island with a bunch of homicidal knitters and—"

"Stop." I held up my hands. "Don't even. The idea of homicidal senior knitters is more terrifying than a professional assassin." I wasn't kidding. There was something supremely alarming about that image.

She grinned. "You are so worried about the things that scare you."

"I think the ocean and homicidal knitters are valid things to fear."

"But gun-wielding assassins aren't?"

She had a point.

At that moment, Hattie noticed us and waved at us. "Mia! Lucy! Get over here."

Right. *Here we go.*

As we headed across the gray wooden deck, I took a closer look at the hopefully-not-actually-dead guy. He *was* attractive, if you could look past the pastiness of his complexion, which didn't bode well for my hopes that this was all a ruse.

Strong jaw, nice tux, good haircut. He reminded me of a fifty-something CEO who walked around with confidence, money, and a hot young thing hanging on his arm. The kind of guy who might stay in the penthouse of a five-star hotel. He'd be perfect for a zombie stripper party favor.

Hattie gestured to the woman beside her as we reached them. "Mia and Lucy, this is my cousin Thelma Gold. Thelma, these hotshots are Lucy Grande and Mia Murphy."

Thelma gave us each big hugs. "It's so great to meet you! Hattie has told me so much about you. You all sound like you have a blast together."

Thelma appeared to be in fine spirits despite the hot tub situation, so that was good. Maybe it really wasn't a corpse. It would just be a fun story to tell the grandkids, mixed in with margarita shenanigans, yoga, and massage treatments.

Lucy grinned. "We do have fun."

"We do," I agreed. "Hattie and Lucy are the best."

Hattie beamed at me. "Smooches right back at you, Mia. You're a treasure."

My heart warmed at all the love. I was so happy I'd braved the ocean to come. "Thanks. You, too."

"And me, three." Lucy draped her arms around our shoulders. "What's going on here, ladies? Looks like a little dead body drama."

I tensed.

"A situation in my hot tub," Thelma said. "I found him just a little while ago and called the police."

My gut sank with the inevitable that I'd known was coming. "He's really dead? He's not a zombie stripper?"

Hattie and Thelma looked at me like I was crazy. "A zombie stripper?" Thelma echoed. "Is that what you have at parties in Bass Derby?"

"No. I just...Blanche said she had fun party plans, and I was hoping..." My voice faded, because it had been kind of ridiculous for me to hope he was a stripper. I mean, he looked dead and there were cops leaning over him. I sighed and capitulated to the facts. "Did you know him?"

Thelma nodded. "He's one of the dance instructors at the resort. He's been here for a few months. His name is Giorgio."

Lucy and I looked at each other. I didn't want Thelma to know him. I wanted the silver fox to be a random stranger who had fallen out of an airplane.

"Why is he in your hot tub?" Hattie asked.

Thelma shrugged. "He was supposed to meet me at the resort last night, but he never showed."

"The resort?" Hattie raised her brows. "Why at the resort?"

"I booked a room there last night because Blanche was setting things up in my house. She kicked me out. I wasn't supposed to stop by but I wanted to grab something, and then I walked in, and there he was."

The three of us looked at each other. Thelma was having a fling with the dead guy in her hot tub?

"I don't suppose those aren't your knitting needles?" I asked, hoping for her to declare she'd never knitted a day in her life.

Thelma made a face. "I was a week from finishing that sweater! I've been working on that thing for six years. Whoever used them to stab him is going to have to suffer. Who messes with a knitting project that's been going on for years? Everyone knows you don't do that!"

Yep. Her needles. Her lover. This was going perfectly.

Hattie squawked and put her hand over Thelma's mouth. "You need to shut up, cuz."

Thelma batted her hand away. "Why? I didn't do anything."

Hattie nodded toward the cops. "Isn't that Sheriff Punting, the one who hates you?"

Of course it was a sheriff who hated Thelma. Lucy and I exchanged glances. Lucy was grinning with far more glee than I felt. A life on the edge of the law was new to Lucy and Hattie, so they still found it fun.

I also found it fun, which is why I was doing my best to stay away from it. Never give an addict a piece of chocolate, right?

"He doesn't hate me," Thelma said. "He just didn't get along with Roger, but hardly anyone did by the end, so what does that matter?"

Hattie put her hands on her hips. "Why don't you take a moment to replay the conversation we just had, from the point of view of the sheriff. How it's *your* knitting project, *your* needles, and *your* lover, in *your* hot tub?"

Thelma frowned at Hattie and paused, apparently doing as Hattie had suggested. After a moment, her eyes widened. "Mother of an oversized lobster! He's going to think he can arrest me for it! Sneaky little worm!"

Hattie looked at us. "Mia? Those cops are going to come over here and interview Thelma in about two seconds, and she needs to lie. You're the expert on lying and deceit. Tell her how to do it."

This was not a good plan. "Lying to the police isn't the best idea—"

"How often have you done it?" Hattie interrupted.

I cleared my throat. "Much more since I moved to Bass Derby, honestly."

"And you're great at it. You lie to Devlin repeatedly, and yet he still wants to date you," Hattie said.

Lucy nodded. "She has a point."

"Look," Hattie said. "All we need is to buy a little time for Thelma, so we can investigate—"

"No. No. And no," I interrupted. "We're not going to investigate a murder." I turned to Thelma. "Just answer the questions they ask and don't offer more. If they ask about him being in the hot tub, just say you don't know why he's in there, and don't offer that he was supposed to meet you at the resort yesterday. If you lie, they will find out, and then you look bad. If you're innocent—" I paused. "Are you innocent?"

"Of stabbing Giorgio?" Thelma looked appalled by the question. "Of course I didn't stab him."

I exchanged looks with Lucy. Hattie's concern was valid about Thelma being a potential suspect. But there were all sorts of levels to how incriminating the evidence would be for her. After all, not every homeowner was responsible for the bodies in their hot tubs.

But some were.

Interesting twist for me. Everyone else who'd been accused of murder since I'd come to Bass Derby was a person who I knew, who I believed in. Whose innocence I was at least moderately certain of.

I knew nothing about Thelma, other than her kinship with Hattie. I had no idea if she was the murdering type. "The cops do like to twist things," I agreed, watching Thelma with more curiosity now. If I had to be the Corpse Whisperer, I might as well keep a positive attitude about it, right? Lean into the opportunity for personal growth that it gave me.

Thelma didn't look particularly upset, but she also was making a point of not looking over to the hot tub. Maybe she wasn't upset because she was a fan of dead people. Or maybe she wasn't upset because she'd killed him. Or maybe she *was* upset but she was holding it together because everyone was around. Or maybe, being Hattie's cousin, she'd had to develop a deep resilience to trauma or else she would have run away screaming a long time ago.

So many options all tangled up.

I found myself morbidly fascinated with this situation. Was I chatting with the killer? Was Hattie's birthday cousin actually a sociopath? Or a spurned lover? Had she murdered her husband? Or was she innocent, a strategically selected scapegoat? So many possibilities.

Dammit. I was turning into Beau, fascinated by the twists and turns of humanity when it came to murder.

Lucy elbowed me. "Mia? Your great advice on handling the cops?"

Crud. I'd been daydreaming. Did I want to give Thelma advice to protect her from being wrongly accused? Or did I want her to be caught before she killed someone else? Hmm..."Look shaken up by finding a body in your hot tub, too. You look way too cheerful."

Thelma put her hands on her hips. "I am cheerful. I have a great weekend planned, and I'm not the one who's dead, so why would I be anything but happy? What if I'd been in the hot tub when he'd been stabbed or dropped off? I'd have been stabbed, too. But I wasn't, so bravo for me!"

I blinked. "Good point."

Lucy nodded. "It's a very resilient attitude."

Hattie beamed at her. "I told you guys you'd love Thelma."

Thelma grinned at us. "From what Hattie's told me, none of

you get upset at dead bodies either, so why pretend we're spineless, over-emotional wimps when we're not? We're strong, badass women who have managed to avoid being murdered so far, so I say we celebrate."

Wow. Just wow. Was she really that happy, or was it a façade? She seemed legit, but there was literally a body in her hot tub. I might not get upset at bodies, but if I found one on my porch, I don't think it would actually put me in an even better mood.

Maybe I needed to work on that.

At that moment, one of the cops walked over. He looked to be in his seventies, but spry and fit. His badge said he was Sheriff Wick. "Mrs. Gold, I'd like to ask you a few more questions."

Thelma nodded. "Of course." She turned to Hattie. "I'll just be a minute. Wait for me?"

"Of course."

Thelma and the sheriff wandered off, speaking quietly.

While we waited, the female cop came over to us. All the Bass Derby cops and my FBI handler were blessed with an overdose of testosterone, so it was a treat to have a woman in the position of power this time. Her nametag read Officer Harrison. I smiled at her, trying to send her some female-power-appreciation. "Hi."

Officer Harrison held up her hand in that way that cops had when they wanted to shut you down and didn't take you remotely seriously as a threat. "Do any of you know the deceased?" she asked.

"No," I said quickly, happy to be able to be telling the truth. "We're from out of town. We just arrived about an hour ago."

Lucy shook her head. "Nope."

"Did he die from the knitting needles?" Hattie asked. "Or were those just added later for effect?"

Officer Harrison didn't fall for that. "Do any of you know Thelma Gold, the owner of this house?"

Lucy and I put on blank faces, but Hattie nodded. "She's my cousin. She's not a killer. Don't waste your time looking at her."

Officer Harrison raised her brows. "Killer? Why do you use that term?"

Good heavens. She thought she was so clever with her questions.

"Because he has knitting needles lodged in his chest," Hattie retorted. "I'm pretty sure that isn't going to be recorded as death by natural causes."

The sheriff looked over at us. "Jane! Take their names and contact info and escort them out. I don't want them contaminating the scene."

Jane. That was so much more fun than Officer Harrison. Officer Jane bristled visibly at the sheriff's tone, and her jaw flexed in irritation as she addressed us. "I need your info, and then you need to leave."

Oh...female power was chafing under the sheriff's autocracy. I did appreciate that. "Sure."

We gave her our names and phone numbers, and then Hattie waved toward the steps. "We'll be on the beach, Thelma, whenever you're done here."

Thelma gave her a thumbs up, not even breaking stride with the story she was rattling off with great animation. As we turned to leave, I noticed that there were coconuts placed around the hot tub, along with a few pitchers with Hawaiian flowers and leis were nailed up on most available surfaces.

There were even tiki torches tied to the deck posts, ready to be lit. I'd been so focused on the corpse and the cops that I hadn't noticed that Blanche had set up a complete Hawaiian party all around the deck.

"I didn't bring my luau gear," I commented "Was this for us?"

"Probably. Blanche is fun like that," Hattie said. "It'll keep."

"Great." I definitely wanted to luau where a body had been only a short while before. It felt like the most sensible action to take.

Officer Jane put her hands on her hips. "Go."

"Right. Yep." We turned away and hustled across the deck.

"Thelma's going to be in trouble," Hattie muttered under her breath. "She's going to need help."

"Our help?" Lucy asked.

"Of course ours. We all know better than to trust cops by now, right?" Hattie looked over at me. "Mia? You in?"

Was I in? That was such a loaded question. Thus far, I'd been unsuccessful at remaining uninvolved in all the murders to date, despite my best attempts.

I decided to go with the assumption that Hattie's cousin was innocent, and our birthday present to her was to clear her name. If I found out later that she was a murderous sociopath, we'd deal with it. But for the moment, I was going with the fact that we were here to help Hattie's cousin feel good on her birthday. I might not be a birthday expert, but I was pretty sure it would be more fun to luau with us than to spend it in a jail cell.

Le sigh. I was in.

"Of course, I'm in. Hang on." I paused to take a few photos of the dead guy, the hot tub, and I even zoomed in on the knitting needles. "It really changes the vibe of the situation to not be a suspect. This almost makes it fun, if you ignore the fact that a man died to give us this joy."

"Right? So much more freedom," Lucy said. "And maybe he was a terrible blight to humanity, so his death is indeed a reason for great joy and celebration."

"We have met some of those," I agreed, as I took a few pictures of the coconuts and the pitchers. And the tiki torches.

Officer Jane looked over at me, and I nudged Hattie and Lucy. "Pose, please."

They both sprung into place, posing like Charlie's Angels with their finger guns. I took a couple pictures of them for a possible holiday card, and then whipped off a stream of pictures of the scene behind them, getting some nice ones of Giorgio.

"Perfect," I said, my gaze falling upon a table of food to the right of the hot tub. "How about a pose with the pineapples?" Not for any investigative purposes, but because I was on a vacation and I was going to take fun, tropical photos on my Maine beach vacation.

My trusty pals raced right over to the table, continuing to showcase their excellent modeling skills while I took photos of the feast on the table. Pineapples galore, some colorful trays of fruit tarts, and what looked like... "Is that a basket of lip gloss?"

"Yes, Blanche believes in moist lips," Hattie said. She grabbed a handful of the little tubes and held them up. "She makes it in her kitchen. All organic, plenty of CBD. You never know who you're going to run into when out with the girls."

CBD lip gloss. I decided not to eat anything that Blanche offered me.

I glanced over at dead-guy-Giorgio. His lips were shiny. Water? Or lip gloss? Hmmm...

Hang on. Blanche had ordered Thelma out of the house. What if Blanche had left Giorgio there for the cops to find? Blanche was sassy and fun. I didn't want her to be a murderer.

Officer Jane stepped between us and the idyllic water scene. "Get out, or I will arrest you."

"Hey." Hattie put her hands on her hips and glared at Officer Jane, without even a modicum of deference. "For your information, Mia Murphy, here—" She pointed to me. "Works undercover with the FBI and our local police force on drug lord cases and murder. She'll be happy to make a call to the FBI if you harass her."

Oh. My. God. Really with that?

Officer Jane's gaze shot to me. "You're FBI?"

"No. Hah. Funny. Imagine me in the FBI? That would be crazy. I don't listen to rules well enough." I tried to look as innocent as possible. "I'm here on vacation with my friends, so we'll be heading back to the beach. Let's go, ladies."

I shoved my phone in my pocket and headed straight for the steps.

It took a moment, but then Hattie and Lucy finally came after me.

Hattie caught up first. "What was that? Why did you back down? Thelma's forever freedom is at stake!"

I glanced over my shoulder as we hurried down the steps. Officer Jane had followed us to the edge of the deck, and she was watching us leave.

We were on her radar.

CHAPTER 8

I GAVE Officer Jane my most innocent look, then turned and hurried across the sand with Hattie and Lucy. "If the cops realize I worked with the FBI and was married to a drug dealer, they're going to put me on their watch list," I whispered. "We can accomplish a lot more if no one is paying attention to us. Being invisible can be extremely powerful."

Lucy nodded. "You did spend your entire childhood being invisible as a criminal, huh?"

"Yep. It works." We hit the beach, and my feet sank into the sand that didn't feel nearly as pristine and peaceful as it had before.

Hattie cursed as we walked three-abreast across the beach, back toward our cabana. "Thelma's in trouble, ladies. Big trouble. Her fingerprints will be all over the knitting needles, obviously."

"Yep," I agreed. "It's a smart choice for a murder weapon. If she did it, she has a reason for her prints to be on there, or if she didn't, then the murderer has ready-made prints on them. Either way, it's well-planned."

Hattie stopped and spun toward me. "You think she killed him?"

I held my hands up, palms out in surrender. "Hattie, I know

literally nothing about Thelma, other than that she's your cousin. I have no idea if she is a killer."

"She's my cousin. Isn't that enough?"

"Well, being that she's your cousin, it really opens the door for a lot, honestly."

Hattie inclined her head. "I will grant you that," she agreed. "We do breed some pretty bold women in my lineage."

I loved bold women. But bold women who murdered in cold blood? Not so much. Killing in self-defense, or defense of others? The line got murky fast.

"I snagged these from the party. We'll pre-dress for the luau." Lucy held out a lei to each of us. "You haven't actually said if you thought she was innocent," she pointed out to Hattie.

"Oh, nice. Thanks." Hattie accepted the orange and white lei and dropped it over her head. "Of course she didn't kill Giorgio. Thelma's not a killer."

I studied Hattie, but she didn't flinch or hesitate. "You believe that." I frowned at Lucy when she nudged me with the pink lei. "I don't want that. It's probably crime scene evidence. Did you check for blood?"

"Blood?" Lucy looked down at the lei in alarm.

"Absolutely, I know Thelma's innocent," Hattie said. "Put on the lei, Mia. We can say we brought them with us if anyone asks. It's not like he was murdered by a flower necklace."

"That you know of." I batted Lucy's hand away as she tried to drop it over my head.

"I know everything." Hattie tossed her handful of Thelma's lip gloss into her bag, then snatched the extra lei from Lucy. She put it over her head, then plopped herself down on her beach chair and waved to our cabana boy, Nate, who was carrying a tray of drinks to a nearby couple who were playing some sort of beach paddle game.

"My ladies!" Nate came jogging up, beaming at us. "You have returned! I'm so thrilled to see you again. How may I be of service to you?"

Nate was positively adorable in his khaki shorts, red polo shirt, and matching little neckerchief. He looked about twenty-two, clean-shaven, and he even had dimples. He made me want to be happier just because he was so happy. Everyone needed a Nate in their lives, especially after basking in the watery aftermath of a visit from the Grim Reaper.

"Nate!" Hattie beamed at him. "How about another round for all of us, plus a margarita for Thelma. You know how she likes it?"

"Oh, I do! Mrs. Gold's Special coming right up. Any food?"

"What do you have?" Hattie asked.

"Oh, many options!" He held out a menu that didn't have prices, because it was that kind of resort. "Mrs. Gold is picking up your tab for the weekend, so she told me that you are to have all that you wish."

We looked at each other, and then spent the next few minutes ordering enough food to make anyone accused of murder feel loved and adored. Or at least full. Because we were friendly and thoughtful like that.

Nate promised to be back soon with fresh beach towels, warm hand towels, ice waters, and our orders, then as he turned to run off, I had an idea. "Nate!"

He spun back toward me. "How may I be of service?"

"Do you know Giorgio?"

Nate's adorable little smile faltered for a split second. "Yes. Giorgio Costa. He teaches ballroom dancing and yoga at the resort."

Ah...I saw that smile slip. Nate was not happy with Giorgio. Or maybe he knew Giorgio was dead, and he was trying to fake his involvement. I paused...no. Not Nate. He was just too freaking adorable to be a murderer. But someone had killed Giorgio, and with great commitment, because knitting needles in his chest took effort. "Good guy?" I asked as innocently as I could.

Nate's smile slipped again. "The staff at our resort is highly selected, and—"

"Nate." I leaned in. "Truth."

Lucy leaned over, and Nate's gaze went to her really cute bikini top, because he was probably a fan of gold stretchy fabric, like any good cabana boy would be. "Nate," she said. "What's up with Giorgio? We've heard things, and we want to know."

"What have you heard?" He looked relieved that we already knew whatever it was he knew.

I glanced at my pals and tried to think of the most outrageous thing I could. "He's a drug kingpin using the resort to launder drug money."

Nate's eyes widened. "He is? I had no idea! That explains so much!"

I'd expected him to say "no, he's only..." and then whatever he was. My strategy had backfired, because I'd apparently just started a rumor instead of gaining info. I had to try to pivot. "What does it explain?"

"All of it! Thank you!" Then he literally ran across the sand to get back to the hotel top speed.

"Well, that was a successful interrogation," I sighed.

"I need to hire him for my café," Hattie said as we watched him depart. "The twins are taking the summer off to do football stuff, so I need a replacement. I love his energy."

"He's so charming," Lucy agreed. "I want to box him up and keep him on my mantle so he can cheer me up whenever I'm in a bad mood."

"It's a little unnatural," I said. "I mean, it's a gorgeous resort, but who gets that excited about being a cabana boy?"

"Let's be honest," Hattie said. "It's not about being a cabana boy. It's about being with us. We're pretty amazing. But let's not get distracted by how adorable Nate is. I can't believe Giorgio is a drug kingpin laundering money at the resort. How did you know, Mia?"

"Shut up." I threw my towel at her, and she ducked, laughing.

"Yeah, you blew that," Lucy said with a chuckle.

"Except we found out Nate isn't a fan of Giorgio, and that Giorgio was up to something significant enough that laundering drug money is a plausible explanation for whatever it was he was doing," I said. "So, he's not a good guy."

"Always good to know murder victims aren't good people," Lucy said. "It makes it less stressful that they died."

"Right? It's always a nice benefit. I'm sure it helps Thelma deal with the fact she found him in her hot tub," Hattie said.

I watched Nate jog across the sand. "Speaking of our possible murder suspect, how well do you know Thelma?"

"Thelma is Thelma," Hattie said. "No words can do justice to her presence."

"So, she's trouble?" I pressed.

"Yes, but only in a great way," Hattie said. "Not the murdering kind of way."

I sighed. There were about a zillion questions I could ask about that statement, but I didn't want to. I really wanted to simply be a normal person this weekend. "Well, great, then. If Thelma isn't a suspect, we don't have to do anything. We can just enjoy our vacation."

Lucy brightened. "Oh, yes, that would be wonderful."

Hattie looked skeptical. "Her knitting needles are in his chest. I feel like she's not going to be okay on this one."

Lucy and I looked at each other. "On *this* one? Were there others?"

"She didn't kill her husband, if that's what you're asking."

"We weren't asking that," Lucy said. "But should we have?"

I blinked. "Was Roger murdered?"

"It's a little unclear at this time, honestly," Hattie said. "How did the peanut butter get into his coffee, and where was his EpiPen? And why was he in the haunted caves in the first place?"

I became slightly more alarmed. Was Thelma actually a serial killer? "Um, Hattie—"

"She didn't do it, but it won't help her here."

I looked at Lucy, who looked increasingly worried as well. "Is there anyone else in her life who died?"

Hattie paused. "She's had a run of bad luck. That's why I'm

here to cheer her up on her birthday. Why *we* are here to cheer her up."

I leaned forward. "Hattie. How much bad luck has Thelma had?"

Hattie looked at me. "You were a criminal for seventeen years, then married a drug dealer, then bought a marina that was being used for drug dealing, and then have gotten involved in multiple murders. And yet, if you were found standing over a body with a gun in your hand, I would make sure your fingerprints were off the gun, and I'd throw you in my car and get you away from the crime scene, because I'd know without a doubt that you were innocent."

I shut my mouth. Point well done.

"I believe in people," Hattie continued, "but I'm not an idiot. If someone's evil, I won't defend them or help them. But I know good when I see it, and Thelma's good." She pointed at me. "Just like you, Mia. You know good people when you see them, and you know bad people, and you take action."

She had valid points. I believed in myself. I'd turned in my own husband, the man I loved, when I realized he was a drug kingpin. Did I have that same faith in Hattie? I leaned forward. "If Thelma did murder Giorgio—"

"Or Roger," Lucy added.

"Would you protect her?" I asked.

Hattie rolled her eyes. "That's an impossible scenario because I know she's innocent. So no matter what evidence I was presented with, I would find out what really happened. No one I care about is capable of murder, because if they were, I'd realize it, and I wouldn't fall for them."

I'd fallen for a man who had probably made the call for many people to be killed. What did that make me? "Would you be willing to change your mind if you found absolute proof that you were wrong?"

Hattie met my gaze. "Like bags of white powder in my china cabinet?"

Like what had happened to me? "Yes."

"Here's the thing, Mia. You knew Stanley was guilty when you saw that, because something inside you had known all along, even if you hadn't been willing to see it."

"So, I knowingly chose to marry a drug lord who had a team of assassins on his payroll?"

She cocked her head, studying me. "On some levels, yes."

"No. Absolutely not. You're wrong." I sat back in frustration. "Look, this isn't about me. I'm just trying to get reassurance that I can believe in Thelma's innocence because you would be willing to see if she wasn't."

"I'd be willing." Hattie said. "Absolutely."

She said it so fast and with such conviction that I believed her. I sighed. "Okay."

Lucy grinned. "It was just a matter of asking the right question, apparently."

"Apparently." All right, I had to go forward on the assumption Thelma was innocent. I had to trust Hattie's judgment. "Then tell us about Thelma."

CHAPTER 9

Hattie wiggled her butt to get more comfortable in the chair. "As she said, those are her knitting needles in his chest, and that sweater that's on them is one she's been working on for years."

"Oh, she's fine," Lucy said as she put her sunglasses on. "Anyone who knows anything about knitting knows that no knitter would willingly sacrifice a project they'd been working on for years. I don't knit, and even I know that."

"Exactly," Hattie said. "She was only a few weeks from finally finishing it. She would never have sacrificed the sweater for his death."

I thought about that. "What if it was a spur-of-the-moment act, and it was all she had with her?"

"Nope," said Hattie. "It's an instinct that knitters have. Protect the project at all costs. It wouldn't even have been a conscious choice. Her inner knitter would have prevented her from using the needles with the sweater on them. She had other needles in her bag. She would have used those. Or a coconut. Or a tiki torch. There were a lot of options around there."

"Agreed," said Lucy.

"I don't think the cops will go with that as proof of her innocence." Maybe it was because I wasn't a knitter, but it seemed to me that it would be the perfect red herring to murder with the sweater, since everyone would assume she wouldn't have done so. Thelma might be very clever. Wait. Dammit. I believed in her innocence. Thoughts like that would distract me from the truth.

"The cops won't buy it as proof of her innocence," Hattie agreed. "Unless they're knitters."

"Which we can't count on." I sat back down and tried to settle. "But at the same time, Thelma doesn't really look like she'd be strong enough to take down Giorgio in a hand-to-hand."

"She could have drugged him," Lucy said.

"Or lured him into submission with sex," Hattie said.

I blinked. "What?"

"Well, she is related to me. The cops will sense her incredible appeal, and it will make sense. The women in my family are all sirens."

"Well, did she have that kind of relationship with him? Was that what she meant when she said he was supposed to meet her at the resort? She didn't deny it when you called him her lover."

Hattie shrugged. "Giorgio wasn't here last summer when I came, but the resort dance instructors often give out private lessons, so maybe she was getting a private lesson. He was in his dancing gear, after all. But I don't actually know if Thelma was doing the horizontal tango with Giorgio. We'll ask her."

Lucy frowned. "We need to find out more about Giorgio."

I nodded at the ladies still knitting on the beach. "I say we start with them."

Hattie and Lucy turned around, and Hattie shook her head. "That's much too obvious. It's not even worth our effort. If they'd stabbed him with knitting needles, the last thing they'd be doing is sitting on the beach with more of them."

"Which is exactly why they might be doing it, especially since it was Thelma's needles in his chest," I said. "Does Thelma knit with that crew?"

Hattie narrowed her eyes and studied them more closely. "I think she might. A couple of them look vaguely familiar. We don't knit when I'm visiting because knitting is boring, but I recall some of them saying hello when we passed them on our way to the bar."

A knitter would feel comfortable with knitting needles. As a murder weapon, it fit. "You're the first to tell me not to underestimate women of more expansive years."

"Women like *me*," Hattie said. "Not women who sit around and knit all day."

"You're so judgy," Lucy said. "Knitters can be badasses!"

"Can they? Honestly?"

"Thelma's a badass," I pointed out. "And she knits."

Hattie stared at me for a long moment, then swore. "Son of a biscuit. You're right. I need to rethink my world view—"

"Good afternoon, ladies of Cabana No. 5!"

We all turned to see a spritely woman with red, curly hair, white sandals, diamond stud earrings, and a black pantsuit standing over us. She was average height, with very white teeth, and minimal makeup. She kind of looked like a lawyer.

She smiled at all of us. "My name is Sylvia Collins. I'm the manager of the Grand Vista Resort, and I wanted to welcome you."

Hattie waved. "Hi, Sylvia. Good to see you again."

Sylvia's smile brightened. "Ms. Lawless, it's our pleasure to host you again, as our VIP guests."

The only time I'd been a VIP in my life had been when my mom and I had conned our way in to assorted elite events. It was completely different to be a legitimate VIP and not worry that I was going to have to make a break for the exit with security chasing me down.

I hopped to my feet. "My name is Mia Murphy. The resort is beautiful."

Sylvia beamed at me. "Thank you so much. We do like to

provide a lovely getaway." She pointed across the beach. "If you need anything taken care of with your equipment, Atlas is your man."

There was a tall, muscular man in his early thirties carrying a huge stack of lounge chairs under his left arm, striding across the sand as if he were carrying a grape. Atlas was definitely strong enough to take down Giorgio with a pair of knitting needles.

"Atlas," she shouted.

He looked over, saw Sylvia, and then changed direction. "Hello, ladies." His voice was insanely deep, and he looked like he could bench press the entire FBI at once. "Good to meet you. If you need anything, please let me know. My cell number is on your VIP card, and you can reach me at any time."

"We have a VIP card?" Lucy asked.

"I have your VIP cards here." Sylvia pulled some cards off her clipboard and handed them out. "On the back is the schedule of all the activities you are currently booked for, and on this—" She handed us another laminated card—"is the resort schedule for the duration of your stay. It lists all the classes, events, meals, and concierge events. You have full access to all the services of the resort, and priority in all scheduling appointments for massages, ocean outings, picnics, ballroom dance lessons. Thelma already booked you for dance lessons with Giorgio—"

"Ballroom dancing?" Clearly the Giorgio news hadn't made it very far yet.

"Oh, Giorgio is lovely," she said. "You'll adore him. The ladies love him."

Oh…I wasn't going to be the one to tell Sylvia that her dance teacher was floating in a hot tub. And I could see from the looks on Hattie and Lucy's faces that they felt the same way. "Has he worked here long?" I asked instead.

"This is his first season, but I assure you, he is fabulous," Sylvia said. "He also teaches sunrise yoga on the beach, so don't miss it!"

Sunrise yoga sounded fun. Maybe I should start offering that at my marina. "Great," I said brightly. "We'll look forward to it all."

"Wonderful." Sylvia paused, then added. "I know I don't need to tell the three of you this, but I just wanted to let you know that we have some special guests at the resort this week, as we often do."

I sat up. "Special? What kind of special?"

Her gaze flickered to me. "The kind you don't bother," she said firmly. "We request that other guests do not ask them for autographs, selfies, or anything of that nature."

Oh…that was just the kind of guest my mom had a radar for.

Hattie put her hands on her hips. "I'm so offended that you feel like you have to warn us. I'm very classy."

Sylvia winked at Hattie. "Ms. Lawless, you are a treasure. But it's protocol. I have to say it. You know how it is."

Hattie shook out her ruffled feathers. "I do know. There are some very unrefined people in this world."

"I know. People who would try to take advantage of celebrities," Sylvia said. "We don't allow people like that here. It's one of the reasons why the rich and famous love to come here. It's a safe space for them." She beamed at us. "All right. You're all good, then? Let me know if you have any questions."

Sylvia gave a little wave and then trotted down the beach toward a couple who were stretched out on lounge chairs at the other end of the beach. There was something about them… I took off my sunglasses and sat up, studying them more closely. "That's them. The VIP guests."

Lucy and Hattie twisted around to look. "Who is it?" Lucy asked. "I can't see from here."

I'd learned from my mom to keep track of celebrities, so it took only a few moments for me to remember. "It's Jennie Diaz and Fernando Valencia." They were both A-list actors, and she had founded a beauty company that had made her a billionaire by age twenty-three. "Recently engaged."

"They probably came here by helicopter," Lucy said.

"And they might even carry a bunch of cash around," I said.

We all looked at each other in relief. Knowing the helicopter could have been theirs felt so much better than the idea of an arms dealer chasing us down. "Who knows," I said, feeling much better. "We might even survive the weekend."

"Oh, we'll survive," Hattie said. "That's not the issue."

I leaned back. "Maybe they murdered Giorgio for being a terrible dance instructor."

"Or Atlas," Lucy said. "He's big enough to toss Giorgio into the hot tub from here. Did you see his muscles? He must work out a lot, don't you think?"

I grinned. Yay for Lucy noticing a guy! After her last boyfriend's untimely ending, she'd been a little gun shy. "It could also be that guy on the beach with the metal detector," I said, pointing to a Hawaiian-shirt-wearing gent scanning the sand with his machine. "He clearly likes metal, and the knitting needles are metal."

"Metal detector people are all a little unique," Hattie said. "We'll have to watch him—"

"A corpse! There's a corpse at Thelma's!" Blanche came hurrying up, dragging her cart of goodies behind her on the beach. "I just came from Thelma's. There's a body in her hot tub! And the cops are there!"

I'd totally forgotten about Blanche.

"That's old news, you slow snail," Hattie said. "We were already over there. Where have you been?"

"I had to stop at home and get the rest of the supplies." Blanche dropped the handle of her cart. "I'm parched. Who has drinks? A body! There's a dead man in her hot tub! Does no one care?"

"Why would we care? We didn't even know him," Hattie said, amusement in her tone.

"A *body*!" Blanche sat down on Hattie's chair, nearly squishing Hattie's feet. "It's that Corpse Whisperer thing, isn't it? I thought you guys were kidding. But no!"

Hattie kicked Blanche in the hip. "Get off my feet! You weigh a thousand pounds!"

Blanche ignored her and picked up a bottle of water that was peeking out of Hattie's bag. "This is going to ruin Thelma's birthday."

"She'll love it," Hattie said. "Murderers make everything more fun."

"No, they literally don't," Blanche said. "A body! Thelma's only a minute behind me. They just finished interviewing her. She told me you were here. What is going on in this town? Money? An assault helicopter? And a body? I need a vacation."

I glanced at Lucy and grinned. Blanche didn't seem that upset. She seemed more thrilled than upset. Which made sense. She was Hattie's friend, so there was no way she'd be some wimpy little thing.

"You're fine," Hattie scoffed. "You love this. You probably killed him just so we could have a fun party."

"I would never kill someone for the sake of a party," Blanche snapped. "That's just silly."

"But you'd kill them for other reasons?" I asked, because who knew what Blanche might have been up to last night before she'd wound up on the mainland.

Blanche looked over at me. "Every person alive would kill for the right reasons, little miss sassy pants. I heard your tone, and I take umbrage. How dare you think I'd kill to make a party fun? I can make any party fun without a single party favor. I don't need a body!"

"This is true," Hattie said. "Blanche is the party queen. That's why Thelma's letting her set up the party."

"Thelma asked me to set up the party because I'm her best friend," Blanche retorted.

"I'm her best friend," Hattie shot back.

"You can't be her best friend. You're related so you don't count."

"I count in everything I do," Hattie shot back. "I matter."

"So do I!"

They stared at each other, then they both burst out laughing.

"Girl, I missed you," Blanche said. "No one keeps up with me like you do."

"Back at you, sister," Hattie said cheerfully. "But you owe me ten dollars for that water."

"You owe me therapy for years of torture," Blanche said, then paused to take a long drag of the water.

Wow. I wanted friends like that. Friends who were forever friends, sassy, silly, and bold. I was going to have to start insulting Lucy and Hattie so we could still be friends in forty years.

"Hey, ladies!" Thelma came trotting up, waving her hand. She wasn't smiling quite as much as when I'd last seen her, but there was still a determined pep to her step. "Thanks for waiting."

"Hey, girl." Blanche hopped up and gave her a big hug, which made my throat get a little thick. There was so much love in that hug, despite all of Blanche's sassiness.

Thelma hugged her back while Hattie frowned. "You all right, cuz?"

"Yes, completely." Thelma patted Blanche's shoulder, then sat down in an empty chair, and leaned on her forearms. For a moment, she looked as old as her years, and I saw the weariness behind the leis and the bright colors. "Giorgio wasn't the nicest man," she said. "But it seems rather terrible to wind up stabbed in a hot tub."

"If he showed you he wasn't the nicest man, he was probably not nice at all," Hattie said.

"Which means, he had it coming," Lucy said.

I bit my lip. "Not everyone who isn't perfect deserves to be murdered."

Hattie looked over at me. "We weren't talking about your mom."

"I know. I just wanted to clarify."

"Right," Lucy said, "not everyone who isn't nice deserves to be stabbed in the heart with knitting needles. But since that's what he got, let's hope he deserved it, right?"

It was a valid point.

"Sheriff Wick is on the hunt to pin this on me," Thelma said. "His questions were very pointed."

Oh...crud.

"The little stink bug," Blanche said. "You're an icon in this town, and he knows it."

"That's right, you are," Hattie said. "He won't get to do it. We'll help. We're so great at this kind of stuff."

Thelma looked around at us. "You guys don't need to help. You're here on vacation—"

Lucy and I looked at each other, but Hattie sat down across from Thelma. "Don't be silly. We love hunting down murderers. That makes the trip fun for us! Who needs to sit around and drink on the beach? That's not us."

I wanted it to be us. I wanted it to be me. I wanted to be the person who went on vacation and sat on the beach, who didn't do things like attract corpses. I wanted to be the person who *wanted* to sit on the beach.

But I couldn't deny the fact that seeing Thelma sitting there looking overwhelmed by Sheriff Wick's need to put her in jail made something inside me sit up and get mad. "Why does he have a thing against you?"

Thelma grimaced. "I dated the sheriff before I met Roger, and the sheriff didn't appreciate that I chose Roger. It's always been a bit sticky ever since."

Ah... "That does complicate things."

"Um, wow." Love was one of the strongest motivators for murder. "Is he the one who investigated Roger's death?" And Thelma had been getting cozy with Giorgio. Was it a jealous lovers thing?

They all looked at me, and I grimaced. That wasn't probably the most cheerful thing to have asked. But it was valid.

"No," Thelma said. "He'd had a bad fall when he was out on a run a few weeks before Roger died, and he was laid up with knee surgery during that time. We had another department send a temporary cop. Just an accident for Roger."

Okay, if the sheriff had been in a hospital bed with a gimpy knee, he probably hadn't killed Roger. But Roger wasn't the issue right now. We had to deal with Giorgio, who was definitely dead. We needed to focus on the victim, to see if we could find a reason for the sheriff, or hopefully, someone else, to have killed him. "How well did you know Giorgio?"

Blanche snorted. "Thelma knows him too well, that's how well she knows him, at least given the situation."

Thelma ignored Blanche. "He came to the resort a few months ago. I took some lessons with him, but honestly, he wasn't the best teacher, and he wasn't suave."

I raised my brows. "Suave?"

She nodded. "To be a dance teacher here, he needed to basically be a Romeo. Make his clients feel sexy, capable, and confident. Charm them. Make them feel like the VIPs that the resort wants them to feel like. He just…wasn't like that. He was rougher, like he was putting on his dance shoes as a costume. Does that make sense?"

Lucy and I sat down. "Go on."

"He was a fantastic dancer, though," Thelma said. "I knew he had potential. So I offered to teach him how to be more successful," she said. "That's why we were meeting. I was teaching him who he needed to be. Not as a dancer, but as a charmer."

Huh. Fascinating. "Why did you offer to teach him?" I asked.

Thelma cleared her throat, and in that moment I knew. She'd been sleeping with him. Trading charm for charm. I couldn't blame her. Giorgio had been handsome, even in death, and there probably weren't a lot of other options in this small, island community. Aside from a long-ago jilted sheriff, of course.

Hattie let out a whoop and clapped her hands. "You little minx! I love that so much! You deserve a hot young whippersnapper. He was so lucky to have you."

Thelma grinned. "Thanks. I was worried you'd judge me."

Hattie patted her knee. "Sweetheart, you deserve to feel your inner female goddess take flight! I'm so proud of you!"

"Honestly, it was really fun," Thelma admitted. "Until I found him in my hot tub, of course."

"Yeah," Hattie agreed. "Been there, done that. I feel you, cuz."

I started laughing. "I'm sorry. I can't help it. The fact that you guys both dated men who you later found dead is funny. I mean, what are the chances?"

They both looked at me, and I swallowed my laughter. "I mean, that's bad luck. Very sad. Big bummer. Traumatizing, even?"

They stared at me, and out of the corner of my eye, I saw Lucy start to giggle. "I dated a guy who turned up dead, too," she said. "Maybe we should start a club. Mia can't be in it, unless her ex gets shanked in prison."

I smacked Lucy on the arm. "Lucy! You can't say that!"

"He probably murdered a bazillion people. Shanking would be a gift to the world," she shot back.

"It wouldn't count," Hattie said. "Mia has to find the body herself."

Lucy nodded. "Right. Mia would have to wait until Stanley gets out of prison and then hunts her down to kill her for testifying against him, only to be popped on your front porch."

"King Tut would kill him," Hattie said. "That cat is a special kind of wonderful."

"King Tut terrifies me," Lucy said. "So, maybe have Stanley killed by a guy from his drug world instead, so I don't have to move out of state to get away from your cat. That would work, right?" She glanced back and forth between us, as we all stared at her. "No?"

Hattie burst out laughing. "If someone could hear this discussion, we'd all probably get locked up. We leave a trail of dead lovers behind us?"

"I haven't had anyone I slept with wind up murdered," Blanche said. "I'll skip joining your little club."

"But we're amazing! We could have a streaming series inspired by us," Lucy said. "We'd all get super rich selling our story. What if Shonda Rhimes picked it up? From *Bridgerton* to us."

"Who doesn't want that?" Hattie said. "Shonda is a guiding light to all women alive to believe in ourselves to be brightly shining stars of awesome. I love that. Let's call her. I'm sure she'd love our story."

My mom had used me to steal from Shonda at a Hamptons party when I was a preteen. She'd stolen from most celebrities at one time or another. "Let's maybe wait to call Shonda until after we get this sorted." I didn't think Shonda would recognize me, but why take a chance, right?

Thelma finally grinned. "I have to admit it feels good to have company." She took a breath. "It's going to work out, right? It'll be okay?"

Hattie let out a whoop. "Of course it will! You've got us at your back. We never lose."

So far. We'd never lost *so far*.

"Maybe Sheriff Wick won't come after you," I said. "Maybe he'll find someone else."

"Maybe we'll *make* him find someone else," Hattie said. "Right?"

"Right," I agreed. "Girl power."

Blanche looked back and forth between us. "Wow. You guys suddenly took on a whole new energy. I wouldn't want to mess with you. You're like *Charlie's Angels*."

"Oh…good idea! We need a team name," Hattie said. "Specific to us."

"I know!" Lucy clapped her hands. "How about Triple Threat?"

"Threat?" I snorted. "More like trouble."

"Triple Trouble," Hattie said. "I love it. I freaking love that so much. We're so much more fun than a simple threat. We're trouble for them, and for life in general." She looked at Thelma and Blanche. "You guys want in? We could call it Circle of Awesome.

Or Circle of Trouble. Or Circle of Chaos. That has some alliteration there, which is always phonetically pleasing."

Blanche snorted. "Heck no! There's no way I want hunting murderers to be such a part of my life that I have a name for it."

Thelma shook her head. "Heavens, no. I agree with Blanche. You guys can have the glory. I'll just get Giorgio his justice and be good."

"Triple Trouble it is, then." Hattie clapped her hands. "Okay, let's focus, ladies. We have dinner at what time? Seven?"

I pulled out my VIP card and checked it. "Cocktails at seven on the patio, and then dinner at seven-thirty."

"Time check?" Hattie said.

"It's four-thirty," Lucy said.

"All right. We have two and a half hours to find out all we can about Giorgio. Mia, you and Lucy break into his room and search it. Thelma, you make a list of everyone you know who might have something against him." Hattie hopped to her feet. "Blanche, come with me to talk to Atlas, the strapping lad carrying the furniture around."

Of course Hattie would choose the muscled, testosterone junkie as her job. "All right."

"A strapping lad?" Blanche clapped her hands with delight. "I'm in."

"I have an all-access key card," Thelma said, holding up a plastic card. "Giorgio's room is in the staff building. Number 3A."

We all looked at each other. "Why do you have an all-access card?" I asked.

"Roger gave me one, and it still works. I like having it for late-night kitchen raids." Thelma grinned. "I'm still friends with the staff. We have fun."

I glanced at Thelma's house. As much as I wanted to hear more about the behind-the-scenes at the resort, I knew it wouldn't be long before the police went to Giorgio's room. "Did you ever meet Giorgio at his room?"

Thelma cleared her throat. "Yes, a few times."

Crap. "Did anyone see you?"

She shrugged. "I don't know. I didn't pay attention. I wasn't trying to hide anything."

Hattie looked at me and Lucy. She didn't have to speak for all of us to know that the case against Thelma was building. We had to assume at least a few people knew she'd been sleeping with Giorgio. Lovers were always great suspects in a murder investigation.

Staff liked to talk, especially about new staff who were sleeping with the much-older widow of the resort's former manager.

In fact, if I hadn't already decided to believe Thelma's innocence, she'd be my number one suspect as well. Which was maybe why she'd been picked as the hostess of his body's last stand. Or…? I wasn't sure.

I took the key from her. "Lucy and I will check out Giorgio's. Do you remember anything noticeable about his room?"

She shook her head. "I wasn't paying attention to his room. I was…giving him lessons."

Hattie snorted. "You need to pay better attention next time you do the tango with a man who's going to be murdered in your hot tub."

"Next time a man is murdered in my hot tub?" Thelma looked alarmed. "Does there need to be a next time?"

"We can only hope, right?" Hattie said.

"No," I answered. "We don't need to hope. Honestly, Hattie. Really?"

"Really. Life can be fun, if you decide to live it." She stood up. "Blanche, let's go find Atlas. Thelma, you stay here on the beach where you have witnesses in case someone else gets murdered."

Blanche and Thelma's eyes widened, but Lucy and I just sighed. Because we knew how these things went. Murder was contagious.

"Mia and Lucy, meet up at our room at six-thirty to recap." She nodded at Thelma. "We're in room 602. Ocean view, which we do appreciate."

Thelma nodded. "I get free rooms there because of Roger. Enjoy."

"Oh, we will." Hattie snapped her fingers at me, Lucy, and Blanche. "Let's go, ladies. Let's find some motive!"

CHAPTER 10

I TEXTED the Keep Mia Alive chat on the way over to Giorgio's room. *There's been a murder. The sheriff could have done it, but either way, he's trying to pin it on Hattie's cousin. We're helping.*

Lucy leaned over my shoulder, grinning when I hit send. "Griselda and Devlin are going to freak out over that. They get so worked up when you put yourself in danger."

"That's my hope." I shoved my phone in my pocket as we walked down the boardwalk that took us behind the resort to the employees' quarters. "Lucy, I'm a little worried about Roger's death. What if the sheriff killed him, too?"

"I thought the same thing, but he was in the hospital for knee surgery."

"Details get murky. Was he actually in surgery when Roger died? I think we need more details."

"I hate that you're right, but you are." She shoved her hands in the pockets of her yellow, mesh cover-up. "We're pretty vulnerable here, without Devlin to back us up."

"I know—" I suddenly heard the sound of a helicopter. We both spun around to see a helicopter flying low along the shallow waters, near the beach. "That helicopter has the same red landing gear," I said.

"And the yellow blades," Lucy said.

"What are the odds it's not the same one?"

"Zero." She paused. "Do you think it's looking for us?"

"Us?" A chill shivered down my spine. "I hope not. Maybe it's for our secret celebrity couple, right?" I saw Hattie at the edge of the beach, watching the helicopter. She was wearing the same bikini top as she had in the boat. "They'll recognize Hattie if they see her. There aren't a lot of senior women around with fuchsia hair."

The helicopter was already even with Hattie. "Too late," Lucy said. "They'll have seen her if they're looking."

"Maybe they're still looking for the trunk. Or doing a security sweep for crazy fans. Not looking for us."

"Maybe."

We fell silent, watching until it flew out of range down the shoreline. It was too far away for me to see if the guy was hanging out with his binoculars again, and I didn't like that I didn't know what he'd been looking at. "We need to buy binoculars," I said. "I feel like we're at a disadvantage with that helicopter."

"Maybe we won't see it again," Lucy said.

"There was a lot of money in that trunk. If they're looking for that, they're not going away." But it was gone for now, and we were still alive, so time to focus. "Let's go."

I kept looking back at the beach as we hurried to Giorgio's, but the helicopter didn't come back. I swiped a couple pairs of latex gloves from an unattended housekeeping cart and handed a pair to Lucy as we reached the door of 3A.

My phone dinged as I was pulling on my gloves. "It's Griselda."

Get on the next ferry and go home. All of you.

I texted back. *Did you guys get the trunk?*

I have a team on the way.

The helicopter just flew along the shoreline again. They're going to see it in Captain Jim's boat.

Mia, I gotta go. Do not get involved. Understand?

I sighed. *I was hoping for help, not a lecture.*

I can't help. It's a local issue. Stay out of it.

I sighed and put the phone in my pocket. "He's being Griselda."

"He sure is." Lucy knocked on the door. "You know, he's hot and all that, but he really doesn't respect your awesomeness. I don't think I can recommend you date him. I vote for Devlin."

I sighed. "I'm not dating either one."

"But you will. A girl can resist a man in uniform for only so long, especially when it's them."

"What's so special about them?" I knocked and pressed my ear to the door, listening to make sure no one was inside.

"Because you like them both."

Alarm shot through me. Did I like them? "I don't like them. Definitely. I don't."

"You absolutely do. You complain about them, but when they're around, you look at them...differently."

Crud. "I've noticed that they're both handsome. It's not the same thing as liking them." I slid the keycard over the electronic pad, and the light turned green. I opened the handle and peered inside. "Hello? Anyone here?"

My phone dinged, and I pulled it out. It was Devlin. *Who died?*

Lucy leaned over, then grinned. "See? He asked who died. He didn't tell you to stay out of it. He's your man."

Giorgio Costa, I typed back. *A dance instructor at the resort.*

I'll look into it. Stay out of it. If the sheriff did it, that's not a good situation.

Lucy sighed. "Okay, neither of them is worthy. We'll have to start from scratch with your dating life."

"I'm not starting anything." I shoved my phone in my pocket and finished putting on my gloves. "Remember, no fingerprints."

After one more look around to make sure no one saw us go inside, we slipped into Giorgio's room and closed the door. The room was dimly lit by the afternoon sun, and I could clearly see that Giorgio Costa was a complete slob. There was nothing remotely debonair or classy about how he lived.

There were pizza boxes on the coffee table. Half-drunk beverages. Clothes piled on the couch. His bedding was on the floor, and the whole room had the stale, soggy scent of a men's locker room. "This doesn't look like the room of the dashing dancing corpse in Thelma's hot tub," I said.

"Well, now we see his rough side." Lucy toed a pair of boots by the door. "He's literally tracked sand all over the place."

There was indeed black, slightly sparkly sand on his boots, and all over the floor.

"Move fast. We don't know how long we have."

"You got it." Lucy headed into the bathroom, and I made a beeline for the dresser.

I yanked open the drawers, quickly rifling through the few clothes that were in there. Giorgio apparently lived in tee shirts and sweat shorts. I didn't find even a single pair of dress socks, or anything remotely related to his job. I found one tuxedo and dress shirt in the closet, and it was still in its dry-cleaning bag. A pair of highly polished dance shoes sat on the top shelf, but no other sign of the debonair Giorgio we'd seen in the tub. "Why would Thelma sleep with him? He's a slob."

"He's handsome. She deserves fun. It's not complicated. Over here." Lucy had moved to the bed. "Come look!"

I carefully made my way across the piles of clothes on the floor, to where Lucy had pulled a large box out from under the bed. I peered inside. It contained numerous pieces of jewelry, watches, and some cash. I grimaced. "My mom had a box like that."

"Stuff she'd stolen?"

I nodded. "Yeah."

"I figured as much. I bet it's items Giorgio stole from the women or men he danced with."

"Or souvenirs from being a serial killer." The moment I said it, we both looked at each other in alarm. "I take that back," I said quickly. "There's no way we're getting involved with a serial killer."

"But if he's the serial killer and someone killed him, then we're not in danger, right?"

"From him, no, but someone killed him."

Her eyes widened. "Maybe he had a partner. A serial killing buddy."

Oh, God. "Or maybe, he just stole stuff." I picked up a diamond ring. I tilted it so the sun caught it, and it sparkled. "I'm not a jeweler, but it looks real," I said. My mom had a good eye for valuable jewelry, and she'd taught me what to look for.

"So, Giorgio stole from someone, and they killed him?"

"Seems excessive." I took out my phone and took some pictures of it. "Who kills over a ring?"

"Right? So, serial killer trophies are what I'm thinking. Who is his buddy? Sylvia? Oh! What if it's Thelma!" She grinned. "This is crazy. Super exciting."

I started laughing. "Lucy! That's not a good thing! That's a really bad thing!"

"We've never dealt with a serial killer before," she pointed out. "It's fun to have new challenges. As long as we don't fit the profile, we're fine."

"Are we really fine? Is that how it works?" I put the lid back on the box and put it under the bed. "Or do you think it's possible that the serial killing buddy would be okay with killing us if we figured out who they were? You know, to avoid spending the rest of their life in prison?"

She cocked her head considering my excellent point. "Yep, they might do that."

"So, not a good thing?"

"You may be right." She looked sadly toward the box. "You think we shouldn't get involved?"

"Honestly, we don't even know if the sheriff is going after Thelma. Even if he was a little pouty about her love life, it doesn't mean that he wants to put her in jail."

"And it doesn't mean he killed her husband."

"Right? There's no proof Roger was even murdered."

We looked at each other. "So, we tag out?" Lucy said. "Just like that?"

"Maybe we lay low," I suggested, "and see if Thelma is actually in trouble."

"Because if she's not, then solving Giorgio's murder is literally not our problem."

"Not at all," I agreed. "We're not cops."

"Or even private detectives."

"We're just us."

"Yep."

We stared at each other, digesting the conversation. It was the right choice. Devlin and Griselda were right. We did need to stay out of it. We really did.

Except that I couldn't stop thinking about the stolen items in that box.

They reminded me of my mother. She had a box just like that. If Giorgio was a small-time con artist and thief, did he deserve to be murdered? If he did, then my mom did, too, right?

If he'd gotten killed over petty theft, then it could so easily have been my mom floating in a hot tub, given the number of people she stole from.

And me, too. I'd been a kid, but I'd still done it.

That could have been us. Me and my mom. Stabbed for stealing some piece of jewelry. My mom didn't deserve to be murdered for what she'd done, so if Giorgio was like her, he hadn't deserved it either.

Lucy was watching me. "What are you thinking?"

"Let me see those items again." I grabbed the box and dragged it out. I pulled the lid off and then crouched down. I peered into the box, looking closely.

Lucy crouched down beside me. "What are you looking for?"

"The value of the items," I said. "If Giorgio is simply a thief, he'll only take items he thinks he can make money from."

"But a serial killer doesn't care about the money?"

"They might, but they might not. I don't know a lot about serial killers, thankfully, but I would think that they'd want something personal to the victim. An item that would make them think of that person. That might or might not have monetary value."

"Got it." Lucy leaned over the box, looking in it. "What do you think?"

"I'm looking to see if all the items look expensive, or if they look like personal items." I noticed one of the rings had a tag attached. "My mom used to attach tags to the items she took. She noted who she took it from and what info she had on it. It was a code we made up so no one would know what it meant if they found it." I picked up the ring and flipped the tag over, and then my body froze.

Shock reverberated through me, and for a second, I couldn't breathe.

"Mia? Mia!" Lucy grabbed my arm. "Mia!"

I sucked in a breath and my fist closed around the ring. "My mom," I whispered, my throat raw. "*My mom.*"

"Your mom, what?" Lucy looked alarmed. "Do you need to lie down? You don't look okay."

I held up the ring. "The tag on this. Look at it."

Lucy peered at the tag. "It's a bunch of gibberish. Designs, maybe? It looks like hieroglyphics."

"It's partially hieroglyphics, but part just randomness." *Holy crap.*

"You recognize it?"

I stared at her. "It's my mom's code," I whispered. "Either my mom was here, is here, or she trained Giorgio." I held it up. "This is our code, Lucy. My code. My mom's. It's *ours.*" I hadn't had any contact with my mom since I'd walked out on her and her way of life when I was seventeen. I didn't even know if she was dead or alive, though I suspected that if she were dead, I would somehow know.

I always figured someday, I'd turn around, and she'd be there, as if no time had passed.

But I hadn't thought it would be at the Grand Vista Resort, in the room of a man who'd just been murdered.

Oh, Mom.

Lucy's jaw dropped. "Holy mother of oyster! What the heck? Are there more tags with your code?"

I shoved the ring into my pocket, and we quickly rummaged through the rest of the jewelry. There were no other tagged items, but all the trinkets appeared to be items of considerable value. There were no obviously inexpensive personal items that I would have expected to see in the trophy box of a serial killer. "I think it's just stolen items. Not serial killer trophies."

"Just that one with the tag," Lucy said, sitting back on her heels. "Maybe Giorgio stole it from someone and it already had that tag on it. Maybe he doesn't know your mom."

"Maybe." The ring was burning a hole in my shorts, I leapt to my feet, scanning the room for any telltale signs that my mom had been there. It had been so long since I'd been in a room with her, it was as if I had to pull that part of my brain out of deep hibernation. "Look for women's clothes. She only wears nice clothes. Expensive brands."

"You bet." Lucy started riffling through the drawers and the closet, while I stood there looking around the room.

My mom always found a place to stash her finds when she was in a room. She hid her identification and cash, and anything else personal in there as well.

Where would she pick in this room?

It was a basic hotel room. Nothing fancy in it. Not a lot of places to hide things.

My gaze fell upon the massive photograph of a lobster on the wall above the bed. There was a faded outline on the bottom right corner of the wall, showing that the painting was slightly askew from where it had sat for a long time. "*Mom.*"

I scrambled across the bed and jerked the painting off the wall.

Cut into the wall, through the particle board, was a hole. Sitting on the bottom board was a small duffel bag.

"Holy cow," Lucy said, coming to stand by the bed. "How did you know it was there?"

"It's too obvious," I said. "That's a fake spot. The cops will stop looking after they find that spot."

I turned away, my heart racing, as Lucy grabbed the bag and opened it. "There's jewelry in here," she said. "None of it tagged, though."

"It's not the expensive stuff," I said. "None of the items in that bag will be traceable. It'll be useless to the police."

There was a painting of a seaside view by the television. That one looked like it was attached to the wall and perfectly aligned. "There." I hurried across to the seascape. I tried to pull the painting off the wall, but it was securely attached. I looked closely and saw that mini nails had been hammered through the corners.

My mom loved those nails.

My mind was reeling with the idea that my mom might have been here. I grabbed a butter knife from the pizza box on the table, and pried the nails out. I yanked the picture off, and just as I thought, there was a second hole in the wall.

But it was empty.

Disappointment rushed through me, and I slammed my hand on the wall. Had she been there? Was that her handiwork? Had she grabbed her stash and run when Giorgio had been killed?

She wouldn't have dated him. He was too much of a slob. For the same reason, she would have refused to train him. My mom was about precision. But those holes were her style, and the tag on the ring was our code.

At that moment, we heard voices outside the door. A man's voice, and a woman's voice.

Lucy and I froze, staring at each other in alarm, as we listened. The voices paused outside the door, and then I heard a knock on the door.

"Out the window!" I whispered. "Go!"

"But the jewelry is all over the bed—"

"No time!" I sprinted for the window and yanked it open. We were on the first floor, but the hill was sloped, making it a bit of a leap.

Lucy leaned out the window. "That's nothing more at stake than a broken ankle at worst. I don't want to be in here if serial killer buddy shows up." Without hesitation, she pulled herself up on the ledge, rolled onto her belly, then dropped.

She landed easily, and gave me a thumbs up. "No problem," she whispered. "Come on!"

Whoever was at the door knocked again, and I climbed up into the window and rolled onto my belly so I'd land feet first. I wanted to pull the window shut, but there was no way to do it.

I inched backward, until I was as far as I could get before letting go. Just as I pushed back, I saw the door open. I saw an arm in a gray sleeve, and a hand with a big ring on it, like a class ring, and then I dropped.

CHAPTER 11

I LANDED beside Lucy as I heard a shout from upstairs. "Someone went out the window!"

"Run!" I whispered.

We took off running, our feet pounding down the gravel pathway, trying to make it to the end of the building so we would turn the corner and get out of sight.

"There!" Someone yelled. "Two women!"

At that second, we turned the corner, slipping between two buildings. Lucy looked back. "What now?"

"We find a place to blend in. Ditch the yellow robe. It's too obvious, and they definitely had to have seen that when we were running."

She hugged it closer. "I love this cover-up."

"Murderer? Serial killer?" I ran to the end of the passage between the two buildings. I saw a Vera's Lobster Shack across the street, with the same signage as the one on the mainland. "Let's go!"

We looked both ways, but no one had emerged from Giorgio's building yet, so we booked across the street and raced into the restaurant. It was dim inside, with lots of picnic tables and paper placements, but not enough people to hide us.

Crap.

"Captain Jim!" Lucy shouted, pointing to a table in the corner.

He looked over, saw us, then gave us a nod. On the table in front of him was a pitcher of beer, several baskets of food including onion rings, fries, and steamed clams.

"Let's go!" I shoved Lucy and we ran over.

I flung myself down on the bench across from him. "We have bad guys after us. Hide us."

His eyes widened, but as I suspected, he got right to work. He ripped off his jacket, and tossed it at Lucy. "Put that on. That yellow robe is like a freaking banana."

She quickly pulled it on, and he handed me his beret. I tucked my hair up as he reached over and grabbed a few empty glasses from the bar. "These women came in with me," he said to the woman behind the counter, a woman who looked very much like Vera. Her daughter?

"These ladies have been with me the whole time," he said. "When people come in asking, tell them they've been here the whole time."

"Lie for you?" The woman raised her brows. "Captain Jim, you are nothing but trouble. Whatever you're into—"

"Are you Simone?" I asked. When she nodded, I continued. "Our best friend is friends with your mom," I said quickly. "Hattie Lawless—"

"Hattie? Well, heck, ladies, why didn't you lead with that?" Simone gave us a big grin. "Of course Hattie's friends have people chasing them. I'll cover for you!"

Hattie's reputation transcended time and space. "Thank you!"

She nodded, and then grabbed two plates and tossed some onion rings on them, then hurried over to the table with them. "Look drunk, snacky and incapacitated, like you've been here all day."

"Got it."

"Drunk and incapacitated? I can do that." Captain Jim sat back down, poured us each half a beer from his pitcher, and then started belting out the words to a hilarious song about a drunk Scotsman and what he was wearing under his kilt. I'd heard the song before, so I started singing too. To my surprise, Lucy knew it as well. It was the perfect song for drunk fools, and we crashed our glasses together as we sang, spilling beer everywhere.

Captain Jim's gaze went between us, and he nodded once. I knew it meant that someone had just walked in, likely looking for us. I wanted desperately to turn around and see who it was, but I didn't dare. We'd literally been caught jumping out the window of a murder victim's room, and the ring I'd taken from there was in my pocket.

Captain Jim gave me a look, and we turned up the notch on our singing. Lucy and I began to sway back and forth, as we sang. "Fall off the end of the bench," I whispered.

She immediately and un-subtly dove to the floor, reminding me that Lucy wasn't the best at undercover work.

Too late. I had to go with it. I burst out what I hoped sounded like stupid, drunken laughter. "Roseanne," I shouted. "Where'd you go?" I crawled along the bench after her, then flopped on my stomach, grinning down at her as Captain Jim kept singing. "Get up!" I yelled. "The song's not over!"

Lucy rolled onto her back, and put her feet up on the bench. She held her glass up over her head, and continued belting out the lyrics.

She had the drunk bar girl down very well. I was impressed. "Get up," I shouted again. "Come on!" I held out my hand. "Grab on!"

She grabbed my hand and yanked me right off the bench. I didn't have to fake my squawk of alarm as I tumbled off the bench and landed on her. She grunted when my elbow hit her stomach, but then we both started laughing for real. "You're such an idiot," I gasped as I rolled onto my side.

"You literally just gut-punched me! Don't you have any grace at all?"

"I'm part ballerina. You're the klutz." I scrambled off her, stealing a glance toward the front door to see who had come in.

It was the guy from the beach with the metal detector, and a woman I didn't recognize. The metal detector guy was still dressed in old, faded jeans, looking like a bum, and he was wearing a long-sleeved gray sweatshirt. *He was the guy who had been reaching into the room.*

The woman was wearing running shorts and a sports bra, and she was fit enough to have just been out for a run. They didn't look like they belonged together at all, but they were standing side by side, scanning the restaurant.

Who were they really? Did they know my mother, too?

They looked right at me, and then Simone let out a holler. "You lushes have been here all day! I'm cutting you off." She stalked over to the people at the door. "I'm so sorry. They tip well, so I let them stay, but I'm kicking them out now. Would you like a table? They'll be gone in a minute."

Simone sounded exasperated, unapologetic, and all business. I was impressed.

Captain Jim held up his empty glass. "More beer!"

She slapped a bill on the table. "Time to pay up. Bar's closing."

"Closing? How can it close? The sun's still out," Captain Jim hollered, while Lucy and I lay on the floor and giggled.

"I'm calling the cops," Simone threatened. "You have three minutes." She turned back to the people searching for us. "It will be handled. Would you like to eat outside or inside?"

"We're not eating. We were looking for two women. One was wearing a yellow dress."

I noticed the hem of Lucy's yellow cover-up peeking out from under Captain Jim's coat, so I threw myself on top of her. "I love you, Roseanne!"

Lucy grunted, and we both started laughing again.

Simone snorted. "The only women here are these two lushes. They came in on the ferry this morning. Day trippers. You know what that's like."

"Mind if we look around?"

"Go for it. But if you're not staying, I'm going to let them stay so they can pay me more money." She walked over to us and stood there, hands on hips, staring down at me and Lucy. "You three are pathetic."

I held my hands out to her. "He cheated on me. Caught him last night. Roseanne said we needed a girls trip. Who needs men?"

"I'm a man," Captain Jim bellowed. "I'm fantastic."

The corner of Simone's mouth quirked, which made me and Lucy start giggling. We almost had her. "Get off the floor."

"It's a nice floor." I was aware of our visitors checking the bathroom, and then peering into the kitchen.

Simone watched them as they came back in from the kitchen. "Would you like some food to go?"

The man walked up to her. "Did you see anyone go by?"

Simone shook her head. "I haven't been watching, though. I'll keep an eye out for a woman in a yellow dress and let you know. What did they do?"

The man and woman looked at each other, and then back at Simone. "Just be careful."

"Careful?" She put her hands on her hips. "I can take care of myself."

"Someone was murdered."

Her eyes widened. "What?"

Captain Jim coughed, spewing his beer across the table. "Murdered? Here? On the island? Who?"

I bolted upright. "What? Murdered? Who was murdered?"

Lucy rolled onto her side, trying to get up. "People get murdered here? We gotta get off this island. How do we get off the island?" She started shouting. "Help! Help! I need to get home!"

The man and the woman looked at us, then the man swore. "We gotta go. Stay safe." Then they bolted from the shop.

I watched them through the front window, as they hurried

down the street, looking around. "Weird," I said as I watched them. "That shouldn't have worked."

"Why not?" Lucy hopped to her feet and brushed herself off.

"They must not have seen us at all," I said. "Because how would they not realize it's us?"

"Maybe they didn't get a good look," Lucy said. "Or just the acting was so good that it derailed them."

"Murder?" Simone sat down at the table. "Was that for real?"

"For real." I scrambled off the floor and wiped my butt off, keeping an eye on the front window in case they came back. "We were searching his room, when those two walked in."

"Whose room?" Simone asked as Lucy stood up with a graceful fluidity that had been nowhere to be seen when she'd been Roseanne.

"Giorgio Costa. He was a dance teacher at the resort. Do you know him?"

Simone shook her head. "I don't. Was he new?"

"Just this season," I said.

"How was he killed?"

Lucy and I exchanged glances, and I decided not to answer. There was no reason to get the entire town pointing fingers at Thelma. "I don't know."

"Why were you searching his room?" Simone asked.

I took a breath, then shrugged. "Lucy, Hattie, and I have a thing for trying to solve murders."

Simone's eyes widened. "Shut up. You do not."

"They do," Captain Jim said. "They told me about it on the way over here. The two of them, plus Hattie."

Simone sighed. "I do believe that about Hattie, but honestly, why would you investigate murders?"

"It's fun," Lucy said.

"Fun." Simone gave her a strange look. *"Fun."*

"But we didn't expect to get caught in his room!" Lucy said.

Captain Jim was watching them through the window. "That was Frank Marchand," he said. "He's always wandering the beach with that metal detector. Lives in a cabin on a bluff near the beach."

I looked over at Captain Jim in surprise. "You know him?"

"Sure do. I know most all the locals around here. Been fishing on these waters for a long time."

"Is he the murdering type?"

Captain Jim leaned back. "Well, that's a question. Do you ever know what people are capable of? You don't. So I don't have an answer. You don't know until you know."

"Oh, you know," Lucy said. "At least sometimes."

"Nope," Captain Jim said. "You don't. You think you do, but you don't. Old Frank has been around a long time." As he spoke, he looked at Simone.

I sat up. "What? Why did you look at Simone like that?"

Simone shot a quelling look at Captain Jim, then turned to me. "I know the woman. Her name is Nancy Michaels. She's the VIP liaison at the Vista Point Resort."

I was very curious about what had passed between Captain Jim and Simone, but I could tell I wasn't going to get any answers at this point. So I let her redirect the conversation, especially since it was helpful. "What do you know about Nancy?" I asked.

Simone shrugged. "Not much. She's been there a few years, but hasn't really assimilated much with the locals. She seems peppy and friendly, but her job is mostly calling me up and asking me to procure outrageous things for her guests."

Captain Jim grinned. "And then you call me and ask me to run to the mainland to get something for them. Remember that time that actress wanted yogurt from that farm in Vermont?"

"Right? And their helicopter was on the fritz so you had to drive there to get it by morning." Simone grinned. "Best money you ever made, right?"

Captain Jim shrugged. "I do anything for a buck," he said with a wink.

I frowned. "Do a lot of the guests have helicopters?"

Simone shook her head. "Most of them do have helicopters,

but the island has a new ordinance against them. They disrupt nature and the serenity of the island, so they banned them about three years ago. It's been great."

Captain Jim nodded. "My business has gone way up since they were banned. Boats are the only way here now."

I considered that. "Did you see the helicopter earlier today?" I asked Simone.

"I did. You don't see helicopters around much because they can't land here anymore. I guess it was a tour or something?"

Huh.

"What about Giorgio?" Lucy asked. "The dance instructor? Do you know him, Captain Jim?"

Captain Jim picked up a fried clam. "Might know his face, but don't know him by name. I don't pay much attention to the staff at the resort. They come and go. Not worth my time until they've been around for a while."

I pulled out my phone and showed Captain Jim a picture of Giorgio from the hot tub. I zoomed in on his face so the knitting needles and location couldn't be seen. "That's Giorgio."

Captain Jim took my phone and peered at it. He stared at it for a moment, then he unzoomed the photo before I could stop him. His eyes widened, and then he zoomed in on the knitting needles. "Is this real?"

Simone looked over his shoulder and let out a gasp. "Holy cow. That man has knitting needles in his chest!"

"Yeah. I guess I should have issued a trigger warning. My bad. Yes, that's Giorgio. Do either of you recognize him?"

Captain Jim didn't answer me. "Where'd you get the picture?"

"I took it."

They both looked at me. "You took the picture?" Captain Jim looked impressed. "What were you doing there?"

I sighed. So much for keeping it a secret. "Hattie's cousin found him in her hot tub. The sheriff might be looking to pin it on her so we said we'd help." I noted that he didn't seem overly concerned about the fact he was looking at a photo of a dead guy.

Maine people were so resilient.

Simone handed me my phone. "He was murdered?"

"I would think so. I mean, it's possible to jam knitting needles into your own chest and then throw yourself in a hot tub by accident, while fully clothed, but the odds are low."

Simone raised her brows. "Don't underestimate people," she said. "I've seen some real doozies in my day."

"Right?" Captain Jim laughed. "You ought to turn that photo into a book cover for that local mystery writer, Hammersley. Doesn't he set his books in Maine?"

Beau. The mention of his name made alarm shoot through me. "Crap. Beau would kill me for not sending him this picture." He might hold King Tut hostage for years to punish me for holding out on murder pics.

I quickly selected a number of photos from the crime scene, including a bunch of Giorgio, and texted them to Beau. *Today's adventures. XOXO*

I put the phone down and I found Captain Jim staring at me. "What?"

"You know Beau Hammersley."

"Yes. He's babysitting my cat while I'm here."

Captain Jim leaned forward, his forearms on the table. "Beau Hammersley is *babysitting* your *cat?*"

"I had to bribe him with the promise to keep him in the loop every time we run across a corpse, but yes."

"Which you totally blew," Lucy said. "We saw that body hours ago."

"We don't need to tell him that."

Simone grinned. "Captain Jim is obsessed with Beau Hammersley. Everyone knows it."

"He's a literary genius with a mind so diabolical that it stuns me every time I read one of his books." Captain Jim's voice was reverent as he gazed at me. "And you know him."

"I do." I studied Captain Jim. "I'll introduce you to Beau if you'll help us."

Lucy raised her brows. "Beau hates people, especially fans. He doesn't want to meet Captain Jim."

I slanted Lucy a look. "That's not helpful."

Two new customers walked in and headed to the counter, and Simone hurried over to help them.

Captain Jim snorted. "You can't get Beau here."

"She can't," Lucy agreed. "Beau hates the world."

Really, Lucy? That was so not helpful. I glared at her, then pulled out my phone and texted Beau again. *I need you to meet a local lobster fisherman so he'll help us with murder.* I showed it to Captain Jim. "He's in love with my mother. He'll agree to it. He's using me as a conduit to meet her when she decides to show up in my life again—"

I cut myself off, suddenly remembering the ring in my pocket. *Mom.* Giorgio had somehow been involved with my mother, and now he was dead. Was my mother next on the killer's list? Sudden urgency filled me, the kind of urgency that twisted around my gut and knotted it with fear. "Captain Jim. I think Giorgio knew my mother, which means she might be next on his list. Help me."

CHAPTER 12

CAPTAIN JIM'S EYES NARROWED. "I was raised by a single mom. She took me out on her dad's old boat and taught me the water and how to find lobsters. It's the boat I still use today."

Well, that last bit made sense.

He had his mom's boat, and I still had the lock picks my mom had given me. "I was also raised by a single mom," I said. "She taught me how to survive." And steal things. And pickpocket. And con celebrities. "We lived on the streets and in cars. I haven't seen her since I was seventeen, but Giorgio had a note written in a code that she and I made up." As I said it, I realized that was my key to Beau. I quickly sent him another text. *The victim had a note in his room written in the code that my mom and I made up. Either my mom wrote it, or she taught it to him. She might be here at the resort.*

That would get his attention.

Captain Jim slammed his beer on the counter. "I'm in. If your mama is in danger, we gotta stop that."

My throat suddenly felt clogged, and emotion seemed to press down on me. "Great. Thanks."

Lucy put her arm around my shoulder and squeezed. "Mia, I was willing to help when it was Hattie's cousin maybe going to prison, but now that your mom might be in danger? You have my all, and I'm sure you have Hattie's too."

My eyes got a little misty, and I nodded. "It's been a long time since I've seen her," I said. "She was my best friend. My only friend, until I met you and Hattie." I wasn't going to count my ex-husband as a friend, even though I'd believed he was, for a while.

"What does the code say?" Lucy said. "Maybe that will help."

"I don't know. I'm a little rusty on it." I looked around to see if anyone was watching us, but the new customers were focused on ordering from Simone. I pulled the ring out. My heart was racing, so I took a moment to look at the ring itself instead of the tag.

It had a large center diamond, and it was surrounded by emeralds and diamonds. The band was an intricate, wavy design that incorporated more diamonds. It was unusual and beautiful, and it sparkled like it was real, which meant it was extremely expensive.

It was exactly the kind of piece my mom would have stolen. "My mom never wasted time on inexpensive items," I said. "Every time you steal something, you're taking a risk. She believed that every risk had to have a big potential reward." I held up the ring. "This would fit her philosophy."

Captain Jim raised his brows. "Your mom was a thief?"

I glanced at Lucy, who shook her head. "She was an entrepreneur," I said.

"What does the note say?" Lucy asked again.

"I don't know." I took a breath and turned over the tag. The familiar markings stared at me, and suddenly, I felt like I was a teenager again, back in the insanity of the life I'd grown up in. Conflicting emotions warred through me: I wanted to burst into tears and race outside, shouting for my mom, and I also wanted to throw the ring in the trash and run for the ferry and get away before my old life could trap me again.

But if she was in danger of being murdered, I couldn't walk away.

She would always be my mom and part of my soul.

So, I took a deep breath, and focused on that tag.

Lucy and Captain Jim leaned in to look at it.

"It looks like gibberish combined with random pre-caveman art," Captain Jim said.

"It's not." I pointed to the triangle. "See the angle of that? It means June." I pointed to the next bit. "See those dots? That's the date."

"June twenty-ninth?" Captain Jim frowned. "That was yesterday."

"It's the date she, or Giorgio, acquired the item." Oh, wow. If my mom wrote it, she'd been on the island *last night.* My heart started racing. I looked at Captain Jim. "Was there a party last night at the resort? She always liked to work parties, because then there were a lot of suspects and a lot of marks."

He shrugged. "I don't hang out at the resort. Ain't my vibe. But there's usually something happening there with high profile celebrities."

Lucy pulled out her phone. "I'll text Hattie. I'll tell her where we are and ask her to find out."

I nodded as I looked at the ring again. There was more written than usual, and it took a few minutes for the rust to come off my brain. "She wrote that's it's a diamond and emerald ring. Estimated value around a hundred thousand dollars." I looked up. "She had a great eye for jewels. She was usually off by no more than five percent on an item's value."

Lucy raised her brows. "If she and Giorgio were stealing things of that value, that might be worth killing over."

I shook my head. "Jewelry is rarely worth killing over. You just collect insurance and buy new stuff. That's part of the appeal of it. People lose jewelry all the time. Everyone she stole from would remember putting it on for the party, and then it would be gone by the time they got home, so they would think they lost it."

Captain Jim was eyeing me. "Your mom sounds like a cagey woman."

"She's smart." I studied the tag. There was another sentence, but it had different markings, ones I couldn't quite remember. "This extra sentence is unusual. She doesn't put anything else on her tags."

"So, maybe Giorgio did?" Lucy suggested. "Maybe he learned from her?"

"Maybe." I studied the tag again, sifting through memories from a long time ago. I could almost remember the symbols, but not quite. "I think she's using original code from when I was little. I just can't quite remember—" I stopped as something flashed through my mind, and my gut dropped. "Holy cow."

"What?"

I pointed at the first symbol on the second row. "That thing right there? It's my name. I couldn't write, so I used to draw this little symbol instead." I leaned back. "She wrote me a note."

My mom knew I'd be coming. And that I'd be in that room and find the ring.

What the heck was going on?

Lucy let out a whistle, and I looked at them. "I always knew that someday she'd show up in my life, but I didn't know how." I raised the ring. "And now I know." I needed to decode that last sentence, to find out what she wanted me to know, but my memory was too foggy.

Captain Jim leaned forward. "I know your mom sounds like a real treasure," he said, with barely any sarcasm at all, "but is it possible, at all, that she is the one who killed Giorgio?"

"What?" I stared at him. "My mom is not a murderer."

"Would she kill to save your life?"

"Yes." I didn't hesitate. "But she didn't need to save my life. I'm fine."

"That you know of." Captain Jim looked back and forth between us. "Maybe Giorgio is dead because he was a danger to you, and your mom had your back."

My stomach tightened. My mom was a con artist. It was a nonviolent criminal endeavor. But she'd also give her life for mine. I knew she would. But she wouldn't kill anyone for any other reason than if someone was about to kill me, right in that moment.

But I hadn't seen her in a decade. How much had she changed? Was it possible she'd—

No. No. *No.* I knew my mom. She was a lot of things, but a murderer wasn't one of them.

"She didn't kill him," I said firmly. "If he were a danger to me, which he couldn't have been, because I've never seen him before, she would have set him up for something and pulled a con on him. But murder? Never."

Lucy looked at me with a sympathetic eye, and I knew she heard the edge of worry in my voice. "We'll find out the truth, Mia. Promise."

"If Mia's mom killed Giorgio, Mia's not going to want to hear that truth," Captain Jim said.

I lifted my chin. "I can handle the truth."

"She can," Lucy said. "She put her ex-husband in prison for drug dealing. If anyone's willing to destroy her own life and happiness to do the right thing by betraying those she loves, it's Mia."

I looked at her, but I didn't have a protest. Stanley was one thing. But my mom?

I wouldn't turn her in. I knew I wouldn't. No matter what she'd done.

But I prayed I wouldn't have to make that choice, an impossible choice that would haunt me forever. "My mom didn't murder him, but she might be in danger of being killed by whoever killed Giorgio."

I just wanted her to be okay and not involved. But the tag on that diamond ring said I wasn't going to get the second part of my wish.

Lucy patted my knee. "It'll be fine. That metal detector guy, Frank, was looking for you. He's definitely involved. We'll go expose him. And we'll figure out what Nancy was up to. Sound good?"

I felt like I needed a moment to process everything, but I didn't have that luxury. "Yeah, okay. Right. It'll be fine—"

The doors to the café flung open, and Hattie, Blanche, and Thelma raced in. "I just saw Frank go by in a pickup truck," Hattie shouted. "He's heading toward the docks. He's making a run for it."

Captain Jim leapt to his feet. "Let's go! I'm ready to get off this island anyway!" He whirled toward Simone. "Simone! We need to borrow your truck!"

She didn't even look over at us. She just kept talking to her customers.

"Simone Eva Jimenez," Hattie snapped. "We need your truck. Now."

Simone looked over sharply, and her face lit up when she saw Hattie. "Hattie! When did you get here?"

"Can't talk. We need your truck. Now."

"Oh, God. Don't crash it, okay?" But Simone dug into her front pocket and tossed the keys at Hattie. "Blue SUV parked in front."

Hattie caught the keys. "Smooches, Simone."

Simone waved us off. "Be safe. My mom will kill me if anything happens to you."

"Be confident, not safe!" Hattie took off for the door.

"Wait! I want to drive!" Captain Jim raced after her, and Lucy and I exchanged grins.

There was no way Captain Jim was going to win that battle. Hattie always got the steering wheel, and she deserved it.

Within moments, we were packed into a well-worn SUV that reminded me of my old truck Turbojet, except mine was a classic and this was fighting for every last mile it could get. Hattie, Lucy, and I took the front seat. Captain Jim was in the back seat between Blanche and Thelma, looking confused about how he'd ended up there.

Never underestimate women, right?

Hattie hit the gas and we shot out into the road, barreling down the small street with astonishing speed, given the old truck. "I can make this work," Hattie said. "She has good bones."

As Hattie drove us recklessly through the small town, I twisted around to talk to Thelma. "What do you know about the metal detector guy? Captain Jim said his name is Frank."

Thelma nodded. "Frank used to work at the resort when Roger first took over. He did grounds and maintenance, but he did a terrible job. Mostly sat around smoking pot when he was supposed to be working. Roger fired him. He got a job at another resort, but when he's not doing that, he cruises the beach with that metal detector."

I grimaced. "Roger seems to have made a lot of enemies."

"Frank is sweet," Thelma argued. "He just doesn't have a big work ethic. I don't think he really cared that he was fired."

Everyone would care. Being fired sucked, even if you hated the job. Rejection was rejection. It was making me more concerned about Roger's death. Had something Roger did come back to haunt Thelma?

"Everyone keep watch for a red pickup," Hattie said, as we approached the docks.

I looked around. "I see three red pickups already. This is Maine. Everyone drives trucks."

"Shell's bells," Hattie muttered as she slowed the truck. "I didn't get a good look at it. Lucy, go check the one on the right. Text if it's him."

"Got it." Lucy jumped out and jogged across the parking lot toward a newish looking truck.

"Thelma, Blanche, and Captain Jim. You guys hit the one on the north end of the parking lot. And Captain Jim? Sacrifice yourself to save my cousin if you need to. She's a treasure and it's her birthday tomorrow. No one needs to die on their birthday."

"I'm not sacrificing myself for anyone," Captain Jim said as he followed Thelma out of the truck. "I'm an island, not a village."

"There are villages on islands," she yelled out the window as he hurried to catch up with Thelma and Blanche. "Men," Hattie muttered to me as she executed a speedy three-point turn. "They're lucky they're like puppies."

"Men are like puppies?"

"Yep. If they weren't so darned endearing, we'd throw them all overboard in the boat ride of life. But they just have this charisma, you know?" She parked the truck near the end of the marina where Captain Jim had docked. "Like your law enforcement throuple. When are you going to get that going?"

Throuple again? Lucy must have told Hattie about her throuple idea. "I don't want one guy, let alone, to be in a throuple."

"Every woman secretly yearns for a law-enforcement throuple. There's just something about the uniform and excellent gun skills. You're just afraid to try, and you need to change that. Life sucks if you go through it on a tank full of fear."

"I'm not afraid." I got out of the truck. "I'm literally hunting a murderer as we speak."

"Not of death," Hattie agreed as she got out. "You have that handled. You fear getting involved with a man again. One kiss, Mia. Just try one kiss and see how it feels."

One kiss. The idea was weirdly terrifying. "I married a man who was a violent drug kingpin who has sent assassins after many people, and I had no idea he was a monster. I don't trust myself, Hattie. If I can be that blind, how can I ever trust my instincts with men again?"

She stopped to look at me. "Mia," she said softly, with surprising gentleness. "I get that. But you're a smarter, more independent woman now, with two amazing besties who have your back. You can't live in fear forever. It'll eat you up."

"You're single and thriving," I pointed out as we began to walk along the boardwalk, scanning for Frank.

"Because I choose it from a position of power, not fear. That's a fundamental difference." She winked. "Plus, I get plenty of naked man time on my terms. I'm not going without, baby cakes. Women have needs, including you."

"I don't have needs."

Hattie cocked a brow. "Well, that's a bald-faced lie, and your soul knows it."

"My soul is still trying to heal, and it's a little busy to be worrying about my lies."

"Is it?"

I glared at her. "It is—"

"Mia!" Griselda's shout interrupted me, and butterflies suddenly shot through my belly.

Of course he was here. One phone call about massive amounts of cash in a suspicious trunk, and he considered that an invitation. All I needed was for Devlin to show up next, and my life would be all neatly tied up on what was supposed to be a *girls* trip.

Hattie grinned. "His timing is perfect, don't you think?"

"No." I turned away from Hattie to see Griselda striding down the dock toward me. He was wearing jeans and sneakers, a Red Sox hat, and mirrored aviators. His tee shirt had a cartoon shark on it, and it sat with the perfect amount of snugness on his upper body. "Dammit. I swear he's working out more. He didn't used to look like that."

"He has a woman he's trying to impress," Hattie said cheerfully. "That's motivation. He may not share the same throuple enthusiasm as you do, and might want to beat out Devlin, instead of recruiting him to the same team."

I shoved Hattie into a pile of boat ropes, which made her burst into cackles of laughter. "Hi, Gris," I said.

"Gris?" He cocked an eyebrow at me, which looked much too debonair for my liking. "My nickname has a nickname now?"

"It's a sign of her love and devotion," Hattie said, popping back to her feet. "You got here quickly."

"I was in the area." He frowned at us. "Where's the trunk?"

I didn't have it in me to be relieved that he wasn't trying to be all flirty or personal with me, because, um, hello? The trunk that was being hunted by people in helicopters was missing? And they'd seen us with it?

"The trunk?" I shot a look at Hattie, who looked slightly alarmed. "Captain Jim left it in his boat. It's not there?" Oh, Lordy. If he had decided to keep that trunk for himself, that was not good for any of us.

"Nope." Griselda pointed toward the dock. "Last boat on the right? *Lady Cassandra*?"

"Let me call him," Hattie said as she pulled out her phone. "Mia, keep looking for Frank."

"Frank?" Griselda narrowed his eyes. "Who is Frank?"

"He's wearing a gray sweatshirt," I said. "Older guy. Maybe in his sixties. He was in the murder victim's room a few minutes ago. Why would he be in Giorgio's room?" I headed off down the ramp, scanning people.

Griselda followed me. "How would you know he was in the murder victim's room?"

"Because I was in there." I didn't bother to lie. It would be so much easier if Griselda decided he wasn't interested in me. I was a pain in the ass. Although he kind of knew that from when he micromanaged my life when I was a spy for him, now that I was free, I would be much more of an uncontrollable maverick than he realized.

He swore under his breath. "I told you—"

"I don't care what you told me. You don't own me anymore. Hattie's cousin is a suspect, and then I found—" I stopped. Pissing off Griselda wasn't worth exposing my mom. She was a known and wanted felon after all, which was the leverage Griselda had used to make me help him go undercover against Stanley in the first place.

Griselda was walking very close to me. "You found what?" he asked, his voice much too level and low. I knew he was frustrated with me, but trying to keep his cool so I didn't shut him out completely.

Too bad for him, my decision to shut him out completely was independent of how he treated me, and one hundred percent a factor of whether it served me.

So I ignored his question. "Are you sure you checked Captain Jim's boat? We hid it under a blanket—" I looked across the dock toward the boat, then froze when I saw Frank step onto Lady Cassandra. "That's him!" I pointed. "That's the guy who was in Giorgio's room!"

Griselda turned, saw Frank, and then took off running. I ran after him, but he was, of course, much faster than I was, and faster than he used to be. I knew how fast he was, because I'd seen him running to save my life before, and he hadn't been as fast as he was now.

"Hattie," I yelled as I raced after him. "Frank's on the boat!"

She turned, then started running toward the boat as well, still talking on the phone.

Frank bent over, doing something on the bottom of the boat. He didn't look like a slouchy, half-crazy pothead with a metal detector. He looked quick, alert, and focused.

Griselda was sprinting down the dock, moving fast. He shouted at Frank, yelling something about the FBI. Frank stood up quickly, saw Griselda on the run, and then leapt overboard.

I wasn't leaping into the ocean. I'd been there, done that, had enough. Griselda reached the boat and jumped on board. He leaned over the water, yelling at Frank, who was swimming away from him. Where did he think he was going?

"Get the boat keys," Griselda yelled at me. "We're going after him."

Hattie was already on it. "Where are the keys?" she asked into the phone. "Well, get them here."

Griselda leapt off the boat and started jogging down the dock, keeping an eye on Frank as he swam along. Frank was swimming along the dock, but far enough out that Griselda couldn't jump in and take him.

Griselda pulled out his phone and ordered someone to get there with a boat as he continued to shadow Frank.

Hattie caught up to me. "Captain Jim is coming."

"Frank was doing something to the boat. I want to see what it was." I headed down the dock, Hattie by my side. We reached the boat, and I could see that the trunk wasn't where we'd left it, which I didn't actually think it would be. Griselda was entirely capable of discerning whether a big trunk full of money was on a lobster boat. "What did Captain Jim say about the trunk?"

"He said he hasn't been back to the boat since he left with us."

"I'm going on." I hopped on and peered at the bottom of the boat, where Frank had been messing around. "He left a bag here," I said.

Hattie was waiting on the dock. "Well open it."

I crouched down and unzipped it, then frowned when I saw a small, black metal box. I picked it up and turned it over. It was heavy, and I could hear a little engine whirring inside it. A recording device maybe? I set it aside and checked the rest of the bag.

There was a small velvet pouch. I pulled it out, and found inside what looked like a diamond necklace. There was another tag on it.

My heart started pounding as I turned the tag over.

Our code. Again.

Fear gripped me. What was Frank doing with it? And why was he leaving it in Captain Jim's boat? Maybe he hadn't meant to leave it. Maybe we'd just interrupted him.

I shoved the necklace into my pocket, then checked to make sure there were no more tagged items. I found a few pieces of jewelry, but nothing was tagged. I left them there.

"What did you find?" Hattie called out.

"A bag with some stuff." I pulled out a small notebook that made me pause. The cover was a tattered turquoise leather with battered gold foil edges. It looked like my mom's inventory journal. Much older and worn, but the design was the same.

I flipped it open, and my heart sank when I saw dozens of pages of code that I recognized.

My mom guarded her journal carefully. Even I had never

known where she kept it. She'd never give it to anyone, and she'd never be careless enough to let it be stolen.

The fact that Frank had it meant that my mom was involved.

And most likely, in danger.

Or...dead.

CHAPTER 13

My gut congealed, and I suddenly couldn't breathe. My mom... dead? She was going to live forever. I'd always thought I had time. More time. Time to find my own space before reconnecting with her. But I had her journal in my hand. There was no way on earth that was good.

"What did you find?" Lucy leapt over the side of the boat, breathing heavily.

"Nothing." I shoved the notebook in my pocket. "It's fine. I mean, I found some jewelry and this box thing. Whatever." I stood up. "What's going on? Hi."

Lucy and Hattie stared at me.

"What?"

"What's wrong?" Lucy asked. Her voice was gentle.

Sudden tears surged, and I shook my head. "I stubbed my toe. Where's Frank? Did Griselda tackle him yet?"

Hattie leaned on the boat. "Mia. I give you a hard time because I know you're tough, and you could be tougher. But whatever just happened put a look on your face that's not good. Talk to us."

"But Frank—"

"Griselda's working on his fitness chasing Frank down," Hattie said. "Captain Jim, Blanche, and Thelma will be here in a moment, so you need to tell us right now."

Lucy climbed into the boat and sat down in the captain's chair. "We're here, Mia. What happened?"

I wasn't used to talking about my mom. She'd always taught me that whatever happened with us, stayed with us. People were our enemy. No one was ever on the side of the criminal, and, in fact, would betray us at the first opportunity.

That was why I had no friends. Because people couldn't be trusted. Only the two of us. No one else.

No one else.

Suddenly, that "no one else" rule felt lonely, depressing, and flat out wrong.

I had people. I had people I could trust with my life...and more importantly, with my family's secrets. Two people who understood me enough to sit there waiting for me to get the courage to tell them.

Hattie smiled. "She's going to tell us. Did you see how her shoulders relaxed, Lucy?"

"I didn't!" Lucy frowned at me. "Is Hattie right?"

I nodded. "Hattie's brilliant, as always."

Hattie beamed at me and took a bow. "Why thank you, my darling. Now talk fast because I can hear the thundering feet of Thelma, Blanche, and Captain Jim."

I quickly dug my mom's journal out of my back pocket. "This is my mom's. It's her inventory notebook. Even I didn't know where she kept it. She'd never, *ever* give it to anyone, for even a second. She'd never show it to anyone, except me. And it was in the bag Frank left in the boat."

Lucy's eyes widened, and Hattie's narrowed. "Your mom's in trouble, then."

"Or dead." The words tumbled out before I could stop them, fear driving them out into the world.

"No." Lucy stood up. "Your mom's not dead. You would know it."

"Would I? I always thought I would but—"

"You'd know," Hattie interrupted. "Strong, powerful women are connected on deep levels. You'd know. She needs you, but she's still okay. I feel it, too."

Tears filled my eyes, and I took a shuddering breath. "You think so?"

Hattie cocked her head. "What would your mom say right now?"

I laughed through my tears. "She'd tell me to stop whining and get to work."

Hattie grinned. "I think I just fell a little in love with your mom."

Lucy laughed. "No wonder Hattie's sass doesn't bother you. You grew up with it!"

I took a deep breath, feeling better. "I did," I agreed. "My mom had no room for any whining or crying. She just lived to the fullest she could in every moment. She always made time for fun, even it if was illegal."

"Hah! Your mom sounds amazing. Fun matters!" Hattie looked delighted. "What else do you have on her?"

I held up the diamond necklace. "This had a tag on it as well."

"What did it say?" Lucy asked.

"I don't know. I didn't look yet—"

"We're here!" Captain Jim ran up. "I have the boat key!"

I shoved the journal and necklace into my pocket. "Let's go get Frank. I need to talk to him."

"Damn straight we do," Hattie said, as she and Captain Jim helped Thelma and Blanche climb into the boat. "Just follow that attractive FBI agent that's running down the dock."

"You got it!" The boat started right up, and Captain Jim hit reverse.

I moved to the bow of the boat and scanned the dock for Griselda. "There!" I pointed to the figure walking along the dock, shielding his eyes as he scanned the water. "He's following Frank."

"I see him!" Captain Jim pulled out into the water and hit the gas.

Thelma and Blanche went to stand beside Captain Jim, but Hattie came up to the front with me. She put her hand on my shoulder. "You okay?"

I glanced at her. "Yeah."

Lucy stood beside Hattie. "We now have Hattie's cousin and your mom at risk. Whatever's going on, we're going to figure it out."

I let out my breath, my heart feeling lighter. Every time we'd teamed up to solve a murder, I'd been helping them out, or a friend. This was the first time I was the one who needed help. I put my arms around their shoulders as we scanned the ocean surface, looking for Frank. "I want you both to know how lucky I am to have you in my life. I'm so grateful for the two of you that I can't even express it."

The three of us didn't get squishy about our friendship, but I'd needed to say it.

Hattie and Lucy each put an arm around my waist and squeezed. "I love chasing murderers with you," Hattie said. "I'm not going to pretend I don't. But it goes deeper than that, and you know it."

"Me, too," Lucy said. "I love you guys."

"Aw...don't get all mushy," Hattie said. "I have no room for mush."

I looked over at Lucy and grinned. "I love you guys, too."

Hattie pushed us both away. "You girls are too soft. I can't even stand it." But she was smiling with deep satisfaction as she turned away. "Griselda's shouting at us and waving his arms. Should we go get him?"

"We need to find Frank," I said.

"Well, do you see him?" When we shook our heads, Hattie turned to Captain Jim and Thelma. "Either of you see Frank swimming?"

"No," Captain Jim said. "He's a good swimmer, though. He can swim for hours. He used to do ironman triathlons back in the day."

"Iron mans?" The man who barely shuffled across the sand with his metal detector could actually swim for hours? No wonder he looked agile when he was in the boat.

My phone rang, and I pulled it out to see Griselda was calling. "Hello?"

"Get over here! He's getting away!"

"Where is he?"

"Just come get me."

I hung up on him. "Griselda's holding info on Frank's whereabouts hostage. We need to go get him."

Captain Jim nodded, and turned the boat toward Griselda, while Hattie grinned. "FBI agents can be so manipulative. I admire that so much in a man."

Lucy raised her brows. "If he has any chance to date Mia, he has to be willing to go there."

"I agree," Hattie said. "It's good to challenge him. See what's he's made of." She waved as we neared the dock. "Hello, Griselda. Do you need a ride?"

He didn't waste time answering. He just leapt into the boat before we were even that close, which was pretty impressive. He didn't even look at me. He just strode over to Captain Jim and pointed. "Drive that way."

We looked in the direction Griselda was pointing, but I didn't see anyone in the water. "We really need binoculars," I said as Captain Jim turned the boat and began to cruise in that direction.

Griselda came up to the bow, standing right beside me, close enough that if I leaned back even an inch, I'd be touching him. I hadn't been that close to him in a long time, not since he was rescuing me from things, and definitely not since he'd said he wanted to date me.

He felt very close.

It felt very different.

"Anyone see him?" Griselda asked, sounding completely focused on Frank and oblivious to how close we were to each other.

I relaxed a little. "You lost sight of him?"

"Yeah. Once he realized I was walking along beside him, he changed direction and headed straight out into the ocean. I lost sight of him quickly."

Crap. "He better not have drowned," I muttered. "I have things to ask him."

Lucy and Hattie chuckled. "That sounded very cold-hearted. Maybe even sociopathic," Lucy said. "Just wanted you to know that, since law enforcement is here, and all."

"Frank can swim for hours," Captain Jim announced again. "He didn't drown. He's out here somewhere."

I looked back at Captain Jim. "What direction would he go? What is there to swim to out here? It's open ocean between here and the mainland."

Captain Jim nodded. "He knows the water. My guess is that he knew exactly how far out he needed to be to blend into the water. It's not far. The water is gray and choppy, and his head would be difficult to discern pretty quickly. Once he got that far, he probably started paralleling shore again."

"Which direction?" Griselda asked. "Back toward the docks or the other way?"

Captain Jim rubbed his jaw. "Not sure. He could get out of the water easily either direction."

Griselda swore. "Keep going this way. I'll have my contact check near the docks." He turned away and pulled out his phone, while the three of us leaned over the bow, scanning the waters.

I kept seeing flashes of black that I thought were a head, but it was just shadows and waves of the water. "How does anyone ever get rescued on the ocean?" I asked.

"Luck," Hattie said. "It's not their time to die yet."

Oy. "Remind me not to get stranded out here," I said.

Griselda came up behind us again, and this time, I felt his arm brush mine as he leaned over the railing. I shifted ever so slightly so I wasn't touching him, and Griselda slanted me a glance. "Scared of me?" he asked softly, returning his gaze to the ocean, scanning for Frank.

I lifted my chin. "No. Why would I be scared of you?"

"Because you're not as tough as you pretend you are." His voice was quiet, his gaze thoughtful, as if he were trying to find out all my secrets. "I'm also not as much of an asshole as you think I am," he said. "My job was to keep you safe, and take down a bad guy. I don't have room to be nice when lives are at stake. But that's not who I always am."

Lucy and Hattie were silent, pretending to be interested in searching for Frank in the ocean, but I knew they were listening.

I lifted my chin. Griselda got me so off-kilter when he was nice. Human. Sane. I didn't trust it. I'd been controlled by him for too long. "Did you see the bag Frank left in the boat?" I changed subject without apology.

Griselda stared at me, and then grinned. "I can be patient," he said. "I know what's at stake."

"She's worth waiting for," Hattie said, staring out across the water.

I kicked her in the shin.

"I know." Griselda said. "I do know that, Hattie."

"Check Frank's bag." I pointed to the floor behind us. "There's an electronic box making a whirring noise and some jewelry."

Hattie and Lucy spun around to look at me. "An electronic box making a whirring noise?" Hattie asked.

"Like a bomb?" Lucy looked horrified.

Griselda dove to the back of the boat, cursing as he grabbed the bag and unzipped it. He yanked open the bag, grabbed the box, and studied it for about three seconds. Then he looked up. "Everyone get a life jacket and get off the boat."

We all stared at him. "Um, we're in the ocean," I said.

"Get off the boat!" He turned to Captain Jim. "Stop the boat.

Get everyone off. Now! You have enough life jackets for everyone?"

Captain Jim didn't move. "It's my boat. I'm not jumping off."

Griselda held up the box. "This could be a bomb. Get. Off."

"Holy cow!" Blanche grabbed a life jacket. "I'm checking out of this adventure. I'm way too adorable to get blown up."

"I'm getting off!" Hattie grabbed a life jacket and pulled it on. "Thelma, get over here!"

As Thelma hurried over, Lucy shoved a life jacket at me. "You'll be fine, Mia. We'll stick together."

Oh, God. My heart was racing as I fastened the buckles. By the time I got it on, Blanche was already in the water and swimming toward shore. Hattie and Thelma were on the transom of the boat. They both jumped in and started paddling away.

Lucy had hers on. And she was at the back of the boat. "Come on, Mia."

The level to which I didn't want to get in that water was stunning. I looked back at Griselda. "You really think it's a bomb?" I couldn't keep the panic out of my voice. We were so far from shore, and the sun was starting to set. The ocean looked gray and cold.

"I don't know." He walked over to me. "I'm staying with it, but if it is a bomb, I'm not going to die without doing this." Then he gave me a look, and I suddenly knew what he was going to do.

He was going to kiss me. A desperate, I-might-die-in-two-minutes-so-I-need-to-stake-my-claim kiss.

He grabbed me around the waist, and for a split second, he met my gaze. I saw the hesitation on his face, the moment where he paused, giving me a chance to stop him.

I didn't.

Realization spread over his face, and he bent his head and kissed me.

Not a peck. He laid one on me that was all about seduction, heat, and a desperate last kiss before exploding into a bazillion pieces.

I expected to hate it. To feel like I was kissing a jellyfish. Or something worse.

But I didn't.

It was…intoxicating.

The man could kiss.

CHAPTER 14

GRISELDA ENDED IT QUICKLY, with the urgency of a man who thought he was holding a potentially death-inducing device. His gaze met mine, and there was new heat in there. But he didn't pursue it. "Get off the boat, Mia. Now."

Lucy grabbed my arm. "Come on, Mia! Let's go!" She dragged me toward the back of the boat.

I stepped over the transom to the little ledge. "Griselda!"

He looked over at me. "Get off the boat, Mia!"

"Don't you dare die before I have time to kick your ass for that kiss!"

He grinned, and then Lucy shoved me into the water. The water was shockingly cold, colder than it had been at the dock. The waves were high, and tossing me around, but I popped right back to the surface, which made me so happy.

Lucy was floating next to me, and she tossed me a rope. "Tie this around your wrist," she yelled. "I want us to all stay together!"

"Good call." I quickly tied it. For whatever reason, my mom had been an advocate of being good at knots, so the knot was secure, and I immediately felt better. "Let's go get Hattie and the others!"

Lucy nodded, and we looked around. I saw orange bobbing

shapes to my left, and I pointed. We stroked out across the water, swimming that awkward life-jacket crawl, but we caught up to Hattie and Thelma quickly. Blanche was already way ahead, swimming with a desperation that gave her wings. Because who wanted to blow up, right?

"Did Griselda just kiss you?" Hattie asked, as I tied a loop in the rope and slipped it around her wrist.

"Yes!" Lucy answered for me as she tied Thelma up.

"Holy cow," Hattie yelled. "Your first kiss since your murderous husband! How do you feel? Did your head explode? Or did your heart implode?"

I grinned. "No, nothing bad happened."

Hattie let out a whoop and put her arms in the air. "Whoohoo!"

"How was the kiss?" Lucy asked. "It was pretty hot how it happened. His last move before sacrificing himself to save us. If he dies, you'll literally be the last person he ever kissed in his life."

"That's so romantic," Hattie said. "Who knew Griselda could be romantic?"

Thelma was floating near me, watching me. "No good?" she asked quietly.

I looked over at her. "It was good," I admitted. "Unexpectedly good." I was mad at him. And me. I'd had time to stop him. But I hadn't. And the kiss hadn't been short. Again, I'd had time to stop him.

And I hadn't.

Why not? Because he might die in the next few minutes? That was a terrible reason to kiss a man who was an annoying control freak.

"Let's swim away from the boat," Lucy said. "Head back toward shore."

Everyone started swimming, but I looked over at my shoulder. Captain Jim and Griselda were still arguing, and then Captain Jim hit the gas. The boat took off and I saw Griselda grab for the railing, miss, and then fall on his ass in the bottom of the boat.

I grinned, feeling decidedly happier. Poetic justice.

Within moments, the boat was out in the bay, getting further and further from shore. I knew Griselda would try to get the boat away from us in case it blew, and Captain Jim was probably trying to shove Griselda overboard. "I hope it's not a bomb," I said as I watched the boat.

Hattie bumped my arm. "We all do," she said. "But we can't help from here. We need to find Frank, and quickly. So, let's go."

"Right." I gave the boat one last look, surprised at how much I didn't like the idea of Griselda being blown into smithereens. Damn him for making me imagine life without him in it.

Lucy tugged at the rope. "Come on. We're not far from shore. It won't take long."

I followed my gals, but I kept looking back. The boat was stopped in the water now, bobbing in the waves. *Please don't blow up.*

By the time I reached the rocky shore, the boat was still there. Still in one piece.

Hattie stood beside me as I faced the ocean and unbuckled my life jacket. "Nothing like worrying about someone you care about being blown up to make you forget your fear of the ocean, eh?"

I looked over at her. "Devlin was my choice," I said. "I was going to try with him."

She raised her brows. "And now?"

This kiss had complicated everything. I would never have been able to cross that line with Griselda in my mind enough to consider dating him, but now that he'd kissed me, and it hadn't been terrible? It was a lot to process. "I don't know."

Thelma walked over, still wearing her life jacket. "Don't let kisses in moments of extreme peril sway you. Wait until he's yelling at you again and trying to control you, and then see how you feel."

I looked over at her. "I hope he does."

She winked at me. "He's not going to die, Mia. It's not his time. He'll still annoy the hell out of you."

Blanche ran up to us. "A bomb? What is happening? This is insanity!" She looked thrilled though. "What next?"

"We look for Frank," I said. "Blanche, you and Thelma head toward the docks. We'll go the other way."

"Right! This is great!" Blanche tossed her life jacket and trotted down the beach. "Frank! Frank! Fraaankkk!"

Thelma didn't move. "I'm staying with you guys. If someone tries to kill us, I want to be with you all. You're much more likely to survive."

"What about Blanche?" Lucy asked.

"She'll be dead whether I'm with her or not. Why sacrifice both of us? That doesn't make any sense."

"A valid point," Hattie said.

Movement to my right caught my eye and I looked over to see a soggy Frank climbing out of the water down the beach away from the docks. Silently, I pointed.

Everyone turned to look at Frank. He was barely dragging himself out of the water, and then he collapsed on the rocks. "He doesn't look like a triathlete," Hattie said quietly.

"He made it to shore without a life jacket," I pointed out. "It's more than we did."

"What now?" Thelma said. "If he sees us coming, he'll have time to run."

"I'll get the truck," Hattie said. "We'll kidnap him."

We all looked over at her. "No," I said. "No kidnapping."

Hattie raised her brows. "Your mom's life and Thelma's freedom are at stake. Frank knows something. That's not worth kidnapping?"

"Then what? Are we going to torture him into answering our questions?" I asked.

Hattie brightened. "I've never tortured anyone," she said. "That sounds like it could be fun. Not actual harm, but maybe some psychological torment."

Thelma brightened. "Oh, yes. We could have fun with that." She did a hip thrust to the left. "A little bit of this."

Hattie thrust hers in the other direction. "A little bit of that."

"And a lot of this!" Thelma broke into a full-on belly dance, while Hattie burst out laughing. "No man could withstand that! We'll sex him to death!"

"Let's go get the truck! You two herd him up toward the road. Meet you in a few!" Hattie and Thelma took off down the shoreline back toward the main docks, which were surprisingly close. We'd been going so slow in the boat looking for Frank that we hadn't actually made it very far.

I looked at Lucy. "Do you want to see Thelma and Hattie sex a man to death?"

She grinned. "It might be even worse than the senior cop stripper we thought we were going to have to see."

I shrugged off my life jacket. "Frank looks like he passed out. Let's see how close we can get."

"Right on." We stashed Captain Jim's life jackets between some rocks so they wouldn't float away, then we casually began to walk along the rocky shore. Frank was mostly hidden behind a couple big boulders, but I could see the top of his head and his feet. He looked like he was stretched on his stomach, using the beach to recover from his swim.

"He must be really tired," I whispered. "Why is he just lying there?"

"Probably waiting for a ride," Lucy whispered back as she scooted over a rock. "He can't exactly walk along the street right now with Griselda looking for him. Plus, he's old now. Probably wasn't up for the challenge."

Griselda. I glanced out at the ocean. Captain Jim's boat was still floating in the distance, intact. "Not blown up yet," I whispered.

"He's not going to be blown up," Lucy said. "He's fine."

"Unless Frank has the trigger in his hand and he's waiting for the right moment." I started to walk faster, hurrying across the rocky shore. The boulders were big, and I had to leap across a few gaps.

Lucy kept up easily, and we were moving with rising urgency.

I couldn't stop thinking of all the movies where the bad guy had his little remote control with that red beeping light, ready to blow up some hot action hero. "The good guy never dies in the movies," I said.

"Never," she agreed.

"If I save Griselda, he'll owe me."

"That's a fun thought. Backrub?"

"Stanley's drug money. I'll buy out Jake's Yacht Club, and I'll own the boat traffic on the lake."

"Perfect. I love it." She held her finger to her mouth for silence as we neared Frank.

He hadn't moved, and I was a little less impressed with him. Did he really think we couldn't see him? His feet were completely visible up to his shins.

We slowed down, and I gestured for Lucy to circle around by his head, so we could trap him. "I wish I had my gun," Lucy grumbled.

"I wish I had my cat." King Tut was much better than a gun. No one could steal him and turn him against me. But I was catless and alone as I snuck toward Frank's feet.

My heart started racing as I neared him. This man had my mother's journal. He had a diamond necklace with her code on it. He had information on my mother, and I was going to get it from him, no matter what it took.

Heck, I'd even let Hattie and Thelma sex him to death if that was what it took.

Lucy crouched at the edge of the boulder by his head and looked back at me. She picked up a rock, showed it to me, and gestured for me to get one.

Oh, *crud*. I'd been so concerned about what Frank knew about my mom that I'd forgotten that he was, most likely, a murderer. Giorgio was victim number one, and my mom could be victim number two.

Frank was strong enough to take down a man who was young, muscular, and fit.

He might be tired from the swim, but if he could take down Giorgio, he could take down me.

I wished I had a corded projectile like my hairdryer, because that was my go-to weapon, but I hadn't thought ahead to potential murderous encounters.

So I grabbed a rock, hefted it, hoped I wouldn't have to use it, then I looked at Lucy.

I held up one finger.

Then two fingers.

Then three.

Then...go!

We both jumped around the rock. "Freeze!" I shouted, holding up my rock.

"Don't move!" Lucy leapt around, brandishing her rock much more aggressively and competently than I was.

Frank didn't move.

His face was smushed in the sand, and his hands were by his hips.

I frowned. "Is he unconscious?"

Lucy tapped his cheek with her toe, but he didn't move. "He must be. His face is literally in the sand."

"Frank?" I reached down to touch his shoulder, then I saw a pair of pink, plastic handles.

They were attached to metal blades.

And the blades of those scissors were in his back.

CHAPTER 15

"Oh...crap. Lucy." Disappointment flooded me. This was the guy who had my mom's journal. He was the one with the answers. He was the one who had been in Giorgio's room.

"I see them." She let her rock drop. "He got stabbed while swimming in the ocean? How is that even possible?"

"No!" I knelt next to him and shook his shoulder. "Frank! Frank! Can you hear me? Lucy, call an ambulance."

"On it."

While Lucy called 9-1-1, I shook Frank's shoulder again. "Frank!" I leaned in. "You can't be dead yet," I whispered to him. "We saw you crawling less than three minutes ago. Where's Tatum Murphy? How did you get her book? Did you kill her?"

He didn't move.

"Frank!" I patted his face, which was still warm and felt alive, not that awful feel of death. "Who stabbed you? Because they'll come back to finish it. Where's my mother?"

He didn't even twitch.

How could he be dead? There was only a little blood on his shirt, not enough to die from. "Frank!" I shook his shoulder again. "Where's Tatum Murphy?"

He still didn't move.

I felt like screaming in frustration. "Frank! Who stabbed you?" Who else was involved? It clearly wasn't just Frank, since he'd been stabbed in the back. Someone else was out there. "Frank. I have the diamond necklace. I'll give it back to you if you whisper one clue about Tatum Murphy. Just one."

If he were alive, the diamond necklace would get his attention. It was worth a lot of money, and criminals liked money.

But Frank didn't even blink.

I put my fingers on his neck and felt for a pulse.

Lucy crouched next to me, watching my face as I moved my fingers around. "Nothing?"

"There has to be something." I kept trying, but I couldn't find a pulse. "Come on, Frank!"

But there was no response.

Sirens echoed in the distance, but I knew they were going to be too late. I looked at Lucy desperately. "He's gone."

Lucy looked over her shoulder, then back at me. "Search him."

"Search him? He's a murder victim!"

"Who knows your mom."

I looked down at Frank. Could I? "Griselda will be on this. And so will the local cops."

I heard a car horn toot, and Hattie appeared on the bluff above us, on the edge of the road. "Where's Frank?"

"Down here," I yelled back. "He's been stabbed!"

"Stabbed! That's so rude! We're coming down. Come on, ladies!"

While Hattie, Thelma, and Blanche made their way down the rocks toward us, I reluctantly patted Frank's back pockets. His socks. His calves. Nothing to find.

"Sirens are close," Lucy said. "Hurry."

I couldn't believe I was doing this. *Mom, you owe me for this.* I shoved my hands under the front of his hip and felt in his front pockets. Both empty. Not even a wallet or a phone. I looked up at Lucy. "Nothing—"

As I said it, I realized that his left hand was balled in a fist. I looked at Lucy and nodded at his fist.

Lucy followed my glance. "Check it."

I did not want to pry open the cold, dead hand of a murderer. "You do it."

"Can't. I'm watching for the cops." As she said it, she hopped up on a high boulder and shielded her eyes, pretending to scan the road.

"I hate all of you sometimes," I muttered, as I crawled across the sand to Frank's hand. I checked his face again, even though I knew he wasn't home anymore, then I grabbed his fingers and pried them open.

In his hand was a scrap of paper. I pulled it out, then carefully unfolded it, doing my best not to tear the wet paper. I opened it, and Lucy leaned over my shoulder.

"It's a knitting pattern," she said. "Why does he have a knitting pattern?"

"Knitting again." I saw the letters TG at the top right. Thelma's initials. I silently pointed them out to Lucy, and we looked at each other. She grimaced, and gestured for me to fold up the paper as Hattie, Thelma, and Blanche came running up.

I turned away, quickly folding the paper. I tucked it in my sports bra, as the others burst out into surprised exclamations at the sight of Frank. I met Lucy's gaze and nodded.

Thelma's mouth suddenly dropped open. "Those are my scissors."

I looked over at the scissors sticking out of Frank's back. Somehow, I wasn't surprised, but...wow.

Hattie made a noise of exasperation. "You're kidding."

"No. They're my knitting scissors. Perfect for yarn. We all have them."

"If you all have them, then maybe they aren't yours," Hattie said.

Thelma pointed at the handle. "I stamped my initials in the handle. We all do that. Otherwise, we might get them mixed up."

I leaned in to look at the scissors. Sure enough, the initials TG were stamped into the plastic, easy to read. It was the same font that was on the knitting pattern. "How do you know that someone didn't stamp your initials into other scissors?"

She put her hands on her hips. "I don't know that, I guess. I keep my stamp in my knitting chest. My scissors, I take with me."

"Doesn't matter." Blanche put her arm around Thelma's shoulders. "You were with us the whole time. We'll vouch for you."

I LOOKED at my friends as the sirens neared. "She was with all of us the whole time. You have a ton of witnesses." But the cops would be very interested in why her scissors were in his back. Especially given the whole knitting needles and hot tub situation.

So was I, especially since I had her knitting pattern in my bra.

Flashing emergency lights lit up the rocks, and I stood up. I looked at Lucy, raising my brows. She glanced at me, then stepped in the sand by Frank's hand, covering my tracks. She looked at Hattie and pointed to the sand.

Hattie looked back and forth between us, then casually walked by Frank's hand as well, mixing up the sand so my footsteps around his hand were now confused with hers.

Should I show the cops the paper? Should I put it back?

I had no right to tamper with a crime scene.

I could get in so much trouble for taking that paper.

But if the cops got wind that my mom was involved, they wouldn't be looking for her to exonerate her or save her.

My mom was a known, wanted felon.

They'd be looking at her as a possible murderer.

I was the only one who'd want to save her. The only one who would care.

If I kept that paper hidden from the cops, I was making a promise to Giorgio, Frank, and my mom that I would follow that clue to the very end and use it to find out who killed Giorgio and Frank, and to make sure my mom was safe.

If I took that paper, there was no going back.

Car doors slammed, and I heard the shouts of the emergency personnel as they looked down the bluff at us. Hattie waved at them. "Down here," she yelled, then she turned to Thelma. "Don't worry about the scissors. Griselda saw Frank jump off the dock without scissors in his back, and you've been with us the whole time. You won't be on the hook for this one."

Thelma looked worried. "It's not good for me, Hattie. We know it's not."

Hattie shook her head. "We got your back, baby. It's going to be fine." As she said it, she shot a look at me and Lucy, and I knew she was worried.

She had a good reason to be worried.

I glanced at Lucy, then I knelt next to Frank. I took his fist in my hand and wrapped my hands around it, creating an obvious reason for my fingerprints to be on his hand.

I didn't put the paper back.

But I held his hand, so that the EMTs coming down the rocks saw me holding his hand.

I also held his hand because, well, he'd known my mom, and now he was dead.

CHAPTER 16

Frank was officially dead.

The EMTs tried to revive him, but I heard their muttered discussion, and they were quick to deduce that the scissors must have hit something vital, which is why it had gone south for Frank so quickly.

Apparently, stab wounds usually weren't deadly, at least that fast. You had to actually hit something important to die from them that efficiently and quickly.

Frank was unlucky…or his attacker was wonderfully skilled at the art of stabbing.

It did make me think back to Giorgio. Another skilled stabbing. I was guessing that a pair of knitting needles between the ribs could be a discussion piece for a while if it didn't hit something important.

Then again, who knew how long Giorgio had been there. I hadn't asked Thelma the last time she'd seen her hot tub empty.

Either way, I thankfully wasn't an expert on ways to die, but I knew enough to know that stabbing was a very intimate way to kill someone. You were up close, personal, and needed a lot of strength and commitment. You had to be okay with inflicting pain, unlike dropping an anvil from a great height. Then you could be like, "Oh, whoops, didn't see that coming."

Stabbing wasn't like that.

I wasn't sure I liked being around a stabber.

It felt like a very angry way to murder people.

The cops kept us there for quite a while, because we were the ones who'd found Frank, and Thelma's scissors were in his back.

It was our word against a local sheriff's bias as to whether Thelma really had an alibi.

Even when Griselda finally made it to shore, intact and alive (apparently, the black box wasn't a bomb, so yay for that), and said that he'd seen Frank dive into the water, and there hadn't been scissors in his back, Sheriff Wick hadn't ruled out the possibility that Thelma and her accomplices (aka us) hadn't lain in wait for him and stabbed him as he'd dragged his weary body onto shore.

Apparently, alibis didn't hold a lot of weight if everyone who would testify as to the alibi was also a suspect.

I didn't like being a suspect, especially given that my bra was holding a knitting pattern I'd pried out of Frank's cold, dead hand, and my pockets were hiding a diamond necklace and a ring with the Murphy family code on it, and an entire journal of Murphy family code that would implicate my mom in a whole bunch of thefts over a whole bunch of years.

Captain Jim had also been detained because Frank had been seen in his boat prior to being stabbed to death, so the five of us got to enjoy a very pretty Maine coast sunset while bonding with our besties, being interrogated by the cops, and having Captain Jim's boat searched.

Griselda had been in full work mode, so we hadn't even spoken. He'd given me a look, and I knew that kiss was going to come up the next time we had a chance to talk.

Which meant I was going to avoid him, because I didn't know what I wanted to say about it.

So, I sat with Thelma, Blanche, Hattie, Lucy, and Captain Jim on the rocks, watching the boats go in and out, enjoying the salt-air breeze, and waiting to be released from the site of Frank's demise.

A perfect evening for a girls weekend.

CHAPTER 17

B𝚈 𝚃𝙷𝙴 𝚃𝙸𝙼𝙴 H𝙰𝚃𝚃𝙸𝙴, Lucy, and I got back to our hotel room, it was late. We'd missed the dinner at the hotel, and we were too tired for the bar, so we'd grabbed takeout from Vera's Lobster Shack (Simone had left for the night so we didn't have to update her) and sat out on our seaside balcony to eat it.

Captain Jim had grumpily booked a hotel room on the beach because his boat had not yet been released.

Thelma and Blanche had gone home to shower and change into dry clothes, leaving the three of us alone for the first time.

"I think Thelma should stay here with us," Hattie said as she laid out the food. "If someone's trying to set her up, she needs an alibi."

"Our alibi didn't work earlier," Lucy pointed out as she dug into the batter-fried shrimp.

"It didn't work with Sheriff Wick," Hattie scoffed. "It would hold up in court. I'm a very upstanding citizen."

Lucy snorted. "Hattie, everyone in Bass Derby knows that you're pure trouble."

"Yes, but also upstanding," Hattie shot back. "I'm going to call her—"

"No," I said. "Don't. I need help."

147

Hattie and Lucy both looked over at me. "The kind of help that we can't give you with Thelma around?" Hattie asked.

"Yes." I dug into my pockets and I laid my stash out on the table, going over each item with them. The diamond necklace. The ring. The journal. The knitting pattern. "The necklace tag lists the same date as the ring," I said. "Someone, whether it was my mom, or Giorgio or Frank, or someone else, tagged those items as stolen last night."

"We checked," Hattie said. "There weren't any notable events at the resort last night, or even on the island."

"What does the tag say?" Lucy asked. "Her note to you?"

I shook my head. "I don't know. Either it's new code, or I don't remember what it is." I looked at them. "It's been a long time."

"And you've done your best to forget that life," Hattie said gently. "You'll remember. There's a lot of rust on those memories."

"I know." I took a breath. "What if my mom's in trouble, and we're sitting here eating?"

"We're eating because self-care is a critical part of life," Hattie said. "And we don't know where to go from here."

I pushed back my seat and walked to the balcony railing. I braced my hands on it and stared out across the ocean. "Mom," I whispered. "What are you here for?" She only worked big parties where she could blend in and be invisible. But there's been nothing here.

"I'm proud of you for stealing all this stuff, though," Hattie said. "Taking control like a badass. My baby girl is growing up."

I turned back to her. "It's on us now," I said, pointing to the knitting pattern. "We have to figure it out. I literally stole a clue because I freaked out about my mom."

Hattie fist-bumped her chest, right over her heart. "I know. Gets me right here. I'd steal from a dead man for you, too, Mia. And you, Lucy."

Lucy grinned. "I'd make Mia steal from a dead man for you, Hattie, but it's the same effect."

I turned toward them. "Do either of you knit? Can you tell if there is anything weird about the knitting pattern?" If we couldn't decode the tags, at least we could follow up on whatever was so important to Frank that he was clutching it even in death.

Hattie and Lucy both shrugged. "I don't know anything about knitting," Hattie said.

"What about the Seam Rippers?" The Seam Rippers were a group of sassy senior sewers for hire from Bass Derby. They liked to cause trouble, drink margaritas, and sell their skills to the highest bidder whose project inspired them.

Hattie frowned, then brightened. "Angelica knits," she said. "Let's Facetime her."

Angelica worked the front desk at the Bass Derby police station, and she'd made it clear she was on Team Hattie & Friends whenever she had to choose between us and the cops.

Hattie pulled out her phone and hit Facetime while Lucy and I squeezed in next to her.

Angelica answered right away. "Hey, ladies! How is your trip going?"

"Hi!" Hattie waved at Angelica. "I can see you're at work. Can you talk?"

"Sure." Angelica nodded. "I'm the only one here. What's up?"

Hattie flipped around the knitting pattern. "We found this in a dead guy's hand today. Is there anything weird about it?"

"A dead guy's hand?" Angelica lit up. "Are you guys involved in another murder?"

"Yep. My cousin Thelma is on the hook so we're helping her out."

"That's so fun. You guys always get involved in the coolest things."

"The first guy was stabbed with knitting needles," I said, leaning in so I could see her. "So there's knitting stuff going on here. None of us knit, so we were wondering if you could see anything significant about the pattern that might make it worth getting killed over."

"Holy cow. A deadly knitting pattern! I love this so much!" Angelica looked thrilled. "Hold it up."

I held up the soggy pattern so it took up the whole screen.

"I can't see it. Text it to me and I'll print it," Angelica said.

I took a picture and texted it.

"Got it. I'm going to run and get it from the printer in the back. The one at the front desk is on the fritz. Be right back." She waved at us, clearly delighted to be involved. "Don't go away, my pretties!"

While we waited for Angelica, I looked over at Lucy and Hattie. "We need to find out more about Nancy, who was with Frank at Vera's Lobster Shack."

"She wasn't in the truck when I saw him heading toward the docks."

"We assume she was with him when they were at Giorgio's room, but we didn't see her" Lucy looked over at me. "Maybe your mom took on Nancy as her adopted daughter after you abandoned her."

I stared at her, horror welling inside me. "She'd never do that."

Lucy's eyes widened. "Oh, God. I'm sorry. I didn't mean to say that. I'm sure she didn't. Did you text Beau pictures of Frank? I assume you took pictures of him, too?"

Crap. I had managed to get off a few shots of Frank before the cops had kicked us to the side. "I totally forgot to text Beau. He's going to kill me." I pulled out my phone to text him, then frowned when I realized he hadn't texted me back when I'd said my mom was in the area. Fear suddenly gripped me. "What if he died and no one is taking care of King Tut?"

"Beau is too rich to die," Hattie said. "He'll buy off the Grim Reaper for years to come."

"But I told him my mom might be here." Frowning, I texted him a few pictures of Frank. *Found another body today. This one has scissors in his back. Can you send me a picture of King Tut? I miss him.*

I waited but there were no three dots indicating he was responding. *Beau. Are you okay?*

Again, no response.

"I'm sure they're fine," Lucy said. "They're probably having a boys night."

I bit my lip. King Tut had chosen me to steal him from his prior home with an owner who wasn't a good person. When I'd purloined him, I'd promised to keep him safe. What if I'd lied? *Beau. Where are you?*

Again, no reply.

"While we're waiting for Angelica to get back to the phone, I want to talk about that kiss between you and Griselda," Hattie said.

I felt my cheeks heat up. "I don't."

"Well, we do." Lucy grinned at me. "It looked hot. Like super hot. He's a good kisser, isn't he?"

I couldn't help but grin. "Yeah, he is."

"*Nice.* If Griselda could manage a good kiss when he was about to possibly get blown up, then that bodes well for what he could do when he had time and privacy," Hattie said.

"I know," I groaned. "It sucks, though. I had convinced myself I was done with men, and then I liked that kiss, so now it's impossible for me to continue lying to myself that I don't want to ever date again."

Hattie patted my arm. "You never really believed that, sweetie. We're humans. We're meant for loving."

Lucy's eyes sparkled. "You know you have to kiss Devlin now, right? You need to compare."

"I'm not going to compare them! That's so mercenary."

"No, not like that." Lucy waved her hand to dismiss my comment. "I mean, to compare your reaction to the kiss. You weren't expecting to like Griselda's kiss, but you *were* expecting that you'd choose to kiss Devlin soon, so you need to kiss Devlin and see how you feel."

I put my head down on the table and groaned, while they laughed. "Can't we just find a murderer first? That's so much less complicated—"

"Devlin!" Angelica's shocked voice jerked our attention back to the phone.

To my horror, Devlin was sitting in Angelica's chair, leaning back, his arm folded across his chest. He was wearing a Bass Derby Police ball cap, and a Bass Derby softball tee shirt. He looked athletic, muscled, and interesting in a whole new way.

"How long have you been there?" I asked.

"A while." His gaze was hooded and intense. "I sat down and said hi, but none of you heard me. You all kept talking about assorted things, like the fact that you and Griselda kissed."

Um…

None of us said anything.

Devlin leaned in toward the camera. "Did you really kiss him?"

A part of me wanted to babble an explanation, like we both thought he might be blown to smithereens, but suddenly, I didn't want to have to explain myself. I had been tiptoeing around who I was my whole life, and I didn't want to do it anymore. "Yes."

He waited.

Hattie and Lucy looked at me.

But I didn't elaborate, and it actually felt really empowering.

"Yes" was a complete sentence, and I was owning that truth. A part of me wanted to feel guilty, because Devlin was a good guy and I didn't want to upset him, but he was a freaking ex black ops badass (or something like that) who had brought me a hot pretzel and agreed to save my life if the opportunity arose.

If he couldn't handle me now, then he couldn't handle me ever, and it was good to know that.

"Are you guys dating now?" he asked finally.

"Nope."

"Does he think you're dating?"

"Nope."

"All right." He grinned and sat back, his body suddenly much more relaxed. "When are you coming back to Bass Derby?"

"Day after tomorrow."

He nodded. "Can I take you for dinner that evening? We never had our date."

I had to bite my lip to keep from grinning. The men were literally pitting themselves against each other. I had to admit, it felt really nice. "I'm going to be swamped getting ready for my grand opening—" An elbow slammed into my ribs. "Oomph."

I looked at Hattie and Lucy. They both gave me meaningful looks.

"Mia."

I looked back at the screen. Devlin was leaning in again, his face looking unfairly sculpted and handsome. "What?"

"You're being a wimp." His voice held an element of challenge that irked me in just the right way.

I narrowed my eyes. "I'm not being a wimp."

"What do you think's going to happen? Either dinner will lead to something, or it won't. You know I'm a good guy. You don't need to worry about that. We'll eat food. We'll have fun. And then we'll see. No pressure. Just a chance for a free dinner."

"From a guy who wants to kiss me."

"I do want to, but I won't, unless you want me to."

I sighed. "Devlin—"

"I have one question for you."

"What?"

"Is there any part of you at all that might be interested in dating me? Because if there isn't, I'll drop this now."

I met his gaze. "You're a pain in the ass."

He waited.

None of my friends said anything.

Everyone waited for me to own my feelings, which I didn't appreciate at all.

Finally, I sighed. "It's a very small, very reluctant, very irritating part of me, but yes."

He grinned, and Lucy and Hattie high-fived over my head, out of view of the camera. "Then dinner? No pressure at all. Friends with possibility."

I'd been through so much in my life, so many things that had terrified me, but after my whole experience with Stanley, I'd reached a special level of fear when it came to dating. But Devlin was right. I did believe he was one of the good guys. I did believe I could trust him to be a good person.

He was a place to start to rebuild.

"I have panic attacks," I said.

He nodded. "Since I picked you up off the floor after one of them, yep, I know that."

"I used to be a criminal."

He smiled. "I know. And you still use those skills. I broke the law a few times, too, if you forgot."

I had forgotten. He'd mentioned he'd grown up in a gang. It wasn't the lifetime of focus on crime like my mom and I, but it wasn't a squeaky-clean childhood either. "And I'll never do what you tell me or ask of me, unless I was going to do it anyway. No matter what our relationship becomes, it would never mean that you got to control me."

His smile widened. "Yep. I realize that as well. I have news for you, Mia. I know who you are, I know what you're like, and *that's* why I want to take you for dinner."

I made a face while Hattie and Lucy grinned. Damn him. "That was a good speech." It was actually kind of great, but I wasn't about to admit that to him.

"Good enough for a dinner?"

I sighed. "I could take an hour. No more. I really do have a ton to do."

His eyes literally twinkled. "Does the hour include drive time?"

"Yes."

"Got it. I'll figure it out. I'll meet you at your marina at seven on Friday. And you don't even need to take time to shower. Come sweaty, covered in dust and grime. It's all good."

I finally smiled. "Okay."

He smiled back. "This time, dinner is going to happen, even if I have to hunt you down." He paused. "And just so you know, I'm extremely skilled at hunting down people."

Oh...that was sort of attractive the way he'd owned his badass. "Then where's my mom?" The question just popped out, and I grimaced.

Devlin paused for a second, obviously trying to switch gears. "Your mom?"

"Yeah. Where is she? I'm guessing Griselda keeps tabs on her." I had no idea if he did or not, but it felt like a good idea.

"I don't know." He frowned. "Why the sudden interest in your mom?"

I was so tempted to tell him, because maybe he could help, he was police. The police never had my mom's best interests at heart. I couldn't make myself trust a cop with secrets about my mother. "Because I love her."

He narrowed his eyes. I smiled at him.

"You're still going to lie to me even if we start dating."

"I never lie."

"You just lied twice in five seconds."

I smiled innocently at him.

He narrowed his eyes, then swore under his breath. "I gotta go." He paused. "See you Friday at seven." He shot me a look that was part long-suffering, and part hot-guy-smoldering, then he shoved his chair back, stood up, and disappeared from the frame.

Oh...dayum.

Lucy hit mute on the phone. "He's in it to win it," she said. "Did you see that look? He basically said you have a green light to be your best criminal self and that's not going to change anything."

"A cop and a criminal can never work."

"They work all the time," Hattie said. "And you're only a part-time criminal, so it barely counts."

"Stealing from murder scenes? I think that counts."

"As I said, part time."

"Hey!" Angelica interrupted us. "This isn't a knitting pattern."

Holy cow. I'd totally forgotten about the purpose of the call. This was why dating was a bad idea. I hit the button to unmute us. "What do you mean?"

She held it up. "Those aren't knitting instructions. Well, this is." She pointed to several rows. "But these?" She ran her finger along a bunch of numbers. "These aren't."

"This is fantastic." Hattie clapped her hands. "It's code. More code. Is it the Murphy code, Mia?"

Frowning I looked down at the original knitting pattern on the table. I hadn't looked that closely before, but as I did now... "No. That's not Murphy code. Lucy? Do they mean anything to you?"

Lucy peered at the section in question for a moment, then shook her head. "I have no idea."

"What are you guys looking at?" Devlin's voice interrupted again.

Angelica slapped her hand over the knitting pattern. "I thought you left."

"I forgot my phone." He appeared in the screen and leaned over Angelica's shoulder. "A knitting pattern? You guys knit?"

"I knit," Angelica said. "Go away. It's girl time. You've already interrupted more than enough."

Devlin grinned. "All right—" He started to leave, then peered more closely at the sheet of paper. "That's not a knitting pattern. Those are GPS coordinates." Suspicion flashed across his features. "What the hell are you guys up to?"

CHAPTER 18

"GPS COORDINATES?" I stared at Hattie and Lucy in shock. "Are you freaking kidding me?"

"Holy crap." Hattie grabbed the sheet and turned toward Lucy, who was already grabbing her phone out to type in the coordinates.

"What are they for?" Devlin asked, leveling a long look at me.

I pulled out my phone and texted Angelica. *We'll distract Devlin. Go shred that before he can get it.*

On the camera, Angelica looked at her phone, then gave me a thumbs up, and slipped out of the camera sight.

I smiled at Devlin. "Hattie and Lucy think I need to kiss you to compare you and Griselda. I feel like that's mercenary. What do you think?"

He stared at me for a long moment, suspicion etched on his face, then he looked around. "Son of a bitch. Angelica!" He disappeared off the screen, shouting her name.

"I hope she has a big enough head start," Lucy said.

"She'll eat that paper before she lets him see it," Hattie said confidently as she hung up the phone. "Angelica's a tough cookie."

I leaned over to look at Lucy's screen. "What did you find?"

"Give me a sec. I'm trying to sort it out."

Hattie leaned back in her seat and picked up a fried shrimp. "Looks like we're going to be heading out shortly. Gotta keep our strength up."

I was too antsy to eat, but Hattie had a point. I had just reached for a French fry when someone pounded at our door.

We all froze, looking at each other in alarm. "Thelma?" I whispered.

Hattie shook her head. "She has a key, remember?"

There was another pounding on the door. "Open the door, Mia!"

Recognition flooded me. "Beau?" I jumped up and ran for the door. I flung it open to find the world's crankiest and richest mystery writer standing in the doorway, holding my cat. "King Tut!"

The massive beast leapt out of his arms straight at my chest, claws bared. I shrieked and ducked, and King Tut shot past me and landed on the floor. He spun around to face me, his tail big, his teeth bared.

"Oh, dear God," Lucy whispered, backing up against the railing. "Your cat partnered with Satan. We're all going to die now, and you're going first."

I put my hands on my hips. "Don't be pouting," I said to my cat. "I thought you'd have more fun eating caviar with Beau than crashing a girls weekend."

"*Two* dead bodies?" Beau strode into the room, not bothering to wait for me to repair my relationship with my cat. "And *your mother?*" He flung the door shut and turned to face me. He was wearing crisp jeans, actual shoes, a golf shirt with a collar, and his hair was slicked back.

I stared at him in surprise. "Why don't you look homeless?"

"Because *your mother* is here. I'll have only one chance for a first impression. I'd have been here sooner, but I had to change my outfit six times." He held out his wrists to show that he was wearing not one but seven expensive watches. "I want her to know that she can pickpocket me anytime. She's like a dragon, attracted by sparkly things." He dug into his front pocket and pulled out a gold pocket watch. "It's not antique, but it cost almost fifty grand." He stuffed it back in his pocket. "It'll be a challenge for her. She loves challenges. How is she? Is she dating anyone? What's going on? Oh, crap! Is she here right now?" He spun around. "Tatum Murphy? Are you here? It's Beau Hammersley. I'm rich, I'm famous, and I've helped save your daughter's life on more than one occasion."

When no one answered, he pointed to the bedroom. "I bet she's hiding in there. I'll go say hi."

Before any of us could answer, he practically sprinted into the bedroom, rattling on about how he was a friend and how glad he was to finally meet her.

As Beau pulled open closet doors and looked under the bed, I exchanged glances with Hattie and Lucy, and then we suddenly all burst out laughing.

"I've never seen that man so animated," Hattie said. "Your mom must be pretty spectacular."

I grinned, watching Beau freak out in the bedroom. "She is," I agreed. "I'm not sure she'd be into a guy who was so into her, though."

"What?" Beau ran out. "She likes men who play it cool? Of course she would. She likes a challenge." He swore. "Why didn't you tell me that? Crap." He ran his hand through his hair and messed it up. "Does anyone have flipflops? I need to dress like I don't care. Wait! I brought luggage! It's in the hall!"

He sprinted out the door and reappeared within seconds dragging two large suitcases. "I got this." He dragged them straight into the bedroom then slammed the door shut.

"Wow." I put my hands on my hips. "That was incredible."

"The power of the Murphy women," Lucy said. "I think Griselda and Devlin are barely hanging on to their self-control. You should keep them away from Beau. The three of them might work themselves into a frenzy. It could get embarrassing for them."

I laughed, suddenly feeling much lighter. Beau's antics had shifted the dynamic of the night, and I had my cat back. I sat down on the floor opposite King Tut and patted my lap. "I missed you," I told him. "There are bad guys around, I wanted you to attack them."

He switched his tail, gave me a long look, and then strode out onto the deck, apparently deciding that being offered victims was not an adequate compensation for leaving him behind. He hopped up onto our table and began to eat the fried clams.

"King Tut is immune to your charms," Lucy said. "He's a monster."

"He's a treasure." I stood up and brushed off my butt. "Let's get those coordinates figured out."

"What coordinates? Is that where your mom is?" Beau flung the door open. He had thrown on his bloody dagger tee shirt, his bejeweled flipflops and he was wearing old jeans that had a hole in the knee and were frayed around the hem.

"Is that paint on your pants?"

"Yes. I decided to be an artist one summer. It was boring, even when I painted murder scenes." He put his hands on his hips. "Where's your mother, Mia? I'm here. I'm ready for her."

"We don't know."

"How is she?"

"I don't know that either. I haven't seen her."

Beau narrowed his eyes with sudden, very angry suspicion. "Is she even here? Was all that a lie to get me here to meet that boat captain?"

"No." I grabbed the journal and the pieces of jewelry and set them in his hands. "The code on those tags is the code that she and I made up. And that's her journal of stolen items. She never lets anyone near it. Even I didn't know where she kept it."

Beau took the items, holding them as if they were the most precious, most delicate blown glass ever made. "These are hers?"

He held them in the flat of his hands, gazing down at them in awe. "These belong to your mom?"

"I found the journal and the necklace in a bag on Captain Jim's boat. They were left there by the guy who was stabbed to death a few minutes later." I pointed at the ring. "Found that in the hotel room of the first victim."

Beau looked up sharply. "She might be in danger!"

"I know."

"We need to find her!"

I was suddenly very glad Beau was there. He was always very focused on following us around and loudly proclaiming he was there only as an observer and not as a participant. But he had money and expertise on murders, so to get him all-in might be super helpful. "I know. We found a list of GPS coordinates in the second victim's hand. Lucy and Hattie are looking them up now—"

"Maybe that's where Tatum is being held at gunpoint!" He ran across the room, leaned over Lucy's shoulder, and then squawked. "You're so slow!" He carefully set his treasures down, then pulled out his phone, grabbed the sheet of paper from her, and started typing.

We all looked at each other dubiously. Was Beau losing his sanity as we watched? The man's entire life was built on hating people, being cranky, refusing to deal with anyone. This was not the Beau I knew and loved.

"You're a GPS expert?" I was sort of afraid to interfere and take back the knitting pattern. Beau was a little bit of a man on fire right now, and I wasn't sure it was in a good way.

"I used GPS coordinates as a clue in *The Night of the Second Knife*." He hurried over to the table, sat down, and began scrawling notes on the back of the knitting pattern.

While he worked, there was another knock at the door. I tensed again, and we all froze.

"It's Captain Jim," a voice shouted.

"And Thelma! Mia, you never gave back my key!"

Oh…I hurried over and opened the door. "Come on, guys!"

Captain Jim stepped back and gestured to Thelma to go first, and I noticed a little bit of a twinkle in his eyes. Oh…a little romance building? I would be so happy for them. "I wanted to check on Thelma and she was on her way here so we—"

He stopped, mid-sentence, and his jaw dropped open.

I turned to see what he was looking at, and realized he'd caught sight of Beau.

I cleared my throat. "Beau? This is Captain Jim."

Beau didn't even acknowledge me.

"Beau!"

He still didn't look over. He was muttering to himself and scratching out notes on the back of the knitting pattern. Lucy was leaning over his shoulder, pointing to the screen, while Hattie hurried over to check on Thelma.

I relaxed slightly. This was the Beau I knew.

I turned back to Captain Jim. "He's in the middle of something. He gets very focused."

Captain Jim didn't answer. He just kept staring at Beau.

I waved my hand in front of his face, but he didn't react.

I put my hands on my hips, my gaze going back and forth between Captain Jim's stupor and Beau's frenetic energy. "Wow. I'm feeling very under-famous right now. No one has ever gone catatonic or crazy at the sight of me like Captain Jim has for Beau."

"It's not as fun as you would think," Hattie said. "Most of the time it's honestly a little creepy. I mean, yes, great for the ego, but it gets awkward. Do you smack them in the face to get them to pull it together? Or spray them with water? Or just walk away and leave them to work it out themselves?"

I raised my brows. "Does it happen to you often?"

"Sure. My cinnamon rolls are very famous, as you know. Plus, well, other stuff, too." She tucked her arm through Thelma's. "How are you doing? You want some food? The cat hasn't eaten all of it yet."

I watched Hattie walk away with Thelma. "What other stuff?" I called after her. "What else are you famous for?"

She winked at me, then ignored my question as she guided Thelma toward the food, asking her whether Sheriff Wick had tried to arrest her yet.

No one, including my cat, was paying any attention to me, so it gave me a moment to take a breath and look around. My little hotel room was filled with people I cared about, who cared about each other, even newbie Captain Jim.

For so long I'd had only my mom.

Then I'd had only my husband, his mom (who had hired an assassin to try to kill me), and my secret ally (who I called Bunny Pumpkin to hide his true identity) in the ranks of his drug lord empire (Griselda didn't count because he was my handler and a pain in my butt).

And now I had all these people: my cat, New Griselda, Devlin, and all the Seam Rippers back in Bass Derby. I had a posse of friends, all of whom would go to the mat for me, including helping me process a crime-scene-stolen item to find my mom.

And I would help them track down a murderer to keep them out of prison.

It felt good.

Some people wanted the kind of friend who would help you hide a body.

I had the kind of friends who would help friends hunt down killers to protect each other.

It wasn't what I would have scripted as my team goal, but now that I was in it, it felt amazing.

Hattie had always told me I had danger in my veins, and a need to live on the edge in my heart. I'd tried to convince myself that all I wanted was a quiet little life on a lake running a marina, but as I stood there, absorbing the energy of all the people in that hotel room, I knew this was exactly where I wanted to be.

These were my people. Each and every one of them.

I would never have predicted it, but I was owning it right here, right now.

Beau and Lucy looked up. "We figured it out," Beau said.

"It's in the haunted caves," Lucy said. "We need to go to the haunted caves."

Thelma looked up. "Tonight?"

I picked up a bottle of water from the table, walked over to the frozen-in-time Captain Jim, then flung the water in his face. He startled and stepped back. "What was that?"

"Can we get to the haunted caves now? Or is the tide too high?"

"What time is it?"

"It's almost one in the morning."

"That's—" He caught sight of Beau again, and stopped mid-sentence, staring at the mystery writer again.

I threw the rest of the water in his face. "Captain Jim! We need you! Get it together!"

I grabbed his shoulder and turned him so he was facing the door. "Just stare at the wood," I ordered him. "Don't turn around."

He leaned his forehead against the door. "Is that really Beau Hammersley?"

I put my face next to his. "Listen to me, Captain Jim. Two people have been murdered. One of them was killed right after leaving stuff in your boat. Why you? Why was that in your boat?"

"My boat? I haven't done anything." He looked surprised by my question.

I paused, suddenly realizing that I'd made a rookie mistake. I'd assumed Frank had left the bag there. But maybe it had already been there when he'd gotten on the boat. "Did *you* leave that bag in your boat? Was Frank trying to get it *back* from you?"

Beau looked over sharply at us, then he quickly grabbed the journal and tagged jewelry off the table. He shoved them into his front pockets, then narrowed his eyes at Captain Jim.

Hattie, Lucy, and Thelma went silent, watching me and Captain Jim.

I couldn't believe I'd been that stupid, assuming that Frank had put the bag in the boat. Just because he'd been in the boat and the bag had been in the boat didn't mean they'd arrived at the same time. "What did you do with the trunk, Captain Jim? You moved it, didn't you?"

Captain Jim turned to look at me. "I didn't take the trunk."

But his eye twitched when he said it, and he started coughing.

"Good gravy," Hattie said. "Even I can tell you're lying. You took the money? Are you an idiot? Everyone's looking for that trunk."

"I didn't take the trunk!"

We all waited.

Finally he sighed. "Okay, fine. I did go back for the money, but I didn't put the bag there. I went back after we all left the boat with a crowbar and popped it open. I just took a little bit from each bundle. No one will notice. The bag wasn't there when I went back."

I fisted my hands. "Did you know I was married to a drug lord? People like that know where every dollar is, and they make an example of anyone who messes with them. Right now, someone is looking for you, carrying a machete, or something worse."

"He has to leave," Beau said. "I refuse to be caught in the blood spatter when they come after him. Murder is fun only in books, and after it's over. I refuse to be present for one, even in the name of research."

"Blood spatter?" Captain Jim looked so alarmed by the words that he forgot to be star-struck by Beau. "*My* blood spatter?" He pulled out his wallet, removed a small stack of twenties, then ran to the balcony. "I don't want it. It's not mine!" He hurled it over the railing, and the wind ripped the money away.

He turned back and held up his hands. "I don't have it. I didn't take it. No one needs to kill me!"

Hattie rolled her eyes. "Oh for heaven's sake, Captain Jim, that's not going to save you! If you took it, they'll know, and they'll come after you."

Thelma gasped and stood up. "We can't let anyone kill Captain Jim!"

Aww...that was sweet. She definitely had a thing for him. That was awesome. She deserved to find love again.

"This man's death is not my problem," Beau said. "We need to find Tatum. Where are these haunted caves and how do we get there?"

"Haunted caves?" Captain Jim frowned. "We need to go the haunted caves?"

Wow. When he was star-struck-catatonic, he was star-struck catatonic. "Yes, we need to go there now. Is the tide low enough? It's a little after one in the morning," I said again, because I wasn't sure it had registered before.

"We can go now." Captain Jim nodded. "We have about three hours until the tide will be too high and we're stuck in there."

"Then let's go!" Beau ran toward the door, but none of us moved. He stopped. "What?"

"We don't have a boat," I said.

Beau frowned. "I chartered a helicopter to get us here. Will that help?"

Another helicopter? "Did you land here?"

"Of course. What was I going to do, jump out?"

"It's not allowed."

He snorted. "I'm rich. I can pay enough to get whatever I want."

I wanted to live that life. That sounded great.

Captain Jim shook his head. "You can only access the caves by water. There's no way to climb down from the rocks above, even if we were able to jump out of the helicopter and land on the rocks."

"We could jump out of the helicopter into the water, then swim in," Beau said. "I'll make a call."

"No." I didn't want to jump out of a helicopter into a pitch-black ocean and swim into a pitch-black cave full of ghosts of murder victims. "We'll boat in."

"I don't have a boat," Beau said. "We're flying in."

I looked at Captain Jim. "Do you know where they have your boat?"

He nodded. "They'll have a guard on it."

I grinned. "The guard's no problem. We have Hattie."

She bolted to her feet. "Bass Derby's most dangerous siren reporting for duty, Murph. I'm on it. Let's go."

"All right!" Beau bolted out the door.

Captain Jim's jaw dropped, then he ran out after Beau, shouting that he needed to show Beau where it was.

The men cleared out in a matter of seconds, leaving only me, Lucy, Hattie, Thelma, and King Tut in the hotel room.

We looked at each other. "Even if it was Frank who killed Giorgio, Frank's killer is still out there," I said.

Hattie shrugged. "We've handled killers before."

Thelma looked a little alarmed. "I haven't been to the caves since they found Roger's body."

I felt her reluctance. "You don't have to go," I said. "Hattie will stay with you—"

"I will not!" Hattie said. "Don't try that 'old ladies stay out of danger' crap with us. Thelma, it's time to face your past. Plus, I saw the chemistry with you and Captain Jim. It's time to start living or get busy dying! Let's go!" She grabbed Thelma's arm and nearly dragged her forcibly out into the hall.

Then it was just me and Lucy.

"Do you think Captain Jim is working with whoever owns that trunk?" Lucy asked.

I let out my breath. "No. I think he really just stole it and then panicked."

"What if he didn't? And we're going to strand ourselves on a boat with him?" she asked. "What if he's the murderer?"

I paused to consider that thought, to really think about it, but the answer was still the same as my initial gut reaction. "I don't think he's a killer. We know for sure he didn't kill Frank," I said. "He was with Griselda the whole time."

"He showed up after Frank was in the water. There was a window."

I stared at her. "It wasn't much time."

"It doesn't take long to stab someone."

Oh, wow. "We need him to get to the caves," I said.

"He could leave us all there to die. The tide will come up, we'll be trapped. No one will come there for days, until they find us all tied together, dead."

I blinked. "We have King Tut now. Captain Jim couldn't take us all on at once."

"He could split us up. Don't you watch television? You and I will go down one tunnel, and then we'll hear Thelma scream. We'll go look for her, and then as we're looking at her dying, gasping body we'll hear Hattie shriek and Beau start shouting desperate offers of bribery. We'll split up to find them, and then we'll be all alone in the dark caves and—"

"Shut up. Are you kidding with that? That's so unhelpful!" I strode past her into the bathroom and grabbed a hairdryer. "We'll go prepared." The hairdryer felt so good in my hand. I felt so much safer. I wrapped the cord around my hand and swung it, testing the weight.

"I want one." She ran into the second bathroom, grabbed that hairdryer, then draped it across her body like a sash.

I did the same with mine, and we both pulled on loose, zipper jackets that mostly covered the bulge. "Hattie will want one."

"There are only two bathrooms."

I looked around, but all the lamps were too big to hide in a jacket. "Any ideas?"

"I knew I should have brought my gun." Lucy put her hands on her hips. "We need a gun."

"We don't need a gun. Hattie can use the fire extinguisher on the boat. I'm sure she's good at that." I took a deep breath, trying to steady my nerves. "You think I should tell Griselda to meet us on the boat?"

Lucy looked surprised. "You don't think we can handle this?"

"I don't know," I said honestly.

"What about your mom?"

I bit my lip. "I know." I couldn't involve law enforcement if my mom was at stake. "Okay, then. Let's go do this." I looked over at my cat, who was still eating our takeout. I wanted to bring him, but I didn't have a life jacket. "I can't take him on the ocean without a life jacket."

"Beau would never have brought him on a helicopter over the ocean without one. He definitely brought it." Lucy ran into the bedroom, then came out a moment later with King Tut's life jacket. "He pretends to be a cranky jerk, but he has a good heart."

Relief rushed through me, so grateful for Beau. I headed toward King Tut. "You can be mad later. Right now, we need to go to the haunted caves." King Tut growled at me as I approached, his yellow eyes hostile.

I paused. "Captain Jim might try to kill us."

He continued to growl.

"I'll let you scare Lucy over in the caves."

He stopped growling, stood up, and strode over to me, while Lucy made a noise of pain. "I think I hate you more than I hate your cat."

"You love us both," I said as I strapped the harness and life jacket on King Tut. Then I hooked his leash on, and tucked him under my arm. "Let's go visit some haunted caves."

"In a boat with a murderer."

"Maybe a murderer. Maybe a drug runner. Maybe a genuinely nice guy."

We looked at each other, then we silently fist bumped and headed for the door.

CHAPTER 19

"I CAN'T BELIEVE Griselda's guarding the boat," I whispered.

We were all crouched behind another lobster boat two docks down, watching Griselda sitting in *Lady Cassandra*. His feet were up on the railing, his arms were folded across his chest, and he was systematically scanning his surroundings.

He was awake and alert.

"I would have thought he was too highly ranked to be on boat duty," Hattie whispered. "I don't think you can date him. He's too much of a lackey."

"I think he doesn't have any staff around, and he doesn't trust Sheriff Wick," I said.

"For good reason," Thelma whispered. "He's so old he can't even see past his glasses."

"We're going to have to take him out," Lucy said. "He'll never suspect a hairdryer."

"You have a hairdryer?" Hattie said, suddenly noticing what we were wearing. "I want one. Did you bring me one?"

"There were only two," Lucy said. "We figured you could use the fire extinguisher."

"A hairdryer?" Captain Jim asked. "What are you guys doing with hairdryers?"

I shot a look at Lucy, and she grimaced. We'd brought them for Captain Jim, not Griselda.

"I want one," Hattie said again.

I looked at Hattie and gave her a slight head shake.

She frowned, and looked back and forth between me and Lucy, clearly trying to figure out what we weren't saying.

"We're not taking Griselda out," I said, trying to redirect the conversation.

"Then what idea do you have?" Lucy said. She had her phone out and she was texting, I assumed Hattie.

Hattie's phone dinged, and she turned away, shielding her phone with her body as she pulled it out.

"Let me think for a sec," I said, trying to focus. I knew Griselda pretty well now. And he knew me. He was suspicious all the time, and I was trouble. We both knew he wouldn't trust me if I showed up at the boat, even if it were to announce I wanted to get naked with him.

Especially if it was to announce I wanted to get naked with him.

Hattie put her phone away and glanced at me. Her face was difficult to read, and I didn't know if she was on board with our suspicion about Captain Jim or not. I wasn't actually suspicious, but we did have to keep all of our options open.

"Why don't we just buy a boat and take that," Beau said.

I looked over at him. "Buy a boat? Where? It's the middle of the night."

"You don't think there's a few drunk idiots sleeping it off right now? I bet I could buy a boat off them for a few hundred bucks."

I suspected Beau had a lot more cash than that on him. I'd gotten my mom's journal and the jewelry back from him, so at least he didn't have that anymore. I was pretty sure he'd keep them forever and enshrine them if I let him.

"You can't take just any boat out there," Captain Jim said. "The waves are tricky. It needs to be a big enough boat, but not so big that you run into issues."

Beau finally looked at Captain Jim. "You speak?"

I grinned. Beau wasted no time with people he considered idiots.

Captain Jim cleared his throat. "Yeah, I do."

"It is useful?"

Captain Jim grinned. "You're an entitled ass. I love it. You deserve it. I've read all your books. I have them in eBook, audio, and print. Will you sign them? I have a couple on my boat right now."

Beau narrowed his eyes. "Every book?"

"Yeah. Every single one. I even have *The Bloody Sunrise.*"

Even stoic Beau couldn't hide his surprise. "That was my first book. It's out of print and sold about three copies."

"Yeah, I have two of them. I don't bring those on the water, though. They're antiques."

Beau narrowed his eyes, and I saw him assessing Captain Jim. "I don't know whether to be honored or run like hell from you."

Captain Jim's smile widened, and he laughed. "Right? Yeah. I get that."

Beau looked at me, and I knew he had noticed that Captain Jim hadn't answered the question.

I tapped Captain Jim on the shoulder. "Look at me."

He turned to me. "What's up?"

"Do you have any plans to harm Beau in any way? Including stalking him?"

His eyes widened. "Harm him? Of course not!"

I wasn't sure if I believed him. Maybe it was because I was worried he was a murderer. Or maybe it was because he was actually lying.

He spun back to Beau. "Was that what you were asking? Because no, I'm just a fan. I love to read. My dad was a mystery reader and he taught me to appreciate a good mystery. When he got old, I would read to him every evening for a couple hours. He died last year, and I haven't read a mystery since. Just can't do it. I miss the books, and I miss my dad. But meeting you..." He shrugged. "Lights me up again. Feels good."

Aww...that was incredibly sweet. He might be a murderer, but that was still sweet. I was a big supporter of the parent-child bond. "Did you hear that, Beau?" I asked.

"I did." He looked at me. "Do you believe him?"

Beau knew that my mom and I were experts in lying. I appreciated that. I nodded. "Yes, he's telling the truth." But as I said it, I met Beau's gaze and tried to tell him with my eyes that I wasn't entirely sure Captain Jim was safe.

Beau stared at me impassively for a moment, gave no indication that he'd received my subtext, then said. "I'm going to go find a boat."

Captain Jim hopped to his feet. "I'll go with you. I know what kind to get—"

"No." Beau pointed at him. "I don't like people. I'll go alone." He looked at me. "Where do you want me to pick you up?"

"At Captain Jim's boat. We'll still try to get Griselda off there. We'll see which way works."

"Got it." He paused. "Watch your back, Mia."

I looked at him. "You, too."

He nodded, bent down to pat King Tut's head in a show of affection that was rare from him, then turned and strode down the dock. He shoved his hands in his pockets and whistled a grizzly, spooky tune.

I saw Griselda sit up, pull out his binoculars, and focus on Beau.

"What's your plan?" Lucy whispered, touching my arm.

I rubbed my jaw, trying to think. I wanted to ditch Captain Jim and Thelma, but we needed Captain Jim to show us how to get into the caves. I didn't know how capable Captain Jim and Thelma were of assorted physical activities, which limited my options.

I was used to coming up with plans that involved me and a limited cast of people whose skills I knew. Four was a lot, especially when I didn't know two of them. Five if I included Beau, but he'd made it clear that he wasn't actually participating in anything.

And Griselda...he was a tough nut to crack.

"How are you going to get him off the boat?" Hattie asked.

"You could start yelling at him for the kiss," Lucy said.

"Or tell him you said you'd go on a date with Devlin Friday," Hattie said. "Get him jealous."

"No. I'm not using that." Griselda would be highly suspicious of anything I did, especially since he was guarding the boat that I would be interested in. Given how much I'd avoided anything personal and intimate, he'd never believe me that I wanted to talk about it.

"He's a hero," Hattie said. "Let him be one."

I looked over at her. "What do you mean?"

"Fall in the water. Let him save you."

Oh, God. "No." I had no idea how to handle him. The fact I'd kissed him changed the level of ruthlessness I could summon with him, which I didn't like at all. I needed to still be able to be myself with him, and that meant being willing to do whatever it took to save people like my mom, and to avenge the murder of petty thieves like Giorgio.

Hattie was watching me. "Don't be soft, Mia. You can't let a man make you less than you are. Don't do that again."

I met her gaze.

"Is that what's happening?" Lucy frowned at me. "Mia, do what you need to do. You have to be you, do you, love you."

Thelma put her hands on her hips. "Wait a sec. Are you thinking of having mercy on Griselda because he kissed you?"

I started laughing. "You call him Griselda, too?"

"Of course." Thelma wagged her finger at me. "I'll tell you what, Mia. I've been around a long time, and I know that the minute you make yourself less to try to fit into whatever mold the world or a person has for you, your soul starts to die. I lived it with Roger, and I'll never go back. Don't do it."

Captain Jim cleared his throat. "I know this is a woman power moment," he said, "but I want to chime in here."

Hattie raised her brows at him. "What?"

"I've got three daughters, and if you were my daughter, Mia, I'd tell you right now that if this Griselda fella is the right guy for you, the only thing that he'd want would be for you to handle this the way that's right for you. If you outsmart him, he'll respect you more. And if he doesn't, then find it out now and leave his ass in the ocean so he can swim home."

"Yes!" Thelma beamed at him. "Exactly. It's a great test, actually. Go kick his butt and see if he can handle it."

"Agreed," Hattie said. "Don't make yourself small. Make yourself bigger."

I grinned. "My mom would love you all. You're right."

Lucy clapped her hands. "That's my girl. Yay! This is going to be fun!" She raised her brows. "Do you see that look on Mia's face? She has an idea."

I did.

It was a good one too.

Griselda was going to kill me if it worked.

All the better.

H

CHAPTER 20

I QUICKLY EXPLAINED my plan to the team, and everyone immediately nodded.

"Love it," Thelma said. "I can do it."

"I'm in," Captain Jim said. "I want my boat back."

Hattie beamed at me. "I'm so proud of you, Mia. That's incredibly ruthless."

Lucy put her arm over my shoulder. "This is going to be great. Let's do it."

"All right." My heart was racing, in that exhilarating way that it always did right before I pulled a con. I couldn't deny that I loved the thrill of the game. Especially taking on a formidable opponent like Griselda.

Maybe Beau would come up with a boat if this didn't work, but maybe he wouldn't.

I was going to have to go forward as if this were our only chance. *Mom. I'm coming for you.*

I texted Beau. *Be loud.*

He was down the dock, still whistling. I saw him pull out his phone and looked at my text. He didn't reply, but he shoved his phone back into his pocket.

We all crouched on the dock, waiting for him to take action.

He passed a few more boats, then paused at a spiffy speed boat with a sleeper cabin. He studied it for a moment, then grabbed the railings and hopped on board. He banged on the roof. "Hey!" he bellowed raucously. "Is anyone here? Hello? Hello?"

"Oh, God," Lucy whispered. "He looks like a homeless drunk. He's going to get himself shot. Someone should go save him from himself."

"No one will shoot him," I said. "He leads a gifted life." I looked back at Griselda. He was standing up now, his binoculars focused on Beau. "Griselda doesn't have peripheral vision right now. Go!"

I tightened my grip on King Tut's leash, and then we broke into a hunched-over run down the dock, trying to stay low while moving fast. Lucy, Captain Jim, and Thelma headed toward shore, and Hattie and I ran right toward Griselda.

"Keep going," I whispered. "Let's see how close we can get before he notices."

"You got it."

We stayed low, moving quickly while Beau jumped on another boat and started hollering at them. "If he gets arrested, we have to leave without him," I said.

"He'll be crushed not to rescue your mom," Hattie said. "I don't know that he'll ever get over it."

"It'll be good for him." We were only a short distance from Griselda, who was still watching Beau through his binoculars. I wondered if he was thinking that rich celebrities were crazy. "Let's do this."

We both slowed to a walk, and I glanced toward shore. Lucy, Captain Jim, and Thelma were climbing into a rowboat that had been tied up near shore. I had a sudden fissure of fear for Lucy's safety. "You think she's okay with Captain Jim? In case he's the killer?"

"She has a hairdryer and the strength of a thousand men. Captain Jim is the one who isn't safe. Focus, Mia. Trust Lucy to do her thing."

Right. Focus. "You ready?"

Hattie grinned. "Ready."

"All right." I took a breath, tightened my grip on King Tut's leash. Then I intentionally tripped on absolutely nothing, let out a shriek of alarm, and did a perfect fake-faceplant onto the boards. "Crap!"

Hattie caught my arm. "Get up," she hissed in a stage whisper. "Keep it down."

"That freaking *hurt*." I stumbled to my feet and faked a limp. "I swear to God, I'm going to kill Thelma. How could she have left her knitting bag on Captain Jim's boat?"

"She was having sex with him. She wasn't thinking. Why are you so slow? You didn't fall that hard."

"I'm not slow. You're slow! I'm waiting for you. No wonder her knitting needles and scissors were stolen. She leaves her bag everywhere." King Tut stopped to sniff at the dock, dragging us both to a stop.

"Get your cat moving." Hattie turned her back on Griselda and put her hands on her hips. "We need to get Thelma's bag before the killer decides to help himself to something else in there."

King Tut ground his face into the dock, which was pretty perfect timing. I also turned my back on Griselda and pretended to focus on the cat. I bent over and tried to pull him away. "Whatever that is, it stinks. Come on, King Tut—"

"Good evening, ladies." Griselda's deep voice rolled over me with less irritation than I wanted.

We both spun around to face him. He was leaning on the railing of the boat, binoculars in hand, watching us suspiciously, with a hint of amusement.

That little bit of amusement immediately grated on me. He was *amused* by me? That felt very belittling. I wasn't amusing. I was a woman on a mission.

Some of my guilt at tricking him faded away, replaced by the irritation that I welcomed. I flashed a smile that was obviously fake. "Heeyyy," I said with an I'm-so-innocent singsong in my voice. "I figured you'd be here."

He raised his brows, not believing me at all, because he was smarter than that. And that's what I was playing into. "Did you?"

"Yes." I tugged on King Tut's leash. "I wanted to tell you first, so you didn't hear from Devlin."

Hattie coughed and turned her head, doing a terrible job hiding her amusement.

He narrowed his eyes suspiciously, definitely not believing me. "Tell me what?"

"I'm going to dinner with Devlin on Friday."

A muscle twitched in Griselda's cheek, and the suspicion on his face grew. "Are you?"

"Yep. He found out you and I kissed and that got him all in a tizzy, so he upped his game, made a great offer, and I agreed to give him an hour."

Griselda's jaw was flexed with irritation, but I could tell he still thought I was lying. "Did you?"

"Yes." I tugged at King Tut's leash. He was still trying to roll on the dock. I was guessing someone had cleaned a fish in that spot. He did like to roll in dead fish smell, as I well knew.

"Why are you out here, Mia?" Griselda asked, refusing to let his ego get drawn into a kissing war with Devlin. "It's the middle of the night."

"Is it?" I blinked innocently. "We were out having a drink at Vera's Lobster Shack. I didn't realize it was that late." I tugged again at King Tut's leash. This would only work if we got close enough for me to pickpocket Griselda. I needed his phone and the boat key.

An arrogant smile played at the corners of his mouth. "I'm not an idiot, Mia. I know you too well. You're—"

At that moment, King Tut let out a yowl that made me jump, and then he launched himself off the dock and into the ocean, jerking the leash out of my hand. "Hey!"

The life jacket kept him from sinking, but he immediately

started swimming right under the dock and out of sight. "King Tut!" I forgot all about our scam and dropped to my belly. I leaned over the dock and looked underneath, frantically searching for him. "Where is he?"

Hattie dropped beside me and held out her phone, shining her light under the dock. "There!" She pointed along the dock, toward the open water.

I located my cat quickly. He was swimming hard along the underside of the dock, heading straight toward the open ocean. "Crap! Keep watching him!" I scrambled to my feet and sprinted to the end of the dock, past Griselda, who was still standing protectively in Captain Jim's boat.

I dropped by my belly and leaned over the end of the dock. Hattie's light was shining toward me, obscuring my vision "I can't see him! Turn off your light!"

"He's still under the dock, heading right toward you!" Hattie turned off her flashlight, plunging the underside of the dock into darkness.

"I can't see him! Help!"

Footsteps raced along the dock, and then Hattie was beside me, leaning over. She shined her light, and I could see King Tut's eyes reflecting as he swam toward us. He was swimming hard, a cat on a mission. "Where is he going?" she asked.

"He likes to swim. Sometimes he does this at home. But that's a lake." I scooched forward, hanging further over the dock. "I'll grab him as he goes by."

"He'll duck if he doesn't want to get caught."

"Then help me!" My heart was racing. I was in pure panic mode right now. This was my baby, in the pitch-black ocean. We'd lost Frank during the day when he was a full-sized man, and he'd wound up dead.

This was a black cat at night, with a life jacket that wouldn't last forever.

His glowing eyes came closer. I kept my hands out of sight, not wanting to give him a reason to change course to avoid me.

"Hey, kitty," I crooned. "What are you hunting? A shark? Because maybe that's not the best choice."

He kept coming, swimming hard. His ears were flat against his head, and his eyes were narrowed, shielding his precious vision against the salt-water waves splashing him. He was fully committed, embracing his new water adventure, and I could tell he wasn't about to stop.

Hattie scooched further forward, so she was also hanging over the dock. "Hey little monster," she said. "Don't scare your mommy like that. We'll let you attack the mean FBI agent if you come out of the water now."

"Yes," I agreed. "Griselda's insufferable. We'll hold him down while you have your way with him."

King Tut kept coming. He was only a few feet away. I suddenly realized that I was too high off the ocean. I wouldn't be able to reach King Tut in the water. I needed to scoot further forward. "Grab my waistband, Hattie."

"I got you." Griselda spoke from right behind me, and then I felt him grip the waistband of my jeans.

I didn't have time to think about how personal that was.

I just launched myself toward the bright orange life jacket as King Tut swam past me. My fingers brushed the life jacket, then King Tut hissed and tried to dive under water. The life jacket kept him up, and I lunged again, my fingers locking around his leash.

King Tut hissed at me when I yanked him to a stop. He spun in circles, trying to outswim my grip on him. I was dangling off the dock up to my thighs, literally hanging over the water. Hattie would have lost me for sure, but Griselda's new workout regime was coming in handy.

I pulled the leash in, dragging the hissing cat closer to me. He bared his teeth at me as I reached for the life jacket.

"That is one pissed-off cat," Hattie said. "Be careful."

"I don't care if he claws me. I just want him safe." I yanked him in, then grabbed him around the waist with both hands, pulling him to my chest. He yowled in protest, his massive paws still trying to swim away from me. "Got him!" I shouted. "Pull me up."

"Raise your upper body yourself," Griselda ordered. "I don't want to rip your stomach open by dragging you across the boards."

"This cat weighs like thirty pounds!" But I did as he said, using back muscles I'd never asked anything of in my life to lift my upper body up and straighten myself out, while clutching an irate Maine Coon Cat to my chest.

Griselda locked an arm around my waist and dragged me back onto the dock. King Tut yowled and tried to squirm free, so there was a brief struggle while Griselda tried to keep me from falling in and I tried to keep the cat from using my arms as a springboard with his back claws.

Hattie threw something over me and the cat, dumping us into darkness. As soon as she did, King Tut stopped fighting, subsiding into low growls of intense displeasure. I didn't trust him for a second, but in that moment of respite, I realized that I was very tangled up with Griselda, and his front pocket was right by my hip.

And there was a bulge in it. My opportunity.

I immediately wrapped King Tut's leash around my wrist several times to lock it in, then I released him. He immediately sprang back into the water, Griselda swore, and I took advantage of the chaos to work my magic fingers. By the time King Tut splashed into the water, I had the boat key and Griselda's phone in my bra.

Jackpot.

A few more mad scrambles and twisted pretzel moments with Griselda, and finally, we were all back on the dock, panting, with custody of a very moody cat. Griselda had muscles, and he knew how to use them for the safety and protection of cats and thieves alike. He was handy and convenient, and all man. And definitely playing the hero role for my cat.

It was a little much. And also kind of perfect. Which made it a little much.

Griselda leaned back against the piling. "Hell," he said.

I grinned. It would be a lot more than one swear word in a few minutes. I cradled King Tut to my chest. "He's used to his nightly swims in the lake," I explained. "He doesn't know that the ocean is different."

"I think he knew exactly what he was doing," Griselda said. "He was hunting something. That laser focus wasn't a casual swim."

I frowned and looked out across the ocean. "He likes fish."

"Apparently."

I looked at Griselda, needing to be honest before I kept going. "Thanks for your help. I know he's just a cat, but he matters to me."

Griselda met my gaze, and something flickered in them. "You're welcome. I still want to know why you're out here, but I'm glad I was here to help."

I noticed Hattie had climbed into the boat, and I saw Griselda had noticed it as well. "Hattie," he said. "Get out of there."

"I didn't come out here to tell you about Devlin," I said. "But it's true. I said I'd go to dinner with him on Friday."

His gaze shot back to mine, and I knew he could hear the earnestness in my voice. "You and I aren't dating."

"I know. That's what I told Devlin." I paused. "It weirds me out to think of you as anything other than an annoying control freak who cares about me only because it helps his career."

He took a breath, his gaze shooting to Hattie, then back to me. I could tell he wanted to get Hattie off the boat, but this conversation mattered to him. Which made me feel a little guilty again. I tried to channel Captain Jim's advice and kept going. "I had sworn never to date again, but then you and Devlin both declared your interest literally within hours of each other."

He nodded. "Yeah. I should have made a move months ago. My bad."

His grumpiness made me smile. "I know you and Devlin are friends. I don't want to play games. But I will honestly say that I'm interested in both of you, but I have no idea what it would be like to date either of you. I don't even know if I want to date, but I find myself wanting to keep an open mind, which is a step I wasn't expecting to ever take."

Griselda regarded me, his gaze shooting briefly to Hattie when there was a splash.

"It's all good," she said. "I dropped a beer. It's fine."

"I need to deal with her," he said.

"I know. I just..." I paused. "I liked our kiss. That doesn't mean anything. We're not dating. But I liked it. And...I don't know. That's all I have for you right now."

He smiled. "It's something," he said softly. "More than I thought I'd get, honestly."

"I'm going to go to dinner with Devlin."

"Are you dating him?"

"No. Just going to dinner."

He nodded. "Then let's just see what happens. He and I are both going in knowing the situation. I think you're worth it, so I'll stick around."

I grinned. "You have to stick around. You're paid to keep me alive."

"I know. So is Devlin. It's not ideal, but we'll handle it." He cocked a brow. "I'm not going to blow up right now, but maybe a kiss?"

My heart started racing. A part of me was tempted, but there was no way I was going to distract him with a kiss. I wanted anything physical between us to not be made of lies. And I was about to mess with him in a major way.

Before I could answer, I heard Lucy's voice from the boat.

Griselda whipped around instantly, then shot to his feet. I scrambled up.

Lucy, Thelma, and Captain Jim were all climbing over the far side into the boat. Their pilfered rowboat was safely tied to a piling.

Griselda's eyes narrowed. "No. Just no. Everyone on the dock, now."

"We can't," Hattie said. "We have a mission."

While Hattie argued with Griselda, I inched over to him. I had to get him off balance and not paying attention. The only way to knock him in would be from behind, otherwise he could grab me as he went in. But right now, if I knocked him forward, he'd fall into the boat, which wasn't really the plan—

A gunshot rang through the night. Griselda whirled around, shoved me to the ground, and pulled out his gun.

"Run!" Beau shouted. "Run!"

I leapt to my feet as Beau sprinted down the dock toward us, arms flailing, his flipflops nowhere to be seen. "What happened?"

"I woke the wrong boat!" He bolted past me, put one hand on Captain Jim's railing, and then vaulted over the edge. "Let's go!"

Another shot rang out, and Griselda swore, moving down the dock toward the shots.

I didn't hesitate to take advantage of the distraction. "Let's go!" I tossed the boat key to Captain Jim, then I jumped into the boat, still clutching my cat, watching Griselda. Lucy leapt out and quickly untied the boat.

Griselda's hand went to his front pocket, and I knew he was going to try to call for back up. *Crap.*

Captain Jim started the boat, and Lucy finished untying.

Griselda looked back at us, and then the look on his face was pure astonishment. "Don't even think about it!" he shouted.

Guilt flashed through me for a second, but I gave him a cheerful wave. "We'll be back soon! Promise!"

Griselda sprinted toward us, moving with alarming speed.

"Go, go, go!" Hattie shouted. "He's coming!"

Captain Jim floored it, and the boat whipped backward. Griselda increased his speed, coming at a full sprint.

I clutched King Tut in alarm. "He's going to jump." I could see it on his face.

"Hurry," Hattie shouted.

Griselda reached the edge of the dock and he launched himself off it with the same commitment as King Tut had jumped into the ocean. Hattie and Thelma shrieked a warning as the FBI agent sailed through the air, like an attack phantom coming right at us.

King Tut yowled and hissed, and then Griselda slammed into the side of the boat, his stomach hitting the railing, and his upper body half in the boat.

"No! Get him out!" Hattie and Thelma whacked at him with life jackets, and I started laughing as he swore at them, trying to grab something to pull himself in.

"I need to video this," Beau said, pulling out his phone. "This is perfect for a book."

Griselda grabbed the back of a seat, but before Hattie could hit him again, King Tut launched himself out of my arms and attacked Griselda's hand with the kind of commitment that I had to admire.

Griselda howled and jerked his hand back, and he started to slide out of the boat. He caught the rail as he went over, so he was hanging on by his fingertips.

"Stop the boat!" I shouted.

Everyone protested, but Captain Jim did as I asked.

I walked over to the edge of the boat and peered over the edge at Griselda. His hand had claw marks on it, and the lower half of his body was dragging in the ocean.

He met my gaze, and then swore. "Don't you dare, Mia. I swear to God, I'll have all of you arrested."

I braced my hands on the railing and leaned over. "Griselda. My mother is involved somehow. I need to make sure she's safe."

He met my gaze. "Your mom?"

"Yeah," I said. "Is the FBI going to be on her side?"

"If she murdered someone, no."

"What if she didn't murder someone? But she's still who she is?"

He ground his jaw. "Mia."

I waited.

Finally, he took a breath. "Someone is killing people, and that trunk is missing. Whatever you're doing is dangerous. I don't want you doing it."

"I don't want to do it either. But my mom?"

He sighed. "I would try to protect her, but I can't promise."

I appreciated his honesty, but I wasn't surprised by it. I suspected he'd tell me the truth. He always had. "Then I have to leave you behind." I grabbed his fingers.

"No, don't, Mia!"

I pried his fingers off, and he slid off the boat into the ocean. "Mia!"

Hattie stood beside me and handed me a life jacket. "Here."

I tossed it to him. "You're only ten yards from the dock. You'll be fine."

He grabbed the life jacket and hoisted himself up on it as Captain Jim shifted back into gear and we began to move away from him slowly. "Tell me where you're going!" he yelled.

I wanted backup. I did. But my mom took priority. "I can't."

"Tell me now!"

"You'll be too close behind us." I raised my voice as we got further away. But then, Hattie nudged me and jerked her chin toward Captain Jim.

Did we really want to be out in the ocean with him, and no one knowing where we were?

Crap.

"The haunted caves," I shouted. "We're going to the haunted caves!"

"What?" He yelled back. "Where?"

"The haunted caves!" I shouted.

"What?"

But we were out of range now. "Circle back, Captain Jim," I said. "I want him to know where we're going."

"Nope. We're going to lose the tide soon. We gotta go now." Then he opened up the throttle, and the boat took off, chugging through the pitch-black ocean into more darkness. The only light was the spotlight from his boat.

I sat down next to Hattie and hugged King Tut to my chest. Thelma was standing with Captain Jim in animated discussion. Lucy sat down on Hattie's other side. "Text Devlin," she whispered. "Tell him where we're going."

I surreptitiously pulled out my phone, then grimaced when I saw the screen. "No cell service."

We looked at each other, then Hattie reached behind her and picked up the fire extinguisher. She tucked it in her jacket.

Beau walked over, grinning. "I must say that you are pure chaos. I don't know how you always make it work, but that was evidence that you have the universe at your command."

I really hoped I did. "Did you get shot?"

"Nope, but it's the first time I've ever been shot at. I can write that feeling with so much more authenticity now. It's brilliant." He walked over to the side of the boat and held his hands up in the air in a sign of victory. "Brilliant!" he shouted. "Brilliant!"

"That man is going to be absolutely crushed if he doesn't get to meet your mom," Hattie said.

"It'll be good for him," Lucy said. "Adversity breeds character."

My mom had always claimed that as well, but she also used to say that too much adversity could kill me, so to choose wisely.

I watched Captain Jim chatting cheerfully with Thelma, and I hoped that we weren't hitting that lethal limit.

CHAPTER 21

It was almost twenty minutes later by the time Captain Jim slowed the boat. "The Haunted Caves are up ahead," he said. "Tide's close and it's pretty windy. We won't have more than an hour in there before we have to leave."

I stood up and walked to the bow. Rising up out of the dark waters was a small, black mountain. Or a massive, black rock, depending on what you wanted to call it.

"Ships used to crash into it back in the day," Captain Jim said.

Hattie and Lucy came to stand beside me.

"That place looks creepy," Lucy whispered.

"Even I don't want to go in there," Hattie said. "And I'll go anywhere."

"This is fantastic!" Beau popped in beside us, his phone out and snapping pictures. "I have the setting for my next book. Absolutely freaking creepy as all heck. I'm thinking I'll call it Skeleton Rock, and the killer takes all his bodies here and hides them. He'll have all sorts of booby traps that look natural, but they're actually carefully orchestrated to kill anyone who tries to get to the cave where he keeps the bodies."

I looked over at him. "That's not helpful."

He snorted. "Do I look like my goal in life is to be helpful? I owe it to myself to use this adventure to my best advantage. This is a muse moment, Mia. Any writer knows you have to embrace them when they come."

Thelma came up behind us. "I haven't been here since Roger was found here," she said.

I looked over at her. "Did you come here often before he died?" I couldn't imagine why anyone would want to come here.

She paused for a split second longer than she should have before answering. "Sometimes."

She was hiding something. Son of a biscuit. What was she hiding?

I instinctively felt for the hairdryer, which was still draped across me under my jacket. It wasn't immediately accessible, but at least I had it.

Captain Jim slowed the boat still more, and his spotlight lit up the land mass in front of us. It looked like a solid rock, and he turned to the right, circling around it, the spotlight continuing to point at it. "Let me know if you see the cave opening," he said. "It's difficult to see at night."

"Is this a bad idea to come at night?" I asked.

"Not if you know how to boat at night."

"And you do?"

"Yep. But it's a bad idea to come at high tide."

"Which we're doing," I said.

"Almost," he agreed.

"There!" Thelma pointed.

I didn't see anything, but Captain Jim immediately turned his boat to the left and began driving straight at the island. "Got it," he said.

I looked at Hattie. "Do you see an entrance?"

She shook her head, silently watching the rock that we were driving straight into.

"This is incredible," Beau said. "I never would have thought of this. It's like a horror movie, where the earth opens up a portal at the last second to swallow us up."

I hit him in the shoulder. "You are not helping."

"Not trying to be helpful. Did you not understand that about me yet?"

Sarcasm from the mystery writer. Exactly what I needed right now.

"I see it!" Lucy exclaimed, pointing straight ahead. "It's a solid inky black on the side."

I looked for a solid, inky blackness, and to my surprise, I was able to make it out. The massive rock was shades of gray with shadows of varying sizes and angles, but there was a deep blackness at the bottom of it, right in front of us. "That doesn't look big enough for us to get through."

"It is for now." Captain Jim took us right toward it. The darkness seemed to swallow up the spotlight, like some horror novel.

And then, just when I felt like we were going to drive right into the rock, we drove through it, into absolute darkness.

For a moment, the spotlight seemed to shine into a black abyss, and I felt Lucy and Hattie move closer to me. We should have kidnapped Griselda and brought him along with us. I'd considered it, but then I'd decided it would have been impossible to immobilize him long enough to tie him up.

Now I wished I'd been more optimistic.

We were utterly alone out here. So isolated. Even if Captain Jim was on our side, we could still be in major trouble if we ran into a pack of murderers. Or even one, depending on how great they were at killing. "I think we should go back," I whispered. "This doesn't feel right."

"No, it doesn't," Lucy said.

"I hate to admit it, but I'm in agreement with you," Hattie said.

"Me, too," Thelma said. "It's eerily dark in here."

Beau cursed under his breath. "What about your mom?"

"My mom wouldn't come to a place like this, no matter what the treasure. She's not here." I turned around. "Captain Jim. Let's do this another time. Let's go home." I was going to delegate this to Griselda, even if it meant I had to confess I'd stolen the document out of Frank's hand.

The spotlight was facing forward, casting the rear of the boat into darkness. I couldn't see Captain Jim at all. For a split second, raw terror hit me. Had he left us? "Captain Jim?"

"You know, I agree with you," he said. "This isn't feeling right. I'm turning around."

Thank heavens. We all let out murmurs of relief, and I heard the clunk of the engine as Captain Jim put the boat in reverse. As he did it, the boat turned slightly to the right, and the spotlight hit the side of the cave, illuminating the wall.

"Wait!" I held up my hand. "What is that?"

I ran over to that side of the boat, scanning the side of the cave. There was a rocky beach, and then rocky steps that led to a rock shelf that was a solid ten or twenty feet above the water. On it, I could see folding chairs set in a circle. There were outdoor pillows on the chairs, and some fake flowing plants. There was even a table along the back wall with sealed storage bins that had bags of chips in them, and some wine glasses neatly arranged. It looked like round white bulbs were strung on the wall above the chairs. "You know what that looks like?"

"It looks like the Seam Rippers were here," Hattie said.

"Exactly what I was thinking." The Seam Rippers were the quilting gang in Bass Derby. They liked to drink margaritas and party. We'd rescued them from a lake in the middle of a storm at night, and they'd been hopped up on Christmas lights, margaritas, and girl bonding. "But there are no Seam Rippers around here."

"But there are knitters," Hattie said.

"I'm not afraid of knitters," Lucy said.

"Me either." I waved my hand. "Captain Jim, pull into the beach. We're getting off."

CHAPTER 22

KING TUT VAULTED off the bow of the boat the minute we were close enough to shore. He landed in the water with a splash, then tried to bolt up the beach, hitting the end of the leash with so much force he almost ripped my wrist off. His excitement to go to shore gave me confidence. He could see and smell so much that we couldn't, and if he wasn't scared, then that was a good sign.

"Let's go." I braced my hand on the side of the boat, then hopped off. My feet landed in the water, sinking up to my knees. The water was cold, but shallow, so I was good.

As I followed King Tut up the beach, the others jumped out after me.

"I'm going to stay in the boat," Captain Jim said. "I don't want to leave it unattended. Check your watches. I'm leaving at two-thirty. Whoever isn't back is going to have to wait out the high tide." He leaned over the edge and held out a bag. "There are headlamps and flashlights in there. And spray paint. The caves are pretty extensive. You want to mark your way back to the boat. It's easy to get turned around, especially in the dark."

Oh, wonderful. That sounded fun.

Beau took the bag, and immediately put a headlamp on and

pocketed a can of spray paint. "I'm hot pink," he said. "No one mess with my trail."

While everyone grabbed a light and a can, I looked back at Captain Jim. He'd tossed the anchor overboard and had turned off the motor. He looked like he was settling in for the stay. But was he? And why was he choosing to stay behind when he had a chance to hang out with his idol, Beau Hammersley?

I nudged Hattie. "Should one of us wait here to make sure he doesn't leave?"

"I'm not missing out," she said. "This feels like it will be fun."

"Me either," Lucy said.

"No way I'm staying behind. This is gold," Beau said.

"We won't drown if he leaves," Thelma said. "We'll just be stuck."

"And if he doesn't tell anyone that he left us?" Lucy said.

"Griselda knows we left with Captain Jim," I said. "He'll find us eventually."

"Plus, we have chips," Hattie said. "We'll be fine."

I looked back at him, indecision warring. I didn't have a good read on him at all.

Hattie leaned in. "On the plus side, if he's the killer, isn't it best if he leaves us here to be rescued by Griselda?"

"Unless he follows us into the cave and takes us out one by one," I whispered back.

Lucy grinned. "See? It was good I said that earlier. It keeps us on our toes."

I needed more information. But did I dare walk over there and challenge him while we were alone in a dark cave with him? No. That was stupid. If he was a serial killer, we were safest if he had no idea we were onto him.

And maybe he was fine. Maybe he was a good guy and I was distracting myself by looking in the wrong direction. If Captain Jim was innocent, then he needed to be on the alert too.

I walked back over to him. "Captain Jim."

"What's up?" He hung a light on his windshield and turned it on, casting the boat into a warm yellow glow.

"Two people have been killed. You have a way to defend yourself?"

He picked up an iPad then sat down on the captain's chair and put his feet up. "Been traveling these oceans for over sixty years, Mia. I have some tricks up my sleeve. Don't you worry about me. Go do your thing. I got my boat back, so I'm happy." He held up his iPad. "Going to read Beau's new book. You think he'll sign my iPad?"

"He definitely won't."

Captain Jim nodded. "He's a bit of an arrogant jerk. Not sure I'm going to keep admiring him. Depends on how good the book is."

I paused, surprised by the hurt in Captain Jim's voice. "Beau isn't an arrogant jerk. He's just antisocial and doesn't handle people well. He's actually an incredibly good man."

"Is he?" Captain Jim eyed me. "He was mean to me."

"He wasn't mean. He was simply being himself. I ignore his rudeness and just hang out with him anyway. I accept who he is, and I don't take offense."

"Really?" Captain Jim peered past me. "All right. I'll take the hint. I'm coming." He stood up and waved his iPad. "Beau! Let's team up! I'll video you so you don't have to write stuff down!"

Oh...wait...I hadn't meant for him to leave the boat and stalk Beau in the dark caves...

Too late. Captain Jim was already out of the boat, running after Beau, who was heading down a dark passageway. He sprinted up the shore, and then ran down the tunnel, still shouting for Beau.

"Dammit," I said. "If he kills Beau, I'll feel really bad."

"Well, if he doesn't kill Beau, then Beau will kill you for sending Captain Jim after him, so you need to enjoy the moment you have, because either way, you're going to be suffering in a very short time," Hattie said.

I raised my brows. "Thanks for that."

"Let's go," Hattie said. "We have an hour. Beau can handle

himself."

"Yeah. At least we know Captain Jim won't leave us behind," Lucy said. "Are his keys there?"

I looked down and saw that Captain Jim had left the keys in the ignition. I quietly took them and stuck them in my pocket. "Not anymore," I said. "Let's go."

W<small>E HEADED FIRST</small> for the arrangement of chairs that were on the landing.

King Tut went straight for the table with the snacks, and I shined my light around the gathering, while the others did the same. The chairs were arranged in a circle, and the remains of an old campfire were in the middle.

Lucy poked her toe at the skewers set on the rock nearby. "You think they made s'mores?"

Thelma held up a package of marshmallows. "Looks like it."

I frowned as I looked around the little clearing. If the Seam Rippers had set up shop here, there would be a nice outdoor carpet, some fun pillows with bright colors, and a generator to plug some blenders into.

Probably some art on the walls too.

It would, basically, look like a place where sassy seniors would want to hang out. It would have charm.

This place didn't.

I didn't want to be judgy, but would a bunch of senior knitters come out here to knit in a place like this?

I put my hands on my hips. "Thelma, did you ever come out here and knit?"

"Heck no. Who would want to knit here?" She held up graham crackers. "More s'mores evidence."

I looked over at Hattie, who was frowning. "What do you think?"

She sat down in one of the chairs. "It's not a comfortable chair.

If it were the knitters, it would be comfortable. Knitters sit around when they're knitting, and they're not going to set up a knitting hideaway and have it be barren and uncomfortable."

I looked over at Thelma, who was still looking through the snack table. "What do you think?"

"I never heard of the gals coming out here to knit," she said. "I think the dampness in the cave wouldn't be great for the yarn."

"So, who's been coming out here?"

Thelma held up a six-pack of cheap beer. "Teenagers?"

"Too neat," I said. "Teenagers would leave trash around." All the trash had been packed out. All that was left was unopened bags of food and drinks.

"Helicopter people, then," Lucy said.

We looked at each other. "I don't want to run into them," I said.

"Me either," Lucy said.

I knew we should leave, but something inside me told me not to leave yet. I'd come out here because of my mom. "Frank wasn't terrifying," I said. "He had this place on his map. So, why?"

Lucy pulled out her phone. "His coordinates were more specific than the haunted caves," she said. "I mapped out the island based on a satellite image. The actual location is on the northwest side of the island, and we came in on the south side."

"Oh." I was impressed. "Did you get a map of the island?"

"Yep." She showed me her phone screen. "I marked the way to the spot." She grinned. "Did you see I put an X on the spot? Because X marks the spot for pirate treasure, right?"

I raised my brows. "That's very clever."

"Right? And I even downloaded everything since I figured cell service would be spotty."

I grinned. Lucy was getting better at this whole spy thing. "You rock, girl. Lead the way."

"Yay! This way." Holding out her phone, Lucy started down a different tunnel than Beau had gone down.

I wondered why Beau had taken off like that. He didn't seem to be the impetuous type. I checked my phone to see if I had cell service, but I didn't, which wasn't a surprise. "You think some of us should go check on Beau?"

"He's got Captain Jim," Hattie said. "Captain Jim will fight to the death to save his idol."

"Or kill him. Everyone has seen the movie *Mercy,* right?"

Hattie put her hands on her hips. "You want to go after them? Because I want to see what's at the end of the rainbow, and we don't have much time."

I bit my lip, but finally nodded. "Hang on." I shook my can of spray paint, then sprayed a message on the rock. "Beau. We went this way." Then I painted an arrow toward our tunnel. "All right."

"Perfect. If the helicopter people show up, they'll know exactly how to find us," Lucy said.

I looked at her.

She grinned. "Just kidding. I like being a doomsayer. It brings out a great reaction in you."

"Let's do this." Hattie pulled the fire extinguisher out from her jacket. "Lead the way, Lucy."

Lucy saw the fire extinguisher in Hattie's hand, and she immediately pulled the hairdryer sash off, wrapped the cord around her hand and swung the hairdryer.

Relief rushed through me. I'd forgotten we had hairdryers, and King Tut. I immediately removed my own hairdryer, wrapped the cord around my hand a few times, then swung it in a circle, testing it. "Good."

Thelma stared at us. "You guys are armed with hairdryers?"

"Yep."

"I love that. It's fantastic."

"All right. Let's do this." Hattie started walking down the tunnel. "Let's find out what's at the end of dark tunnel number two. Hopefully another body."

"I'm hoping for a pot of gold," Lucy said.

Thelma said nothing, but she followed Hattie and Lucy. I watched her walk, wondering how it felt to be where Roger's body was found. Had she seen him there? Where had he been found? If this had anything to do with the resort, maybe his death was relevant? I wanted to ask, but at the same time, it felt weird to bring it up.

I let the three of them walk away without asking.

I looked down at King Tut. "You warn me if there's any danger."

He looked up at me, his yellow eyes glowing in the beam of my light.

"And don't attack my mom, if she's there."

He swished his tail, and said nothing.

"All right." I gripped his leash in my left hand, the hairdryer in my right, and then followed my friends down the tunnel.

―――――

I WAS WATCHING THE CLOCK, and it took us almost fifteen minutes of crisscrossing tunnels, mostly because not all the tunnels were on Lucy's map, and we wound up going over our own trail a couple times.

But finally, she paused. "Right here. This is the spot."

We all looked around. "We're in the middle of a tunnel," Thelma said. "There's nothing here."

I shined my light at the walls and the ceiling. It was rock on all sides. "There has to be something. He held onto that paper in death."

Everyone shined their lights around, and wandered down the tunnel a bit, looking for something.

I stood there with King Tut, who had sat down to clean his claws.

Frank had died for those coordinates. Giorgio, a petty thief, was dead. My mom's journal had been in Frank's possession.

There was no way that there was nothing here.

"Maybe someone already took it," Lucy said.

I went down on my knees and pressed my hand to the ground. It felt like cold rock. Solid. What the heck? I shined my light along the floor of the tunnel, looking for drag marks, or a dry spot, or anything that would suggest something had been there and then been removed.

It was on the third pass that I saw something glitter.

I passed my light back over and saw the source of it. Another ring. I silently picked it up. It was a diamond ring. He couldn't have wanted just that ring, right? There had to be more.

"What do you have?" Hattie asked.

I handed it to her, then shined my light in the crevice that the ring had been in. There was nothing else there.

"What did you find?" Lucy came over.

Hattie handed her the ring. "You think that's it?"

"It looks like a regular ring. Nothing special." I stood up, running my light over the ceiling. "It's a rock tunnel. There's no secret passageway here." I was so disappointed. We'd come all the way out here in the middle of the night, and found just a ring and an abandoned s'more's party? "There has to be more."

Hattie put her hands on her hips. "Channel your infamous mom. If she's involved, there's always a con going on, right?"

I looked over at her. "Well, yeah—"

"So, what's the con? You're always talking distract and redirect. What if this whole thing is a distraction? What if there's nothing there but that ring because everything is somewhere else?"

I stared at her. "What else is there?"

"I don't know. You're the Murphy woman. You figure it out. You've got two dead bodies, knitting needles, knitting pattern, your mom's journal, some tagged rings." Hattie put her hands on her hips. "What's going on that we don't see?"

"Don't forget the trunk of money and the helicopter people," Lucy added.

"And the knitters, that VIP Liaison Nancy, Atlas, Sylvia the resort owner," Hattie said.

"And Vera, Simone, and your mom," Lucy said again. "If your mom is involved, then there's something big going on. What would she be doing?"

"She's only involved if there's expensive items, a possible five-star vacation, and zero risk of actual danger." I shook my head. "This doesn't fit her at all."

"It's been ten years," Hattie said. "People change."

"Not her. Not in that way." I rubbed my hand over my jaw, trying to think. The jewelry was my mom's style. But nothing else was. I held out my hands in frustration. "I don't know."

Hattie sighed. "Maybe it's time to forget about your mom. We've been so focused on her that we completely forgot to look into Giorgio. What's he been up to? Why did our little man Nate think he was such a turd?" She looked around. "Thelma! We need more info on Giorgio."

There was no answer.

Alarm rushed through me. "Thelma!"

No answer.

Hattie cursed. "Thelma!"

We all shined our lights around, but there was no sign of her. Just the empty, dark tunnels. My heart started racing. "Thelma!"

"Captain Jim!" Hattie shouted, but her voice echoed back to us.

"Beau!" My turn to yell, but again, no answer.

We looked at each other in rising alarm. "We're sticking together," I said. "We need to find Thelma."

"She had to have gone that way," Lucy said, pointing in front of us. "We would have noticed her squeezing past us to go the way we came."

"Right, Let's go." Three abreast, we hurried down the tunnel, staying close to each other while she shouted for Thelma.

We made it only about thirty feet, and then ran into a dead end.

I spun around. "What the heck?" I agreed with Lucy. There was no way Thelma could have made it past us. The tunnel was narrow, and we'd all been looking around actively, searching for whatever it was Frank had been after.

But the tunnel was a dead end and there was nowhere she could have gone.

CHAPTER 23

WHILE HATTIE BACKTRACKED down the tunnel, calling for Thelma, I stood there with my hands on my hips. Thinking. Trying to channel the seventeen-year-old Mia who knew how to see things that weren't visible.

I shined my light around the dead end again. Rock on all sides. But Thelma had gone somewhere. "Where did she go?"

Lucy rapped her knuckles against the rock wall. "Maybe she's a ghost. Maybe she died when Roger died, and we've been snookered by a ghost all this time. Maybe she lured us here as a sacrifice to bring Roger back to life."

I grinned. "She's not a ghost." I turned around, scanning the cave walls. "What do I need to see here?"

Lucy raised her brows. "You think asking that's going to help?"

"Yep. My mom used to always say that you need to ask the questions that you want answers to, the questions that will serve you. Like, instead of freaking out that Thelma's missing, you ask a question that will get your brain focused on the answer." I'd forgotten about that trick of my mom's, but now that I was standing here in complete confusion, it had come back.

"Huh. Like, how do you choose between Griselda and Devlin?

Instead of just complaining about how two gorgeous law enforcement men want to date you?"

I rolled my eyes. "More like, what do I need to know to figure out how to move forward with them? Because I don't know that I want either of them, so that's not the answer I want."

"Ah…interesting." Lucy looked around. "What did Thelma notice that we didn't?"

"Yes, like that." I shined my light around the tunnel ending. "What doesn't fit in here?"

Lucky looked around. "The ring we found doesn't fit this setting."

"Yep. What else?" As I asked, I scanned the rocky walls. I could practically feel my brain trying to find an answer to my question. "What do I need to hear?"

"Hear?" Lucy asked.

I nodded. "When you ask the right question, your subconscious will lead you, and that question popped up." I closed my eyes. "Listen."

We both went quiet, and all I could hear was Hattie shouting for Thelma. "Hattie! Quiet for a sec!"

She stopped yelling and I heard her footsteps coming back toward us. "Hattie," I said. "Stop where you are and listen."

"For what?" she called out, her voice echoing through the tunnel.

"What we need to hear." I closed my eyes, focusing on listening, and Hattie and Lucy must have been doing the same thing, because they were quiet as well.

For a moment, I could hear only my breathing and Lucy's.

Then I became aware of another sound. A faint tapping that was a steady rhythm. I cocked my head, trying to pinpoint the direction of the tapping.

I began to move to my left, inching my feet across the floor, trying to be silent. As I moved, the sound became fainter. I stopped. Listened. Moved back to where I'd been.

It was so faint. *Where was it coming from?* I asked the question. Put it out there.

Instinct told me to drop to my knees, so I did. It became louder, but still faint. I pressed my ear to the floor of the cave, but it wasn't coming from there.

"What is Mia doing?" Hattie asked, startling me.

"Shh," Lucy said. "She's asking questions."

"What questions?" Hattie asked.

"Just be quiet for a second."

They became quiet again, and I focused on the tapping. I moved to my right, and it became louder. I moved a little further to my right, and it got even more audible. Not that it was loud, but it became more audible. I pressed my ear against the wall, and I could hear the tapping. I touched the wall and opened my eyes. "Here. On the other side."

Lucy shined the light on the wall. "It's solid rock."

"It can't be solid." I ran my fingers along the rock face, searching for a crevice or a crack that shouldn't be there. "Come on," I whispered. "Show it to me."

"The pirates," Hattie said. "The pirates must have put in a secret room, and someone found it. Come on, Mia!"

I sat back, surveying the wall. "If it is from the days of pirates, it would be mechanical. Nothing fancy. Just a..." I suddenly noticed a rock that was a little bit sunken, as if it had been carved out and then put back in. "There—"

Hattie lunged for it and pushed at it.

The rock immediately slid backwards about ten inches, silently, revealing an opening that led to darkness. "Wow," Lucy whispered. "You're amazing, Mia."

King Tut meowed. "Wait no—" I lunged for him, but he shot through the gap before I could grab him. "King Tut!"

But he was gone. *Crap.*

"You really need to put a leash on that cat," Lucy said.

I held up the chewed leash that was still in my hand. "He eats through them all." I jumped to my feet. "How much time do we have?"

"About thirty minutes until the tide gets too high," Lucy said. "It took us twenty minutes to get here, so we really only have ten minutes."

"Then let's go. There's no way I'm leaving him." I shined my light through the gap, peeking past the rock. "It's another tunnel. There are scrapes on the walls, making it look like someone built it." I turned sideways and slid through the gap. The rock scraped my back and my stomach, trapping me. For a split second, panic hit me, then I was through.

I shined the light around as Lucy squeezed in. It was indeed a tunnel, but there were fresh footprints in the sand. The tapping sound was loud now, echoing from down the hall.

"I think I hear Beau," Hattie shouted. "I'm going to go check on him!"

"No, Hattie!" But I could already hear her footsteps running down the tunnel. I looked at Lucy. "We can't lose her. Go after her."

"And leave you? No—"

"It's Hattie. You have to go with her."

Lucy stared at me. "All right, but I'll be back as soon as I can. Meet me here."

"No. Time is running out." I quickly pulled my sweatshirt over my head. "Leave this outside the rock. If I leave, I'll take it with me, and you'll know I headed back to the boat."

"Okay. Be safe." Lucy grabbed the sweatshirt and hurried back to the gap in the wall. As she squeezed through, I turned back and began to run down the tunnel.

I didn't take time to think about the fact I was alone and there was at least one murderer around. I just gripped my hairdryer, stayed focused on King Tut and Thelma, and ran toward the tapping sounds.

———

INSTINCT MADE me slow down as I reached the end of the tunnel, and the tapping sound became louder. I pressed back against the side of the tunnel, and I peered around the corner.

It was a large cavern that looked like it had been carved out of solid rock. There were several trunks in the room that looked like the one we'd found in the ocean. Thelma was kneeling over one of them, hitting the lock with a hammer.

I didn't see King Tut anywhere, but I hadn't passed him in the tunnel, so I knew he was ahead of me.

Thelma was muttering under her breath and hammering at the lock as if her life depended on it. She looked frantic, furtive, and determined. She had the vibe of a woman who knew exactly what was in that trunk and was determined to get it.

It wasn't the body language of a woman scared that a murderer was going to sneak up on her.

Thelma Gold did not look like an innocent victim right now.

Crap.

Did I go out there and accuse her? Or go out there acting worried for her safety?

I was alone with her. It would be idiotic to do anything but make her think we were on the same side. I took a breath, tightened my grip on my hairdryer, then backed up a few steps so I was out of sight. "Thelma!" I shouted. "King Tut! Can you hear me?" I jogged in place, making my footsteps heavy and loud. "Thelma! King Tut!"

There was a yelp from Thelma, then a loud thud, then footsteps.

What the heck? I sprinted forward, and then stopped when I saw Thelma sprawled on the floor, face down on the rocky floor. The trunk was open and empty. The hammer was gone. "Thelma!" I sprinted across the floor and knelt beside her.

Her face was ashen, and her eyes were closed. Suddenly, she looked old. Weary. Tired. I saw in the wrinkles in her face, the burden of a woman who had lost her husband and had fought to keep going. Guilt flooded me, guilt that I'd doubted her long enough to back out of that room and give whoever had been in there with her the chance to hurt her and leave.

"Dammit." I pulled her onto my lap and shined my light in the trunk. There were a few twenty-dollar bills in there, and a few smaller denominations, scattered carelessly. What had we stumbled into? A drug smuggling ring?

Sudden fear gripped me, an icy cold fear. I knew what the drug trade was like. I knew how expendable lives were. I knew how well-trained in death their people were.

Was Captain Jim smuggling on his boat?

Had Roger figured it out?

Or had Roger been involved and paid the price?

I looked down at Thelma, sprawled on the floor, and then I saw her eyelids twitch. Son of a biscuit. She was faking it. *She was faking it.*

I shot to my feet, my heart hammering. What the heck was going on?

"Mia?" Thelma's whisper drifted to me.

I looked down. "What?"

"Oh, God. It was you?" She sat up. "I thought I was dead."

I stared at her. "Did someone hit you?"

"No. I faked it." She scrambled to her feet, then looked down. "You got the trunk open?"

"No. You did."

"I didn't." She leaned in, then let out a very pirate-like profanity. "It's empty!"

There were still a few hundred dollars in there, so I was curious as to what was better than that. "What were you looking for?"

She spun around, searching the room, then ran to another trunk and tried to open it. "Locked! Where's the hammer?"

I stood there, watching her frantically try to open the trunk. She was like a woman possessed. "What is going on, Thelma?"

She sat back. "You can open this, can't you? Unlock it?"

"Probably." I made no move to do so. "What's going on?"

"Unlock it! We don't have much time."

I took a firmer grip of my hairdryer. "Thelma," I said softly. "What is going on?"

She stared at me, and I saw her realize that I had no intention of helping her until I got answers.

"Roger." She sat back on her heels. "He told me that he found money in the caves. He was going to go to the police. He was out here to meet the police on the night he died. But by the time the police showed up, he was dead. I never believed it was an accident. I've come out here so many times to try to find the cave he told me about, to find the trunks of money. I've found nothing, until I accidentally bumped into that rock today and it opened, and I knew I'd found it."

I stared at her, understanding dawning. "You think Roger was murdered?" She'd completely lied about coming out here after he'd died apparently, but I understood why. She'd been on a secret mission for a long time.

"He was in great health. I don't know what happened, but I know that he was trying to do something right, and it killed him." She held out her hands and gestured at the trunks. "What is all this? This is the room he described. If we figure out what it is, we'll know who killed him."

I still didn't move. "Did you kill Giorgio, Thelma?"

She lifted her chin. "Absolutely not. Why would I kill him?"

"Because he had something to do with Roger's death?" I knew the time was ticking fast. We would be stuck here soon, and I was becoming increasingly certain I didn't want to be stuck here. At all. But I couldn't leave without King Tut, and I couldn't look for him until I knew Thelma wasn't going to stab me in the back when I turned away.

"He did?" She looked stunned. "What did he do?"

I was great at reading people. I was fantastic at sorting out lies. And I knew that Thelma was holding out on me. But what wasn't she telling me? That she was a murderer? Or something else? "You tell me."

Thelma stared at me, and then understanding dawned. "You think *I* had something to do with Roger's death?"

I blinked. "I didn't say that."

"You implied it."

"I literally didn't. I implied you might have killed Giorgio, but I wasn't thinking about Roger."

"Oh." She cleared her throat. "Well, I didn't kill either one of them, but I want answers." She reached behind her and, to my shock, pulled out a gun, and pointed it at me. "Open the trunks, Mia. I don't have time to try to prove my innocence to you."

My heart immediately started hammering. Holy crap. "Why do you have a gun, Thelma?"

"Because my husband was murdered and when I find out who it is, they'll come after me." She flicked the muzzle of the gun at the trunk she was next to and stepped back. "Open it, now. I want answers."

Did she want answers, or did she want loads of cash? If I opened it and there was a bunch of cash, I might get a bullet in the back of the head while she took off with the money.

If I opened it, and it showed that someone murdered Roger, then justice would be served, a widow could move on her with her life, and I would be alive.

Thelma raised the gun. "Now, Mia."

Hattie had sworn by Thelma's innocence. Did I trust Hattie? I did trust Hattie. Did I trust her judgment? No. She was pure chaos and adrenaline.

But did I trust her heart?

Yes, I did. One of the reasons I loved Hattie was because she had the biggest heart in the world. She helped anyone who needed it and saw the best in people. She'd believed in me, and many people didn't. If she thought Thelma was a good person, then I had to trust her.

God, I hoped I wasn't wrong.

"Okay," I said. "I believe you. But if you didn't open that trunk, and I didn't, then someone else did."

Her mouth opened, then she unleashed another pirate-worthy curse. "Where'd they go?"

I took my gaze off her gun and looked around the little room. King Tut was nowhere in sight, but there was an opening in the rocks off to my left. "Keep an eye on that, my vigilante friend. I'll open the trunks."

Thelma nodded and hurried over to the other crack in the rocks. She shined her light through, then leaned on the rock, gun ready, watching down the hallway. "All clear."

"Okay." I hurried over to the first trunk, popped the lock, and opened the trunk. "Holy cow." It was full of antique trinkets. I wasn't an expert, but I have enough of an eye to know value when I saw them. They were all tossed in there, not packed neatly like I would have expected. Some pieces of jewelry, some candlesticks, and they all were tagged with my mom's codes. *Crud.*

I hurried to the next trunk and popped it open.

More of the same.

My mom only did jewelry, because she could slip it in a pocket. She'd never do candlesticks and larger items. "Mom," I whispered. "What's going on?" I lifted up a tag and looked at it. It wasn't my mom's writing. But it was our code. It was the same writing that was on the pieces I'd found in his room.

"Giorgio," I said. "Giorgio put these here. These are his."

Thelma looked over. "What is it?"

"Stolen items, I think."

She left her post and hurried over, searching through the trunks. "What is this? This is—" She paused and picked up a vase. "This is from the hotel. It's in Sylvia's office."

"Sylvia's office?" I thought of the resort manager that had replaced Roger. "It wouldn't be in this trunk if it wasn't expensive." Why would an expensive artifact be in the hotel manager's office?

I stood up. "We already know Giorgio stole from the hotel and people. What's the money for?"

"Illegal selling of goods?" Thelma looked through the trunk.

"The hotel hosts auctions twice a year for private sellers. They've been doing it since Roger was here."

Illegal auctions? Auctions of stolen goods? And this was the transition point? "Did he run the auctions?"

"No." Thelma looked at me. "Sylvia was head of events under Roger," she said. "She ran the auction even back then."

My gut sank. "Crap."

Thelma rose to her feet, anger flashing in her eyes. "Roger must have found out, and she killed him. That little wench! She killed both of them! And framed me because she knew I was getting close. Let's go!"

I caught her arm. "You can't go kill her."

"I'm not going to kill her. I'm just going to terrify her into admitting it."

"If she is guilty, then she killed at least two, maybe three, people already, that we know of." It did make me think back to the other members of the resort who had turned up dead in the caves. How long had this been going on? "She wouldn't hesitate to kill you to stay out of prison. You're not going to be that scary. You'll be dead."

Thelma stared at me, then lowered the gun. "So, what do we do?"

"Tell the cops. Tell Griselda. Tell other people who can manage it."

"We can't just leave this stuff here. She'll move it, and we'll never catch her." Thelma closed a trunk and sat down on it. "I'll wait here. You get the cops."

I had a sudden vision of Sylvia walking into the room, finding Thelma there, and deciding it was the perfect set up to stage Thelma as responsible for everything. "You can't stay here."

Thelma folded her arms over her chest. "My husband was murdered. I'm not leaving."

I checked the time on my phone. "Thelma, we have to go."

"No."

"What if Sylvia's here? Someone opened that trunk and took what was inside."

"I would love for her to come after me." Thelma raised her gun and pointed it at first one entrance, and then the other. "Send her in."

The tone of her voice sent prickles down my arm. How long had she been plotting her revenge for Roger's death? "Thelma," I said softly. "Killing her won't bring Roger back."

"I told you, I'm not going to kill her. But if she tries to kill me, I'll be ready."

I was suddenly so grateful my mother had been who she was. A con artist, yes, but never violent, never dangerous, never crossing those lines. I loved adventure, but I never, ever *wanted* someone to come after me with murderous intent so I could respond in self-defense.

So much anger in Thelma. I got it. I did. But at the same time... "Thelma, we need to leave. Now. If Sylvia is still here, she'll be trapped. All we need to do is get outside the caves. We can wait out there until the cops come. Roger wouldn't want you to die for him." I had no idea if that was true, but I was hoping. "He really wouldn't."

She glanced at me. "I owe him."

"You owe him making smart choices. Put the gun away, Thelma, and let's go."

She took a breath, then looked down at her gun. "I feel him here," she said softly. "Every time I come, I feel his presence."

I could feel her sadness. "Thelma, he wants you safe. Can't you feel that? More than anything?"

She closed her eyes and took a breath.

"Thelma?"

She opened her eyes and stood up. "He said you're right. He wants me to leave. He says we've done enough."

"Great! Let's go!" I pointed toward the exit we'd come in. "Go that way. Head back."

She raised her brows. "You're not coming?"

"I can't leave my cat."

"Your *cat*?"

"He's my Roger."

She looked at me. "You're much too young to be that much of a cat lady."

"No one's trying to kill *me*, Thelma. If I'm not back at the boat, make them leave without me so you guys can call the cops." I handed her the boat key that I'd swiped from Captain Jim. "Have Hattie call Devlin, and he'll get a message to Griselda."

I thought Thelma would argue with me, but now that she'd decided Roger wanted her to leave, she apparently was all-in on following his orders. "All right! Try not to get killed!" Then she turned and disappeared down the passageway we'd come from.

The moment her footsteps faded, I suddenly felt very alone.

The cavern was silent, pitch dark except for my light. I didn't even have the spray paint to find my way back.

But it was fine. My friends knew I was somewhere in the caves, and they'd come back for me if they had to leave. All I had to do was find my cat and play innocent if I ran across Sylvia.

I was a great actor. It would be fine.

CHAPTER 24

"KING TUT!" I strode toward the second passageway. "King Tut!"

He didn't reply, and frustration flashed through me. He was always very good about staying with me when we were out and about. It wasn't like him to take off. "King Tut!"

I headed down the tunnel, which was narrow and dark, of course.

And then I reached a dead end, which meant my cat had made it out of the tunnel before the door had been closed, because there had to be another hidden door.

So someone *had* been in the cave with Thelma.

This time, I knew what to look for, so it took me only a few minutes to find the release lever. But by the time I pushed it and the rock wall slid toward me, I knew that unless I'd inadvertently circled back around so I was close to the boat, I was going to miss my ride out of there.

I hoped they'd left.

And I also, selfishly, hoped they hadn't. I was independent and resourceful, but I didn't want to be stranded with whispers, ghosts, and a possible murderer.

I'd gotten used to tackling life with my friends, and I no longer wanted to do it alone.

I hurried down the tunnel, not even bothering to call for my cat. He had to be in front of me, and he clearly wasn't interested in coming. What had intrigued him?

The tunnel wound on longer that I would have expected, but there were no forks so I knew I was still following my cat. What the heck was he doing down here? The tunnel kept going down, and I had a bad feeling I was underneath the ocean now, which didn't make me happy at all.

What if there was a leak? Would I suffocate?

I wanted to turn around, but I couldn't leave my cat.

I didn't dare run, because if I fell and hit my head, I felt like no one would find me. I'd be another one of the ghosts that haunted Whispering Caves—

I suddenly heard a whisper.

I stopped dead, my heart racing.

Definitely the sound of whispering up ahead.

For a split second, I wanted to turn and run.

And then I remembered that I wasn't entirely convinced ghosts existed. Maybe it was time to find out.

I wrapped the cord of my hairdryer around my hand and turned off my flashlight, instantly trapping myself in absolute, impenetrable darkness. I'd been in darkness before, but this was surreal. I felt like the air had become a thick black sludge, pressing down around me.

In the darkness, the whispers felt louder, fluttering around my head and into my ears, like a faint, spooky breeze.

Oh, heavens. *Calm down, Mia.*

I made myself take a breath, then put my hand on the wall. Using the physical presence of the rock as my guide, I inched forward, checking for footing before each step, knowing that falling would be a bad idea on a bunch of levels right now.

I kept moving forward, and the whispers kept getting louder.

But at the same time, a faint glow of light began to penetrate the all-consuming darkness trying to suffocate me.

I pressed myself against the wall of the tunnel as I went

around a bend, not knowing what was coming. As I rounded the corner, the light became much brighter, and I knew that around the next bend was most likely my answer.

Ghosts? Sylvia? Someone else?

I inched oh-so-carefully to the final corner, and then peeked around the bend.

The first thing I saw was a boat. Not our boat. A different boat. In water that wasn't the same water we'd arrived in.

A second entrance!

Sylvia and Officer Harrison, the female officer, were loading supplies onto the boat. The cop. Crap. The cops were involved! That wasn't good.

The two women were whispering and working hard, so I leaned out slightly to look around. My gut dropped when I saw Captain Jim, Hattie, and Beau lined up along the edge of the water, tied and gagged. They were all sitting with their knees up and their hands tied behind their backs. Their backs were toward me, so they couldn't see me.

If anyone pushed them, they'd be in the water...with no way to swim.

Oh, dear heavens.

I didn't see Lucy anywhere. Or Thelma. Had they gone back to the boat on the other side, or wherever it was?

I felt something move against my ankle, and I froze, only years of training by my mom keeping me from screaming and running.

I forced myself to look down, and relief rushed through me when I saw King Tut looking up at me, with his unblinking yellow eyes. He'd come for Beau and Hattie. Of course he had. He pretended to be so tough, but he was as loyal as I was.

We both knew what it was like to be alone, unsafe, and scared, which meant we both knew how lucky we were to have people in our lives who loved us. I held out my arms, and he jumped up into them.

He didn't snuggle and purr, however. He just looked at me,

unblinking, and I knew he was telling me that we needed to save them.

"I know," I whispered. "Give me a sec." I scanned the area, trying to think. There were two of them, one of me, and all my friends were tied up. If I went after either Sylvia or Officer Harrison, then the other one could get me before I could accomplish anything.

I leaned back against the wall. All I had was my hairdryer. I could lure them back into the tunnel, but then I'd have to attack in cold blood.

I'd used my hairdryer in self-defense on more than one occasion, but to lure someone into a dark tunnel and smash them in the face with a hairdryer felt a little aggressive. I'd sent people to the hospital with my hairdryer before.

But then again, Sylvia had my friends tied up, and she was apparently a murderer. And her partner was a cop with a gun. Could I get in trouble for assaulting a cop? Yes, yes, I could.

Crap.

A hand came down on my shoulder, and I screamed, whirled around, and swung my hairdryer. Lucy yelped and ducked, but I got her in the shoulder. She grabbed my arm and then dragged me back down the tunnel as Sylvia shouted out a command to go search the tunnel.

We sprinted back down the tunnel, using our flashlights so we could go fast. We burst into the cavern with the jewelry, and we each slammed ourselves up against the wall next to the entrance and turned off our lights.

I could hear the footsteps coming, and a light bouncing. A cop was coming. How were we supposed to jump a cop? You can't jump cops! I had zero proof she'd done anything.

I leaned my head back against the wall and frantically tried to think. I had only seconds, milliseconds…

Officer Jane burst into the cavern, and I screamed.

She leapt sideways toward Lucy, and shined her light on me. "Mia!"

"I'm so glad you're here!" I raced over to her and grabbed her arm. "We lost everyone! I think the ghosts got them. I can hear whispers and I'm *freaking out!"*

Behind us, Lucy jumped out. "Help us!"

Officer Jane startled and jumped away from her, slamming right into me. I grabbed her around the waist and we both fell to the floor in a tangle of awkwardness. During the fall, I disarmed her, got her phone, and snagged the boat key. By the time we stopped rolling and were on our feet again, I'd stashed all her stuff in the back of my jeans, and then spun to face her, putting my back toward Lucy. "Did Hattie call you?" I asked, still grabbing her arm, while Lucy helpfully pulled the gun and the phone out of the back of my jeans.

"Get off me!"

"The whispers are down there!" I spun her away from Lucy, pointing down the tunnel. "Did you hear them?" I did a stage whisper. "We have to find Hattie and the others! The tide's coming, and they'll be stranded!"

Officer Jane looked at me, and I saw understanding dawn that I hadn't seen her with Sylvia or the others, which I was hoping meant we could live. "I'll look for them," she said. "Do you know the way back to your boat?"

"We do," I said. "I have the keys."

"Get on the boat and go back for help," she said. "I'll look around and see what I can find!"

"Okay." I whirled, as if to sprint toward the tunnel, and then I spun back to her. "Where's your boat?"

She stared at me for a long second. I wasn't impressed. Shouldn't she have had an answer prepared?

"Oh," I said, "you must have arrived after us."

"Right. We came after you."

"Who's 'we?'"

Behind her, Lucy removed the clip and tossed it aside.

Officer Jane blinked, then swore. "You *know.*" She grabbed for her gun, but it wasn't there, obviously.

She swore and looked down at her little holster thing, and then cursed again. "Give me my gun."

I held up my hands. "I don't touch guns." I really felt like we couldn't attack her, given the whole cop thing. She was scrawny and young, and I was pretty sure that she was Sylvia's little minion.

"What do you think is down this tunnel?" I asked, pointing toward the one that led to my friends.

"I don't know. Let's go find out." Lucy followed me down the tunnel.

We both listened behind us, but Officer Jane was searching the cavern for her gun, not following us.

I looked over at Lucy. "Let's *go.*"

She nodded, and we took off in a run for Hattie and the others.

"Any ideas?" Lucy asked as we ran.

"I'm winging it." King Tut was no longer in the opening, and we burst out of the tunnel. "Sylvia!" I shouted. "Officer Jane tried to kill us! Run!"

Sylvia whirled around, and I saw her reach behind her. For a gun? Screw that. She wasn't a cop. And she had my friends tied up. "No!" I shouted as I launched myself at her.

CHAPTER 25

Sylvia stepped to the side, and I shot past her, fell, and skidded off the ledge into the ocean. The water was icy cold, closing over my head with familiar horror.

I swam back to the surface, but as soon as I reached the surface, she shoved me back down under before I could take a breath.

Dear heavens. She was going to kill me right now!

"Get off her," Lucy shouted.

Sylvia's hand disappeared from the top of my head, and I burst out of the water, sucking in air as Lucy tackled her. But just as they hit the ground, Officer Jane came running out of the tunnel.

"Mia's in the water," Sylvia shouted. "Don't let her out."

Were they freaking kidding?

Officer Jane's gaze fixed on me, and she charged right at me. I lunged for shore, but she got there and stomped my fingers just as I grabbed the rocky shelf. "Hey!" I jerked my hands back, and then ducked as her foot came down on my head. *What the heck was wrong with these people?*

They were trying to kill me in front of a bunch of witnesses, which meant we were all going to wind up haunting these caves. *Not my friends.* I reached up, grabbed her foot, and yanked.

She shrieked and I twisted her leg again and yanked. She landed beside me with a splash, and I grabbed the edge again and tried to drag myself out. She came at me from behind, grabbed my hair, and yanked my head back. I lost my grip as she hauled me backwards. She was strong as heck, and a much better swimmer.

And she wanted to drown me.

Screw that. I'd had my almost-drowning for the day already.

I ducked down under water, fighting to get out of her head-lock, but she went under with me, gripping tightly. I fought harder, and then I heard a splash next to me.

Yellow unblinking eyes swam toward me, and I almost started laughing. *Never underestimate a girl and her cat!* I twisted around, dragging Officer Jane in a circle, so she swung toward my cat.

I don't know what he did, but suddenly she screamed and threw me aside.

I swam toward the surface, and when my head broke free, I saw her surface as well, my cat locked around her head, his claws digging into her scalp. He was like a sodden, black phantom sucking her soul right out of her head.

It was brilliant.

She screamed and swatted at him, trying to get him off, but he flattened his ears against his head, bared his teeth, and dug his claws in. I was pretty sure I could almost hear him laughing with pure glee.

Best cat ever.

"Good kitty!" I lunged for shore and this time, when I dragged myself out, no one tried to stop me. I got to the hard ground, and I saw Lucy had finally pinned Sylvia. Hattie, Captain Jim, and Beau were all frantically trying to get free. Hattie had rolled herself over to Lucy, and was leaning her elbow into Sylvia's hamstring, shouting unintelligible things through her gag.

I scrambled to my feet and spun around to the water. "Come on, King Tut!" I held out my arms. "Get out of there!"

He tensed, then launched himself off Officer Jane's head. She screamed as his claws dug in, and then he landed in the water. He swam efficiently toward me, and I crouched down and scooped him up as he pulled himself out of the ocean.

Officer Jane lunged for his tail as he got out, and he spun around, hissed, and slashed at her hand.

She jerked her hand back and cursed at him, blood running in rivulets down her face.

I couldn't attack a police officer, but my cat sure could.

I ran over to Hattie and pulled off her gag.

"Zip ties," she said. "We need scissors. Watch her!"

I spun around as Officer Jane scrambled out of the water. She stumbled several steps, and then went down on her knees, coughing and gagging. I ran over to her and swung my hairdryer. "Down on your face," I said. "Now."

She looked up at me. "You're going to jail for the attempted murder of a police officer—"

King Tut hissed and took a step toward her.

She glared at him, then lay down on the rock. "I win," she said. "My uncle's the chief. You all will lose. All of you."

King Tut let out a low growl, drawing her attention back to him. Shooting him looks of death, she put her head down.

He sat down in front of her and began cleaning his claws.

I grinned and patted his head. "Caviar for the rest of your life, kitty cat." I looked back at the group. Beau and Captain Jim were watching me, and they both looked somewhat horrified and shocked.

Satisfied that King Tut had Officer Jane under more control than I ever could, I hurried over to remove their gags.

"Holy mother of murders," Beau said as soon as I got the gag down, "that was bloody magnificent. I'm definitely murdering someone that way as soon as I get home. Your desperation was so visceral I could almost feel myself choking on that ocean water.

Did it get in your lungs? Are you traumatized for life? What if you fell in now? Would you freak out? Jump in. I want to see."

I eyed him. "You're very alarming."

"Did anyone video that?" He looked around. "Did anyone get that?"

"I'm fine, thanks."

"Of course you're fine. You're standing here. I might have to invent a cat assassin. Your cat is brilliant."

I grinned. "Yep." I walked over and pulled down Captain Jim's gag.

His face was stunned. "She tried to drown you. She almost succeeded."

Ah…yes…the sympathy I needed. "I know, right?"

"You need to become a stronger swimmer. She's a scrawny thing. There's no way she should have been able to take you down like that."

I sighed. People in Maine were much too tough. "No sympathy anywhere?"

Lucy looked over. She was sitting on Sylvia, her knees pinning the resort manager's hands to the ground. "I'll be honest, Mia. I know what your water skills are like, and I thought you were going to die before I could get over there to help. Don't ever come that close to dying in front of me again. I can't handle it."

My throat tightened at her earnestness. "Thanks."

"No, I'm serious. Don't ever do that again. Swear to it."

"She can't swear to that," Hattie said. "She attracts these experiences, the same way we do. It's part of the fun. Not dead yet, right?" Hattie was sitting on Sylvia's feet. "I need scissors. This wench zip tied us. Find the zip ties and lock up these beauties. I think they're in the boat."

I checked King Tut. He was now licking his butt right in front of Officer Jane. His tail was twitching, smacking her in the nose with each move. She tried to move her face away from him, and he let out a low growl, staring her down, his face inches from hers.

She closed her eyes. "I hate cats. I really, really hate them."

I didn't. I loved them. "Good kitty."

He didn't look at me. He just kept staring at her, as if daring her to move, begging for her to give him an excuse.

Did I have a sadistic cat? Maybe. And I was okay with that.

I found the pile of zip ties that Sylvia had tossed aside, and I handed them to Lucy to tie up Sylvia. Weirdly enough, Sylvia had a knitting basket on the boat, so I grabbed those scissors and cut Hattie free, who then went on to cut the others free.

I sat down in front of Sylvia. We had a situation, but we still had no facts.

"You killed Roger, Giorgio, and Frank to keep your auction going," I said conversationally.

Her eyes widened. "No! I didn't kill anyone. I'm an auctioneer, not a murderer."

"A criminal is a criminal," Hattie said, but I knew that wasn't true.

There were types of criminals, and violence didn't always follow. "You were going to kill my friends."

"I wasn't," Sylvia snapped.

"You tried to drown me." I had her on that one.

Her eyes widened? "What? You were trying to drown me! I was trying to stay alive!"

What? Was she insane? No one would believe that. I leaned in. "Murder, Sylvia. Both you and Officer Jane tried to murder me. She literally stomped my fingers. Regardless of what happened with the others, you tried to kill me and there are a bunch of witnesses."

"Jane is a lunatic. I don't know what she did, but I wasn't trying to hurt you! I was trying to save myself from you and your murderous friends!"

"What? My murderous friends? You attacked me when I was in the ocean and stood on my head."

"Your friends are lying to protect you," she said. "Officer Jane saw the whole thing and attacked you to try to save me, and you dragged her in and tried to kill her."

I looked at Lucy, and she grimaced.

Sylvia wasn't entirely wrong.

"We followed you out here and found all these stolen items," Sylvia continued. "We subdued Hattie, Beau, and Captain Jim, and then started to load them up to take them back to their rightful owners, and then you all attacked us."

"Impressive," Beau said. "She's good. You guys have any actual evidence against them, Mia?"

"I wouldn't lie to protect these out-of-towners," Captain Jim said. "I just met them."

Sylvia looked at him. "We cut your lobster contract six months ago. You're pissed, broke, and wanted revenge. Anyone would get that. Your business is trash because we were your only client."

I looked over at Captain Jim. "Really?"

"I don't need them," he said.

"But they fired you?"

His jaw went out. "I don't need them."

But he had motive to try to bring them down. "We didn't take any of this stuff. We aren't even from the area," I said. "No one would believe that we did anything."

Sylvia scoffed. "Hattie is Thelma's cousin, and she comes out to Harmony Island every year for the week following the summer auction. Thelma is the one who is running this whole ring, and she brought you guys in to help unload all the stuff from the latest auction. Captain Jim has been transporting for her for years. She's been running her own illegal auction right under our noses this whole time, and we caught her."

I looked at Captain Jim, and thought of the twenty-dollar bills he'd been carrying.

Oh, no. I could see how everything Sylvia said could be true, with the exception of me, Hattie, and Lucy helping. But...then, suddenly, I recalled that Hattie's house and boat were much nicer than what she could possibly be earning from her café.

No, no, *no*. I believed in Hattie. She was my friend.

But…

"Where's Thelma?" Hattie asked suddenly. "Did anyone find her?"

"I did." I explained what happened, keeping my voice low enough that Sylvia and Officer Jane couldn't hear. "I sent her back to our boat," I said. "She must be waiting for us there."

Hattie stood up. "I'll go find her."

Sylvia looked at me. "See? Hattie's going to go find her, and they're going to disappear."

"Everyone's under arrest," Officer Jane shouted. "Put your hands up and lie face down on the rock."

No one listened to her, mostly because she was still lying face down on her own rock, trying not to make eye contact with my cat.

"We need to find evidence," I said. "We have how long until the tide shifts and help can get here?"

"About four hours," Captain Jim said.

"All right." I took a breath. "Beau and Captain Jim, you guys search the boat. See if you can find anything."

"Nope." Beau sat down and leaned against a rock. "That could be evidence in there. If you touch it, then you could have planted it. And I don't get involved. I just observe." He pulled out his phone and started recording. "Continue your discussion. Don't mind me."

I put my hands on my hips. "Beau. Sylvia literally said you were to blame."

"I'm not. I have enough money to defend myself to whatever level I need. I'm not worried."

Hattie put her hands on her hips. "I'm not worried either. We haven't done anything."

Unfortunately, I knew all too well that innocence did not guarantee anything. "You guys, we need to address this. Seriously."

"Mia, if your mom is really involved, then *you* could be in real trouble," Lucy said.

"Your mom?" Sylvia perked up. "Who's your mom?"

"Oh, right." Beau leapt to his feet. "I can't believe I forgot about Tatum. Where is she? Is she around here? Sylvia, where's Tatum Murphy? Did you kill her? Did she kill Giorgio?"

"Tatum Murphy?" Sylvia echoed with a frown.

"She's your *mom?*" Officer Jane started laughing. "This is priceless. *Priceless.*"

My stomach twisted, and I ran over to Officer Jane. "You've seen her?"

Officer Jane raised her brows. "I saw her with Giorgio a few times. She looks like she's your sister, not your mom."

"She had me young." I suddenly found it difficult to breathe. My mom had really been here? Working with Giorgio? *Mom. What did you do?* "When was the last time you saw her?"

"She was here this weekend," Officer Jane said. "Working the auction. I was paid security, and she was there."

My mom would be at an event with a lot of celebrities. That was exactly where she'd be. "Where is she now?"

"Haven't seen her since Sunday," Officer Jane said. "But then you showed up. God, this is good."

Lucy pulled me aside. "You could be in trouble," she said under her breath.

Hattie hurried over. "It sounds like Officer Jane believes Sylvia's story," she whispered. "If the two of them really did show up here and find everything, then they will fight to make us pay."

I looked at them. "And if they did kill Giorgio, Frank, and Roger, or any of them, they'll also fight to make us take the blame." I thought of the ring with my mom's tag in my pocket. Her journal that I'd taken. If they found them on me, I'd be connected.

Heck, I was here. I was my mom's daughter. I was connected.

Lucy, Hattie, and I looked at each other. "We have four hours to figure out what's going on. Griselda will be waiting when the tide goes down. You know he will. He believes in me, but there's only so much he can do."

"What should we do?" Lucy asked. "Search their boat?"

"Find Thelma," Hattie said firmly. "She's been around this resort for decades. She must know more than she's telling us."

My gut twisted tighter. "Why would she lie?"

"I don't know."

I caught Hattie's arm. "Are you questioning her innocence?" I asked.

"I don't know. Something's not right about that story you told about her in that room with the trunks. She'll be honest with me. I'm going to go find her."

I looked at Lucy and she shook her head. No way were we letting her face Thelma alone. "Captain Jim? Beau? Can you guys watch these two?"

"No." Beau was still filming. "I'm going with you guys. We need to find your mom."

"I got it." Captain Jim waved us off. "No one's going anywhere."

His voice was low and hard, and I suddenly saw the rugged, rough lobsterman who had survived decades on the ocean. I would never mess with him. "King Tut? You got Officer Jane?"

He looked over at me, then continue to lick his back leg.

"Okay." I turned to Hattie and Lucy. "Let's go."

"Split up or stay together?" Lucy said. "Hattie and Beau could go the way they came, and we could go the way we came. See what we missed."

"I'm going with Mia," Beau said. "She finds the bodies."

"Beau and Mia will die if they run into trouble without us," Hattie said. "They're not seasoned. We stick together."

"Let's go the way Lucy and I came," I said. "That's the way I sent Thelma."

"Right. Let's do it." Hattie grinned. "This is fantastic. Good job, Captain Jim."

He saluted us, but didn't take his gaze off his captives. He looked fierce and ready to handle anything they tried. He might have wrinkles on his face and years on his body, but he was a man who had spent his life in hard labor.

We headed down the tunnel, but Beau stopped us right when we went around the bend. "Someone give me a phone," he whispered. "Someone with a full battery."

"Why?" I asked.

"Because, depending on who you believe, you might have just left two women with a guy who murdered a bunch of people in a revenge lobster killing. I want to set up the phone to record what happens in case we come back and there's carnage.

We all stared at each other. "This is incredibly awkward," Hattie whispered. "I feel like we should give them all a gun and let them shoot it out. The good guys won't kill, but the bad guys will, so once we see who's dead, we know they're the good guys."

I raised my brows. "You're terrifying sometimes."

"Only sometimes?" She grinned. "I'm hoping to get to one hundred percent, but it's a process."

"I'll stay and watch them," Lucy said. She pulled Officer Jane's gun out of her pants.

"You can't shoot them," I hissed.

"I know. I tossed the clip. But Captain Jim doesn't know that. As long as Captain Jim is the good guy, I won't need to do anything. If he's not..." She shrugged.

"If he's not, you can't stay here and face him alone," I whispered.

"I'll stand in the tunnel," she said. "I'll stay out of sight and won't interfere unless I need to save their lives."

Dammit. "I don't like this at all," I whispered.

"It doesn't matter," Lucy said. "We need to find Thelma and get answers. And someone needs to protect Sylvia and Officer Jane if Captain Jim is the bad guy." She raised her brows. "I'm a big girl, Mia. No one messes with me. Who pulled the trunk out of the ocean? Me or Captain Jim?"

"You."

"Right. You might not be stronger and more capable than an

old, weathered lobsterman, but I am, so shoo, shoo, go find Thelma and find out what's going on." She waved us off.

Beau didn't move. "You'll set up your phone to record it? I still want that."

She raised her brows. "It's a good idea, in case I do need to kill anyone. Self-defense and all that."

Oh, God. "I don't want you burdened with a lifelong trauma from killing someone."

She raised her brows. "I would never feel guilty for killing someone who was trying to murder someone. That's silly."

"It is silly," Hattie agreed. "Lucy isn't that silly."

"I'd feel guilty and traumatized," I said.

"Would you?" Hattie put her hands on her hips. "How guilty did you feel after you put that assassin in the hospital with your hairdryer? Did you visit him to see how his facial reconstruction went? Did you send him flowers?"

I started laughing. "No."

"See? If the people are heinous enough, then you're good." Hattie made a circling motion in the air with her index finger. "Let's go, people. Time is ticking. And watch out for the whispers of the dead."

We all stared at her, suddenly aware of how dark every inch of the caves were, except the areas reached by our flashlights or Sylvia's spotlight. "Really?" Lucy said.

Hattie grinned. "Just want to keep you all on your toes. Let's go."

She blew Lucy a kiss, and headed down the tunnel.

Beau waited for me while I spoke to Lucy. "Don't risk yourself, even to save their lives. I love you, and I want you alive."

Lucy's face lit up. "I love you, too!" She threw her arms around me and hugged me tight. "Let's do this, girl. We got this!"

She let go, turned away, pulled out her phone, heading back toward Captain Jim and the others.

CHAPTER 26

I STOOD FOR A MOMENT, watching Lucy go, my heart tight. "I'm scared for her safety."

"She's the toughest of all of us," Beau said. "You should be worried for everyone else, especially since your assassin cat is still out there." He turned his camera on me. "You do look pretty forlorn. I love the complexity of your character. Tough. Sassy. Funny. Ex-criminal. And yet behind all the façade, you're just a scared little kid afraid of being alone and rejected."

I looked over at him. "Is psychoanalysis really necessary?"

"How do you think I've sold so many millions of books? My characters are brilliant miasmas of the broken side of the human soul, combined with a fierce resilience that every single reader craves for themselves. It sells books because everyone is traumatized on some deep level, and everyone is also a hero at the same time, and they burn to see that broken part turn into a victor. Every time a person reads that story in one of my novels, the broken part of them becomes stronger. I give life to my readers because I see inside the human soul. So, yes, psychoanalysis is necessary. It's my superpower."

I raised my brows at him, giving him a sassy look. "And to think you pretend you hate people. You're a student of them."

"I am. Doesn't mean I don't hate most people, too. It's a complex relationship. Are we walking or standing here talking? Because now is the time for action, my reluctant protagonist."

I took one last glance in Lucy's direction, but she was out of sight. I sighed and turned and began to stride down the tunnel. "I'm not a character in one of your stories, Beau. This is real life. My real life."

He kept pace with me easily. "When people read stories, the books are real life while they are immersed in them. Fiction becomes truth. So, the two are intermixed. You inspire my stories, so your truth becomes my fiction, which becomes my reader's truth. It's the labyrinth of the human experience."

"I think I need to read one of your books."

"You haven't?" He sounded amused. "I thought you were trying to win me over. Did you really think you could do that without fangirling over my books?"

"I don't need to win you over. You're in love with my mother."

"Not in love. Morbidly curious."

We rounded a corner. "Obsessed."

"Fascinated on a scholarly level."

We reached the trunk room, and I shined my light around. "What's so fascinating about her? She's a criminal." The trunks I'd opened were now empty. Who had taken the contents? Hattie? We weren't that far behind her. Thelma. My mom? Who else was in the caves with us?

"Your mother is a criminal who raised a child with insurmountable ethical standards and morals, intense love for others and her own mother, and brilliant wit," Beau said. "Any mother who can raise a child in a life of crime and still be respected, loved, and adored by that child, even after the child rejected that lifestyle, is a woman who is so much more than a simple criminal."

My throat tightened at his depiction of my mom. "You were obsessed with her before you met me."

"Because I saw all of those nuances in the documentary about the two of you. Meeting you simply reinforced it."

I looked over at him. "I'm worried that she's crossed the line," I said softly. "That she's become…someone else."

"Someone you can't respect?"

I nodded.

Beau was still filming me. "You mean, you're worried that if she's turned out to be a bad person, then maybe you're not as good a person as you want to believe you are?"

"It does make me look at my life through a different lens." I walked over to one of the open trunks and felt along the sides, checking for anything that had been hidden.

"What are you looking for?" Beau asked, following me with his camera.

"My mom's strategy has always been to hide the most important stuff and let people see the less important. No one ever looks past the obvious to the hidden if you give them enough obvious to see."

"I love that. See? She's brilliant."

"She is." If my mom was involved, there would be more than what it appeared, and I was willing to bet Thelma, or whoever cleaned out the trunks, didn't know that. I checked the lining but found nothing.

I walked over and checked the second trunk. I also couldn't find anything.

I sat back on my heels, trying to think.

People would be in this room looking for and at the trunks. Which meant they wouldn't look in the corners.

I stood up and looked around. People tended not to look above their heads. They looked down and at eye level. Which meant she'd put it up high. I began a slow circuit of the room, shining my light to the upper edges of the cavern. The rock was mostly smooth, so it was easy to see that there was nothing hidden.

"What are you looking for?" Beau asked.

"My mom hid something in here," I said with more confidence than I felt, but I knew it would get Beau to help me. "It's in a crack or crevice above eye level. Help me find it."

"Heck, yeah! I love this!" He started in the other direction, shining his light, narrating excitedly.

I suddenly saw a little spot above my head. It was dark and high, set back. There were no footholds to get up there, so no one would have an easy time checking it.

My heart started racing, and I ran over and grabbed a trunk. I dragged it back over to the wall, then put the second one on top.

"Did you find something?" Beau asked, hurrying over.

"I don't know yet." I climbed up, bracing myself against the wall. The hole was above my head, so I reached in blindly.

My hands closed around something small immediately. I pulled it out. "It's a phone. It looks like a burner phone."

"Open it. See who it called."

I tried to open the phone, but it was locked. I took a breath, then typed in my birthday, month and day.

The phone unlocked. *Holy crap.*

It opened to the text messages screen. On it, was the string of text messages with the XXX warning that I'd gotten yesterday. My hand started shaking. "She sent me the messages yesterday." God. I was so glad I'd left Bass Derby when I had. What was happening at my marina that had been so dangerous? Chills ran down my spine at the thought of what could have been worth my mom choosing to break more than a decade of silence between us.

"What?" Beau sounded delighted. "Let me see!"

"Wait a sec." I opened the phone and checked the emails. Nothing had been sent.

I checked the photo albums. There was one video, and the still image was the interior of my marina store. Holy crap.

My heart racing, I opened the video and played it.

The video had been shot from the upper corner of the store, above the front door. I didn't have a camera there. Had Griselda missed a camera when he'd searched my marina after finding the first one?

Beau climbed up next to me. "What do you have?"

"There's one video on the phone. I'm watching it."

"Holy crap. Your mom left you a message! This is incredible."

I hit play, and Beau leaned over my shoulder to watch.

In the video, I was sorting life jackets and King Tut was sprawled in a patch of sun.

Hattie walked into the store, her back to the camera. "Mia. You need to come with me. Harmony Island is amazing."

I looked up at her, and I could see the weariness on my face. "Hattie, I want to go, but I'm not ready for my grand opening."

"Work expands into the amount of time you allot for it," Hattie said. "Get off your butt and come. Grand Vista Resort is calling you."

"I can't."

"You can."

"I can't."

"You can! I'm leaving tomorrow midday to catch the ferry. I'll come by to pick you up around noon. Great. See ya!" Then she turned and walked out, and the video ended.

"Holy crap," Beau whispered. "Your mom sent you that triple X to get you to leave, knowing that you would come *here*. She texted you right at noon, when Hattie would be coming to get you."

"She didn't want me to simply get out of the marina," I said quietly. "She wanted me to come here, specifically."

"She's been the one watching you?"

My throat tightened, and suddenly I felt like crying. She'd been with me all this time? "Hattie's been talking about this trip for a month. My mom would have had plenty of time to know that she could get me here for these three days."

Beau let out a low whistle. "This whole thing has been a set up by your *mother*? Why?"

"I don't know."

"She's trying to get you back in the game."

"No." I rubbed my jaw, trying to think. "She respected my decision. She never once tried to talk me out of it. She wouldn't call me back in to work." I scrolled through the phone, but there was nothing else to find. "She told me when I left that it was up to me to reopen communication with her, that she'd never force me back into that life."

"So, then why would she contact you?"

I looked around the cavern. The stolen jewels were right up her alley. The auction with wealthy people was her jam. This scene had many elements that fit her. But the violence didn't.

I tucked the phone in my back pocket, and my fingers brushed her journal, which I'd kept with me. Wait. If she'd known I was coming, maybe she'd *wanted* me to find the journal. Maybe she'd asked Frank to put it in our boat…maybe he hadn't stolen it from her. Maybe he'd been working *with* her.

"I think," I said slowly, "Frank was on my mom's side. I didn't understand how anyone would have gotten her journal away from her, but if she gave it to him to put in the boat, that would make sense."

"I thought you said she wouldn't give it to anyone."

"She wouldn't, unless she had a reason big enough."

"Like?"

I looked at him. "Keeping herself, or me, alive."

His eyes widened. "What if she was in danger, and she needed you to save her. Would she bring you back into her life for that?"

I pulled out the journal. "She would," I said. "Not because she's selfish, but because she knows I need her. She'll always be my mom, and I'd do anything to keep her safe."

"And she'd do the same for you," Beau said, not even bothering to keep the admiration out of his voice.

"Yes."

"So the life of you or your mom, or both, was at stake," Beau said. "That's why you're here."

"Maybe not 'was' at stake," I said. "Maybe it still is. Maybe the danger is still there. If Frank was helping her, and he was killed..." A chill ran down my spine and I looked around again, suddenly on edge in a way I hadn't been since I arrived. "My mom had a lot of enemies," I said. "All criminals do."

"And you, do, as well."

"Yes." I bit my lip. "I'm guessing she knew about my marriage to Stanley and the trial, but Griselda is handling that. He's on top of things." I didn't mention Bunny Pumpkin, who was my secret inside contact in Stanley's world. I'd called him recently to see if there was an assassin after me. If anyone found out he'd helped me when I was undercover, he'd be dead.

"Which means this is about her."

I looked at Beau. "If Frank was helping my mom, and someone killed him as soon as he got that journal to me..."

"Then whoever your mom is dealing with would probably kill her as well."

"Giorgio had stuff in his room that had my mom's writing on it."

"And he's dead now, too."

Oh, God. "Maybe this wasn't about Roger. Maybe this is all about my mom." Panic hit me hard, the kind of panic I'd experienced many times as a little girl, when my mom had been in danger. I remembered sitting in the shadows, waiting for her to show up at our arranged meeting spot, terrified she'd been caught and I was going to be alone. That I'd lost the only family, the only safety, the only love, I had.

And I was back in that moment again, that little girl, terrified that she was going to lose the only anchor she had.

My heart started to race, and the walls started to spin.

"Oh, no you don't." Beau grabbed my arm. "Get off the trunks, Mia. Get down to the ground."

I bent over, my hands on my knees, fighting for breath. My lungs were too tight. Couldn't breathe. *Mom.*

CHAPTER 27

"ARE YOU KIDDING ME? I hate having to get involved!" Beau climbed down off the trunks. "Mia!" His voice was sharp. "Get down."

My legs were shaking. I felt like I was going to pass out.

"Mia! Give me your hand!"

His voice was raw and rude, and I put my hand out. He grabbed it, cupped my arm, and dragged me off my perch. I landed on him, and we both hit the floor of the cavern.

I pressed my face to the cold rock and closed my eyes. Tears clogged my throat, and I felt a scream rising. A scream of protest, of panic, of raw terror. The agonizing howl of being so alone that that it felt like the darkness would suffocate me. *Mom!*

"Mia." Beau sat down next to me and put his hand on my shoulder. "Mia." He leaned in, so his voice was next to my ear. "Your mom needs your help right now. You can collapse later, but right now, you need to get up. *Your mom needs you.*"

I squeezed my eyes shut and hugged my arms around my belly. I was cold. Shaking. I couldn't think. Couldn't breathe.

"What's wrong with Mia?" Hattie's voice.

"Panic attack. She thinks her mom might die."

Their voices were echoing in the distance, a faint noise so far away.

"Mia." Hattie's voice was close now. "Honey, you're safe. You've got all of us with you. Me. Beau. Lucy. Devlin. Griselda. You have a team. You don't have to face this alone."

I reached for her hand, and she caught it and squeezed tightly.

"We're your family now," Hattie said. "Which means your mom is our family, too, so she's in our circle of protection. We can't be stopped. You know that. Right? You know we can't be stopped."

I nodded once. *We can't be stopped.*

"That's my girl. Rub her back, Beau! Make yourself useful, you old cranky pants."

"I'm not cranky, and I was already rubbing her shoulder."

I felt Beau's hand on my shoulder, while Hattie gripped my hand.

"Mia," Hattie said gently. "This is your moment when you leave behind the scared little girl. You're a badass now. You're not scared. You're not a victim. You're powerful and fierce, and you own a hairdryer."

I did own a hairdryer. I nodded again, but I still couldn't breathe. My chest felt like a vice, but this time, I felt anger under the panic. Anger that the panic had that kind of control over me. Anger that the panic kept me from functioning.

Then I heard a meow, and a soggy cat butt sat on my face. *King Tut.* I started laughing and blew his tail out of my mouth.

"How could I forget your attack cat?" Hattie said. "He'd save all of us without even breaking a claw."

I let go of Hattie's hand and wrapped my arms around King Tut, squishing him against me and burying my face in his wet fur. His loud purr seemed to reach inside my chest, and my breathing and heart began to match the slow, steady rhythm.

"She needs to register that cat as an emotional support cat," Beau said. "Never seen anything like this feline."

"That cat is definitely not of this world," Hattie said. She touched my shoulder. "Mia? You with us now?"

I opened my eyes and saw Hattie and Beau both leaning over me. They both looked so worried that I started laughing. Not real laughter, but the kind of love-filled, emotional release that spilled out in laughter. "You guys look so worried."

"Not worried," Beau said. "Just irritated. No one has time for you lying on the floor of a cave."

"Not worried," Hattie said. "I'm fully aware of how capable you are. Just delighting in watching you find your power."

I took a shuddering breath, relieved to find my lungs were working again. Yay for breathing. "You guys are liars." And it felt good.

"I make up stuff for a living, so my entire life is a lie," Beau said. "But get up."

Hattie grinned. "I agree. Time to get up." But her touch on my arm was gentle as she helped me and my emotional support attack cat sit up.

I leaned against the stack of trunks and hugged King Tut, who was still purring. "Sorry about that."

"Sorry?" Beau looked annoyed. "Why would you be sorry about having an emotional response to your mother being in danger? Being sorry about that is a waste of everyone's time. I rip into the deepest recesses of my soul to bring my characters to their knees like that. Be proud of that."

I narrowed my eyes. "Did you video that?"

"No. I saved you from falling and cracking your head open, and I'm not happy about it."

I laughed softly. "Thank you."

"I hate to say it, but Beau's right on this one. Own your trauma, girl. It makes you who you are. It's your fastest path to unleashing your greatest self."

King Tut squirmed in my arms, and I let him go. He scampered off down the tunnel, no doubt back to guard Officer Jane. He'd left his duty because I'd needed him, and I'd never forget that. "Well, I'm putting my trauma back inside its black box for the moment." I stood up, and shook out my legs. The strength was returning to them, and I felt better. "Probably just a lot of pent-up angst about my mom."

"You think?" Hattie sat back on her heels, giving me such a skeptical look that I burst out laughing.

"All right, fine. It was." I filled Hattie in on the phone and what we'd figured out. By the time I finished, Hattie was frowning.

"Where is your elusive mother? That's what I'd like to know," Hattie said. "She dragged you here and then stashed the phone and went into hiding? No little welcome party from her for her favorite daughter?"

"It's not her style." My head was aching, but I could tell the panic attack was over. It was time to get focused.

"What *is* her style? Putting her daughter in the middle of a bunch of murders and then hightailing it out of town without leaving a single clue about what's going on?"

I raised my brows. "Why are you so mad?"

"I feel manipulated, and that pisses me off. I like to be in control, and now I discover that we've been your mom's little puppets. I don't like it." Hattie stood up. "Don't get me wrong. I meant it when I said that your mom's family since you are, but I'm still irritated with her. I'm going to have a little chat with her when I find her."

I looked at Beau, and we both started laughing. The thought of Hattie and my mom squaring off against each other was hilarious. Two strong women who both liked to be alpha dogs. "You guys might kill each other."

"I never kill anyone, but I *am* annoyed." Hattie sat down on the trunk. "What now?"

"Did you find Thelma?"

"I didn't make it very far. I heard Beau squawking so I came back." Hattie ran her hand through her fuchsia hair. "I'm not going to lie. I'm very unclear on what all is happening around here."

"We have two bodies," Beau said, "plus Roger from a couple years ago."

We both looked at him.

He grinned. "Just wanted to keep everyone on track. This is so much fun. Amazing research. And…where is your mom, Mia? I want to know, as well."

"I don't know—"

"Of course you know," Beau said. "The two of you ran about a million cons together. You know exactly how she operates. All you need to do is put the pieces together. She has given you a welcome party, Tatum Murphy style. You just have to find it."

I thought about that. He had a point.

"Frank got that journal to you," Beau said. "What else was in the bag?"

"A diamond necklace." I pulled out the ring, the necklace, and the journal and laid them out on the ground.

Beau picked up the journal and opened it. "How is it not ruined by the water?"

"My mom waterproofed it. She'd never take the chance that water would wipe away her legacy."

"Of course she'd waterproof it. She is so impressive." Beau sounded almost reverent, as he pointed to the symbols on one of the pages. "What does this say?"

"It's a code she uses. I don't remember it well enough to translate."

Beau handed the journal to me. "If she risked Frank's life to get it to you, it matters. Figure out why." He sat down next to Hattie. "We'll wait."

I stood up. "We can't wait. Thelma's out there in the tunnels somewhere, and my mom might be out there."

"Or all the answers are in that journal," Beau said. "Read the journal."

I felt restless to move. Instinct was telling me to get out of that room, and with my mom's legacy weighing on me, I was going to trust the instincts she'd cultivated in me. "I'll read it on the way." I put the rings in my pocket, clutched the journal, and headed toward the crack in the rocks.

Beau and Hattie didn't move.

"Read the journal," Beau said. "Just take one moment and scan it. See if you can tell why she gave it to you. Clues matter in mysteries, and this is one heck of a mystery. Nothing is a coincidence."

"Fine." I shined my light on the journal and started flipping the pages.

Hattie came over and took over the light so I could use two hands.

"It's just names and dates of things she stole," I said. "It goes all the way back to when we were together," I said impatiently, thumbing through the pages. "There's nothing different—"

"Go to the end, then," Beau said.

I flipped to the last page. "Blank."

"Second to last, then."

I turned the page, and still nothing. "There's nothing—"

"If your mom knew you were getting this, where would she put something in that journal that only you would see?" Beau asked.

I looked at him, then closed my eyes, trying to channel my mom. "She'd hide it."

"In the middle?"

I opened my eyes. "No. She liked hiding places. Puzzles." I opened the journal again, and this time, I felt the front and back covers between my thumb and forefingers. My heart jumped. "The back cover is thicker."

I checked carefully. Both the front and back covers were two layers of leather. But the back one was definitely thicker.

My heart racing, I opened the journal again, and I began searching the back cover for an opening, but it was neatly stitched all along the edge. Stitched? The front cover was also stitched, but my mom paid attention to small details, like making sure the front and back cover stitching matched after she'd opened the back cover and stuck something inside it.

My heart started racing. "Scissors?"

Hattie held up a pair. "I took them from the boat. I didn't want anyone stabbing anyone."

"Great." I put the journal on the floor of the cave and carefully slipped the tip of the scissors underneath the top stitch. It slit easily, but none of the others came loose.

Obviously, because my mom would have made sure that one accidental ripped stitch wouldn't expose anything.

Long-forgotten respect settled in me. She was so good at what she did. I quickly ripped out all the other stitches down the side, one by one. As the stitches came out, the cover didn't split, because again, she would take no chances. "Glue," I said. "It's also glued."

"Cut the edge off," Beau said. "Let's take some action."

"Don't need too. She loves this journal. She'd never do something that would require destruction of it." I inserted the tip of the scissors along the edge and wiggled them. Sure enough, the glue gave way easily, and the cover split open.

"Hot diggety," Hattie said. "What's in there?"

Beau leaned forward, still videoing.

I flexed the cover and shined the light inside. There was a piece of paper folded in there. I pulled it out and unfolded it. The first thing I saw was my name, written in my mom's handwriting.

Sudden tears filled my eyes. *Mom.* It had been *so long*.

"Read don't weep," Beau snapped. "Let's go!"

I scanned the page.

Mia—

Giorgio = Gus Fish. Former dirty cop. His camera is at your place. Auction for stolen items. Has local partner. Don't know who. Thought it was Sylvia, but not her. I can't get out until you're safe. XXX0.

. . .

I STARED AT THE NOTE, stunned. Not Sylvia. Then who? She'd been up to something, zip tying my friends.

"What? What does the XXXO mean?" Hattie asked. "I'm guessing it's not a bunch of kisses and hugs."

Beau grabbed the note and took a picture of it.

"XXXO means get out at all costs and make myself so hidden that even she would never find me."

Hattie's eyes widened. "Your mom could find you almost anywhere."

"Yeah." I paced away from her, my heart racing.

"So, this Gus Fish set up a fake identity here as a dance teacher?" Hattie said. "That's so nefarious. I love it!"

"Looks that way." I wished I had cell service. I needed to bring Griselda and Devlin in on this. A dirty cop? *Wow.*

"The cameras at your place and that bit about how she can't get out until you're safe could indicate that he's threatening you to force your mom into working with him," Beau said.

"Yep."

"But he's dead now." Beau raised his brows. "It's not *Thelma* who was set up for this guy's death. It's your *mom.* Son of a biscuit! That's not okay!"

"I didn't see any indicators it was my mom at Thelma's house," I said, "but I wasn't looking."

"Your mom had good reason to kill Gus," Hattie said. "If he was threatening her daughter, any mom would do whatever it took to keep her safe."

"Which is why she was working with him," I said. "She'd sell her soul to the devil to protect me, but she wouldn't kill anyone. I don't think she could."

"Not even to save herself?" Hattie asked. "Anyone could kill to save herself."

"Or her daughter," Beau said. "The stakes are high enough. She could have done it."

"Yes," Hattie said. "She could have done it and set my cousin up for it."

"Inadvertently set Thelma up," Beau quickly chimed in. "Tatum Murphy would never send an innocent person to jail. She might set up someone for her crimes, but only if the person deserved jail for other reasons."

"Thelma doesn't deserve jail!" Hattie retorted.

"Then Tatum didn't set her up!" Beau snapped back.

I stepped away as they argued about my mom, Gus, murder, and Thelma. My head was reeling from what I'd learned. It made more sense. This wasn't my mom's scene, but if Gus/Giorgio had stumbled across my mom somewhere, he would have found her talents very useful. It would have taken something to the extent of video surveillance of me to convince my mom that she couldn't protect me from him.

A dirty cop would have connections. She would have known that.

Stupidly, I suddenly grinned. My mom loved me enough to sacrifice her faint morals for my safety. I hadn't heard from her since I'd left, and a part of me had always wondered if she'd disowned me for choosing a different life.

Maybe she had, but not to the extent that she would have let some jerk hurt me if she could help it.

I felt so loved.

I took a deep breath again, but this time it was a breath of energy and excitement. I'd been validated with my life choice, because I hadn't lost the only person who mattered to me. Well, one of the only people, because I now had a crew that warmed the cockles of my little heart on a daily basis.

I watched Hattie and Beau argue. My people. Plus Lucy. And my cat.

Then my smile faded. If those cameras had caught me, they'd also definitely seen my friends, my found family, on those recordings as well. Were they also in danger?

I balled my hands into fists. First my mom and now my friends? And my cat? No. *No.*

I wasn't sitting back for this one. I wasn't playing scared. No more freaking panic attacks. I didn't have time for that. I needed to think, decide, and take action. Now.

I paced away from the arguing duo and took a few steps down the tunnel to check on Lucy. I whistled once, and she looked over her shoulder at me. She gave me a thumbs up, and I nodded.

Lucy was safe.

Time to focus.

I walked back into the cavern. "Let's go find Thelma." I had questions for her.

I headed off down the tunnel, and it took a moment for Hattie and Beau to wrap up their argument and hurry after me.

"What did you figure out?" Hattie asked as she came up behind me, following me down the single-file tunnel.

"There's no way Gus had cameras on me when I was in the safe house or undercover in Stanley's house, which means that he didn't set them up until I got into the marina." I was walking fast, propelled by urgency. "He'd probably been looking for me, but it wasn't until I got to Bass Derby that he could get to me." Gus Fish. Who the heck was Gus Fish?

"And now he's dead," Beau called out, hurrying to stay close behind Hattie.

"Yep. I know that." I reached the opening that we'd slipped through before. My sweatshirt was still on the ground, so I grabbed it pulled it over my head as we walked. "Frank could have killed him."

"And now he's dead, too," Hattie said.

"Yep." I paused, looking at all the paint on the floor of the cave. It went in all directions, because we'd gotten lost. Except there was more paint.

"Wow." Beau caught up. "You guys suck at creating a paint trail back to the boat."

"We didn't make it this messy. Someone added to it." I paused, looking around the cavern, then started down the tunnel on the right. "This way."

"You're sure?" Hattie asked.

"Yep. I always had to have an exit plan growing up. I learned to memorize maps from an early age. Always know your way out." I hadn't realized how closely I'd been paying attention on the way in, but I was absolutely sure of the way back to the boat. "Gus was a dirty cop who was tough enough to control my mom. Frank was a local with a thousand years of Maine in him. Who would be strong enough to kill people like that?"

"Atlas," Hattie said. "The maintenance guy at the resort."

"If someone set up Thelma on purpose, we need to look for people who have a thing with her. Vera is her best friend."

"Vera?" Hattie frowned. "She is a tough woman, and Simone has been a challenge for her."

"And Blanche is jealous that Thelma married Roger." I turned the corner, knowing we were getting close to the boat. "If my mom was right, it wasn't Sylvia, but she knew about the auctions. Everyone at the resort had to have known about them."

"But maybe she didn't know they were stolen goods," Hattie said.

"Someone does. Someone who either brought Gus into it, or who Gus convinced or blackmailed to help him."

"Frank used to work there," Hattie said. "For a long time, until Roger fired him."

I looked over at her. "What if Roger was running the auction with the stolen items? With Gus? And then something happened? What if Roger started them?"

She stopped. "You think Thelma knew?"

"I have no idea what Thelma knew, but I think it's time we asked some more pointed questions. The boat's right around the corner." We hurried around the corner, and then stopped, staring at the empty water.

"The boat's gone." I know it was stating the obvious, but...what?

"I thought you took the key," Hattie said.

"I did. It's right here—" I put my hand on my pocket...and felt nothing. "Oh...right. I gave it to Thelma."

Beau started laughing. "This is fantastic. The one time a pick-pocket needed to keep her treasure, she gave it away!"

I thought back to when I found Thelma sprawled on the floor, pretending to be hurt. Maybe she hadn't been trying to avoid some boogieman. "Maybe she cleaned out the trunks, took the stuff to the boat, and then made it out before the tide closed off the entrance."

Beau turned the camera onto Hattie. "Still claiming your cousin's innocence, Hattie?"

Hattie looked stunned, and my heart went out to her. I knew exactly what it felt like when someone you loved and trusted turned out to be a murderous criminal. I pushed Beau's camera aside and gave him a look. It was too personal for recording. Betrayal like that was like a knife in the heart that never fully healed. "Maybe she's trying to solve Roger's murder, like she said."

"By leaving us all here?" Hattie walked over to the water and stared at it. "Thelma," she whispered. "What have you done?"

I walked over and put my arm around her shoulder. "It might not be what it looks like," I said. "I'm the queen of illusions. I've created dozens of distractions in my life to fool people. Maybe she thought the tide was too high and she left to get help."

Hattie was quiet for a moment. "She's been different since Roger died. I assumed it was sadness and grief. I didn't for a moment think it was guilt."

"Maybe it's neither. Maybe it's revenge to solve her husband's murder."

"She would have told me," Hattie said. "If she believed Roger was murdered, she would have told me. She knows I love that kind of stuff. It's not like I hide it."

The sadness in her voice tore at my heart. Hattie believed in people with all her soul. She made them better people because she believed in them and saw the goodness in everyone, including me.

I didn't want that side of her destroyed. Her faith in humanity was one of the best things about her.

I'd already had my faith in the goodness of people torn from me, and putting it back together was brutal, as evidenced by my recent panic attack.

I wanted more for Hattie. She'd been my protector since I'd come to Bass Derby, and suddenly, I wanted to become hers. I wanted to fix this for her, in a way no one had been able to fix it for me. I wanted to be that faith in humanity for her. "I believe Thelma is innocent. She didn't murder anyone."

I knew I was saying it because I wanted it to be true, and not because I necessarily believed it, but the look of gratitude on Hattie's face made me glad I'd said it.

"The brain always looks for what you tell it to look for," I said. "If you decide to look for all the blue in a room, you will see so much blue. Along those same lines, if we look for evidence that Thelma is guilty, we'll see it. If we look for evidence that she's innocent, it's how we'll find it." If there was any to be found, but I wasn't ready for doubt yet.

This whole trip was turning into a plunge into the depths of my soul, challenging everything I knew about love and faith, but that was what drove me, so I was leaning into it. I didn't ferret out murderers for fun. I did it to protect those I loved, and to make the world a little bit fairer.

Hattie looked over at me. "So, what next?"

"We assume Thelma found something in those trunks that gave her information about what happened to Roger. She's in the boat because she wants to handle it. Would she go to the cops?"

Hattie bit her lip. "If she thought the cops would help, yes."

"And if not?"

"She'd handle it herself."

Alarm shot through me. "What does that mean?"

"She's my cousin. What do you think it means?"

I sighed. "We need to stop her!"

CHAPTER 28

WE SPRINTED BACK into the cavern where the trio of awesome was holding Sylvia and Officer Jane hostage. I burst into the cavern, and ran over to Sylvia. "How were you going to get out? Can you get out with the high tide from here?"

She gave me a murderous look and said nothing.

"Seriously?" I ran over to Officer Jane, who was now sitting cross-legged. King Tut was sitting directly across from her, staring at her with his unblinking yellow eyes. "Can we leave from here now?"

She narrowed her eyes at me. "Don't bother me. I'm making a list of all the charges I'm going to file against you and your friends when we get out of here. If you distract me, I'm going to have to start over."

I looked at Captain Jim. "Can we get out?" I was literally asking three possible murderers how to get out to chase down another possible murderer. The irony was not lost on me, but my gut said we needed to get out fast, and this was the best way.

Captain Jim hadn't tried to murder either of the women, so I was going to go with the win for that one and claim him as the innocent we thought he was. He shrugged. "I didn't know there was an entrance over here. I've been trying to think of where they came in, but I haven't seen it from the ocean."

Dammit. "Look," I said. "I think Thelma blames Blanche for Roger's death and she stole the boat to go handle Blanche herself. We have to stop her, or one of them might wind up dead!" I didn't actually believe that Thelma thought Blanche did it, but I wanted to see how the people in our little bubble reacted.

I was especially watching Officer Jane when I said it. My mom had said it wasn't Sylvia, and I trusted my mom. Captain Jim felt okay to me. But we had one dirty cop involved so, cops support cops, right? I mean not, all cops. Devlin and Griselda were good guys, regardless of who the bad guy was.

But not all cops were.

Officer Jane frowned at me. "Roger?" She echoed. "Roger Gold? Her husband?"

"Yes," I said. "Thelma thinks Roger was murdered, and she's been looking for evidence all this time. I think she found it, and she left with it." I had a sudden idea, and gave a look at Hattie before continuing. "Wait a sec. I assumed she went to go after Blanche, but what if she didn't?"

Hattie, being a clever cookie, gave me a confused look. "If she didn't go after Blanche, where did she go? It must have been important to strand us here."

"I bet she went to the FBI."

Officer Jane's eyes widened. "The FBI? Why would she go to the FBI?"

"Because they're here on the island looking into the trunk of money that was found in the ocean." I pointed back to the cavern. "Trunks like the ones in there." I grinned. "Honestly, I'd be so happy for Thelma if she got closure on Roger's death. Agent Straus is awesome. He'll take her seriously and investigate whatever she brings him." I sat down on a rock. "I guess we just wait, then. Agent Straus knows we're out here, and he'll come looking for us when we don't come back. Anyone want to go get chips from the other side?"

"Oh, I do." Lucy had walked into the cavern. I didn't see the gun anymore, and I figured she had it tucked away, hidden until and unless she needed it. "Let's have a party."

"Um, hello?" Captain Jim waved at us. "What about these two? They had us tied up."

"And tried to drown Mia," Lucy said. "They were both very determined."

I narrowed my eyes. "That's right. Why did you try to drown me? Both of you. That's really aggressive. Is it my hair? Because most people don't find my hair that offensive."

Hattie grinned. "I think it's because you're such a sparkly light in this world. Some people are threatened by positivity and good- ness. They just want to chop it up into little, tiny pieces and grind their cranky faces into it."

"Is that it?" I sat down and crossed my foot over my knee, watching my kitty cat, who was still sitting next to Officer Jane, just out of her reach, but well within range of his claws. "I'm too sparkly for you? Toxic positivity, and all that?"

"I didn't try to drown you," Sylvia said. "I was trying to save you, and I tripped."

I looked over at her, replaying the moment in my head. I didn't quite believe her. "Really?" I asked, giving voice to my skepticism.

She nodded. "Really."

"Why did you tie up my friends?"

She made a noise of exasperation. "There's at least one murderer running around. Who am I going to trust?"

"Two senior citizens and a crazy mystery writer? You think they're the killers?"

Hattie, thankfully, decided not to choose that moment to take offense at being called a senior citizen incapable of murder. I winked at her, and she smiled. We both know that I fully believed in her capability of murder, so all was well.

Sylvia glared at me. "My dance teacher was *murdered* in the home of a seventy-five-year-old widow. We all know Thelma could do it, as could her cousin. Someone killed him, and it wasn't me."

Her anger felt legitimate, edged with fear. Sylvia was scared.

"And Frank," I added. "He also used to work at the resort, and he was murdered, too—"

"What?" She bolted to her feet, alarm on her face. "When? What happened to Frank?"

Oh…whoops. I hated being the one to announce these types of things. I nudged Hattie to answer, so I could watch Officer Jane.

"He was found stabbed on the beach by the main dock," Hattie said. "Earlier tonight."

"*Frank*?" Sylvia sounded horrified. "*Why?*"

Officer Jane's face didn't twitch. Literally, no reaction. Which made a very deep *oh, no* begin to well up inside me. I realized suddenly that she hadn't been at the crime scene. Only the sheriff had been there.

"We don't know why Frank was killed," Hattie said.

"Yes, we do," I said, trying to be all dramatic and inflammatory. "Or, at least, I do."

Everyone looked at me. "You do?" Beau was filming again. "Why?"

"He had a paper clenched in his fist," Lucy said. "It had the coordinates of the cave on it. What else?"

Officer Jane was watching me closely, her face intent. She was no longer relaxed. She was sitting up, her fingers digging into the rock she was sitting on. "What else was on it?"

"It wasn't what was on it," I said, completely lying. I reached into my pocket and pulled out my mom's journal. "It was what was in the journal he left me. My mom's journal."

Sylvia, Captain Jim, and Officer Jane's eyes all widened.

"What's in there?" Sylvia asked.

"Code," I said. "It's—" I stopped suddenly. *Code?* I pulled out the ring I'd taken from the trunk and I looked at the tag. I'd seen that number before. It was in the journal. My heart reaching, I opened the journal and flipped through the pages until I found it. I held the tag next to the listing in the journal.

It was a match.

My mom had recorded all the items in the trunk. All of which were stolen, because that was all she recorded. But there were more notes next to each one. Notes written in code, but I could figure enough to decipher them. "She's listed every stolen item, when it came in, and how much it sold for. Who bought it." I looked up, and then added one more item which was a complete lie. "And who brokered it."

"Stolen item?" Sylvia sounded confused again, but this time, I didn't believe her.

I looked at her. "You've been running an auction for stolen items and you know it," I said. "Giorgio trapped my mom into helping, and then he was killed, and Frank was killed."

"Your mom killed them?" Sylvia looked so horrified, I started laughing.

"No, she didn't. She's not a killer."

"Then who's the killer?" This was Officer Jane, watching me intently.

I met her gaze. "You tell me. You know who it is."

Everyone looked at Officer Jane. "You know?" Sylvia said. "Who is it?"

"Thelma." Officer Jane said. "It's Thelma."

I sighed. "Oh, sweetie, you know it's not."

"Then who is it?" Captain Jim said, looking mystified.

"This is fantastic. The dramatic reveal," Beau said. "Even I haven't figured it out."

I wasn't sure either, but I had a suspicion. "Officer Jane's uncle. Sheriff Wick."

Officer Jane's face morphed into a split second of horror, and my gut sank. I'd guessed right. She was protecting him. She jumped to her feet, and King Tut stood up, his fur puffing up, as a low, menacing growl bristled along his spine. "He didn't do anything. He's old and infirm."

"He's not old and infirm," Hattie said. "He's completely capable."

"I'd be willing to bet that we can find a history between Giorgio and the sheriff," I said. "A place they knew each other from—"

"Shut up."

We all turned around, and fear clumped in my stomach when the sheriff walked out of the tunnel, his gun aimed on me. *Oh, crap.*

"Well done," Beau said. "I'm so impressed. You ferreted out the bad guy with lies and manipulation."

"Get over by the water," the sheriff ordered us, his gun pointed at me.

My humor faded at the look on the sheriff's face. His gaze was icy cold, remorseless, and mean, with an edge of smug impunity.

He was willing to kill and fully believed he would get away with it. If he'd murdered all the former employees of the last ten years who'd died in the caves, then he had reason to be confident.

Lucy raised her hand. "Hello? Sheriff? Mia is dating an FBI agent and a cop. They both know she's out here. If something happens to her, they'll be super pissed."

"Vengeance," Hattie added. "They'll be out for vengeance, and they're very talented former black ops."

"They're both in love with her," Lucy said.

"What?" I looked over at her. "They're not in love with me."

Hattie rolled her eyes. "Dear heavens, Mia. Are you blind?"

"No. But you are. They don't love me."

"You know," Beau said. "Devlin does have that look when he's talking to you."

"Look? What look?" I kept the conversation going while I frantically tried to think of what to do. They were correct Griselda and Devlin would come after the sheriff, and they would find him, but that would be too late to do us any good because we would be dead and all.

Officer Jane scrambled to her feet. "Uncle Stan," she said

urgently. "Put away the gun. The folks are innocent. We don't need to arrest them."

Oh…clever ploy. She was urging him not to kill us, but doing it in a way that cleared his path. She had framed all of her actions and his as the actions of people who were trying to save themselves from us. Victims, not aggressors. She was making it sound like he'd pulled the gun on us because he thought we were murderers, not because he was going to kill us. How long had Officer Jane been trying to control her uncle? It was chilling, actually.

The sheriff walked into the cavern. "Finish putting the items on the boat, Jane."

She looked at me with alarm. "The cat will kill me."

"The cat?" The sheriff looked at King Tut, then aimed at him.

CHAPTER 29

"No!" I screamed in protest and dove on top of my cat, shielding him with my body. I cradled him against my belly, bracing myself for the impact of a bullet, but it didn't come.

Officer Jane met my gaze, and I saw real worry in her eyes. My heart suddenly went out for her. We don't choose our family. What would I have done if my mom had caused real harm? Or had she? How many people had been hurt by her thievery? Should I have tried to stop her? Should I have turned her in?

My gut turned over for Officer Jane. I knew what it was like to betray someone you loved. I had never thought to turn my mom in, but my husband had forced me to act.

Officer Jane had to act. People had died because of her uncle. She couldn't keep making the choice to protect him.

I gave her a look, but as soon as she understood what I was saying, she looked away.

She'd made her choice. Family before the lives of countless others.

I had to say, I disagreed with her choice. Very much so.

"Uncle Stan," she said again. "They are innocent. It turns out that Blanche is the one who killed Frank and Giorgio. Thelma went to stop her. We need to go stop Thelma from killing her."

His brows went up, and I saw him thinking about her point. Allow Thelma to kill Blanche? That was such a tidy little bow. I honestly had no idea where Thelma had gone, but I'd apparently been successful in giving them something else to think about.

King Tut growled again, and Hattie gave me a look, then jerked her chin toward the boat and nodded emphatically.

She wanted me to claim the boat. I was right on the edge of the water, but the boat was drifting a bit. The front end was tied, and the boat had swung sideways. There was no way for me to climb on the boat without good ol' Uncle Stan noticing and getting a clear shot off.

"Are there knitting needles in the boat?" Uncle Stan asked. "Like I told you?"

Knitting needles? Dammit. I didn't want us all to be stabbed to death by knitting needles. That sounded like a terrible way to die, and so melodramatic. Death by knitting needles? It was a freaking craft.

Lucy had been correct. No legit knitter would have sacrificed Thelma's years-long project just for murder. Good to know. Knitters had craft morals.

Hattie nodded at me again and flicked her gaze empathically toward the boat again.

King Tut growled, and I tightened my arms around him. Dammit. Now I definitely had to get into the boat first. Knitting needles could not be allowed to be unleashed. I felt like I was in a spy movie, and I had to keep some toxic chemical from being unleashed into the world's drinking water. A race against time! Death or victory! There was no in between.

Hattie elbowed Lucy and Beau, then put her hands on her hips. "Honest to goodness," she announced, her quick movement drawing everyone's attention toward her. "This just feels insane. Who wants to knit right know? I mean, I know it's a stress reliever, but can't we take action?" She then broke into a series of martial arts moves that had Uncle Stan raising his gun at her.

"Stop it."

I really, really hoped she didn't get shot. But I wasn't about to let her brave sacrifice be in vain. Wrapping my arms around King Tut, I quickly rolled over the side of the rock and then sank under the water.

The cold water hit me like a PTSD party, and suddenly I was back in that moment by the ferry. Or the one when two people tried to drown me. The moments when ocean meant death, destruction, and the raw terror of being trapped below the surface.

Panic hit me hard and fast, then King Tut slapped his paw across my cheek, claws out.

The shot of pain jerked me back to the present, and survivor instinct took over.

Let's go! I let go of King Tut and kicked through the water, holding my breath as I swam around the back of the boat. I went under the propellers, and fear slapped me as my arm brushed against the metal.

But my arm didn't get chopped off. No one was starting the boat yet. *I had time.*

I kicked harder, my lungs squeezing as I rounded to the back side of the boat. It was dark, but I kept close to the boat, bumping it with my shoulder to keep track of where it was. I couldn't see King Tut, but I knew he was way better at swimming in the dark and underwater than I was, so I had faith.

I came up for air right next to the boat on the far side. I surfaced as carefully as I could, breaking the surface of the water like a mermaid in a game of hide and seek, because that was me. A freaking mermaid. Right?

I paused, listening. Hattie was shouting about something, and actually sounded like she'd lost her mind. I could hear Stan yelling at her to shut up, which Hattie took offense to, which is exactly what I'd expect form Hattie.

"How dare you tell an old lady to shut up?" She shouted. "Don't I deserve respect? Do you know all I have survived in my life?"

No one appeared to have noticed I'd disappeared. Hattie was so impressive as a terrifying, irrational lunatic.

I reached up and grabbed the side of the boat as King Tut surfaced beside me. He immediately climbed up on my shoulder, his weight temporarily shoving my head under water.

I sucked in my breath in a very brief moment of panic, but then I pulled myself back up, using my rock-solid grip on the boat.

Beau suddenly started yelling absolute gibberish, and I had a feeling someone had started to look toward where King Tut and I had been.

"You first, kitty cat," I whispered.

King Tut immediately used my shoulder as a springboard, digging his claws into my skin as he launched himself upward and over the edge of the boat.

I waited for someone to yell that they'd seen him, but Lucy had started screaming that Beau was having an episode and they needed to save him. It was pure chaos and mayhem.

I slung my other arm up and grabbed the edge of the boat. It was so freaking high. I'd never managed to pull myself into a boat or onto a dock. Lucy could do it with her pinkie. Even Hattie could do it.

But my upper body strength was...not enough.

King Tut leaned over the edge and peered down at me, his yellow eyes regarding me with visible disgust to find I was still down there.

I had to do this. My cat, my friends, and my own life depended on it.

I adjusted my grip on the boat, took a breath, then hauled myself up. I got my head over the edge, saw Beau on the ground gyrating, met Lucy's gaze, and lost my focus.

I immediately fell back down into the water.

Come on. I could do this. I had to do this.

My arms aching from holding onto the edge of the boat, I stared up, remembering how terrified I'd been when the assassin had broken into my safe house. That fear. That panic. And that absolute *focus*.

I closed my eyes and went to that space. Calm. Focused. And absolutely unwilling and unable to fail.

I am doing this right now.

I opened my eyes, focused on King Tut, and then hauled myself up with every last bit of strength I could summon. I shot over the edge and fell right into the boat, landing on my face.

King Tut jumped down beside me, and we both froze, listening to the mayhem, waiting for someone to scream that I was in the boat.

But the only ones screaming were Lucy, Hattie, Beau, and Uncle Stan.

The light in the boat was faint, but my eyes adjusted quickly. There were already four trunks in the boat, plus a duffel bag. I opened the bag, and my gut sank when I saw it was a knitting bag. Several sweaters underway, and many knitting needles. I quickly grabbed the bag and tossed it over the far side of the boat.

I am sure I was breaking some knitter's heart that I was tossing aside almost-completed projects, but I was a ruthless non-knitter, so that was the way life was.

Plus, I was a hairdryer person, not a knitting needles person, and I wasn't even going to begin to mess with that. I looked around the boat quickly.

The keys were in the ignition. For a moment, I stared at them. Was it better to keep them in there and try to get my friends in the boat to make a run for it? Or better to take the keys and trap us here with murderous sociopaths so they didn't get away?

Definitely better for us to leave and let Griselda and the others handle this.

But there were no others, because the only two cops in this little town that I knew of were here.

I looked around frantically, trying to figure out a weapon, a plan, or anything.

There was a paddle.

Some life jackets.

I opened the glove box, and my gut dropped when I saw a gun. I didn't want to touch that. What if it went off? I wasn't a gun person. But there was no way I wanted that used on me.

My heart racing, I reached for the gun to toss it overboard...

But what if it was a murder weapon that could incriminate them?

Like the murder weapon used in our deaths?

Um...uh oh.

I hurried over and popped the lock on the nearest trunk. It was full of money, like we'd seen on the ocean. I covered my hands with the edge of my shirt, then, I moved the gun into the trunk, then, on a whim, grabbed several stacks of money, then closed the trunk and locked it.

I scanned the rest of the boat quickly, but there were no more obvious ways to kill us.

All that was left was the guns that both officers had.

I peeked over the edge of the boat, and saw that Uncle Stan had Beau flat on the ground. His foot was between Beau's shoulder blades, forcing his face into the rock. And most alarmingly, his gun was aiming at the back of Beau's head.

CHAPTER 30

OH, oh, oh.

"Stop right now," he snarled. "Or the mystery writer dies this instant."

Lucy and Hattie were too far away to get to the gun, so they went quiet, both of them breathing hard from their exertion of appearing insane.

"I have a ton of money," Beau said calmly. "I'm happy to pay for my safety. What would it take?"

"You don't have enough," Uncle Stan said.

"I do, actually. I'm a hugely successful author and I invest my money wisely. I have partial ownership in a team in every major sport in America. I'm happy to sign over my ownership for a dollar."

To my surprise, Uncle Stan paused. "NFL?"

"Baltimore Ravens."

Officer Jane had her hands on her hips. "It's a good deal, Uncle Stan. You could let him go and watch football from the owner's box."

I admired her pluckiness. Standing up against her sociopathic uncle. Well-done.

"We could just have the three ladies do a murder-suicide," she added.

I revoked my support of her.

"Oh, can I film it?" Beau said. "That's great research."

Oh...Beau was just buying me time. Of course he wouldn't own an NFL team. Dammit. I'd been standing there listening instead of coming up with a plan. They'd endangered themselves to give me time to save them, and instead I'd been listening. I needed to find an opportunity.

"You're a sociopath," Uncle Stan said.

"Of course I am," Beau said. "I'm obsessed with murder and write about it all the time. Every mystery and thriller writer is a sociopath. You should see our basements."

"Bodies?" Uncle Stan asked.

"I'll never admit that. You're a cop. But I would like to video it."

"Wait a sec!" Sylvia interrupted. "Where's Mia? And her cat?"

And...there we had it.

I leaned back against the side of the boat. I held up a stack of bills. "King Tut," I whispered. "Hop up where they can see you. Shred the money."

He gave me a look that was so chilling, I could actually hear him saying, "I'm a cat. I do not *ever* take orders."

"It's to save lives."

He still didn't move.

"Caviar every night."

He still didn't move.

Right. Because I'd already promised that—

He suddenly went into a crouch, staring upward as a low growl burned in his chest, waiting for his prey to show itself over the edge of the boat.

I realized the boat was moving, being dragged back to shore. No one was talking. It was completely silent, and I knew they were trying to sneak up on me.

I looked at my cat and held up my hairdryer, wrapping the cord around my hand. "Ready?" I whispered.

He crouched lower, his tail switching. I inched back underneath the steering column, tucking myself into the space. I stayed crouched on my toes, ready to spring, trying not to feel completely trapped. I gestured to King Tut to stay hidden, but he ignored me, staring up at the edge of the boat, waiting for the chance to pounce.

I heard something brush against the edge of the boat, and my heart started to race.

I stared upward like King Tut. Waiting.

A hand appeared on the edge, and King Tut suddenly bolted into the shadows. I shrank back, watching through the steering wheel as a face came into view.

It was Officer Jane. *Yes.* We needed to take her out more than we did Sylvia.

"I don't see them in here," she called out.

I quickly tossed a wad of money to the back of the boat. It landed with a thud, and she leaned over the boat again, watching the stern of the boat. There were tarps and trunks piled up, enough that I could easily be hiding between them.

"Yep, no one here," she called again. "They must be somewhere else." As she spoke, she hopped over the edge of the boat and landed softly, all of her attention focused on the stern of the boat, where the money had thudded.

I tightened my grip on the cord of my hairdryer. Her back was to me.

Shoot. How could I jump a woman from behind? I didn't have control over the hairdryer. All my strikes were level 10. A sucker punch from behind felt super aggressive.

There was a creak from the rear of the boat, and then two glowing eyes appeared.

King Tut. He'd made himself a target.

Officer Jane aimed her gun. *At my cat!*

I moved before I'd even processed that I'd made the choice. I swung the hairdryer in that arc I'd perfected. It slammed into the side of Officer Jane's shoulder, throwing her against the side of the boat. The gun fell from her hand, and King Tut and I both leapt on her. He landed on her back and dug his claws in. She screamed and I slammed my hand over her mouth. "If you lie still and silent, I won't let him rip your face off," I whispered, giving King Tut a firm look of do-not-kill.

He growled. At me? At her? I wasn't sure. But he didn't claw out her eyeballs, so I figured I'd won.

Officer Jane went still, and King Tut put his paw over her left eye and growled.

Dear God. He was terrifying.

Officer Jane clearly felt the same way, and went utterly still.

"Jane!" Uncle Stan shouted her name.

King Tut growled.

"Don't answer him," I whispered.

"Jane!" He yelled again, but this time there was an edge of anger in his voice, an anger that sent chills down my arm. He was terrifying, and I had sudden, real empathy for Jane. Would he have killed her if she'd turned him in? He might have.

King Tut kneaded her eyebrow, the pad of his paw resting against her closed eyelid.

She started whispering a prayer, and I almost started laughing. *Good kitty.*

"Sylvia," Uncle Stan snapped. "Go check the boat."

"I'm not checking the boat. Did you hear her scream?"

I stayed crouched, listening.

"Check the boat!"

"Haven't you heard about Mia? She worked undercover against drug dealers for the FBI! She killed four assassins with her hairdryer! I'm not an assassin! All I was doing was running an auction. I'm not getting involved with murder!" I heard the sound of running feet, and I realized she was taking the chance that he wouldn't take his gun off Beau long enough to shoot her.

I held my breath, waiting to see if she'd guessed wrong—

There was the crack of a gunshot, and my heart dropped. *No.*

There was a shriek, then silence.

My heart was pounding. Fear gripped me so tightly I could barely breathe. Who had he shot at? *Please let everyone be okay.* How did I get out there? How did I save my friends? He was too far away.

I hit Officer Jane's arm. "Tell me how to stop him," I whispered.

She kept praying.

"If you helped him with murder, you're going down as accessory," I said. "But if you help stop him now, that helps your cause. This is your chance."

She kept praying.

I leaned in. "I know what it's like to be trapped in hell by someone you love," I whispered. "My husband was a sociopathic drug dealer who was responsible for the deaths of many, many people. I get it, Jane. But the only way to get free is to take him on. I put mine in prison. I can help you do the same."

She finally stopped praying, but she didn't open her eyes. Dammit. How did I reach her? I knew people. My mom had taught me to assess people and find their pain points. Who was Jane? I didn't know her well enough to know. But I had to guess.

This was a woman who didn't agree with what her uncle had done, but she hadn't gone to the feds, which was an option, as I knew. That meant that she wasn't all that caring about doing the right thing or saving lives. But she maybe did care about the benefits she got from it.

I put a brick of twenties in her hand. "Take the money and run," I whispered. "Go find a new life. Just help me save my friends and you can go. No one will find you."

She opened her eye that wasn't under imminent threat of removal.

"I can open the trunks. I can get as much as you want." I put the last stack of bills in her hand. "Just save my friends."

Her hand tightened around the money. "I want the boat. I want to be able to leave."

I nodded. "I have the key. I'll trade it as soon as my friends are free. I'll unlock all the trunks and then you can go." I leaned in. "You'll be free of him, Jane. *Free.*"

She looked at me, and I could feel her warring with her decision. "Okay," she said finally.

Dammit. I didn't trust her. She was lying to me. She was probably planning to leave with Uncle Stan.

"Get out of the boat," Uncle Stan shouted. "Or I will start shooting your friends one by one."

Jane looked at me. "Surrender," she said. "He doesn't want to shoot. He prefers stabbing. Then when you get close, get him with the hairdryer."

Freaking liar! She wanted me shot! The little beast!

But he was about to shoot my friends. I had to act now. "Keep her down there," I whispered to my cat. Then I grabbed her gun, hid it behind my back, and crawled to the steering wheel. I jammed the key into the ignition. "Let my friends leave or I'm taking the boat and all the contents," I called out to Uncle Stan. "You won't see the money and you'll have no way to escape."

"I can get more money," he said. "You can't get more friends."

None of my friends were saying anything. None of them were giving me guidance. My heart was pounding. I had to read this situation correctly, or we would all die.

Who was the better liar? Me, or him?

Did he really not care about the cash?

He cared.

Did he want to keep his scam going here? No. He couldn't. The gig was up. Too many people involved, including me with my FBI contacts.

He knew he had to get out.

He needed the boat. He needed the money.

He was lying.

I grabbed the wad of cash from Jane and held it up. "I opened the trunks," I shouted. "Release my friends!"

"You have three seconds, or I start shooting them."

My heart was pounding. So much at stake. My world. My life. My friends. I couldn't screw this up.

I couldn't afford to be wrong.

I closed my eyes. *Mom. How do I save my friends?*

I heard her voice in my mind immediately. *Money. He values the money.*

I immediately stood up and hurled the stack of bills over the stern of the boat, into the ocean. "Release my friends!"

I ducked back down as a shot rang out, and the windshield on the boat shattered.

Jane tried to hide the other wad of cash from me. "No!"

King Tut growled, and I hurled the next wad over the back of the boat. "Set them free, or it all goes in the ocean!"

I ran over and unlocked the trunk which contained the money. I opened it, then hurled another wad of cash over the back of the boat.

"You stupid wench! Leave the money alone!"

"Free my friends!" I threw another one over. He hadn't shot again, and I was hoping I'd guessed correctly that he didn't want to shoot up his only way out of the caves. "Let them go!" I screamed.

"He's coming," Hattie shouted. "He's coming for you!"

I heard splashing, and I knew he was close. Oh, God. Was I ready for this? "Don't let her up, King Tut!"

I went low, hiding where I'd hid before, but as soon his hands grabbed the edge, and he hauled himself over, Jane shouted a warning. "To your right! Argh!" She screamed as King Tut smacked her in the temple with his paw, slamming his foot against her face repeatedly, as only cats could do.

Uncle Stan launched himself over, moving with an agility I was beginning to expect from the senior citizens in Maine. He looked over at me, his wrinkled face trying to make me hesitate.

But it was too late.

I'd left the emotional space of humanity. He was simply a demon coming for those I loved.

I swung hard, and the hairdryer hit him in the face before he even saw it coming. He dropped immediately, landing on top of Jane.

She lunged for his gun, but King Tut's paw shot out and he ripped his claws along the back of her hand. She screamed and jerked her hand back, then tried to shove him off her. I lunged for the gun, and she tried to grab it again. Uncle Stan's inert body tumbled over the edge, landing between us, bending my wrist back.

Jane's eyes lit up, and she grabbed the gun—

A hairdryer came over the edge of the boat and smashed down on the top of her head. She gasped and fell on top of me. King Tut leapt on her back and dug his claws in. She screamed, but she still fought for the gun.

And that's when I realized that Uncle Stan wasn't the only crazy one. King Tut was ripping her back up, and she didn't even care.

Oh, God.

"I got her!" Lucy vaulted over the edge of the boat with an agility of a panther. She landed on her feet, grabbed Jane by the hair, and literally hauled her off me and threw her off the boat and into the water.

I gasped, scrambling to my feet. "Is everyone okay?"

She nodded. "All good." She held up zip ties. "Get Stan. I'll get Jane when she comes to shore!" She blew me a kiss, then jumped off the boat.

I zip tied Stan's ankles and wrists, then jumped to my feet, needing to see for myself.

Hattie and Beau were standing on the shore, their hands still tied behind their backs. Both of their faces lit up when they saw me. "Mia," Hattie shouted. "You good?"

I waved. "I'm great. You guys?"

"Awesome!" Hattie shouted. "Great job!"

"Brilliant," Beau shouted. "Best research I've ever done for a book. I'm never leaving your side again!"

"Get scissors," Hattie said. "I don't know how Lucy managed to break her ties, but the rest of us have human level strength. Get us free! Find something!"

I thought of the knitting bag I'd tossed overboard. "I'll find something."

But I didn't check. Instead, I sank down on the captain's seat and bent my head as the moment finally took over. My throat tightened, and my eyes filled with the tears of gut-wrenching relief. "Everyone's safe," I whispered. "We did it."

King Tut meowed, and I opened my eyes. He was sitting in front of me, staring at me, flicking his tail.

I held out my arms, and he jumped into my lap, did a little circle, then settled down. I wrapped my arms around him and pressed my face to his wet fur. My hands were shaking now, and I knew it wasn't from the cold.

"Come here, you little monster," Lucy said.

I hugged King Tut and stood up, watching as Lucy dragged Jane out of the water. She tossed her face-down on the rocks, then zip tied her right up. When she finished, she stood up and looked over at me. "You dove into the ocean voluntarily to save our lives. I'm so proud of you."

I let out a breath and grinned. "Thanks. It was important therapy to overcome my terror of the ocean."

"Everything always works out as it's meant to," Lucy said.

"Hello? Scissors?" Hattie said.

"I tossed them overboard," I said. "Sorry."

"Apology not accepted. Go get them."

I laughed. "I'm not going in again." I looked over at Captain Jim, who was still sitting on a rock. "You okay?"

He grinned. "I'm going to use this on my tours. I'm going to be rich. Thanks for including me."

I looked around at my little group of friends. "No one here is traumatized by what just happened?"

"Traumatized?" Hattie asked. "This is what makes life worth living. I don't want to die being old. I want to die having fun!"

"This is what I write about," Beau said. "It's literally brilliant in real life. Fantastic."

Captain Jim laughed. "I've been on these oceans for decades. I'm no lightweight. You see stuff out here that makes you tough."

I looked at Lucy. "And you?"

She grinned. "I'm a little traumatized," she admitted. "I don't sleep as well as I did before meeting you, but overall, I feel like it's a worthwhile trade off."

"Why?" Hattie spoke up. "Don't even tell me that you're traumatized?"

"You literally just saw me have a panic attack back in the trunk cave. I'm not cut out for this."

Hattie smiled, and there was a gentleness in her eyes. "Sweetie, just because you have panic attacks doesn't mean you're not cut out for this. It means you're braver than the rest of us, because of the courage you have to summon to make these choices."

"Yes," Lucy said. "You're our anchor, Mia. You always are."

My chest grew tight. "I love you guys."

"We love you!" Lucy shouted.

"We do," Hattie said.

"Even I love you guys," Captain Jim added.

"I don't love any of you," Beau said. "But you're great for research. Speaking of that, we need to find your mom, Mia. She's around here somewhere."

I thought of the journal, and the phone in the wall. "I don't think she is around."

"What?" Beau looked shattered. "Where is she?"

"She's gone." I knew she had moved on. That was what she did. She'd stuck around to keep me safe, but once Gus was dead, that was it. The threat to me was over, so she left. Of course, the threat hadn't been over because I'd stayed here to finish it, but from her perspective, the threat was over. She was gone. For now.

My throat got a little thick, and I wished I'd gotten a chance to see her. Hug her. Speak to her.

But now that I knew we were still connected, I knew I'd see her again.

I knew it.

And in the meantime, we had to find some scissors, track down Sylvia, grab some chips, and wait for low tide.

Griselda would be waiting.

CHAPTER 31

Hattie and I found Sylvia in the cavern where we'd first arrived.

She was sitting in one of the chairs, eating chips and drinking beer. When she heard us burst in, she screamed and dove behind the chair. "I have a gun," she shouted. "Get back, Stan! Get back!"

"It's Mia and Hattie." I shined my flashlight on her, and quickly determined she didn't have a gun.

She didn't come out. "Did Stan kill everyone? How did you get away? Is he dead?"

"Tied up," I said. "So is Jane," I said conversationally. "So we came looking for you."

"I didn't kill anyone," she said immediately, easing out from behind the chair. "I didn't know Stan had killed anyone. I had no idea. I'm not taking responsibility for any of it." She stood up and brushed herself off.

I sat down across from her, and Hattie took the seat beside her. We'd left Captain Jim and Lucy guarding our zip-tied hostages. Beau had decided to try to interview Chief Stan about why he killed people, so it had just been me and Hattie venturing out into the tunnels.

We'd found our way back pretty quickly. We were getting good at it.

Which meant we had time to kill before the troops floated in to rescue us.

I wasn't entirely sure Sylvia was innocent, so it was the perfect time to chat her up. We both had hairdryers, and King Tut hopped up on my lap as soon as I sat down.

Between my hairdryer and my cat, I was feeling very safe. Sylvia wouldn't be able to murder me from where she was unless she had a gun, which she didn't, so I was quite relaxed. "You knew the auction had stolen items, though."

She gave me a look as she sat back down. She didn't pick up her chips. She perched on the edge of her seat, looking ready to bolt. Were we that scary? I didn't think so. Which meant there was something else happening.

Oh, goody. I loved puzzles.

Sylvia evaded a direct answer to my question. "Roger had already been running the auction when I took over. It's extremely profitable for the resort, so the owner had me continue to run it. I don't keep track of who the attendees are or where the items come from."

The owner. Hmm…who was the owner? I hadn't thought of that. "Do you get a cut of each item sold?"

She pressed her lips together.

Hattie leaned in. "Girlfriend, you tried to drown Mia. We all saw it. That's attempted murder. I'm pretty sure Beau was still videoing at that time. Attempted murder goes to prison for a long time."

Sylvia's eyes widened, as did mine. I'd already forgotten that Sylvia had tried to drown me. I was getting so resilient with that kind of thing. "I didn't try to kill Mia."

"You did," I said agreeably. "I remember it quite clearly."

"If you tell us what you know," Hattie said, "we might develop selective memory about what happened when the non-murderous police arrive."

Really? We might? Let an almost-murderer run free? I was pretty certain we weren't going to develop selective memory.

But Sylvia seemed to think that was possible. "I meant it when I said I didn't run the auction," she said. "I provide the venue and make sure that all the logistics are in place. They fill the rooms, order a lot of food and drink, and tip very well. I don't take a cut."

"They who?"

She blinked. "I don't know who organizes the auctions. I never speak to them directly. I just get emails."

She was lying. Seriously.

I stood up. "Forget it, Hattie. We'll just report to the FBI what we saw. I don't feel like dealing with this—"

"Wait!" Sylvia stood up, and I tensed, waiting for her to launch herself at me. "Stan and Jane did get me involved. They were hired to provide security, and Stan's a dirty thief, and he took protection money. He roped me into it. He would have killed me if I'd ratted him out."

Would he have? Maybe. If he had, it's tough to go to the cops on another cop. "So, you worked for him."

"I didn't know he was killing anyone!"

Maybe. Maybe not. "Did you kill anyone for him?" I asked.

"Besides Mia," Hattie said.

King Tut growled and kneaded my thigh.

"No." Sylvia paced away from us, restless. "I can't talk about this."

Sudden alarm crept down my neck. Sylvia was scared. That was why she'd attacked me. She was *scared*. I leaned forward. "We caught Jane and Stan," I said, watching her face. "We tied them up." Stan had regained consciousness, so I thankfully hadn't killed him.

Sylvia didn't relax.

I looked at Hattie, the hair on my arms standing up. Whoever Sylvia was scared of was still free. He or she could still get to Sylvia. Hattie's eyes were wide, and I knew she'd realized the same thing. "Who are you scared of, Sylvia?"

She shook her head. "You can't protect me."

She wasn't wrong. "No, but the FBI can."

"The FBI won't protect me."

"An FBI agent is in love with Mia," Hattie said. "If he thinks it'll get him laid, he'll help."

I looked over at her. "Seriously? Griselda would never break the rules for me."

"He literally does it all the time! This whole trip has been a rule breaker for him. He's the biggest stickler ever, but he looks at you like you're the sparkling light that ignites his soul."

I started laughing. "You're insane. Griselda wouldn't know a sparkling light if it hit him in the face."

"I beg to differ. He knows sparkling lights. He just doesn't show it." Hattie turned back to Sylvia, who was watching us as if we were insane. "Either way, Griselda will help you. He had Mia in a safe house for months to protect her. He's a safe house guy."

"He did?" Sylvia looked over at me. "For real?"

"I did live in a safe house," I agreed, not bothering to clarify that that was only *after* two years undercover when the only safe thing I had was the breath I was taking in each moment that I survived.

Sylvia leaned against the wall.

"Did Stan kill Gus? I mean Giorgio?" I asked. "Did you?"

She looked over at us. "No."

My heart started to race. *Oh dear heavens.* "Who is in charge?" It had to be big if she or he was strong enough to control two dirty cops, plus Gus.

She looked at us. "I don't want to die."

"Dying is easy. Do you want to go to prison?" Hattie asked. "I heard it's not as fun as you might think. Much harder than a quick, nifty little death."

"I don't want to go to prison." Sylvia looked at me, desperation etched on her face. "What do I do?" she whispered. "She'll kill me like she killed Roger."

I narrowed my eyes. "She? She who?"

Her eyes flicked upward, and she bit her lip. I knew whatever she was about to say was a lie. "Thelma."

"No!" Hattie shot to her feet. "No! Thelma is not a murderer!"

"She is! She killed Roger because he wanted to expose her!"

I sat back, scratching King Tut's head as I watched them argue. Studying Sylvia. Trying to read the words she wasn't saying. She kept rattling off details about Thelma that sounded incredibly accurate. Too accurate. They sounded like details that had been set in place to make sure Thelma took the fall.

I realized Thelma had been set up from the start. From the very first moment. The scapegoat that would be blamed when things got too hot, and then people would move on, leaving Thelma hanging.

What was Sylvia's role? Was she the top dog? Or was she a peon, like the others were? She knew Thelma had been set up. She knew the rule was to point the finger at her. But was it her rule or someone else's?

I leaned forward, my mind racing as I watched Sylvia gain confidence. She wasn't scared anymore. She was fully immersed in arguing with Hattie, intent on making Hattie believe her cousin was a murderer.

Sylvia was on a mission right now.

I realized that it had all been an act. Her fear. Her running. Her acting like she wasn't in control with Stan and Jane. I was watching a smart, savvy woman winding a web around my friend, and it was working.

I knew what I was seeing, because I'd grown up with a smart, savvy mom who could wind a web around anyone, and they had no idea.

But my mom had said it wasn't Sylvia. So I'd discounted Sylvia, because my mom was smart.

But what if my mom was wrong? What if Sylvia was behind it all?

What if Sylvia was even better at being a criminal than my mother was?

Or what if my mom was right? What if there was someone else we hadn't seen?

How could I expose her? How could I know?

I could leave it to Griselda, but if Sylvia had been as careful as she appeared to lay a trail to Thelma's doorstep, then Griselda would have no choice but to pin it on Hattie's cousin.

I saw Sylvia glance over at me and realize that I was just sitting there. Her eyes narrowed, and I stood up. I met Hattie's gaze and gave her a look. She flipped me the bird, which almost made me laugh, then she went back to yelling at Sylvia.

I walked up behind Hattie, and pushed her to the side. She raised her brows, and I gave her a look. Curiosity flickered in her eyes, but she stepped to the side, giving me space to do my thing.

What was my mom great at? The con. Deception. Showing people what they expected to see so they didn't see the truth.

Every great murder needed a con, and this was that moment.

King Tut was sitting by my ankle, staring up at Sylvia. "Do you know who I am?" I asked.

She narrowed her eyes. "You're Hattie's friend."

Hattie snorted. "First mistake is to underestimate a woman. You know better than that, Sylvia."

Yeah, Hattie was the best. She didn't know what I was up to, but she was more than willing to roll with it. I was so lucky to have a friend who trusted me like that. Big hugs to girlfriends! "I'm Tatum's daughter, remember?"

Sylvia inclined her head, suspicion growing in her eyes. "I do recall."

"I'm better than my mother."

She said nothing, but Hattie nodded. "She is."

"I married a drug lord, ratted him to the feds, got him put in jail, and now I run his business, and I have the FBI on retainer."

Her eyes widened slightly.

"Lucy and I help run the operation," Hattie added. "Lucy's the muscle, and I'm the charm. Mia's the CEO. Women-run businesses are the best. So much love, support, and wisdom."

I had to bite my lip to keep from laughing. "Hattie can bend the world to her will. She's a freaking siren. Never mess with her."

"I am a siren," Hattie agreed. "To men, to women, even to sociopathic cats. I can dismantle someone's will, morals, and resistance in less than a minute, every time."

Sylvia's gaze flickered to Hattie and then back to me.

"I bought a marina that the prior owner was using as a pipeline for drugs brought up from Florida," I continued. "I took over that business as well. It fit in well with my infrastructure."

"She did leave a few bodies behind in her quest to take over," Hattie said, "but it was worth it. They were both men, and they were both murderers. Hashtag girl power."

I grinned. "I have assassins on speed dial." Bunny Pumpkin was on my favorites list. I wasn't lying. Of course, I'd never call him and ask him to kill anyone, but I could, and he would. That was empowering, wasn't it? Everyone should have that feeling of comfort that comes with having an assassin on speed dial. Not just any assassin. One that was a personal friend, who had risked his life to help keep me alive when I'd been undercover. But that was a secret. Shh…

Sylvia looked back and forth between us, and I could tell she believed us. Of course she did. We were telling the truth, and she could sense that. Well, not about taking over the business, but the rest of it was true. "What do you want?"

"I want in."

"In what?"

"Your auction business. I saw the trunks full of cash. I like cash." I almost started laughing as I said it. I sounded like a freaking mercenary. *I like cash.*

"Me, too," Hattie said.

Sylvia snorted. "You want to come in and take over. You literally just said that's what you do."

"It is what I do," I agreed. "But I have big plans, and I don't have time to micromanage all my businesses. You know the show *Shark Tank?*"

She nodded. "The one where business owners present their product and then try to get the Sharks to invest in them?"

"Yep. That's me. I'm a shark. You bring me in, and I give you all the resources and contacts I have, in exchange for some of the money."

"An angel investor, if you will," Hattie said. "Who said venture capitalists all have to be men? Girl power all the way."

"I don't live here," I said. "I don't want to manage this business. I just want to make it bigger and get money from it."

Sylvia looked back and forth between us. "You're serious."

"I do have the FBI on speed dial. Griselda is my lover..." I almost choked on the words. "I own his heart and soul, and he'll do anything for me."

"He's the one who put Mia's husband in prison," Hattie said. "That's how they met. She made his career with that bust, and he'll never forget it."

Sylvia raised her brows. "Is he dirty?"

I wanted to say yes, but there was no way I would spread that kind of lie about Griselda. I couldn't. He'd worked too hard in his business. "No. He's clean. But he trusts me, and he'll help me." I was starting to wish I hadn't brought him up at all. I didn't want to do anything to compromise him, especially since he *had* gone out of his way to help me on more than one occasion.

I needed to move on. "I want to meet your boss and make an offer. We need to do it before the FBI arrives."

Sylvia raised her brows. "We're locked in here."

"We're not. You guys clearly have an exit plan with that other boat. Let's go now. The offer expires the moment the feds show up, and I know Griselda will be waiting for that tide to come down."

Sylvia looked back and forth between us. "I don't want your help."

"It's not up to you, is it?" I asked, trusting my mom that Sylvia wasn't the one in charge. There had to be someone else above her. "If you don't present our offer, you'll be killed. I'm worth it, and you know it."

Sylvia blanched. *Yes.* The fear was back.

"The minute the feds show up to arrest Jane and Stan, the offer expires," I said.

"Fine," Sylvia said. "Accepted. Let Jane and Stan go."

She'd just admitted to being involved. Holy cow. When she'd asked for Jane and Stan to be freed, she'd just tied herself to them. *Wow*.

But she wasn't who we wanted.

I looked at Hattie, and we both started laughing. "You're not the boss," I said to Sylvia. "You lose. Too late. Let's go, Hattie."

To my surprise, Hattie whipped out a gun and pointed it at Sylvia. "Citizen's arrest for attempted murder of my bestie."

I let out a squawk of alarm. "Whose gun is that? Where did you get that? Put that away, Hattie!"

Hattie didn't even look at me. "It's Jane's gun. I had to disarm her. I couldn't leave guns around." She wiggled the nose of it at Sylvia. "Down on your knees, girl. Attempted murder charge is coming for you."

"Do you know how to use that?" I asked Hattie. "I don't want you accidentally killing someone!"

"Of course I know how to shoot. I'm me. Being a badass is one of my many superpowers."

Sylvia didn't move. "You're not going to shoot me."

"I'm not," Hattie agreed. "I don't want to go to jail for attempted murder, like some people I know. But Mia's cat is another story. He is immune from jail, and he does like violence on behalf of those he loves."

"And violence in general," I added.

Sylvia looked at King Tut, and he growled.

She backed up a step.

I smiled, sat down in a chair, and patted my lap. King Tut hopped up. "Call your boss," I said, knowing full well that there was no cell service in the caves.

Sylvia's brows went up, and then she sighed dramatically. "Fine." She pulled out her phone and looked at it. "No cell service."

"Call anyway," I said. "Try." Um, hello? She'd just acknowledged she had a boss! Or…she'd pretended she had a boss. How clever was she?

She frowned at me. "You're an idiot."

"Who has a killer cat," I said cheerfully. "And a hairdryer. Call."

She unlocked her phone and called. "No cell."

"Fine." I tapped King Tut's butt. "Get her," I whispered.

I didn't know what I expected, but I didn't really think he was going to leap off my lap and charge her.

But he did.

She screamed and bolted to the right. I jumped up and tackled her, slipping her phone out of her hand. I showed it to Hattie and then turned away, using my body to block that I had it.

Hattie shouted at her and created a scene while I looked at the screen of Sylvia's still-unlocked phone.

Blanche. She'd called *Blanche.*

Thelma was possibly on her way to Blanche's house.

I looked at Hattie, and her face paled. "What's wrong?" she asked.

"She just called Blanche, and Thelma's on the way to see her."

"She'll kill Thelma," Hattie said. "We need to get there first!"

Sylvia started laughing. "You idiots. It's not Blanche. I just called her because she was the first name in my phone. If I was a criminal mastermind, I wouldn't have everyone's information on my phone."

I looked at Hattie, and she shrugged. Crap. Why could I not figure out what was going on? Because whoever was running this thing was good. They'd fooled my mom, and I'd always thought my mom was so much better than I was at this kind of stuff.

If she couldn't figure this puzzle out, how could I?

It was such a freaking mess right now. We have two cops tied up, with no evidence against them, other than that we claimed they tried to threaten us, and they'd just say that we were guilty and they were trying to restrain us.

Literally, we had nothing, and the tides were going down very soon. And heaven knew what Thelma was up to out in the real world.

We were sunk, and Thelma was going to pay the price.

And maybe us, since we'd attacked cops and tied them up.

Even Griselda might not be able to get us out of this one.

CHAPTER 32

WE DECIDED to zip tie Sylvia and gag her. Why? Because we were already in trouble, and it seemed the lesser of two evils, when the other option was that she might be the ringleader and try to kill us.

We tied her to one of the chairs, left her there, and then headed back toward the other side. We found Lucy on our way back.

"Hey, guys," she said. "Did you find Sylvia?"

I nodded and explained what had happened. "What's going on with you?"

"Beau and Captain Jim have them under control. Beau's beginning to alarm me. He's role-playing an evil captor right now, and scaring the bejeebers out of Stan and Jane." She grinned. "It's actually pretty hilarious. I started laughing, and he told me that mocking a writer while they are in the midst of their creative process was like stabbing a wound in their soul. He made me leave."

"Beau is insane," I said.

"Definitely," Hattie agreed. "That's why he fits in with us."

Lucy put her hands on her hips. "What do you think is going on? How do all the puzzles fit together?"

I shook my head. "I don't know. And honestly, if my mom

couldn't figure it, we don't have much of a shot. She's so much better at sorting people and situations than I ever was."

Hattie smacked me on the side of the head. "Stop it."

"Ow! What was that for?"

"You're acting like a baby. Honestly. Because your mom couldn't figure it out, you can't? I have news for you, Mia. You're not some teenager anymore. You're a grown-ass woman who took down a drug lord. Underestimating yourself isn't sexy, attractive, or admirable. So pull yourself together."

I frowned at her as Lucy started chuckling. "Really?"

"She has a point," Lucy said. "Your mom's the teacher, but you're the protégé."

"My mom is the master. I quit when I was seventeen."

"But *did* you quit?" Hattie asked. "You quit her, but did you quit you?"

"What are you talking about? I never quit me. That's why I left her, because I *didn't* quit me."

"Exactly." Hattie stared at me, expectantly, clearly waiting for me to understand.

I frowned. "You're saying that I'm a criminal in my soul, and I've been doing it all this time? Because that's a lie. I help out my friends, but I have a literal stranglehold on that side of me."

"You avoid being a criminal for the sake of being a criminal," Hattie agreed, "but you've continued to develop all the skills. People observation. Logic. Creativity. Boldness."

"You're even learning how to be a boat person," Lucy said. "Fighting off assassins. Facing down murderers."

"Elevating your conviction of doing whatever it takes to make sure good people are protected," Hattie said. "You're becoming more and more *you*, and pretty much all of that makes you a better criminal."

"Yes," Lucy said. "So just because your mom couldn't figure it out and let herself get trapped or conned or whatever by Gus doesn't mean you can't unravel this mess."

"This is your moment to step into the role of the leader," Hattie said. "Where the baby girl becomes the next generation. I'm so proud of you. This is a very heartwarming moment." She beamed at me. "Let 'er rip, Mia."

I held up my hands in frustration. "I'm not part of this world anymore."

"This world is a part of who you are," Hattie said. "But that's nothing to be ashamed of. That's what makes you special. Embrace the beauty of who you are. Don't make yourself plain vanilla to fit into society's narrowed-minded views of the extraordinary. You're extraordinary, and it's time you own it."

"I'm not—"

"You are," Hattie said. "I'm also extraordinary, and it's because I own it. Do you think everyone I ever met encouraged me to drive race cars, disrespect all social norms for women, and to sell my recipes for millions so I can live life however I want? No. If I'd listened to what people told me I should be, I'd be dead by now, because my soul would have shriveled and died. That's one of the reasons I love hanging out with you, because you ignite the essence of who I am and keep me growing. Without you, I might be dead."

"Me, too," Lucy said cheerfully. "I love our little group. It's amazing."

"Be a criminal, Mia," Hattie urged. "Be a freaking criminal mastermind, and use those skills to save those we love and take down the beasts that try to hurt our honeypots."

I clasped my hands on my head and took a shuddering breath, trying to calm my racing heart. I hated everything Hattie was saying about how I was still a criminal. How my soul was entwined with being a criminal. Did it make a difference that I was trying to do good now when I was using the same skills I'd learned to steal from people?

"I don't want to be a criminal," I said softly. "I left my only family behind so I could become someone else. I sacrificed my marriage to avoid it. I don't want to be that person."

Lucy put her arm around my shoulders and squeezed. "We love you, Mia."

My throat got thick. "Do you love me because I'm a criminal? Because I don't want to be one. I hate that about me. *I hate it.*" I didn't want to be in these caves. I wanted to be on the beach, celebrating the birthday of a widow who wanted to be with her friends.

"No," Hattie said. "We love you because you have the hugest heart on the planet, and because you're brave, and bold, and will fight for what's right, no matter what the cost."

"That's a hero, not a criminal," Lucy said.

I looked at them. "I'm not a hero. I'm just me. That's all I want. To simply be me."

"I think," Hattie said gently, "that you need to stop hating yourself and start seeing the beauty in who you are. There's a reason why we all love you, and it's not because you're the Corpse Whisperer, although that's great, too."

"You are simply you," Lucy said. "But that you is meant to have an impact in this world. This is your impact. Imagine what you could do if you stopped fighting who you were?"

I looked at them. "I'm scared," I whispered. "I'm scared that if I stop fighting who I am, then I'll become like Stan or Jane or my mom. Or Gus. A criminal, twisted up in a life of terrible things. I love the adrenaline."

Hattie nodded. "You love the adrenaline, not doing bad things. There's a difference, Mia. You need to accept that you don't have to be scared that if you set yourself free that you'll become a murderer or a monster. You won't. You'll just be more you, and that, my friend, is a beautiful thing." She winked. "And trust me, it feels amazing when you embrace your true self and give it wings. You'll be amazed at who you are and how it feels."

I paced away from them, my hands clasped behind my head. I felt like my world was spinning. Running into my mom in this kind of setting had derailed me. Dragged me back into my past. Mocked me for who I thought I had become.

"She's not buying it," Lucy said to Hattie.

"It takes time to learn to love and trust yourself," Hattie said back. "But it's a start."

"But we need to figure this out now," Lucy said. "Not in ten years when she's spent hundreds of thousands of dollars on therapy."

I started laughing. "I can hear you."

"Of course you can," Hattie said. "At least you're not in denial of your ability to hear. So, not all is lost. Celebrate the small wins."

Lucy gave a little fist pump. "Go us."

"Look, Mia," Hattie said. "You don't have the luxury of years of therapy right now. Lucy's right. We're going to get arrested very soon for things that we actually did, and my cousin is going to be put in prison. We need to figure this out, and it has to be now."

"Now," Lucy echoed.

They were right. It had to be now, and there was no one but us to solve it. I took a breath. "I do have something my mom didn't have."

Hattie nodded. "That's my girl. What do you know?"

"It's not what I know." I grinned. "It's who I have. You guys."

They both grinned. "Damned straight you have us," Hattie said.

"That's so true," Lucy agreed. "That does make you about a zillion times more powerful."

I took a breath. I'd been such an idiot, trying to do it alone. I'd been taught my whole life not to trust anyone and to count only on myself, but not anymore. I had my secret weapons right there in front of me, cheering me on. "Okay." I took another breath, this time to focus. "Whoever is in charge here trapped my mom and fooled her. So they're very good."

They both nodded. "Obviously," Hattie said.

I was telling the truth that I hadn't been an active criminal in a long time, but I'd been around people. "The top reasons for murder are money, power, survival, and love," I said.

"Money is at play here," Hattie said. "We have that."

I walked away, thinking. "One of the biggest skills for a con artist is to distract people from the truth. Give them what they want and they never see what you want to hide."

Lucy nodded. "You've said that before."

"So...let's play that angle. Power is tied with money," I said. "My mom would have seen that."

"Survival? Is anyone's life at risk?" Lucy asked.

"Not that we know of," Hattie said.

"Which leaves love, which my mom, as an outsider, wouldn't necessarily see." I looked at Hattie. "Thelma was targeted as the scapegoat for this. We need to know why. Let's assume it's love. Tell me all the juicy romance gossip about Thelma. Did Roger have an affair on her?"

"Never. They were great together." Hattie frowned.

"Did Thelma dump anyone after he died? Or to marry him?"

Lucy raised her brows. "That would be a long time ago."

"The burn of a broken heart can last forever," Hattie said, with just enough emphasis that it made me wonder if she was carrying that mark on her own heart. "Thelma met Roger when they were in their forties. They'd both been married and divorced before. No kids from either of them. Late love, but true love."

Huh. That gave a lot of time for a history. "Who were they married to before?"

Hattie shook her head. "No one that's around here. Thelma moved here originally to help Vera in her store. They'd known each other in college and had stayed friends. Thelma lived with Vera and Simone until she married Roger, actually."

I looked at her sharply. "Wasn't Vera married to Frank?"

"Never married. But they shared a daughter."

"And now Frank is dead." Holy crap. "What if Frank getting killed wasn't about my mom? What if it was about Vera and romance?"

"What about the auction?" Lucy asked. "Someone was running that."

I paced away from them. "Did Thelma ever date Frank?"

Hattie nodded. "Briefly."

I looked over at them. "And she also was sleeping with Gus."

We all stared at each other. "Everyone that Thelma has been linked with romantically is dead."

"Not everyone," Hattie said.

"What do you mean?"

"She and Captain Jim were flirting. I think there's something happening there."

"Were they flirting in front of Vera?"

"Simone," Hattie said. "At the lobster shack."

"Wait!" Lucy held up her hands. "You think Vera has killed everyone Thelma dates? Why? Is she in love with Thelma?"

"I don't know," I said. "But with that lobster shack, Vera can easily bring cash on and off the island through all the fish she sources. She could easily be running that auction."

"Or maybe there are two things going on," Lucy said. "The whole auction thing, and then Vera is using it as a cover to take down Thelma."

I listened to them go back and forth about Vera and Simone. Yes, love was possible. Yes, my mom wouldn't have had their history, so she wouldn't have seen it. Yes, my mom had said Sylvia wasn't involved.

All the logic pointed toward Vera, Blanche, or Simone.

But my gut was telling me Sylvia.

But my mom had said not her.

I realized suddenly that Lucy and Hattie had stopped talking, and they were staring at me. "What are you thinking?" Hattie asked.

"I think my mom was wrong." The words felt like tears in my heart. I'd held my mom on a pedestal my entire life. I didn't want to be better at crime than she was. I didn't want her to be flawed any more than I'd already judged her to be. But I felt in my gut that she was wrong this time. "Gus was better than she was, getting her trapped. I think...I think she is out of her league with them."

Hattie and Lucy turned to face me, and Hattie quirked a brow. "You think it's Sylvia?"

"I do." Even though my mom had said it wasn't, I did. "Did she work here when Roger was here?" I asked.

Hattie nodded. "She was assistant manager."

"So, she killed Roger, Gus, and then Frank," I said. "It's always been her." I felt flat saying it. Not excited, like I'd been when I figured it out before.

"How do you know?" Lucy asked.

I shook my head. "Instinct."

"The cops won't take action on instinct," Hattie said.

I noticed that she hadn't said instincts weren't enough. She respected my opinion.

Lucy nodded. "What do we do then?"

I paced away from them, thinking. I'd already tried to talk Sylvia out of it, to get her to expose herself, to trick her, but she hadn't wavered at all. I suspected that there would be no evidence in her house. She was smart. Smarter than my mom. Smart enough to take down an ex-dirty cop and control two others.

Would they rat her out?

Maybe. Maybe not.

I crouched down and pressed my forehead to my palms, trying to think. "What does she want?" I asked aloud.

"Money and power," Hattie said.

"To escape from this without getting blamed for it," Lucy said.

I thought about that. Those were the words I'd said literally moments ago. But that wasn't why my mom had become a criminal. "My mom could have done a lot of jobs and gotten by, but she'd chosen crime because she liked it. Because she was addicted to the high...like me."

Hattie nodded. "So, Sylvia doesn't want money and power then?"

"She wants to win," I said softly, thinking about the situation. "She picks cops and top criminals because she wants to be the best. My mom did the same thing. She picked the high-profile targets because they were the most lucrative, but also because there's no better high than beating the best. That's what Sylvia wants." I sighed. "That's why my mom couldn't see it. Because she's the same, but could never admit it."

My mom. Like Sylvia. A murderer. Oh, boy. That didn't feel good.

Hattie put her hand on my shoulder. "Your mom has never killed anyone. They're not the same."

"Definitely, not," Lucy said.

I took a breath. "Doesn't matter. What we have to focus on is Sylvia. She wants to beat someone 'better.'"

"You already told her that you're better than your mom," Hattie said. "You'll be her next target. She'll want to take you down."

"No. She didn't believe me." I looked at them. "We'll have to make her believe me," I said. "Make her believe she's going to lose, and it's going to be to me. She'll have to act."

Hattie and Lucy nodded without hesitation. "What do we do?"

"Set her free."

They stared at me. "What?"

"Set her free. We have to catch her in the act."

"No." Hattie put her hands on her hips. "If you're right, she's already killed three people. You can't take the chance."

"I agree with Hattie," Lucy said.

"Then what else can we do?" I rubbed my forehead as I asked the question aloud. "She thinks she's safe. She thinks she can't get any of this pinned on her. And she probably can't." I looked at them. "So, we steal everything from her."

Hattie grinned. "I love it. Perfect."

"I'm in," Lucy said. "Let's do it. What's the plan?"

I told them.

CHAPTER 33

An hour later, I went to get Sylvia. She was still tied up, but she seemed amused when she saw me walking back into the cavern. "Still here?" she asked cheerfully. "You haven't rushed off to find my boss?"

"Let's go." I snipped her ankles so they were free, and then pulled her to her feet.

"Go where?"

I didn't answer. I just pointed her toward the tunnels.

She sat down where she was. "I'm good."

"Hattie," I called out.

Hattie and Lucy walked out of the tunnel. They were carrying one of the trunks with all the money. The trunk was open, and the money was visible. Sylvia tensed ever so slightly, but she didn't move. "We're taking the money," I said.

"It's not my money, so whatever."

I waved at them and they carried the money back into the tunnel. Sylvia watched them go.

"Get up, Sylvia," I said.

She didn't move. "The cops will be here soon. You'll all be going to jail. I did nothing except get tied up and try to save you when you fell in."

She was so calm. So relaxed. Like ice.

A chill ran down my spine. Was she pure sociopath?

I sat down across from her, spinning the scissors on my index finger. The scissors that cut her free would be a great weapon to kill me. "You can't beat me, Sylvia."

"I'm not trying to." Her gaze was sharp as she watched me spin the scissors. I could almost feel her timing my moments to figure out when to grab them.

"You set up the cameras in my marina," I said.

She blinked innocently. "What cameras?"

"The one you used to blackmail my mom into helping." I leaned forward. "She didn't think it was you. You were better than her. I'm impressed."

She smiled slightly, but didn't answer.

She was too good. She'd never crack, at least not with me tossing questions at her like this. There was nothing at stake for her, other than some cash. And beating me. "I'm taking all the money," I said.

She shrugged. "Money is easy to get."

"I'm taking all the items you were going to sell."

She shrugged again.

I leaned in. "And I'm spreading the word that you made a deal with the cops. They're letting you go in exchange for finger-pointing. Your reputation will be shot, and you'll be dead in a week."

This time, her eyes widened slightly.

The greatest asset my mom and I had had was the cloak of invisibility. People didn't notice us. We could slide under the radar. Sylvia's greatest asset was her reputation. People trusted her, or at least respected her.

I held up my phone. "I know people who can destroy your reputation in thirty seconds. I don't even care if you go to jail. You killed people, so now you get to die." I stood and tossed the scissors to the side, out of her reach, like I was an overconfident idiot. "We'll be gone when the cops arrive." I held up the keys to the other boat. "We're heading out. The second we're out of the cave and I have cell service, I'm making that call. See you on the other side, Sylvia."

Then I turned my back on her and walked away. My heart was racing. I hadn't checked Sylvia for a gun. I was sure she had one. If she was the leader of this, she'd have one.

Or knitting needles.

I heard movement behind me, but I didn't turn around. I kept walking toward the tunnel, sauntering as if I had all the confidence in the world.

All the time.

All the safety.

There was a sudden click. "Mia."

I kept walking. Sweat was dripping down my temples, but I didn't dare wipe it away. "What?"

"Turn around."

I flipped her off and kept walking. If I was wrong, she'd shoot me in the back. But I believed I'd read her correctly. Shooting me in the back would never work for her. Never. She needed to be up close and personal, and to claim her victory.

The stabbings had given her away. She needed death to be personal.

The dirt exploded next to my foot, and I squawked and jumped to the side despite my efforts to appear nonchalant. I spun around to find Sylvia pointing the gun at me. "Did you just shoot at me?"

"I did. I missed on purpose." She strode toward me. "You don't get to win, Mia. That's not how it works."

Ah...*win.* She cared. I'd been right.

"It is how it works," I said. "I always win." The gun was coming closer. All she had to do was pull the trigger and I'd be dead, dead, and more dead. *Please let me be right.*

"Not today." She came to a stop in front of me. "I win today, Mia Murphy. It's my resort, it's my auction, and it's my business.

No one gets to stop me or rat me out. No one. Gus tried to take over, so he had to die. Frank was helping your mom. And then Roger didn't want the business to go in the direction I wanted to take it. You go along with me, or you die. That's how it works."

Yay! That was basically a confession!

She put the gun to my forehead. "Boom."

I flinched.

Then she backed up, fished around behind the chairs, and then came up with a pair of knitting needles. "Stole these from Thelma, too, so they have her prints on them. A big fight, Thelma took you down, and then she left. I saw the whole thing from my tied-up chair before I escaped."

She walked over to me, and I tightened my grip on my hairdryer.

"Carnage everywhere," she said. "Enough scandal to bring in tourists for years. Captain Jim will handle Hattie and Lucy, and then we're all going to watch you guys burn."

My mouth dropped open. "*Captain Jim?*"

"Didn't see that one coming, did you? Is he with your friends right now? Bad call to leave them with him. Bad call indeed, Mia. Bad call—" She reared back and slammed the knitting needles toward my chest.

I swung my hairdryer and hit her in the shoulder, knocking her off balance. She fell sideways, and the minute she hit the dirt, Lucy and Hattie charged out of the tunnel. I jumped on Sylvia, and pinned her while Lucy and Hattie jumped on top. We had her tied up instantly, and by the time we finished, Beau was standing there close to us, recording the whole thing.

"That was fantastic," he said. "You were brilliant."

I sat back, my heart pounding. My hands were shaking, and I felt like I was going to throw up. "It's so much less stressful to do that when Griselda is standing behind me with a gun."

Hattie patted my shoulder as Sylvia muttered behind her. "Is it really? I thought he was never actually close enough to rescue you. No one's faster than a bullet, Mia."

"I know."

Beau came to stand above me, still recording. "I knew you were Tatum's daughter, Mia, and that made you special. But I've never seen courage like that. You could have died."

"Wasn't my day." I still felt like I was going to throw up. That had been so much closer than I'd thought. "But I'm never doing that again. I'm done. I'm out."

Hattie put her arm around me as the sound of a boat engine echoed through the cavern. "Thank you, Mia. Thelma would be in jail if it wasn't for you."

I closed my eyes as the sound of a boat engine got louder and pressed my face to my hands. I could feel genuine appreciation in Hattie's voice, and my throat tightened. "I hate it when innocent people go to jail."

"Or when bad people get away with stuff," Lucy said. She grinned. "Well done, Mia."

"You faked that reaction so well when she said Captain Jim," Hattie said. "I almost believed you didn't know."

I smiled. "His only crime was stealing that money. She was trying to distract me with fear for you guys."

"I know. He has a good heart. Being a lobsterman is tough. Not a lot of income from it." Lucy sat next to me and put her arm around my shoulders.

We sat together as a boat chugged into view. Thelma and Blanche were sitting on the bow. "Hattie!" Thelma shouted when she saw us. "You're okay!"

I was so happy to see them together, so happy that Thelma had gotten it right with her friend. She had gone after Blanche... but in the right way.

Griselda walked up from the rear of the boat, and I realized she'd gone to get him. *Way to go, Thelma.*

I saw him before he saw me. I watched his gaze sweep across the shoreline, first to Sylvia tied and gagged, then to Hattie, and then to me. He stopped searching when he found me. He just kept his attention on me, only on me, stopping on me. "You okay?"

I nodded, and sudden tears filled my eyes.

We were safe.

It was over.

CHAPTER 34

THE MUSIC WAS LOUD.

The lights were sparkling.

The beach was glowing in the moonlight.

Thelma's birthday rave was rocking the beachfront at the Grand Vista Resort.

Blanche, Vera, and Simone were roasting marshmallows for s'mores, and others were mingling. Gossip was traveling fast with all the murders and Sylvia's arrest, but people were cheerful about it, because good gossip always made for a fun time.

Nate was busy waiting on everyone, and he had even more sparkle in his eyes than he had before. Atlas was there, running the firepit, and Nancy, VIP-Liaison-turned-Interim-Manager, had stopped by to check on us.

She was Sylvia's replacement for the moment, and she was charming. I watched her working the guests, making sure everyone was all right. It turned out that she'd been with Frank because he'd asked for her help when he'd heard that Gus was dead. She'd been working as VIP Liaison, trying to do damage control for the resort, not trying to murder anyone.

The resort was rolling onward without Sylvia, and I knew that Roger's legacy would be rebuilt.

I nudged Hattie and Lucy, who were sitting with me on a lounge chair, waiting for Blanche to reveal the birthday cake, which she had told us was wildly inappropriate. The party had been moved to the beach so that we didn't have to sit around the hot tub and imagine Giorgio's body, and the luau decorations had been abandoned in favor of a fresh start.

Hattie nudged me. "Look at Thelma and Captain Jim. I think there's a romance budding."

I grinned, watching as Thelma and Captain Jim stood barefoot in the water at the edge of the beach, laughing and talking. "I wonder how long it takes to recover from finding out that your husband was murdered."

"She's been saying it for a long time," Hattie said. "I'm sure it's more relief than anything at that point. And vindication. No one believed her."

I looked over at Hattie. "Did you?"

"Of course."

"Is that why you invited us on this trip with you?" I asked. "Because you thought we might be able to help her figure it out?"

Hattie grinned. "I didn't know there would be fresh corpses, but yeah, I thought that might be a really great birthday present for her."

"That's a heck of a birthday present," I said.

"Right? She's so happy." Hattie raised her glass. "A toast to justice prevailing once again."

Lucy and I raised our margarita glasses and tapped hers. "Cheers!"

"So, what's happening with you and Griselda?" Lucy asked. "That look you gave him when he showed up at the caves was pretty intense. That kiss complicated everything, didn't it?"

"Ah...that kiss," Hattie said. "You think he knew all along that it wasn't a bomb?"

"Right?" Lucy said. "He's an FBI agent. Shouldn't he have recognized that it was a recording device?"

"He was being a protector," I said. "It's what he does. He didn't want to risk any of us."

Hattie grinned. "Damn that protector side of him. It's way too appealing. You need to tell him to cut that out."

I laughed. "I agree. I haven't really talked to him since the kiss, though. He's been busy and had to work to sort out this mess." Which was good. My curiosity had been dancing in Devlin's direction, not Griselda's, and I wasn't sure I wanted to open any doors with the FBI agent. But I was thinking about him now in a way I never had been before.

"Huh." Hattie leaned back. "Griselda's playing hard to get. I wouldn't have expected that of him. Clever man."

Lucy laughed. "Scared is more likely. Mia's terrifying if she's your enemy."

"That she is," Hattie agreed.

I grinned. "It's not just me. It's all of us together." I put my arms around them and kissed each of them on the cheek. "We finally got our girls trip," I said. "All I wanted was the beach and my girls." I felt so happy. These women were tough, smart, and had the hugest hearts. I didn't even care that Hattie had lied to us to get us to help Thelma. Of course she would do that. Of course it was right.

That's what we did: make sure bad people didn't get away with things.

Beau had left the island already. Once he'd realized that my mom was gone, he'd said he had to go home and start writing. The trip had inspired him, apparently.

"What about your mom?" Lucy asked. "Have you heard from her?"

"Nope, but I'm sure I will." The connection between us had never faded, and this little escapade had showed me how tightly woven our bond still was. It had also given me a new appreciation for the woman she was, and the woman I'd become as a result of having her for my mom. Competent. Loyal. Capable. Smart.

It felt good to win. To defeat an actual crime ring. Granted it had been a small one, but it still felt good.

See? I was my mom's daughter. I got off on the win. But at least my win was putting bad guys away now, not stealing from celebrities.

"Maybe you'll run into your mom under better circumstances" Lucy said.

"What's better than murder?" Hattie scoffed. "That's the best part."

I pushed her off the chair. "No more murder. I was actually terrified at the end there. I don't need that again."

"It was close," Lucy agreed.

Hattie stretched out on the sand, unbothered by the fact I'd pushed her. "Whatever adventures come our way, we'll embrace them. We have each other. We're good."

"And Mia's terrifying cat," Lucy added, as King Tut trotted over and hopped up on my lap, a hot dog in his teeth. "Between the four of us, we're unstoppable."

Unstoppable.

No one was unstoppable.

Not even my mom, at least this time.

I'd been the one to bail her out, for the first time ever.

I had a lot of emotions about that, but I hadn't had time to process them yet.

Hattie touched my knee. "How are you doing, Mia? In all seriousness."

I was surprised by the question. Hattie didn't go for vulnerability. "Processing."

She nodded. "It'll take time. But I want you to know that Lucy and I were talking about it, and we both want you to know that you're ours forever. We're not letting you go, no matter how much of your past shows up in our lives."

Tears filled my eyes. "It could get messy. I'm sure I'll hear from her again."

"You're our girl," Lucy said. "The three of us are a unit. A triple threat."

"Triple trouble, more accurately," Hattie said.

We all looked at each other, and then burst out laughing.

Triple trouble indeed.

That was entirely too accurate.

"I don't know about you guys," I said, "but there's no one I'd rather get in trouble with than the two of you."

"I love that," Hattie said. "You didn't deny that we live a life of excitement and adventure. You just owned it and showed us love. That's the only way forward, my dear. To us!"

"To us!" Lucy cheered.

I grinned at these two awesome women, who had seen me at my worst and best and accepted it all. I'd never let them go. "To us!"

Do you want to know what happens when Mia gets back home for the grand opening of her marina, only to have it derailed by a poisoned margarita? And are you burning to find out what happens on Mia's date with Devlin, and what Griselda does about it? If so, grab the next Mia book, *Margarita Mayhem,* today!

Sign up for my newsletter here to be notified when the next Mia story is released, and to get bonus Mia content! New to the series? Grab the first Mia Murphy mystery, *Double Twist* today!

If you enjoyed the Mia vibe and also enjoy mixing it up with a little magic and romance, try my *Immortally Sexy* romantic comedy series (a little steamy!) or the *Guardian of Magic* paranormal mystery (contains some profanity!).

If you love cowboys, try my deeply heartwarming, family-oriented (but with a little spice!) *Wyoming Rebels* series or the spinoff *Hart Ranch Billionaires* series. Grab the series starter for the Hart family, *A Rogue Cowboy's Second Chance,* or start with the first first book in the *Wyoming Rebels* series, *A Real Cowboy Never Says No.*

If you want more small-town stories with heart-melting, emotional romances, you'd love my *Birch Crossing* series! Get started with *Unexpectedly Mine* today, in which a billionaire hero gets stranded in a small town and gets his world upturned by a sassy single mom and her daughter.

Is dark, steamy paranormal romance your jam? If so, definitely try my award-winning *Order of the Blade* series, starting with book one, *Darkness Awakened.* Jump into the world of soulmates, passion, danger, and immortal warriors who will do whatever it takes to save the woman who steals his heart, no matter what the cost. Don't we all want a guy like that?

WHICH BOOK IS NEXT?

What's the easiest way to know when a new book is out?

My newsletter.

It's a quick read, it goes right to your inbox, and it has the info you're looking for. No ads or commercials flashing in your face! Just me and books you enjoy!

I also make sure you know when I have a free book, a cover reveal, or any other important book info. I post reader surveys, give away Advance Review Copies, and provide insider scoop on my books, my writing, and the author life (it's super glam, trust me...).

Give it a try. See if it works for you. If not, you can always unsubscribe at any time!

Go to www.stephanierowe.com and click on the newsletter link to sign up!

Stephanie

SNEAK PEEK: TO DATE AN IMMORTAL

AN IMMORTALLY SEXY NOVEL

"I couldn't put it down! It was funny, heartwarming, sexy, and badass all rolled into one. Keep em coming!!!!" ~Christa S (Five-star Amazon Review)

———

DEREK LAVALLE HAD less than four minutes to save his cousin's life, break the Curse that would kill him and his twin in a week, and prove to his family that he wasn't insane for believing in curses, dragons, and immortality.

It was kind of a loaded four minutes.

Which was why the billionaire, no-carb-soft-pretzel mogul was in a bit of a rush as he vaulted up the crumbling steps of the hovel that his less-than-impressive cousin, Les LaValle, was currently living in.

As a general rule, it might seem pretty easy to make sure an unemployed pothead doesn't die in the next three and a half minutes. But when it came to thirty-one-year-old LaValle men, it was a little tricky. Like the kind of tricky that boasted a zero percent success rate for the last two hundred years. Dead. Dead.

Dead. Dead. Dead. And dead a few more times. For four generations. As odds go, those aren't exactly fantastic ones.

But Derek had an advantage, because he was the only one who'd realized it was a curse that had been knocking off each LaValle male at the precise moment he turned thirty-one years, forty-six weeks, four days, six hours, three minutes, and five seconds old.

Yeah. A freaking *curse*. What are the odds?

Maybe not that high, under normal circumstances. But if you have in your hot little hands a two-hundred-year-old journal by your ancestor that explains very clearly that the men in your family are cursed, then, yeah, the odds are pretty high that could be what's going on.

Derek had the journal.

His family? Not so much on the bandwagon. As in, spend-the-last-ten-years-trying-to-get-Derek-committed not on the bandwagon. Lucky for Derek, he had vast amounts of disposable income and had bought his way to freedom several times.

In truth, his entire extended family had disowned him because they thought he was a freaking whack job who besmirched the family name with his insanity. Understandable on some levels, but for Derek, breaking the Curse that had damned his entire lineage trumped trying to win his family's approval.

It was a no brainer. Screw playing by the rules when the rules wind up with you dead, right?

Derek wasn't super interested in dying in a week, and he sure as hell didn't want his math professor twin brother, Quincy LaValle, to die two minutes after him.

Which meant he had to break that damned Curse.

For those unclear on how curses work, it's hard as freaking hell to break a damned curse. Derek was a master of chasing down leads on how to break curses, but guess how many times the assorted mumbo jumbo tricks and other stuff had worked?

That's right. Zero. A big fat goose egg.

So, now, it had come down to this: break the Curse by beating it mano-a-mano in the battle for his cousin's life or death. Derek had come armed (thank you, baseball bat, for being a deadly weapon masquerading as sporting equipment) and ready to fight.

Yeah, granted, keeping Les alive wasn't exactly a public service, and might even be considered criminal in some societies with basic human morals, but death was death, and Derek was so not going there right now.

But Les was not making it easy.

The disbelieving bastard had been avoiding Derek for the last two weeks, from the minute Derek had showed up and told him he was keeping him alive.

And now, death was three minutes away, and Derek still couldn't find his cousin anywhere, which was, obviously, a major impediment to defeating the Curse.

He was down to his last chance.

If he didn't find Les here, he'd be out of time, and death would roll on through, thumbing its nose at Derek once again.

Derek had been by twice already today, but he was trying a third time, because there was literally nowhere else Les could be. He'd been by Les's favorite bars, the park bench, and a couple alleys he liked to pass out in, but Les had been nowhere. The dude had to be home. His life literally didn't include any more possibilities. "Les! It's Derek! Open up!" He gripped his baseball bat tighter as he hammered his fist on the peeling front door.

Still no answer.

He tried the doorknob.

Still locked.

Derek glanced at his watch. Less than two minutes. *Shit.*

Fuck it. He was breaking in.

Derek shifted the bat to his right hand and sprinted around the side of the house. The rusted gate was closed, wedged in place with a pile of old kegs, a couple bald tires, some strange looking lead pipes, and other thoughtful lawn décor.

No problem.

Derek scrambled over the gate, clearing it easily, courtesy of his slight obsession with assorted martial arts and fitness. Hey, if something was going to try to murder him next week, he was going to make damn sure he was fit enough to fight for his life, right? Amen, brother.

He raced up the rickety stairs to the back deck, and nearly tripped over his cousin, who was sprawled in a lawn chair. Elated disbelief rushed through Derek. He'd found him! "Les! Didn't you hear me?"

"Jesus. You just don't know when to drop it. Fuck off." Les was holding a reflective cardboard piece across his chest to catch some rays. A horrifyingly small bathing suit stretched to the limit across his hips, the yellowing fabric barely visible beneath his expansive gut. His hairy feet were partially covered by the green, murky water of a plastic wading pool.

Oh, damn.

That was just not a sight anyone needed to see.

Honest to God, the things a guy needed to do in order to break a family curse, right? Derek averted his eyes before the sight could be entrenched forever in his brain. "It's time, Les."

"I'm not interested in your shit." Les didn't even bother to open his eyes.

Derek scanned the backyard, searching for rabid chipmunks and homicidal yard implements that might develop a mind of their own. "You're supposed to die in less than two minutes. I'm here to save you."

"I already told you. I don't need saving. I'm a fantastic model of male perfection exactly as I am." He paused to belch. "Take your insanity off my property, dude."

"Damn it, Les. I'm not insane."

"Are too."

Are too? Really? Because every grown man should throw out retorts worthy of a six-year-old brat. "Listen to me, Les," Derek said urgently. "You're going to hit the expiration date for LaValle men in just over a minute." He raised the bat into the ready position, settling it on his shoulder. "You might want to get off your ass and grab a metal rake or something to help me defend you." *I know you're out there, you murderous son of a bitch. I'm ready for you.*

"Fuck that." Les took another drag of beer and waddled his ass deeper into the lawn chair. "Everything always works out for me."

"Everything? Really? You're so sure about that?" Derek eyed the rusted motorcycle sunken into the weeds. Could that come flying at Les? That would be deadly, for sure. Shit. There was so much junk in the yard that could be lethal.

"Hell, yeah." Les waved his hand around the broken-glass and weed-filled backyard. "Look at this glory. I sit out here, drink beer, and get high, then go play Internet poker. I haven't punched a time clock in six years, because I'm a freaking genius at working the disability game. I'm one of those lucky bastards, Cuz. Hell, they just made pot legal in this state. I have shitloads of cannabis in my house, and my health insurance *paid* for it. I live a gifted life, my friend. *Gifted.*" He stretched his arms up and then clasped his hands behind his head. "The other LaValle men were unlucky sons of bitches, but that's not me. I'm a fucking *god.*"

"*Unlucky*? Hell, Les, it's not a matter of bad luck." Derek's dad had made the same claim, but that hadn't stopped a wayward butter knife from taking him down, right in front of seven-year-old Derek, while they'd been sampling a no-calorie waffle together. Derek had managed to perfect a no-carb-soft-pretzel recipe by the time he was eighteen, but replacing his dad? Not so much.

And how could bad luck explain his Uncle Jack, who'd been lethally impaled by a cotton-ball? Or Grandad Howie, who'd choked to death on lemonade? And let's be honest, folks, newborn babies don't usually generate enough power with their kicks to give fatal brain damage to tenth degree black belts, like his cousin Tony. The fact that his fifth cousin, twice removed, had shot himself in the head while cleaning his gun could have been bad luck, except, of course, for that precise age he'd been when it had happened. And pet hamsters? Really? How many of them maul a three-hundred-pound iron worker to death?

Every LaValle man had died, and every single one of them had died at the same age, down to the *second*. There was no chance that could be anything but supernatural, as if fate was grabbing whatever was available at that precise moment. Who the hell could be stupid enough *not* to realize that there was something supernatural going on? "I'm staying, Les."

"Then I'm calling my mom and telling her you're over here talking about the Curse again," Les whined. "And then I'm going to call the cops and—"

"Shut up and let me concentrate." He glanced at his watch. Forty-five seconds to go. "Maybe you should go inside. You could drown in that pool." His bat wasn't going to be much good if the water suddenly swelled up in a massive tsunami and swept Les away. Mouth-to-mouth resuscitation with Les was just not something that he wanted to be thinking about right now.

"You go inside. Get me another beer." Les let his head drop back against the lounge chair straps. "Order a pizza while you're at it."

Derek looked up at the sky. No lightning bolt could come out of that blue sky, could it?

Ten seconds.

He kicked an old pizza box off the deck. He wasn't sure how cardboard could be deadly, but he wasn't taking any chances.

Les yawned. "I'm gonna take a nap."

Five seconds.

Les belched again and picked up his beer.

"Give me that bottle. I don't want glass near you." Before he could grab the bottle, Derek's phone alarm went off, and a huge rock came careening over the back fence, heading straight for Les's head.

Les screamed and dove out of his chair. Derek swung for the rock. It shattered his bat but ricocheted away from Les and smashed through the living room window.

Derek whirled around, ready for another incoming assault, but the yard was quiet.

Nothing else was happening.

Nothing else was coming in for attempt number two.

Slowly, a stunned disbelief settled over him. He'd done it. He'd intervened and stopped the Curse from getting his cousin. Son of a bitch. *It was over.* Letting out a deep, shuddering breath, he lowered the handle of the bat, barely able to let himself relax. "Believe me now, Les?"

There was no response, not even an obnoxious, ungrateful whine.

Derek spun around, then swore. His cousin was lying on the deck, motionless, his neck twisted at an angle that was unnatural and very, very wrong. His eyes were open and staring, without nearly enough alcohol-induced haze for him to still be alive.

Son of a bitch. Dead. Right on time. "Dammit, Les. Why didn't you listen?"

No one listened. And everyone died.

Well, Derek wasn't going to die, and his twin wasn't either.

So what if he had less than a week to solve a problem that he'd spent his life failing to fix? Deadlines were fantastic motivators, right? So, it was all good. He was going to figure this shit out, and he was going to do it in time.

He glared at the overgrown backyard. "You've just taken your last LaValle man, you hear me?"

There was a weird cackle, almost like maniacal, possessed *laughter.* It didn't sound human. It didn't even sound like it was of this world. It sounded like a freaking nightmare coming for him.

Chills crept down his spine.

A Curse with a warped sense of humor?

Or he was officially starting to crack.

Neither option felt really fantastic, so yeah, he was going to just pretend he hadn't heard that.

But as he pulled out his phone to call 9-1-1, he couldn't deny the truth.

He'd heard it.

Someone…or rather…some*thing* had laughed.

SNEAK PEEK: A ROGUE COWBOY'S SECOND CHANCE

★★★★★ "Absolutely swoon worthy, lovable and emotionally driven. Family is everything." ~Madison (Five-star Amazon Review on *A Real Cowboy for Christmas*)

———

Brody was late.

And he still wasn't sure if he was staying.

He kept his head down, his shoulders hunched, and his cowboy hat tilted as he strode through the quiet tunnels leading into the stadium.

There were a few people in line for beer or pretzels, but it was mostly empty.

Everyone was in their seats, screaming for Tatum, who had been on stage for a half hour already.

Brody knew, because he'd sat in his truck and watched the social media feeds. He wasn't about to go in before she was on stage. But once she came on...he'd just sat there in his truck, watching as fans posted grainy clips of her performance.

Then, thirty minutes in, someone had posted a clip from up

close, close enough for Brody to see her face. She'd looked up, as if she were looking right at him, telling him to come in.

So he'd shoved his phone in his pocket and gotten out of his truck.

And now, he could hear the thud of the music as he neared the doorway that led to Floor Section 4, Rows 1-10.

He paused to show his ticket to the usher, and then was waved inside.

He shoved his hands in his front pockets and stepped inside the stadium. The music hit him like a wave of raw power. The lights flashed. Smoke rose from the stage. An assault on his senses that he ignored, his gaze going right to the stage to find her.

His breath seemed to catch in his chest when he saw her in person, for the first time in fifteen years. She was at the far end of the stage, one arm over her head, her stance wide and strong in red, sparkling heels. Her halter top matched the shoes, showing off her muscled torso, while her black leather pants showed off every curve. She radiated a passion and gloriousness that the photographs never did justice to.

She was moving to the fierce beat, working the fans up into a frenzy.

Her voice was glorious, radiating through the stadium like heaven itself had unleashed its greatest glory through her. It wasn't country. It wasn't soul. It wasn't pop. It was all of those together, mixed with a magic that no one else had ever been able to mimic.

Tatum Crosby was legend, and she was right there, fifty feet from him.

The front row was less than five feet from the stage. She would see him. And the moment she did, he would be close enough to read her expression and know if she'd sent the ticket and back-stage pass. He would know whether to stay.

But still he didn't move.

He stood there, silently, watching. Breathing in the woman who had been a part of his soul for fifteen years. With the lights from the stage, he knew she wouldn't be able to see him from where he was standing.

He could watch her entire concert, and then slide away into the night.

She would never know.

But then, neither would he.

Keegan was right. He had to know. This was his chance to begin to live again.

He waited until she was at the far end of the stage again, singing to the crowd on that side of the stadium. The moment she turned her back on him, he pulled his hat down to hide his face, and then he went on the move.

* * *

Brody wasn't coming.

The realization wound tight around Tatum's chest, making it difficult to get enough air to sing.

She fought for the energy her fans deserved. She shouted her love for them. She poured all she had into her music. But she couldn't keep looking at the empty seat in the front row.

She'd known it was a long shot he would come. It had been so long since she'd seen him. Since everything had fallen apart. Since she'd run.

Movement in the wings caught her eye, and she saw Donny shouting at her, gesturing with his palms up for her to step up the energy. He would be angry at her performance.

Her chest tightened even more, dreading the after-show recap with him.

Beside him stood Nora, her clipboard clutched to her chest. She shrugged at Tatum, indicating that she, too, had noticed the empty seat in the front row.

He wasn't coming.

She had to get over it. She'd come this far on her own. She didn't need him. Wasn't that the point she'd been trying to prove her whole life? That she didn't need anyone? Her mom had quit on her, choosing drugs over her own daughter. Her dad? She didn't even know who he was. Foster care? All hell, except for a gray-haired old man named Roger who had given her his old guitar and changed her life.

No. The guitar hadn't changed her life. *She'd* changed her life, and she didn't need anyone.

It was fine if Brody didn't show. Absolutely fine.

She could do this. She'd been on her own since she was ten, tossed between foster homes when her mom was in jail for drugs, sitting in their crappy apartment, watching her mom's chest to see if she was still breathing, or if she'd finally died of a life not worth living.

Her mom had finally died. And on that rainy day in June so long ago, Tatum had decided she was going to become the star she'd always dreamed of, the celebrity who was so incredible that everyone would love her. That everyone would see how special she was.

And she'd done it.

She had money. She had success. She was a star. She didn't need anyone or anything, especially not Brody. But even as Tatum told herself that, she stumbled, panic starting to close in around her.

Emotion caught in her throat, filling her eyes with the tears she worked so hard to keep at bay every moment of every day. The loneliness, the fear, the isolation—they were all lies and illusions. She *had* what she needed. She was *enough,* all on her own.

She spun away from the wings, away from Donny and Nora. She focused on her fans, on the people who filled her soul and kept her going.

Still singing, she moved to the edge of the stage and bent down, holding out her hand for a high-five. A woman in her forties with red hair screamed and high-fived her, making Tatum smile. She moved along, holding out her hand to her fans.

Two adorable young men, early twenties, stopped holding

hands long enough to high-five her. "We love you, Tatum!" One of them yelled.

"I love you, too!" she shouted back.

The next in line were three girls that looked like they were in college, screaming and shouting and jumping up and down, filming her as she high-fived them.

Next up, a man in a cowboy hat with his head down.

In Brody's seat.

At that moment, he raised his head and met her gaze, dark brown eyes that she'd never forget.

Brody.

Tatum was so shocked she forgot the words for a second, the music thundering on without her. She caught up almost immediately, and she knew that no one except Donny would notice, but she couldn't take her gaze off Brody.

He looked the same. And different. A beard. Muscles. Heavier. Fancier.

Still singing, she held out her hand to him for a high-five, her heart pounding.

He reached up and caught her hand. It was a split second of skin brushing over skin, but it was the touch of a man she'd never forgotten.

A QUICK FAVOR

Hey there, my friend!

It's Mia! Tell me, tell me! What did you think of *Triple Trouble?*

I hope you loved it, and my suffering wasn't for naught.

Just kidding. No suffering here! I love my life. And my hairdryer. And my cat. And my friends. And… well… the list goes on and on. And just wait until my next book comes out. More fun on the way!

I hope I gave you some feel-good entertainment in these pages! If I did, it would rock if you'd do me a favor and help get the word out, so that other folks can find their way here.

Tell a friend. Tell an enemy. Leave a note for your barista.

Reviews are also incredibly helpful to encourage new readers to make that leap and try a new book. It would be super fab if you'd consider taking a couple minutes and jotting one or two sentences on the *the etailer* and/or Goodreads telling everyone how freaking amazing I am. Or King Tut. Because we all know that he's the best. Even the short reviews really make an impact!

Thank you again for reading my story! I can't wait for you to see what happens next!

Smooches,

Mia

BOOKS BY STEPHANIE ROWE

MYSTERY

Mia Murphy series
(Cozy Mystery)
Double Twist
Top Notch
Gone Rogue
Triple Trouble
Margarita Mayhem

CONTEMPORARY ROMANCE

Wyoming Rebels series
(Contemporary Western Romance)
A Real Cowboy Never Says No
A Real Cowboy Knows How to Kiss
A Real Cowboy Rides a Motorcycle
A Real Cowboy Never Walks Away
A Real Cowboy Loves Forever
A Real Cowboy for Christmas
A Real Cowboy Always Trusts His Heart

A Real Cowboy Always Protects
A Real Cowboy for the Holidays
A Real Cowboy Always Comes Home
SERIES COMPLETE

THE HART RANCH BILLIONAIRES SERIES
(CONTEMPORARY WESTERN ROMANCE)
A Rogue Cowboy's Second Chance
A Rogue Cowboy's Christmas Surprise
A Rogue Cowboy Finds Love
A Rogue Cowboy's Heart

LINKED TO THE HART RANCH BILLIONAIRES SERIES
(CONTEMPORARY WESTERN ROMANCE)
Her Rebel Cowboy

BIRCH CROSSING SERIES
(SMALL-TOWN CONTEMPORARY ROMANCE)
Unexpectedly Mine
Accidentally Mine
Unintentionally Mine
Irresistibly Mine
Secretly Mine

MYSTIC ISLAND SERIES
(SMALL-TOWN CONTEMPORARY ROMANCE)
Wrapped Up in You (A Christmas novella)

CANINE CUPIDS SERIES
(ROMANTIC COMEDY)
Paws for a Kiss
Pawfectly in Love
Paws Up for Love

SINGLE TITLE

(CHICKLIT / ROMANTIC COMEDY)
One More Kiss

PARANORMAL

ORDER OF THE BLADE SERIES
(PARANORMAL ROMANCE)
Darkness Awakened
Darkness Seduced
Darkness Surrendered
Forever in Darkness
Darkness Reborn
Darkness Arisen
Darkness Unleashed
Inferno of Darkness
Darkness Possessed
Shadows of Darkness
Hunt the Darkness
Darkness Awakened: Reimagined

IMMORTALLY DATING SERIES
(FUNNY PARANORMAL ROMANCE)
To Date an Immortal
To Date a Dragon
Devilishly Dating
To Kiss a Demon

HEART OF THE SHIFTER SERIES
(PARANORMAL ROMANCE)
Dark Wolf Rising
Dark Wolf Unbound

STANDALONE PARANORMAL ROMANCE
Leopard's Kiss
Not Quite Dead

BOOKS BY STEPHANIE ROWE

Funny Urban Fantasy
Guardian of Magic
The Demon You Trust

Devilishly Sexy series
(Funny Paranormal Romance)
Not Quite a Devil

ROMANTIC SUSPENSE

Alaska Heat Series
(Romantic Suspense)
Ice
Chill
Ghost
Burn
Hunt (novella)

BOXED SETS

Order of the Blade (Books 1-4)
Protectors of the Heart (A Six-Book First-in-Series Collection)
Wyoming Rebels Boxed Set (Books 1-3)

For a complete list of Stephanie's books, click here.

ACKNOWLEDGMENTS

Special thanks to my beta readers. You guys are the best!

There are so many to thank by name, more than I could count, but here are those who I want to called out specially for all they did to help this book come to life: Alyssa Bird, Bridget Koan, Britannia Hill, Deb Julienne, Denise Fluhr, Dottie Jones, Heidi Hoffman, Helen Loyal, Jackie Moore Kranz, Jeanne Stone, Jeanie Jackson, Jodi Moore, Judi Pflughoeft, Kasey Richardson, Linda Watson, Regina Thomas, Summer Steelman, Shell Bryce, and Trish Douglas. Special thanks to my family, who I love with every fiber of my heart and soul. And to AER, who is my world. Love you so much, baby girl! You are brilliant, kind, funny, sassy, and a fantastic athlete. I am so proud to be your mom, and I look forward to watching you grow and thrive through life! And to Joe, who keeps me believing myself. I love you all!

Thank you to Elizabeth Turner Stokes for the most AMAZING cover. I am in awe of your vision and your talent.

ABOUT THE AUTHOR

NEW YORK TIMES AND USA TODAY bestselling author Stephanie Rowe is the author of more than fifty published novels. Notably, she is a Vivian® Award nominee, and a RITA® Award winner and a five-time nominee. She loves her puppies, tennis, and being as as sassy and irreverent as her heroines. She's pretty sure dead bodies are better in fiction than real life, but hey, never say never, right? She has a pretty fantastic newsletter thing happening, so if you want in some good entertainment, go to www.stephanierowe.com and click the newsletter link!

Printed in Great Britain
by Amazon